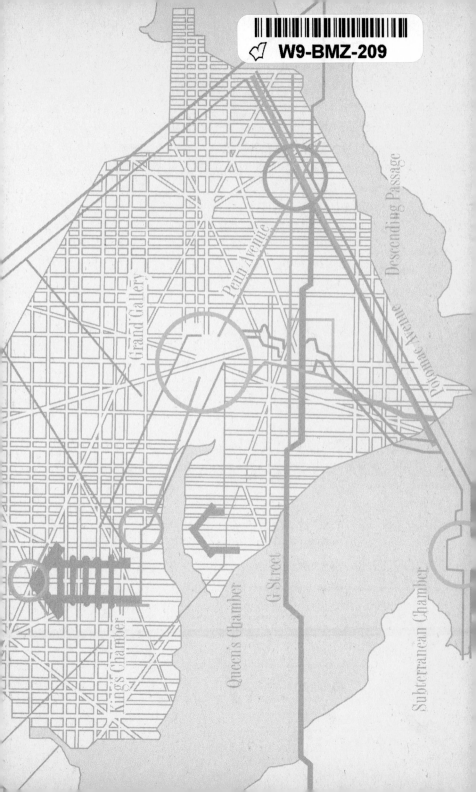

W9-BMZ-209

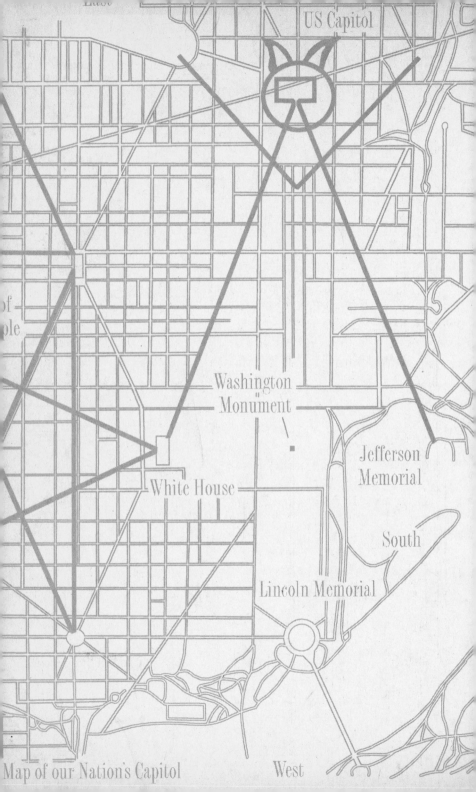

US Capitol

Washington
Monument

Jefferson
Memorial

White House

South

Lincoln Memorial

Map of our Nation's Capitol                    West

# THE SHADOWS

# THE SHADOWS

L. A. BANKS

 ST. MARTIN'S GRIFFIN ✠ NEW YORK

THE SHADOWS. Copyright © 2008 by Leslie Esdaile Banks. Illustrations and maps copyright © 2008 by Dabel Brothers Productions, LLC. All rights reserved. Printed in the United States of America. For information, address St. Martin's Press, 175 Fifth Avenue, New York, N.Y. 10010.

www.stmartins.com

*Illustrations by Chase Conley*
*Maps by Dabel Brothers Productions, LLC*

Library of Congress Cataloging-in-Publication Data

Banks, L. A.
    The shadows / L. A. Banks.—1st ed.
      p. cm.
    ISBN-13: 978-0-312-36875-3
    ISBN-10: 0-312-36875-5
  1. Richards, Damali (Fictitious character)—Fiction.   2. Vampires—Fiction.   I. Title.
PS3602.A64S49 2008
813'.6—dc22

                         2008012388

First Edition: July 2008

10  9  8  7  6  5  4  3  2  1

This eleventh book in the series is dedicated to all those who know that "the Secret" of manifesting joy and love and abundance begins with unshakable faith, and to those who have held on to their belief in the inherent goodness of humankind through all the darkest periods of history. We know tragedy exists . . . we know the worst and most catastrophic events have been caused by the horrors people have visited upon one another. But we have also seen some of the most surreal acts of kindness, of gentleness, of love, and compassion. Therefore, while the shadows will always gather, let us hold on to hope and manifest the Light.

# SPECIAL ACKNOWLEDGMENTS

I would like to give thanks and special recognition to a dear friend—and one of (if not *the*) smartest ladies I know—Wendalyn Nichols, for turning me on to "Black Bodies and Quantum Cats," as well as some serious viewpoint art and science. . . . You, lady, took my research to a whole "nuther" level. (*Big smile!*) Of course, I must always give a bow and a shout out to "the usual suspects," LOL—my mentor and agent, Manie Barron; my editor, Monique Patterson; Ms. Kia, who keeps everything shipshape; Colleen and Harriet for keeping me on the road; and to Michael for always hooking me up with fab book covers! Bless you, team St. Martin's! I want to also express my deepest gratitude and respect for the teachings and fellowship I received from the members of the Ausar and Auset Society in Philadelphia, as well as to the Nile Bookstore in Philadelphia. (Derrick Richardson, a.k.a. Meki Ra, you are "da man!") But the VHL Street team, there are no words . . . you all are the Ones who *make it do what it do*—thank you!

# PROLOGUE

Dead Harpies, messenger demons, and human helpers lay strewn across the granite floor, victims of the Beast's wrath and involuntary black blood donations. The smell of burning, sulfur-ridden flesh filled the air and the sound of agonized wails was clotted by the sizzling meat frying against the dank cavern bottom.

Lilith worked feverishly to staunch the dangerous flow of blood that gushed from the heir's side while her husband continued to work triage, summarily calling forth more blood and more bodies for his progeny to consume in order to keep their prized patient hydrated.

Another blast rocked the cavern and a winded Lilith looked up from the task as her patient howled in pain.

"Keep working!" her husband commanded and then looked up. His nostrils flared with blue-black fire and the clatter of his hooves echoed in the chamber as he paced, setting her teeth on edge. "If you lose him due to your ineptitude, you die!"

Lilith cautiously continued to excavate the eerie, glowing white light out of the heir's side. The brilliance of the white light emanating from the Neteru blade bolt was blinding. There was no way to stare at it directly, and even touching inches near it could permanently injure her limbs. What she could never make her husband understand was that if she placed her mouth over it to tear it out with her fangs, both she and their progeny would die and it would have been all for naught.

This was delicate surgery, but in his state of mind, she knew the Dark Lord was beyond logic. He couldn't touch the injury; she couldn't touch the injury. Only a black magic blade could be used to make an incision outside the glowing white ember that was spreading on the heir's skin like a rapid cancer. The light lesion was also imploding, damaging vital organs beneath it, which meant she had to cut wide and deep and quickly. The patient couldn't be anesthetized, for she needed his fury-will to help keep his dark life force going. However, the pain from his injuries compounded with her ministrations was sending him into shock.

Tears of frustration stung her eyes. Part of the chrysalis had been damaged. The heir had been born too soon. He was fully formed on the outside, but his internal demon organs had yet to harden. His exoskeleton had only recently been absorbed and covered with his human masking capacity. Even his fangs were new, hadn't hardened, nor had his wing bones turned to steel-hardness yet. His spaded tail wasn't even retractable at this point, and it flailed about piteously, trying to push her away as the source of his agony.

Their poor baby was still night-blind, his eyes had yet to adapt to complete darkness . . . and his lungs were not strong enough for the underground sulfur and heat. His heartbeat had yet to die. There was so much that had to be corrected before it had been time. Damn the Neterus!

Vital blood supply veins in the placenta that had been connected to the roof of the birthing cave, which were needed to wash the heir's system clean of the dreaded silver and light toxin that contaminated him, had been severed. Their patient's breathing labored in the subterranean air. He needed fresh, earth-plane oxygen in his fragile, living-species lungs. The chrysalis would have given him that, too.

Ruefully, Lilith looked at their gasping, struggling patient and the partial chrysalis skin that still covered his face. That was the only thing they could quickly improvise while under siege to give him what little air could be siphoned from topside during the onslaught. Beads of black sweat rolled down her face as she leaned over his body. Another blast rocked the cavern, causing stalactites to come crashing down and stalagmites to uproot from the cavern to begin a dangerous subterranean avalanche.

Lilith's and her husband's eyes met as he shielded her and the heir from falling rocks. She was certain that for the first time in history, probably since the initial battle he had fought in Heaven before being cast down, a lack of surety burned in his bottomless black eyes. He turned away from her, the vulnerability shaking them both. She could feel his power being torn between guarding his future and protecting his current empire from the onslaught of warrior angels ransacking his realms.

"Go, fight," she said as calmly as possible. She stared at him and then down at the patient. "If there is nothing for him to inherit, then he is as good as dead to us, anyway."

"Your life for his," her husband said between his teeth in *Dananu,* beginning to pull away from the table as he smashed another body into the feeding rocks to be sucked dry by the few remaining placenta-attached veins.

"It was going to be that in any regard, so why fear leaving me here to do my very best?" Her gaze narrowed, for once all fear had fled her.

"At this point I trust no one," he said, seething. "As if I ever did. And were it not for your lax security measures they would have never—"

"Hold it," she said, her voice strong and not wavering. Rare truth burned in her mouth like acid and she spit on the smoldering floor, unafraid. "They followed *your* black energy trail, not mine." When her husband turned away, she pressed on, making the most of the extraordinary moment of having bested the Devil in his own game. "They were able to do that because you underestimated the old priest's power of love." She clucked her tongue, making a tsking sound that caused her husband to whirl on her. "You need me, even if you punish me later for my insolence—so be it. But as the only entity in all of Hell that will tell you the truth, and not just what you want to hear in the midst of a crisis, I implore you to consider me a valuable resource and not waste me in a sudden rage."

When he walked away from her, she knew she had him. Satisfaction spread through her body, filling her with renewed power, even if it was potentially short-lived.

"Can you save him?" he finally asked, his shoulders slumping from fatigue and worry.

"Saving him has always been in my best interest, too, husband, regardless of your opinion of me. However, if you do not prevail then we're *all* dead, even you. So go, fight, and leave me to my work. Preserve what little is left and seal the breaches. There will be time enough to settle the score if I fail . . . where on earth shall I run from you, anyway?"

"There will be no shadow dark enough to hide from me if you fail."

"Failure was *never* my plan. You should know me well enough by now. I *always* play to win." She lifted her chin and stared at him directly. "I told you, Lu, I was in this with you till the very end."

The patient stopped breathing. The two powerful entities stared at each other. Her husband's fangs lengthened.

"Listen," she hissed.

"He's gone," the Beast growled, beginning to circle her.

Lilith pointed up at the network of veins clinging to stalactites that were still pulsing. "Listen," she hissed again. "The shelling by the Light has ceased."

"Just as my heir's breaths have ceased!" A section of cavern wall flew at her and she ducked. Undaunted, she leapt up in a rare show of insubordination. "Stop it. You'll kill him!"

Silence settled between them. Poised for a final black-energy extinction strike, her husband watched as she went to the marble slab and checked vital signs.

"They were linked to *his* dark-energy life pulse." She smiled slowly and closed her eyes, beginning to chuckle. "He's self-aware and finally helping to heal." She glanced up at her husband, who was now towering over her, trying to get a closer look at their patient. "Don't you see . . . he's flatlined to deceive them."

With a wave of the Beast's hand, four more bodies were impaled on the stalactites.

"Be proud, Lu . . . he has your cunning and endurance for pain. I must finish my work of cleaning the wound. You must finish your work of sealing the realms and reinforcing all the gray-zone shadows. Let us not be at odds, but be in collusion toward the same goal." She touched his stonelike chest, glad that he simply closed his eyes for a moment and steadied his breathing, rather than ripping the limbs from her body. "I will not fail you."

Slowly he reached out and a length of barbed-wire chain filled his hand. He closed his fist around it as the chain yanked away in a scorching whir through his palm. Attached to the end of the twisted metal was a huge manacle that cuffed three baying hound heads that were connected to the same dog's body.

The vicious creature's jowls were filled with acid-dripping fangs, and it scrabbled against the smoldering floor, trying to pull toward the breach in the realms. Thick cords of muscles striated the animal's back legs and barrel chest, its barking now near deafening. It was on the scent of angels. Frustrated at being held back by its master, the creature finally gave into a mournful howl, red eyes glowing with pure outrage at the assault against the nether region.

Lilith studied her husband's renewed composure as his gaze scanned the vaulted ceiling, deciding where to strike. She watched him slowly wind the chain in his fist, holding the guardian of his primary gate to Hell back, a strategy developing in his mind. That he'd called his favorite pet, Cerberus, to his side, meant that he'd refocused himself for war.

"I will not fail you," Lilith repeated.

Her husband simply nodded and looked up again, and then was gone.

# PART I

THIS IS OUR HOUSE

# ℮ CHAPTER ONE

It was what it was. Shit!

Carlos turned off the big-screen HDTV that was mounted on his and Damali's bedroom suite wall and then flung the remote control across the coffee table. The images continued to burn inside his head even after he shut off the television. Flames engulfed everything, appearing like fast-moving lava as they ate up countryside, homes, streets, abandoned cars, and people who couldn't make it out of the unrelenting smoke. Orchids, farms, olive groves—nothing stood a chance. Entire economies were disrupted, from small village infrastructures to that of the larger national interests.

Athens had been burning for weeks after he and Damali had severely injured the Dark Realm's heir apparent on a remote Greek island. Fair exchange was no robbery, according to the laws of revenge and reciprocity in the underworld, and since the offense had occurred on Greek soil, unfortunately the innocents of that land would pay the ultimate price. Greece was under spiritual siege, no matter what the news reports claimed. Yeah, right . . . wildfires. Scores of people had died from fires that raged out of control. The international news said it was a combination of arid weather and high Mediterranean winds, along with overwhelmed local fire departments. The battle between Heaven and Hell on a remote Greek island obviously didn't make the six o'clock news.

If they could have just gotten off a direct white-light bolt to make the attempted hit on the Antichrist a clean kill . . . *damn!* Today he'd get back on a mission. After weeks of nearly paralyzing fatigue, he could feel something shifting within the energy of the house. They'd all rested, even if they hadn't all recovered, it was time to go hunting again.

No doubt the Greek capital was now taking the brunt of the Beast's fury. Then again, in all likelihood, razing the land with billowing flames was just a ploy by the Devil to distract the warrior angels, to get them to pull up from their wrecking search for the wounded Antichrist throughout the bowels of Hell. It made sense that they'd redirect their efforts to attend to their primary mission—saving humanity. Brilliant. Dark. Twisted. But absolutely genius. Carlos stood and then walked across the room.

As soon as he opened the door leading out to the main hall, the soft filter of voices and the general hubbub of compound activity greeted him. The mild chaos was soothing. His nerves had been shot ever since he'd known for sure that his wife was pregnant. In rare glimpses he saw the strain of that reality in Marlene's wise eyes, but she hid it well. Shabazz was another story. His brow was constantly knit, like his. Of course Mar was gonna see it and then tell her husband—but Shabazz never spoke on it or stepped to him about it. Worry wafted off the senior Guardian brother in quiet, tight waves, but Shabazz was old-school enough to keep up a cool façade in front of the team. Every now and then Shabazz would give him a subtle nod that said it all without words: *I gotchure back.*

Carlos dragged his fingers through his hair as he walked down the hall. Damali being pregnant was the biggest open secret in the house that he'd ever witnessed. He was just glad nobody else beyond Marlene and Shabazz had picked up on Damali's condition yet.

The team would be happy, but they'd also freak. They all knew how dangerous it would be to have one of the Neterus in a vulnerable position this close to the end of days. But with a house full of seers, sooner or later the cat would be out of the bag. He was just glad that everyone was observing the house rule not to look into anyone else's personal auras or business without consent. But sooner or later, it would be obvious to anybody with a normal pair of eyes. Then what? Panic on a team fighting the kinds of entities that had now surfaced from the pit was an extremely dangerous thing.

Fallon Nuit paused for a moment to admire his newly reconstructed Los Angeles high-rise. Human bodies milled about in the landscaped courtyard, casting a succulent array of flavors onto his palate. He inhaled slowly as he entered the building through the huge revolving glass doors, enjoying the fragrance of pulsing life that had been baked to warm perfection by the sun's rays. Cattle. Some grain-fed beef, some garbage-fed meat on the hoof—what did it matter as long as they bled in the end?

Blood Music International would reign again, now more so than just a lucrative hip-hop label, but renamed and transformed into a multimedia empire—Council Group Entertainment. His gallantry in battle, as well as his shrewd observation of a potential double cross by the Neterus, had been rewarded. He'd been the only Vampire councilman who knew that Yolando had been a fraud from the start, thus his territory had been expanded to control all of topside communications for the Dark Lord. In addition to his considerable holdings, he now owned everything that Yolando had once had principality over. Nuit smiled as he surveyed his expanded territory. Death was good. *Très bon.*

Black-and-white marble and clean chrome lines stared back at him under the gleaming sun that poured through the massive open atrium, much to his satisfaction. The entire building was made of huge plates of glass inviting in the sun. The irony of it all made him heady. To stand in the sun as a daywalker while retaining all of his vampire powers had been a fantasy for centuries; now he was living it.

Flanked by several patient human bodyguards, he chuckled privately as his gaze roved over the jarring signature splash of scarlet color in the middle of the floor that was supposed to resemble royal embossing wax . . . but for those who truly understood, it was spilled blood. And plenty of it. Right in plain sight—the same way he'd corrupt the minds of the cattle all around him, feeding them propaganda, polluting their minds, and driving them in the direction the underworld needed to herd them. Perhaps he and the council had been going about it all wrong. Rather than attack the Neterus directly, attack humankind and watch the Neterus twist in the wind. *That* would draw them out.

They would pay for what they'd done to Lucrezia and Elizabeth, two gorgeous councilwomen wives who were now injured so badly that if they came out by day, they couldn't retain their illusion of beauty. Nuit lifted his chin, throttling back the unproductive rage beginning to surface within him, and pulled down on his monogrammed cuffs so that just the right corporate length showed beneath his custom-tailored Armani suit.

Although his mate, Lucrezia, was trapped again by the night, where her beauty still flourished, she'd survived the heinous attempt at silver poisoning. Sebastian's wife, Elizabeth, fared no better. It was a horrific crime against his vampire family. However, time was on his side to settle the score. That was the one thing he and Sebastian could seem to agree on. The tragedy that had befallen their wives oddly quelled their incessant rivalry.

Joining forces was the only way to best the Neterus, especially since Sebastian had also been maimed. And when he finally found Yonnie . . .

As Nuit brushed invisible lint off his lapels he sent his gaze around the lobby one last time. Another bit of irony lifted the corner of his mouth into a sinister half smile; Carlos and Damali's aggressive move on the chessboard of war actually put him in position to be the strongest vampire on the council.

Lilith was indisposed, feverishly working to heal the Dark Lord's heir. The Dark Lord was walking the planet, creating topside chaos to keep the angel corps frenetically working to save humanity, thereby effectively thinning their resources to hunt for his injured son. The other members of the Vampire Council had been exterminated, discredited, injured, or hijacked by the Light. That left him as the only legitimate holdover from the old regime of Dante.

Nuit straightened his already perfect posture, finding an additional millimeter of height to add to his six-foot-two, aristocratic bearing. What made it all the more glorious was the fact that he'd been the only one to predict the outcome of the events that had recently unfolded. Even Lilith took solid consideration of his counsel now, as did their ultimate ruler. One day, or night, when he finally ripped out Carlos Rivera's entrails, he'd have to thank him for positioning him so well.

Satisfied, he smoothed back his expertly barbered thicket of salt-and-pepper hair that he'd purposely allowed to become silver-flecked to add to his new daytime demeanor. Gone were the nights of perpetual, visceral youth; his new façade was strictly that of an entertainment industry maverick. As he began walking, he was closely followed by a retinue of henchmen that looked like secret service agents. Every human that swarmed around his seemingly forty-five-year-old visage donned wires in their ears, dark suits, and barely concealed weapons.

Ignoring the mild stir they created in the lobby, he crossed over the gold inlaid crest in the floor that glittered against the red hue like a maker's mark. He opened his graceful hand that held the horrific potential of black lightning and bloodletting, staring down at the gold crest ring of office that he wore like a wedding band. The craftsmanship of the piece was befitting of royalty, of age-old entitlement, and he admired how the near resemblance of that crest to the one on the floor looked against his café au lait skin.

He almost laughed at how the new corporate logo had been slightly toned down from the one in the Vampire Council's pentagram-shaped bargaining table in Hell, but it still was what it was: a sign of absolute power.

J.L. looked up with a smile as Carlos passed his equipment room in search of Damali. Guts of computers, television innards, cell phones, stereo system circuitry, and other varying bits of technology that he couldn't immediately recognize littered the long workbench in front of his Guardian brother.

He could tell by J.L.'s broad grin that a cursory greeting wasn't going to be enough—J.L. wanted to talk. His Guardian brother's entire vibe practically yanked him into the room. Problem was, he didn't feel like talking; he just wanted to find Damali. He wanted to know how she felt and to get her take on starting a new demon hunt.

Renewed energy made him impatient. He hadn't felt this clear and this good in weeks. But the way J.L. popped up like an excited jack-in-the-box to round the table made him laugh. Maybe the big secret had finally gotten out? The entire room was crackling with J.L.'s tactical sensory charge, as pure adrenaline made it waft off his skin and begin to lift the edges of Carlos's hair.

"What's up, man?" Carlos said, chuckling as J.L. pulled him

into a quick Guardian brother hug. "You've got blue static jumpin' all over you. I think you've been cooped up in the compound too long."

"That's no lie—but I finally figured it out," J.L. said excitedly. "The downtime made me focus. Now I know what's up."

Carlos beamed and just nodded. "Yeah . . . sooner or later I knew you would, man."

J.L. playfully punched Carlos in the shoulder with a lightning-fast martial arts spar and then dashed back over to the table where he'd been working. "You know I got skills, brother," J.L. said, laughing. "Check it out." He held a tiny silver object that looked like a small transistor the size of a pencil lead on the tip of his index finger. "No cheating . . . make a clean guess, man. You're gonna love it!"

The smile slowly faded from Carlos's face. J.L. hadn't figured out his secret . . . this was about something else. Carlos nodded, trying to play it cool, and then stepped farther into the compound's brain center—the tech lab.

J.L.'s smile widened and Carlos shoved his hands into his jeans pockets. Damn, he'd almost slipped and told on himself. In that moment he realized just how badly he'd wanted to share the good news about the baby with the household, and he had to really be on guard not to go against the advice of the Neteru Council On High. They'd said to wait; this time he was following the rules to the letter. Marlene and Shabazz had found out on their own. That was something different. But no grand announcements at this juncture were authorized. The older couple instinctively knew that, too, even before Damali had asked them to keep the info on the downlow.

"Okay, enlighten me, oh genius one," Carlos said with a half smile after a moment.

There was no way to know what new gadget J.L. had developed

for the team security systems, short of going into J.L.'s razor-sharp mind for a subtle thought scan, but that would be cheating. He could tell that he'd made J.L.'s day by being stumped, so he allowed his Guardian brother to revel in the triumph. Curiosity pushed Carlos's other thoughts aside as he stepped closer and peered down at the tiny object J.L. held out for him to inspect.

"You know how all of us have been in a funk ever since we came out of that last battle in Greece?"

Carlos nodded. "Yeah . . . but you know who we were up against, too, so it stands to reason. But the Covenant said we were all clean and would shake it soon."

"True," J.L. said with a wide smile. "If we had a chance not to mentally get weighed down again for a little while."

Carlos just stared at his Guardian brother for a moment, studying the quiet warrior burning deep within his almond-shaped, brown eyes. It was as though thousands of years of ancient Asian wisdom had coalesced into one soul as the two men stood facing each other, both expectant of the other's reaction. J.L.'s smile faded, giving way to his more serious side. Everybody's energy had been zapped after that battle, and it felt like they'd been walking through quicksand. Not even Marlene's white baths were helping.

"Talk to me," Carlos said quietly.

"It's been coming through the airwaves . . . the assault. You-know-who is the Prince of the Airwaves."

"Shit . . ." Carlos murmured, more closely studying the tiny bit of silver metal on J.L.'s finger.

"Yeah," J.L. said with triumph. "Once again, Inez's baby girl was our canary in a coal mine. All of us thought we were burnt-out from battle, and Inez's mom just from age and the pure shock of being inducted into this life. But neither of them went to war with us over in Greece. They stayed back home in New York in the Covenant safe house until we got back, right?"

"Right," Carlos said, extracting his hands from his pockets to fold his arms.

"Yeah, well, I get up real early every morning to do my tai chi on the back deck—gotta pass through the kitchen. I have a routine . . . make my green tea, let it steep, while I do my thing. The three-year-old gets up real early like that, too. I pass her every day in the kitchen eating her cereal and every morning her grandmother can barely make it into the kitchen and the kid is always sniffling. So a few days ago I asked the little bird why she was always so sad in the morning . . . and get this, man. She said the cartoons make her cry."

"Huh? Cartoons?" Dumbfounded, Carlos simply stared at J.L.

J.L. gingerly set down the small silver-coated chip on a piece of black velvet on the workbench. "That's what I said, man. So I asked her which ones she watched and the kid said everything makes her cry on TV now. She said it wasn't good anymore."

"That's . . . *crazy*."

J.L. nodded. "Yeah, and you and I both know the kid is a seer, right?"

"Right . . ."

"Inez's mom said she was just being dramatic because she wouldn't allow her to bust into Inez and Big Mike's room first thing in the morning, so it was just a daily tantrum . . . but I didn't *feel* that, bro. I wasn't feeling like the kid was making it up. There was genuine melancholy."

"This is too deep," Carlos said, raking his fingers through his hair.

"Uh-huh. My take exactly. So I got some old DVDs of *Barney* and other stuff she likes, and the kid was happy. Then I'd try a direct broadcast, and the poor little thing would hide her face and say it was scaring her."

"Whoa . . . man . . ."

"Yeah, yeah, I know," J.L. said excitedly, waving his hands. "It was freaky. So I asked Mom Delores if I could babysit Ayana for the day. I didn't want to say anything to anybody until I had hard evidence, ya know—in case I was just tripping. But I tested her on everything. I used old DVDs of her favorite cartoons and shows and Disney movies *before* the Greek isle battle as a control group of items, and then I showed her direct broadcasts over cable, satellite TV, images off my cell phone, and songs on the radio versus off older CDs as my test group, feel me?"

"Yeah, I feel you," Carlos said, worry making him clench his jaw for a moment. "What happened in the test?"

"Every time out the kid had the same reaction. Whatever was being broadcasted made her sad or afraid. Then I asked her what she saw and how she felt, and the poor little thing would only shake her head and say it made her want to do bad things to people. The kid was so horrified she wouldn't spit it out . . . so maybe Inez is gonna have to go in, as her mom and also a seer, to lift it out of her head . . . maybe purge it and then translate what the kid witnessed for us."

"Okay, we're gonna have to have a full team meeting about this, you know that, right?"

"Yeah, Carlos, I know. Because think about it, man . . . if after Marlene sent up some serious prayers with the members of the Covenant so that the angels would do their thing to cloak Ayana's little mind from going into the more, uh, sensitive areas of house business," J.L. added with a wry smile. "I mean, even Heaven knows the kid doesn't need to accidentally see what happens between couples . . . TMI at her age."

"At any age," Carlos said, forcing a smile.

"True . . . and if they've kept her shielded from any war strategy we have in the Situation Room, so the kid can live with us, then if she's picking it up that strong through a shielded mind . . ."

"Whatever's jumping through the airwaves now has some serious kick to it."

"You telling me?" J.L. shook his head and picked up a pair of tweezers. "The average human without any powers of sensitivity would be oblivious to the subliminal messages being broadcasted—but they'd feel the effect. They might even start to act out. It could be pure chaos . . . but I'm not a seer, just a tactical sensor, bro. So I didn't want to turn Krissy or any of the other seers onto her, because Ayana isn't our kid. Inez would have every right to be pissed off with us going that far with testing her daughter . . . I figured the exposure to TV and radio and whatnot was okay because that was already happening. But to send my wife into the little girl's head without her mother's consent might be crossing the line."

"So what you got, man?" Carlos said, nodding toward the silver item J.L. had lifted. "You did right, by the way . . . Inez might kick your ass."

J.L. nodded and laughed. "I might know karate but 'Nez knows kar-ray-zay."

Carlos pounded J.L.'s fist as they shared a private chuckle. "Especially when it comes to her baby girl. Mike might kick your ass, too."

"That's why I didn't go there, but instead worked on a small distortion device," J.L. said proudly. "It basically sends the broadcasted signal through the silver first, before it hits the screen and/or the speakers. Went to my geek buddies over at the University of San Diego, where they have da bomb labs already set up for nanotechnologies and new computer technologies—and where they love to work on wild-ass conspiracy theories . . . all I had to do was give them the specs and some cash, and it was all good."

"You've got some mad skills, man," Carlos said, impressed, as he leaned in closer to inspect the tiny object J.L. held over the velvet. "How did the kid react?"

"Like a normal kid . . . laughing, smiling, and clapping at her favorite parts of whatever show was broadcasted. But get this . . . she also wasn't mesmerized."

Carlos straightened and stared at J.L. He'd seen little kids in his extended family and in the old neighborhood watch television before he'd left them for this life. They normally sat two feet away from the screen, eyes wide, practically unblinking, staring up into the light, jaws slack and in a daze.

"You know how dangerous this shit is, J.L.?"

"I know," J.L. said, gently setting down the miniscule filter again. "I've seen little kids watch TV, old people, too. How many people you know sit with the remote control in their grip, just staring, like they're in a spell or a trance?" He smoothed his hair back from his forehead. "And don't forget nursing homes, prisons, hospitals, captive audiences, the broadcast zone is limitless."

"Plus, how many people download music and walk the streets with earphones stuck in their ears, music blasting?" Carlos said, his mind envisioning the busy sidewalks of every urban environment he knew.

"Or have a cell phone glued to their ears?" J.L. said quietly.

Carlos looked at J.L. for a moment. "Or have the computer on surfing the Net, while talking on the telephone with the speakers on blasting music MP3 downloads while the TV is on in the background? Or cops, with loaded weapons in the streets, getting signals off their radios. . . . This shit could be epidemic."

"My point exactly," J.L. said, lifting his chin with dignity. "So I went around the house filtering everybody's equipment room by room, gadget by gadget for the last twenty-four hours. How do you feel?"

Carlos stopped and thought about it hard. "Way better, man. Like, I got my energy back or something."

J.L. simply looked at him. "Good, man, 'cause you did."

## CHAPTER TWO

After an exhaustive search of the house he found Damali in the last place he'd expected—the kitchen. Carlos came to a silent halt and watched his wife for a few precious moments before she noticed him.

He let his eyes take in the graceful curve of her back, the way her shoulder blades added contour where wings could majestically emerge when she was provoked or impassioned. Gorgeous, cinnamon-brown skin kissed by early morning light seemed too soft to even make contact with her casual getup of white sweat shorts and a wife-beater T-shirt with no bra. Barefoot, hair swept up in a ponytail of soft brown dreadlocks, and a voluptuous figure that would soon be evidence of growing life . . . the sight of her stole his breath. And she was hungry; that was a blessing.

Since the last battle, her appetite had been off. Anything edible sent her into the bathroom to secretly hurl. Keeping her symptoms from the team had been difficult. Nausea had plagued the poor woman so badly that she was actually beginning to look gaunt. At least that's what he'd thought had been the culprit until his enlightening conversation with J.L.

Carlos remained in the archway of the kitchen entrance,

watching his wife bend and survey the refrigerator shelves. The sight of her luscious backside tweaked his libido, making him remember how many weeks had gone by since they'd done more than cuddle. Sure, he could have just mentally scanned the compound to find her, but he'd needed to walk and think and process what he'd learned from his Guardian brother. He reminded himself of that fact as his gaze caressed the sleek backs of her thighs.

Perhaps more important, he didn't want to connect into anyone else's vibes by touching their energy with his own. He couldn't trust the seers not to pick up his tension regarding this latest threat and begin probing, and he prayed to God that none of the negative radiation coming through the airwaves had affected the baby. But now even his and Damali's abstinence made sense—they were being poisoned through the airwaves. Maybe all of humanity was. Those facts kept his nature in check; there was important shit to attend to.

But as he basked in this brief stolen moment watching Damali without her knowing he was there, an eerie, yet soothing calm soon slid over his taut nerves, making him begin to relax. Her third-eye radar was down and her calmness fed his. She was humming a little tune that he couldn't quite place and the refrigerator door was wide-open as she stood in front of it considering her options. One graceful hand clutched a huge family-sized bag of barbecue potato chips—heresy in Marlene's camp—and the other was dug down deep in the bag up to her elbow. The sight of Damali extracting a single large chip from the bag as though she were a diamond dealer checking a precious stone for flaws, and then popping the whole thing in her mouth with a sigh, made him smile.

This was the part of her pregnancy he'd been waiting for, the part he'd imagined a hundred different ways . . . where he could be useful, where he could help. He couldn't do the heavy lifting by carrying the baby for her, but he could make the craving runs for her. He could be her personal army of one. He could take a bullet for her, hunt down and kill anything that even thought about hurting her. Hell to the yeah—he could do that. He could feed her, keep her safe, and make sure she didn't want for nothing. Could be her soldier or die trying. That would at least give him something constructive to do. He was so glad she felt better. . . . God he loved her so much.

"Marlene's gonna have a cow," he said with a chuckle, finally entering the kitchen.

Damali spun around and hid the chips behind her back, laughing.

"You're busted," he said, peeking around her back and trying to grab her contraband.

Her pretty brown eyes sparkled with mischief and her cheeks were full with what appeared to be a chipmunk's loot. She covered her mouth with one hand, chewing quickly and crunching loudly, and using her body to block him from taking her chips. "Don't tell Mar I smuggled these in," Damali finally gasped, laughing hard enough to make him laugh, too.

Carlos closed the small gap between them and hugged her, whispering in her ear while still laughing. "Your secret's safe with me, señora . . . but I'll need a bribe."

"Always a catch," Damali quipped playfully, kissing his neck, but holding her chips away from him.

Carlos cocked his head to the side. "You know where I'm originally from, girl . . . fair exchange . . ."

Damali gave him a lopsided smile and opened her bag of chips, ignoring him. "Kettle Chips . . . there's no negotiation. They're all mine," she said with a sigh. "I don't know what happened, but this morning I woke up and that's all I wanted."

"You got out of bed too early, that's why," he said, still chuckling, then giving her a wink and closing the refrigerator behind her.

"Yeah, well," she said, waving her hand at him and prancing away. She raised her eyebrows, glanced around the kitchen like a thief, and then lowered her voice. "That's how I got like this in the first place—not getting up when I should have."

They both laughed and he leaned against the refrigerator door with a shrug.

"What can I say?"

"Nothing." She placed her hand on her hip and devastated him with her megawatt smile.

"What you want to eat, baby? I'll go get it." The playfulness suddenly left his voice and was replaced by a tone so gentle she just stared at him. That seemed to cause her smile to fade into a softness that touched her eyes.

"I don't know," she said quietly. "But I love you."

He pushed off the fridge and opened his arms. She filled them and he rested his cheek against the crown of her head. She smelled wonderful, a concoction of shea butter and almond oil and barbecue chips. The satiny feel of her skin beneath his palms as he stroked her arms and the soft, velvety texture of her locks against his face made him close his eyes.

Her warmth had married his and they stood that way for what seemed like a long time; him just hugging her in the middle of the kitchen floor; her just hugging him back with a bag of chips crushed against his spine. It was Heaven on earth, a gift granted in small slivers of time between worry and fighting and sharing the planet with duty and other people. He so wanted her to eat something healthy before they had the team meeting, and well before he had to disclose to her the conversation he'd had with J.L. After that, she probably wouldn't be able to keep anything down.

"What's the matter, baby?" Damali murmured, finally pulling away from him.

"Nothing," he lied. "I'm just glad your appetite is back and you're feeling better."

"I do feel better," she said, staring up at him. "It was awful . . . and I didn't want to upset you by telling you how bad I
was really feeling. Headaches that felt like an ice pick was going
through my brain, and the nausea was a bitch."

Her gaze searched his face and he kissed the center of her
forehead.

"I'm sorry . . ." he said awkwardly.

"Wasn't your fault, puhlease," she said, dramatically scowling
at him, trying to make him smile. "Goes with the territory."

"Yeah . . . I guess," he said offhandedly. "But, like, did you
notice it at any specific time?" he added, fishing for information.

Damali nodded and released their embrace so she could go
back to munching on her chips. "Every time I'd get comfortable to watch the news or a movie, or even listen to the radio,
within five minutes, I was as sick as a dog."

He watched her carefully as she crunched on potato chips
and tried to talk at the same time. Mild panic began to brew
within him again; what if the baby hadn't been getting enough
nutrients because of all this? Chips just didn't seem right. What
if the poisonous messages had attacked her or the fetus beyond
just nausea? If the old Chairman of the Vampire Council could
claw out her womb to make her miscarry before, what could
the Ultimate Darkness do to Damali or the baby? He quickly
shoved every mental outburst into the black-box within his mind
and sealed it shut like an ancient sarcophagus. She never needed
to know about or feel even a hint of his concerns while she was
carrying.

"Carlos, maybe I'm crazy," she mumbled through a mouthful
of chips, oblivious to his growing concern, "but I swear talk radio kicked my behind . . . I could play my old music on the
stereo or on my iPod, but all the new stuff on the radio just made
me evil, and it seemed like I was allergic to the computer—I

couldn't download jack off the Net without jumping up fifty times to go hurl. So I just tried to walk and sleep . . . baby, I'm sorry I've been such a trip. I know these past few weeks have been really hard on you, with the mood swings and the sickness." She held his gaze for a moment. "And I know I've been all teary-eyed and not real . . . you know . . . romantic. Just wanting to hug, but that's it . . . I don't know."

"Hey," he said, coming to her to cradle her face. "I love you, all right. You haven't been feeling good. I want you to feel better—that's my number one priority. Everything else can wait."

"Yeah . . . but . . ."

He kissed the bridge of her nose. "Yeah, but what?" He pulled back so she'd look at him. "I waited five years for you before, what's waiting till a little morning sickness passes?"

He smiled; she smiled.

"It's been morning, noon, and night sickness, though, Carlos . . . and—"

"And you know how I am—go 'head, say it, 'cause I know that's what you were going to say." He gave her a lopsided smile, even though he was feigning outright indignation. The combination made her laugh and he released her face and hugged her off her feet. "Like, where am I going, huh? My wife carries a blade and don't play."

She pushed at his shoulders, laughing harder. "Will kick your butt. Got me all knocked up and acting crazy. You'd better not leave me."

"Ain't going nowhere and can wait till you feel better," he said, burying his face against her neck to kiss it gently. He set her down on her feet and allowed his hands to slide over her shoulders in a gentle sweep.

"I'm gonna try to do better so you don't have to deal with nine months of this mess. Damn I'm hungry . . . but I don't know what I want."

"It's cool," he said, quietly surveying her. "I signed up for this tour of duty, so you just tell me what you feel like you have a taste for and I'll go bring it home."

"Salty—it's gotta be salty," she said emphatically. "Sesame seeds and salty . . . with like, lots of soy sauce. You know that vegan place that does the soy chicken stir-fry with sesame seeds . . . and they make the vegetables crunchy—they don't overcook them."

"I'm on it," he said, heading toward the door. Suddenly he wanted to hunt something, wanted to expend lots of energy on a quest to feed her. He could have transported anything she desired into the kitchen, but his body needed to move. She'd ignited something very primal within him that was reminiscent of his old life, and that was also a little disturbing.

"No, wait," she said, waving a hand stained orange from barbecue flavoring. "Tahini. That's the taste. Falafel with lots and lots of tahini on it . . . that's the sesame seed and soy taste, I think, and the garlicky, grainy, other thingies in it that I want—the chickpeas." She closed her eyes and ate another chip. "Yeah, in a thick, warm pita wrap."

He gave her a brief nod. "I'll be right back."

She opened her eyes, looking confused. Her suddenly serious expression and knit brow said it all; she was obviously wondering why he was going to the trouble of physically leaving the house to go get her grub. But he couldn't explain the complex emotions coursing through him right now. Profound knowing slammed into his mind with each footstep as he crossed the great hall, and then crossed the marble foyer and opened the oak French doors. Bright early morning sunlight met him, but he knew that the darkside would never stop coming for them, and with each passing week, it would be harder and harder for Damali to hide the fact that she was pregnant—then what?

Even though he remembered what Adam and Ausar had said,

the Neteru Kings telling him not to worry, how was he supposed to do anything *but* worry? The fact that he was so twisted up in knots pissed him off. Panicking was not an option; it was the best way to tip his hand, show the other side vulnerability, and *that* was definitely not an option.

He had to remember that serious hallowed ground that not even daywalkers could breach protected his wife and the rest of the team. All of them had been under self-imposed house arrest since they'd returned from Greece. He had to remember that they'd reinforced the compound with silver, holy water, protective prayer barriers, and every conceivable anti-demon technology available. He had to remember that the darkside was blind to this location, as were their human helpers, courtesy of a little Divine intervention by the angels. Then it dawned on him . . . why was he worrying so much? Was he poisoned?

More than anything at the moment, however, he needed to drive, needed to move, needed to break through his own fears and reenter the world—the restored silver Bugatti was Damali's sweet, sweet thing, but the gleaming red Saleen S7 in the garage was his precious. Fuck all this lying low. That was never his style, dead or alive.

Carlos rounded the garden pathway to the garage, preferring to enter it that way rather than by going through the entire house to enter the spacious carport. His head felt like it was about to explode, and he didn't know why. Worry was one thing, but this was something much more intense.

Salt, she wanted salt. The baby was building blood volume in the first trimester. It was a fact that anyone could read online or in a parenting magazine article while sitting in a doctor's waiting room. But a very old part of him sensed it, perhaps worse, he'd literally smelled it . . . the minute changes in the hormone concentrations in her blood . . . in the baby's blood. Maybe that was what was freaking him out—if he could still smell that acutely after no longer being a full vampire, what could very old councilmen pick up in the hundredths of particles per billion coursing through his wife's veins? Lilith would know . . . her husband would know—then it would be on.

Sesame seeds. Damali had said she had a taste for sesame seeds. Carlos wrested his mind away from the brink of an outright panic attack as he walked. Sesame seeds were chockful of nutrients, especially those that fed a growing baby's brain. He punched in the code and impatiently waited for the long garage door to open.

What he couldn't understand was, where did the sudden kill-rush come from?

Carlos walked between the lines of custom-kitted parked vehicles and then opened the butterfly door on his red racer. His S7 had been put back together lovely after all the body damage she'd sustained in Death Valley, just like Damali's Bugatti had. Rider's boys from the Arizona Guardian team had done a fantastic job.

Remembering the run-in with Fallon Nuit almost made him snarl as he slid against the butter soft leather interior, yanked the door closed, and gripped the steering wheel. Yeah, now he knew why he'd wanted to kill something—just thinking about what had happened to Heather on the back of Dan's bike that night sent a chill through him. Damali couldn't miscarry again, and at the same time, as her belly grew, the harder it would be for Heather . . . maybe even for Juanita, who desperately wanted a child, too. There was so much bullshit to think about it was making his mind crazy.

"Damn!" Carlos started the engine and shifted the gears hard, peeling out of the garage. Driving with one hand, he leaned over and popped open the glove compartment to pull out his sunglasses, hurriedly put them on, and pushed them up the bridge of his nose. If they wanted to play . . . and this time, if they hurt her, there'd be no redemption for him. Yeah, he and old Lu could go one-on-one till the end of time and blow up half the planet—but he was not going down without a fight or be held hostage to fear.

Speed was his demon at the moment, the one he wanted to conquer right now. It was easy to blind police radar guns as he took the scenic route at a hundred-and-ten miles per hour. The vehicle handled like a rocket and didn't even start to vibrate as the speedometer crept to one-eighty with a bullet. It was pure engineering genius.

Carlos focused on the desolate road, his senses sweeping the terrain for bikers, other drivers, deer, and morning trucker traffic, anything that could flip his car or be killed by it. Five miles out from his destination, he backed the S7 down to a reasonable suburban speed. But he'd had to get the rush out of his system first.

Adrenaline sweat had made his T-shirt cling to his back. A deep burgundy V formed a pattern in the crimson T-shirt. Carlos glanced in the rearview mirror as he brought the S7 to a purring stop. A noticeable, intense silver glare showed through his dark lenses and a hint of fang had begun to crest in his mouth. He had to pull it together—what the hell was wrong with him? He definitely couldn't go into the small diner like this. Coming out of the compound had been a really bad idea, but after weeks of being cooped up, he'd needed this run.

Summoning calm before he opened the car door, Carlos allowed his forehead to rest against the steering wheel. He'd actually wanted to do battle with Lucifer—*was he outta his damned mind?* Had actually, for a moment, felt that old vampire urge to bring his woman a feeding kill. Had felt so many old bad habits coming at him that he'd thought for a moment he'd smother in them all.

"Help me, God," he murmured with his eyes tightly shut. "What's wrong with me?"

"Nada," a quiet, familiar voice said, making Carlos snap his attention toward the passenger's seat.

The translucent image of Padre Lopez stared back at Carlos. For two seconds, the interior cabin of the sleek sports car was way too small. It took everything within him not to bolt or attack, and for his mind to catch up with the image his eyes took in. Immediately his hot silver gaze burned through the apparition to scan it for authenticity. Padre Lopez waited, his patient stare an answer to the invasive burst of silvery white light. Carlos's shoulders relaxed by several inches and his sudden battle bulk slowly ebbed as he realized his dangerous thoughts had summoned a friend and not the Devil himself.

Carlos let his breath out hard and rubbed his palms down his face. "Padre, you've gotta give a man a little more warning if you're gonna make a visitation from the other side." He then smoothed the bristled hair down on the back of his neck, never taking his eyes off the apparition.

"I am among many who help guard the child," Padre said softly. Even in his spirit form, Padre Lopez's youthful eyes held the same wonder and awe they had when he was alive. "I have missed the family, Carlos, but I stop in to pay my respects from time to time." He smiled tenderly and looked at Carlos for a long while before speaking again. "How have you been, brother?"

"I'm not sure," Carlos admitted quickly, knowing that if the Light had sent in a dead priest after he'd prayed for help, things were definitely not looking good.

Padre Lopez nodded and Carlos watched the sunlight that was coming in the windows beam right through the young priest. Seeing that was as eerie as having Lopez read his thoughts. This clearly wasn't just a social call.

"You are not reverting, Carlos, just remembering. There is nothing wrong with that which Damali carries. As it grows, every defense mechanism that is a part of your DNA will get stronger. So will hers."

"You sure? The baby is fine? My wife is cool, too, right?" Carlos massaged the tension out of his neck. "Positive?"

"This time, you will be able to trust the human doctors from the Covenant. They will not betray you again."

Carlos shook his head. "Last time, when they weren't sure what I was, they tried to sterilize Damali. So you'll have to forgive me if I'm skeptical. I'd rather leave it up to Marlene, Aset, and Eve, because in this frame of mind, I *will* take a body—human or otherwise, if they mess with my wife."

Padre Lopez nodded, but didn't smile. "I pray over her food, even when she forgets. Her system cannot take another poisoning. We all watch for murderous attempts from the darkside." His eyes remained sad and his unrelated comment was clearly avoiding the sore subject of the earlier betrayal of the team by misdirected humans.

Carlos released his breath in another hard sigh of relief and let the subject drop, picking up on the young priest's evasive statement. "Good looking out, man, thank you."

Still the apparition of one of the lost members of the Covenant didn't smile. The strained look in Padre's eyes prompted Carlos's next question.

"Then why am I remembering the old days when I was dead? I know I'm getting stronger . . . but I'm feeling some of the old things that I thought were finally purged out of my system, Padre."

Padre Lopez looked down at his hands for a moment and his image began to fade. "You are still our best asset. From the line of Dante, who was the progenitor of Cain—who thus helped beget that which we now hunt . . . the spawn of Lilith and the Unnamed One. You can still feel them directly when we cannot. You were once tethered to their dark thrones and know how they function; you are experienced in their ways. Once their drain to your energy lifted, you could again pick up impressions. That is why they sent me, your line brother, from life . . . one who can interpret those images and messages, too. Just call on me, Carlos, to gather up whatever you feel and I will carry it up to the battle stations in the Light."

He stared at Carlos when Carlos didn't immediately reply. "Remember Psalm Ninety-one, 'He will command His angels concerning you to guard you in all your ways . . . they will lift you up lest you strike your foot against a stone.' Never forget that—we have been instructed in your behalf."

"Cool." His voice was monotone. He didn't like still being remotely connected one bit, but what could he do. Carlos slumped back in his seat and briefly shut his eyes as he let out a hard exhale. "They're feeding him—the Beast's son—which means it's still alive, strong enough now to eat. I know that's good intel but I don't wanna feel it. Maybe I didn't even wanna know it. Does that make sense?"

When Carlos opened his eyes, Padre Lopez was gone, but his faint voice hung in the cabin, leaving behind an eerie gentle answer.

"Yes."


When Carlos came back into the kitchen with her meal, she could tell by the mechanical way he walked into the room that something was seriously wrong. He moved like a robot. His normally fluid motions were now jerky. Gone was the smooth, almost feline stride that gave him a graceful, pantherlike quality that was one of the sexiest things about him. It was his trademark and it was gone, along with any ability he owned at stealth.

Tension had made the muscles in his handsome face rigid and he avoided looking directly at her—a dead giveaway. He seemed flushed, as though he'd battle bulked and then repressed it. Beads of perspiration rimmed his hairline, causing his precision cut onyx waves to glisten under the sunlight. Adrenaline sweat had obviously made his red T-shirt stick to him, showing off every brick in his stonecut chest and abdomen, because it wasn't hot enough outside this early in the morning for him to be looking like that. Even his muscular thighs now seemed to be straining, trapped beneath the black jeans fabric as he walked deeper into the kitchen. His Tims created heavy, weary thuds against the floor. This was not the same man that had left the house a little more than a half hour ago.

Damali quickly jumped up from the deck lounge chair she'd been sunning herself in and slid open the glass door that led into the house. What was wrong with her husband? She said a quick mental prayer—*Dear God, don't let anything bad have happened.* Then she amended the request with a whisper, knowing that something awful had already obviously gone down. "Please, God . . . just help us."

She stared at Carlos's intense expression and the way his deep brown eyes were still hidden by black sunglasses as he entered the house, studying every detail about him. The muscles pulsed in his jaw; his biceps twitched every few seconds like he was straining not to punch something unseen. The muscles in his broad shoulders were so tight that they'd bunched into thick cords. She surveyed his golden-bronze complexion, searching for any signs of demon attack, and came away wanting.

Damn. Why did she ask him for tahini . . . ? She could have figured out something else, eaten anything else—it wasn't that important. She should have stopped him! The entire team had been lying low for weeks; nobody had ventured off the compound grounds. But he'd seemed so happy to be finally getting out for a drive. So confident. She'd never forgive herself if she'd sent him on a stupid grub run and he'd gotten ambushed. She took a steadying breath and closed the door behind her.

"You okay?"

"Yeah, yeah, I'm good . . . did you pray over those chips before you ate 'em?" Carlos glanced at her and then raced to the trash can as he slung her falafel platter onto the counter. "Benedicti—"

"Hold it, hold it, hold it, Carlos." Damali rushed up to him and held on to both his arms. "If you're doing ancient Latin benedictions over a dead potato chip bag like an exorcism, you mind telling me—*your wife*—what's going on?"

"Everything's cool," Carlos said, wiping at the sweat on his brow. "No need to get yourself all worked up. We just have to be diligent, have to be sure you don't get poisoned again. If you pray over your food—"

"Who came to you?" She stared at him without blinking.

"Nobody, it's just for good measure."

"You used to be able to lie so smooth . . . humph, humph, humph," she said with a half smile, shaking her head. "I guess there's been improvement, growth. You can't lie to me anymore without me knowing."

"Baby, I got your platter the way you wanted it," he said, guiding her to the counter and then pulling out a stool for her to sit down on. "Let's say the Lord's Prayer over it, then you can eat, and I'll pour you something to drink—"

"No offense, but the Lord's Prayer is a little intense over a falafel platter, don't you think? What about the normal grace that takes all of five seconds?" She was baiting him, but he just shrugged and tried to play it off.

"Naw, it's just that we need to be more careful nowadays."

"Carlos Rivera," Damali said quietly, folding her arms over her chest. "Who did you see and what's going on?" She let her breath out hard when he didn't immediately answer. "Keeping things from me doesn't protect me—it makes me worry. I'd rather know if something bad was about to jump off than get blindsided by it . . . you oughta know me better than that by now."

Carlos took off his sunglasses and dragged his fingers through his hair, sliding the glasses across the counter. He looked both ways and then stepped in close to her, keeping his voice low.

"My job is to help protect you through all of this . . . to keep you chilled out. The whole time you're carrying, everything happening around you needs to be real peace so the baby doesn't go through any trauma because you, my lady, ain't gotta go through no bullshit."

Damali reached up, cradled his face, and gently kissed him. "Impossible job, given who we are and what we do, but I appreciate the sentiment." She leaned closer, almost falling off the stool to hug him while he stood next to her, roughly rubbing her back. Even his touch was off. Both of his huge hands felt like anvils as they tried to pat her shoulders before he stepped away from her, spiking her alarm at the amount of tension riddling his body.

"Tell me," she said in a firm but gentle tone.

"Padre," Carlos finally admitted in a quiet voice. "He prays for you before you eat anything, even when you forget."

Damali caught his hand and pulled him in close, then laid her head on his shoulder and hugged him hard. "I know you miss him . . . is that what this is about?"

"I miss a lot of people, D," he admitted, pushing a stray lock that had worked its way loose from her ponytail behind her ear.

"Then what's wrong?" Damali pulled back and looked deeply into his eyes. "Why else did Padre Lopez come to you? If it was just to make you feel better about missing him, you wouldn't have walked in here all jacked up."

"I'm still linked in," Carlos said on a hard exhale. "Still a fucking GPS system, which is dangerous for anybody near me. . . . If I'm tapped into them, they might be tapped into me and mine."

"You'll always have a tie there," she said quietly. "We both know that. It's our best defense and I'm not afraid of that."

"Yeah, well this time I am," he said in a sudden rush, slapping the center of his chest. "I am, D. Why can't they just give me temporary clearance where I'll know for sure that nothing bad can seep from me to you or from my old life to you? I did *not* need to hear that shit this morning!"

"Hey . . ." she said softly, holding on to his arm so he didn't widen the space between them. "I'm silver-plated."

Her attempt to minimize the risk didn't work and she immediately felt bad that she'd even tried that tact. Carlos just looked at her. His mood was sobering, and although she'd known how deeply worried he'd been when she'd conceived, she'd mistakenly thought he'd purged that pain when they'd discussed it before. Clearly he hadn't, or maybe it was that something new had brought it all back with a vengeance.

"It's gonna be all right, Carlos," she said softly, not knowing what else to say. "The Neteru Councils promised . . ."

"The baby *has* to get here this time," he murmured. "You have to make it, too. It's not an either/or choice. Both of you gotta make it, or I won't."

"Gonna do my best, and with you having my back, what's the worry?" She forced a smile and caressed his cheek.

"Damali, there's been an incident. We have to have a family meeting after you eat."

"Eat? Hell . . . no time like the present. Let's get everybody in the Situation Room and—"

"Not till you eat."

She began to pull away, but he held her firm by hugging her where she sat. "C'mon, Carlos, that can wait."

"This is exactly why I've been acting like I have. I need to know that you'll do things a little differently—not a lot differently, just a little differently—like you'll listen to me when I ask you to please sit down and eat."

Slowly, her body yielded within his embrace. "Okay," she finally said. "But can you debrief me here while I eat?" She didn't have the heart to tell him that after scarfing down an entire family-sized bag of chips, the last thing in the world she wanted to do was eat a falafel platter. The mood had passed.

He forced a smile and she could tell that it took a lot for him to make his mouth accept it. "I'll talk, you eat, but that's the deal."

"Deal," she said, reaching around him and picking up the dinner bag he'd left on the counter, glad that the impasse was solved.

"Good, 'cause it don't make no sense trying to raise my kid on barbecue chips."

# CHAPTER THREE

Surreal calm overtook her as she listened to Carlos. Rather than the sensation entering her, it oddly emanated from within her. She'd promised him that she would eat. Damali moved her hands by rote to appease him . . . stalling for time by picking up the paper bag, slowly opening it, taking out the plastic container, opening that with care, and then allowing her meal to sit before her untouched as she listened intently to what her husband was saying. Something about the smell of the food now turned her stomach.

It was only when she saw him blink that she became aware that time had actually slowed down all around her. His lids slid closed as though a heavy curtain of onyx lashes had been dropped to thud one against the other. His voice was now like distant thunder—a rumble of unintelligible words, they were being spoken so slowly.

Background sounds thrust their way to the forefront of her senses. Her breaths and heartbeat, his breaths and heartbeat, were each so slow and so loud they created a collision inside her head. Even though she couldn't quite make out what he was saying, she gathered what she could from his private, urgent tone and then watched how he slowly leaned in close to her to speak.

Carlos's physical warmth suddenly felt as though she'd been wrapped in a blanket and then soon became a searing barrier like one would expect if one stood before an open oven that had been left on broil for hours. She settled back from the uncomfortable body heat radiating off him, and as she did, the sound of her clothes rustling against the chair was jarring.

He swallowed hard, pausing midsentence, and she almost cringed from the change in decibel that had transitioned the low rumble of his voice to the mucous-thick sound of saliva coating his throat. Yet through all of it, she oddly knew what he was saying, not from the words, but the impressions that began to form behind her wide-open eyes.

Never taking her gaze from his, she saw it. The poisonous vapor. The way it slid out of technology orifices and opened dark portals within houses, buildings, and within human minds. The airwaves were polluted. Devious propaganda had living entities entwined within it, and the embedded messages spewed thick black emissions into the human realm. The gray-zone, the earth plane, was becoming denser, darker, more twisted and violent.

Shadow entities spilled over the very edges of Hell and into the psyches and spirits of the unaware, diving into the pools of light that are normally within each human being.

Damali sat transfixed as she watched how the demonic forces entered a living body and then swallowed up all the clean light within it, slowly corroding it until there was simply no living aura left. At the point of total eclipse, the person was no more. Gone was their will, along with every shred of humanity that had once defined them.

"Tell me your names," she whispered, horrified. This was so much worse than the plague of the Damned. It was such a quick transition, no incubation period. No abstinence of touch could keep a person safe. The airwaves were being infected exponentially, and even people in the most remote villages had radios and televisions in small general stores!

Carlos had cocked his head to the side and had asked her a question. She could tell by his worried expression that he was asking something important of her. But the reply that should have been hers was instead a shadow turning to her before it entered the body of a man on the streets. It smiled a sinister smile, baring mangled, yellow teeth in a hollow black pit devoid of a face.

Her husband's voice drifted farther and farther away until she was spinning in a panicked daze within a crowded market, then she was on a crowded street. All around her people were being taken over. All around her chaos was simmering beneath the surface of human potential. An army was being raised right on the streets and right before her eyes. Vertigo claimed her as her vision jettisoned her from New York to Copenhagen, to Kenya to Milan. Remote islands, metropolises, it didn't matter, the invasions were unrelenting.

Arms outstretched, she ran toward a school yard and then skidded to a halt as high school students fell into darkness. She couldn't breathe. *Not the children.* Her gaze fell upon a middle school and she watched as dark entities swarmed the windows like locusts.

Damali covered her face and turned away. *Tell me this plague's name so we can send it back into the pit!* Within seconds she was in a hospital, her hands pressed flat against a nursery's glass window and she saw the shadows slide eerily into the nurses' bodies, but none touched the babies. Yet that provided no relief. One nurse simply smiled and turned off an incubator's oxygen.

"No!" Damali's voice escalated with her panic. She had to know what this entity was in order to fight it. Not vampire, not succubus, the team had never seen a manifestation like this. "Tell me its name!"

Suddenly every person on the streets everywhere she looked had a sinister companion and they all smiled at her simultaneously and whispered back, "My name is legions."

"Damali. Damali!"

A tight grasp held her upper arms and she was mildly aware of being shaken. Time snapped back. She caught Carlos by his elbows, panting and covered with sweat.

"You all right? Damali, talk to me!"

"I saw it," she gasped. "It's already starting."

As soon as she'd made the statement, she shrugged out of Carlos's hold and covered her mouth and nose.

"Get that out of the house!" she demanded, jumping down from the stool and backing away from the counter, pointing at her untouched food.

"Oh, shit!" Carlos toppled his stool as he backed up quickly and stared at the larvae teeming over the edge of the container.

The moment his silvery line of vision hit it, the entire platter exploded, sending disgusting, maggoty gore everywhere. Instantly shielded by a golden disc, the couple took refuge as they watched the wriggling mass rain down on the translucent surface and sizzle and disappear with a sulfuric stench. Everything the larvae plopped down on made them fry and evaporate. Marlene's kitchen was well anointed, and Inez had undoubtedly backtracked through it and given it a second blessing.

No less than they'd expected, they immediately heard heavy footfalls and knew the team was headed into the kitchen in a call to arms. Carlos and Damali shared a glance.

"Inez is gonna have a cow," Damali said, dry-heaving from the residual sulfur smell.

"After Marlene has a heart attack," Carlos muttered, checking twice before lowering the shield to be sure it had stopped raining maggots. "This happened in her kitchen." He looked at Damali. "You okay?"

"Yeah," she said, swallowing down the feeling of nausea and then stepping around his shield to assess the damage.

"I don't understand. I prayed over it." He looked at the scorched counter where the platter had been. "Lopez even prayed over it from the other side."

"That's why it never made it to my mouth," Damali said in a tight voice. "But it came from the outside . . . they were laying for you, baby. They've been laying for any of us to leave the compound for weeks, so I guess now it's officially on. Vacation is over."

Carlos nodded and set his jaw hard as fellow Guardians came to a halt at the kitchen's threshold.

"What the f—" Rider stopped mid-expletive as he spied Inez's mom and toddler, and he held out his arm to bar them from fully entering the kitchen. "Sulfur's so thick in here you'd think we'd entered a hellhole."

"Jesus H. Christ," Berkfield muttered as his gaze scanned the black pockmarked kitchen cabinets, floor, counter, and appliances.

"I'll just be damned." Marlene's words seethed between her teeth as she entered the kitchen with Inez, both women placing their hands on their hips. Marlene's gaze narrowed as she surveyed the damage. "Up in *my* laboratory . . . where I do my sacred work?"

"Aw, hell to the no," Inez said, unable to curtail her rage as she walked across the smoldering floor and folded her arms over her ample breasts. "A breach in here, *my kitchen,* where I feed my family?"

"What happened?" Shabazz said, putting the safety on his Glock 9mm. His long dreadlocks were static-charged with fury and the muscles in his toned arms, shoulders, and back kneaded like that of a stalking panther's as he walked deeper into the abused room.

Yonnie's and Carlos's eyes met.

"Were they looking for me?" Yonnie asked, making the group turn and stare at him. " 'Cause if it's my time, I'll go out there and let them take me rather than bring this bull on the family, yo." He glanced at Valkyrie and lifted his chin. "Bound to happen sooner or later, so if they're—"

"They'll always be looking for you, man," Carlos said in an angry rumble. "Just like they'll always be looking for me and everybody else on this team. We ain't sacrificing no family to appease the Beast—got that, man?"

"Cool. Then I'll take that as a no, this wasn't personal then," Yonnie said, sniffing the air and retracting his fangs.

"Oh, it was personal," Carlos assured him. "They personally want me, you, and everybody else on this team dead."

"Yo," Damali said, frowning, and then nodded toward Ayana.

Carlos paced to the window and sent his gaze beyond it. "My bad. Team meeting in the Situation Room."

Rider and Jose walked to the sliding-glass doors, opened them, and then hocked and spit out over the deck rails.

"Definitely in another room, *holmes*," Jose said, shaking his head. "You know us guys with the noses for sulfur can't deal with this."

"Mom," Inez said, looking at her daughter. "Why don't you and Yaya go put on some cartoons . . . I'll fill you in later."

The child shook her head and rushed to hold on to her mother's leg. "Don't wanna go with Nana. I wanna stay with you, Mommy! I'm scared!"

"C'mon, boo," Big Mike said, lifting the child up and giving her a hug. He held her high off the floor, his six-foot-eight cinder-block frame of solid muscle a promise of sure safety, and he looked at her with a tender smile. "Did Uncle Mike ever tell you a lie, suga?"

The patience of the team's gentle giant who doubled as a

killing machine held the group in thrall. Inez's eyes conveyed such a level of intimate gratitude that Mike simply traced her cheek and pushed her long microbraids behind her ear before turning to her daughter again.

"Do Uncle Mike lie to his Yaya?" Giving the three-year-old his complete focus, Mike waited until the child yielded and finally shook her head.

"Then I'm not gonna tell you a lie right now. You trust me?"

It took a moment, but Ayana nodded.

"We gonna be right in the next room. In fact, we'll keep the door open while you put on your shows with Grandma. I bet she's sorta worried and needs a big girl like you to sit on her lap to make her feel better."

"I sure would like that, honeybird," Delores said, coming in close to rub her frightened granddaughter's back. She looked up at Big Mike's towering frame. "Thank you for such a good idea, son."

"See," Mike said, nodding with confidence, his voice steady and soothing as he spoke to his stepdaughter, "then, when we finish, Mommy will be right there to scoop you up . . . but smell it in here," he added, wrinkling up his nose. "It's all stinky, making Uncle Rider and Uncle Jose sick . . . Aunt Damali ain't looking too good neither . . . so we need to go where it don't smell so bad. Does that make sense? We need to let Uncle Carlos air this room out and fix it nice and pretty again. Is that okay with you, little lady?"

Ayana popped her thumb in her mouth and hugged his thick neck, mumbling over the digit. "Yup, it stinks."

Big Mike forced a laugh to ease the child's very real fears. "Eiiieww."

The moment Ayana giggled, the team let out a collective sigh of relief and started walking to the new location. Mike's diplomacy had worked. Inez and Damali mouthed a silent thank-you toward the huge Guardian, while Inez's mother simply hugged herself as she walked—clearly too terror-stricken to do much more.

Within five minutes, the group had settled into the Situation Room with the blare of cartoons coming into the room from the hall. Damali scanned the team, giving each person a knowing look to be cool, lest little ears overhear. They all understood that they needed to give it a few minutes before launching into gory details of death, Hell, and destruction. The kid needed to relax and be otherwise engaged. Nobody wanted her psyche scarred by the insanity of the life the team lived, but it seemed like it was becoming increasingly difficult to avoid that.

Although expressions conceded to Damali's silent terms, each pair of eyes held a different mix of emotions that she knew she and Carlos would have to wade through during the discussion.

Tara and Rider, like Shabazz and Marlene, were old-heads, respectively, and were from the old-school of Guardian thought that said no kids—ever. Guardians weren't allowed said luxury for a reason; it kept them near sane and there'd be no leverage point the darkside could use to totally break them. Having a lover or spouse was bad enough.

Damali looked at the two senior Guardian couples and tried to fight the anxiety brewing within her. Well more than forty and sans kids, those guys were going to start in about the hazards of children in the compound . . . she could feel it. They'd made their position clear early on; they understood that it was what it was, but didn't like it. They also knew the grief of loss, and how it would break the team's back if anything happened to little Ayana or Mom Delores. Marlene and Shabazz had the added worry of knowing that there was another child to be concerned about—hers. At least Tara and Rider hadn't figured that part out yet.

But keeping the scent of her blood changes away from Tara

was going to be tricky. Tara had been a vampire once, understood the darkside, just like Yonnie did, and even Rider had had
his brush with the vampire realms. Those guys had the vamp ol-
factory system still resident within them, and Jose as a nose was
no slouch, either. Any Guardians that had once been vampires
or had been tied to a vamp distant line, like Jose, knew the scents
of the pit and had probably seen as many manifestations as she
and Carlos had.

As she scanned the group during the tense silence, waiting for
the child's happy voice to begin filtering into the room, she
took in how the older team members' eyes held no patience for
having to dance around the subject of imminent war due to
civilians being in their camp. Early on they'd expressed their
misgivings, and at the same time, they also understood that sending Ayana and Mom Delores away indefinitely was no longer an
option. It was what Carlos had called that rock and a hard place
position. At the moment she was standing in the middle of it.

The struggle was subtle. No words, just body language. Tara
lifted her chin ever so slightly and folded her arms over her
chest as she sat in a leather computer chair, tension making her
lean, athletic frame seem taut enough to snap. Her silky, jet-
black bob haircut barely swayed, her movements were so minute.
A pair of deep-set eyes stared back at Damali unblinkingly, and
the blend of African American and Native American cultures
warred within Tara's exotic features. Her high cheekbones and
hard-set jaw made her expression virtually unreadable. But
Damali knew exactly where her Guardian sister was at—
conflicted by her desperate fear for the child's safety and Inez's
sanity if anything happened to little Ayana, and extreme annoyance for having to also deal with that on top of everything
else.

Rider's reaction was much clearer than his wife's. The man
was tired of the bullshit, plain and simple. Weary with life in

general and drama in particular. She could dig it. The older Guardian just sighed and grabbed a ladder-back chair away from the weapons table, turned it around backward, and sat down hard, then raked his fingers through his dirty blond hair that was now littered with silver-gray strands. A pair of wise, hazel-brown eyes followed the team's every move. Carlos offered Rider a nod and a silent understanding passed between them. Clearly they were both mentally wrung.

However, Marlene moved slowly through the room, finally settling into a seat with care. She was obviously, and without apology, picking up vibes from every person in the room, monitoring the situation silently like a radar scanner. Her silver dreadlocks practically cracked with tension and the emotion of worry for Damali's secret circumstance. Her ebony skin, which was normally vibrant and smooth, had gone ashen. Shabazz glanced at Damali, then Carlos, and then finally at Marlene, his worry just as palpable behind the hard mask of his regal African features.

Carlos and Damali shared a quick glance. This was going to be tough, trying to go over the situation with every team member's special gift on high alert, and not tip their hand. But the Neteru Council had been adamant for them to wait before disclosing Damali's pregnancy, so that was the end of it.

The problem was that all the seers had frowns—even the younger members of the team.

Heather's wide gray eyes raked the couple. Her husband, Dan, absently sat down beside her and stroked her profusion of auburn curls. By nearly thirty, like Juanita and Inez, Heather had come into her own. Of the three midrange Guardian sisters, Heather was the strongest in picking up non-dream-state information. She'd be much harder to evade than Krissy or Jasmine, who had just recently made it to their twenties. Damali kept her eyes on Heather, not wanting to look at Juanita or Inez. Marjorie was another tough customer; she was Marlene's age . . . but the only saving grace was that Marj was somewhat naïve and her gift wasn't as developed. Marj didn't go looking for stuff the way the others did.

Damali watched how her Guardian sister, Heather, almost shrugged away from Dan so she could study the source of her confusion better. It was like watching a bird dog hunt; Heather had picked up something but wasn't sure what it was. Carlos noticed it, too, and Damali could feel him sending in a subtle block to wrap around her aura.

Almost as though he'd heard his wife's request to pull back his tactical charge, Dan's hand left Heather's body space and he placed his palms on top of his spiked blond thicket of static-ridden hair, trying to calm it. Dan's crystal-blue gaze nervously assessed his wife for a moment, but he seemed to give up the quest for more data with a weary shrug.

It was no different with Bobby and Jasmine. Damali watched her Guardian sister's almond-shaped eyes rove over her, and then Jasmine leaned against the wall, refusing Bobby's nonverbal offer of a chair. She folded her arms over her petite breasts and her delicate, rosebudlike mouth formed a concerned pout. With an annoyed shrug, Jasmine tossed her long, blue-black hair over her shoulder, and stood there immovable, seeming very much like a fragile, tense, Asian porcelain doll. Unsure what to do, Bobby stood by her and finally dragged his fingers through his dark hair, glancing at his parents, Marj and Berkfield, for a moment, and then toward his sister.

Krissy caught her brother's glance, and gave a slight shrug. Clairvoyance was not the young wizard's strongest suit. Frowning as she spied the tension among the seer females on the team, Krissy fidgeted with the end of her long, blond ponytail, her gaze constantly checking with J.L., who practically had blue-static charge spilling onto the floor in a pool around them.

J.L. gave Carlos a direct look that contained a plea to start the meeting soon. The older couple, Marj and Berkfield, glanced at their daughter, the state of agitation their son-in-law was in, and then at Carlos and Damali.

"For the love of Christ," Berkfield said between his teeth, smoothing a flat palm over his bald head as he whispered. "We've gotta have a better way of doing team communications. My nerves can't take this crap much longer."

"I'll drink to that," Rider said, standing and heading toward the wet bar. "Even at seven in the damned morning."

"Yo, yo, yo," Shabazz said to Rider, laughing. "It ain't that dramatic, man. Can't be . . . can it?" He gave Damali and Carlos a curious stare as Rider halted in the middle of the room.

"They violated the five-second rule, dude. Didn't answer fast enough," Rider said. "You guys who don't have the noses have no idea." He poured five shot glasses of Jack Daniel's and handed them out to Tara, Jose, Carlos, and Yonnie, keeping one for himself. "A little something while we wait for the Cartoon Network to kick in the kid hypnosis. This ain't about alcoholism or morning indulgence. This is about getting brimstone off our palates." He threw back the shot and then shuddered hard. "Works like a charm—ask me how I know."

Four more Guardians tossed down a shot and shuddered.

"Thanks, *holmes*," Jose said as Yonnie pounded Rider's fist as he passed him.

"Much obliged," Tara said, giving Rider her shot glass, but never taking her eyes off Damali. "So what the hell's going on?"

Juanita cut Tara a silent thank-you with her eyes and then slid her voluptuous body onto the edge of the weapons table. Her dark eyes pinned Carlos to the wall beside Damali and she set her lush mouth with an unspoken question while gathering up her long brunet tresses into a clip on top of her head.

"Whatever it is, your ass is lying, Carlos Rivera. No offense, Damali, but I know my Guardian brother."

Damali had to laugh and took no offense. Of all people, Juanita would know. Once lovers, some things were just obvious. Even Carlos cracked a half smile, but kept it respectful, glancing at both Jose and Damali to be sure he hadn't crossed the line.

"You're right," Damali said, allowing her back to hit the wall with a thud. "I'm sure Carlos was about to say it wasn't that bad, and it is, folks . . . that's why we were waiting until the little bird got engrossed in her cartoons."

The half-truth made bodies relax all around the room. Carlos gave her a quick glance filled with amazement.

*You're getting as good as I used to be.*

Damali swallowed a smile and didn't answer his telepathically sent message. Inez walked over toward the door and peeked down the hall briefly, and then quietly pulled it closed behind her short, curvaceous frame.

"Okay, now I'm really worried," Inez said in a low tone. She gnawed on her bottom lip for a moment and then wiped her damp palms down the back pockets of her jeans.

"Any time sulfur and brimstone is blowing up in my kitchen, it cannot be a good thing," Marlene said, folding her arms over her chest.

"Then you would have loved the maggot explosion, followed by a larva rain," Carlos said dryly, pushing his body off the wall to begin pacing.

"A what!" Marlene and Inez gasped in unison.

"Damn, Carlos," Damali muttered. "Why'd you have to go there?"

"Because it was what it was," he said, his tone defensive. "Look—I made a run this morning to get D some grub that she had a taste for. I was sick and tired of being cooped up in the compound and I took a drive . . . came back, prayed over it, and began telling her about something J.L. showed me, and boom. The shit blew up nasty."

"That was because everything he's been importing for the last few weeks comes in his silver light sweep. So, if your food or whatever hasn't been right, it wouldn't have gotten here . . . but this was hand-carried in. The prayers made it erupt into what it was once I was out of my vision daze and about to pick up a plastic fork. So, on that note, we don't need to panic. Unless someone physically from our side brought it over the threshold, it couldn't have gotten in."

"Aw'ight, that's cool," Yonnie said, lolling a toothpick around in his mouth. "But, uh, homeboy . . . like the lady said, you accidentally brought it over the threshold, so how you know some residual shit ain't still in here?"

Valkyrie gently touched Yonnie's arm, her large brown eyes slowing his words as her graceful, ebony palm traced his cheek. "I'm a half-angel, and can go after it so that it does not harm the team nor the child. You don't have to ever go back to Hell."

Rider groaned as Yonnie filled his hands with Val's platinum dreadlocks, and her athletic body melted into his.

"In the midst of the Armageddon . . . brand-new couples with the hots, babies, grandmothers, what next, Lord?" Rider said in a sarcastic tone. He turned to Tara and folded his arms. "Would you be too terribly pissed off if I went out to get a pack of Marlboros and never came back? I swear I need a cigarette!"

"The kitchen is cool," Carlos muttered. "You see the silver scorch damage up in there?"

"Word," Shabazz said, pounding Jose's fist. "But an extra layer of protection before you go in and white light it back together wouldn't hurt."

"True," Damali said, glad that the team's focus had been

derailed from her personal circumstance. "Marlene, Val, 'Nez . . . the power of three . . . cool?"

"Done," Marlene said, but she held Damali's gaze for a moment, opening a mental channel to her and Carlos. *And until we sweep it, you stay out of there.*

Damali simply nodded as Carlos began to pace. "Cool."

"Then, since I was outside," Carlos said, holding Marlene's gaze with mild terror in his eyes, "I'll need you to hook me up a white bath, and make it do what it do . . . I don't want anything I could have made contact with coming *anywhere* near D or the team."

"I'll blast you, no problem," Marlene said as the team grew tense again. "But I've got something on the doors that would have made you sick as a dog if you were carrying, trust me."

"Cool. I can take that to the bank?" Carlos stared at Marlene.

"You can take it to the bank and cash that sucker with no ID, brother," Marlene said, her tone unwavering. "I know *exactly* what's at stake up in here and I ain't playing with the bullshit, either."

"Aw'ight . . . then we're good." Carlos dragged his fingers through his hair again as a very quiet team stared at him. "Next issue," he said, beginning to walk down the row of semiautomatic weapons that were mounted on a far wall. "It was really a backhanded blessing that Damali sent me on an errand and then as a result, this shit bubbled up in the kitchen, or we coulda went out there and gotten blindsided as a team. What kicked everything off in the chain of events was the fact that J.L. found something interesting in the airwaves."

Before Carlos had finished his statement, J.L. had jumped up from the stool he'd been sitting on in one lithe move and had begun walking in front of the seated team, waving his hands as he spoke. He looked like a crazed martial arts instructor, using jabs and karate cuts to the air to emphasize each point. Both

Neterus watched the team absorb the implications one by one, and only when J.L. was finished and the questions being fired at him had died down did Damali speak.

"That was the good news," she finally said with a weary sigh. "Now let me fill you in on what's waiting for us outside."

# CHAPTER FOUR

This was not at all how she'd planned to spend her day, much less her life. The end-of-war hiatuses were always the same—abrupt. Gut-wrenchingly so.

Hours of white-light-bleached communications with members of the Covenant and Guardian team safe houses had left her with a throbbing headache, almost as much as debating about what to do with Inez's little girl and mother had. There was no clear resolution; the team still didn't know what they were going to do. Chaos and the undercurrent of blatant indecision had a stranglehold on the household. Then there was the energy-depleting task of holding an orb of white light around the kitchen while Carlos gutted it and then silver-singed the entire area before rebuilding everything from the wall out.

All this on a bag of barbecue Kettle Chips while waiting to be sure the transaction to procure supplies had gone off without a hitch. Carlos couldn't bring in food until he'd been white-bathed, power hit by the Neteru Councils, and otherwise deemed a non-contaminant. That meant a message requesting grub had to be hot-prayer-jumped from her to local church kitchens on the safe list that would in turn send out deliveries through a Covenant prayer line with food loaded onto armored trucks.

Damali rubbed her temples and stared out the window, wondering if this was what people that'd crossed the prairie felt like in the covered wagon days. Would the food arrive, would the water arrive, what if the truck was ambushed or followed by hostile forces? Supplies had been packed in holy water ice, placed in silver containers surrounded by Red Sea salt, and blessed five ways from Sunday under the auspices of each of the major religions. Once it arrived, Marlene had been given instructions as the elected house chaplain to literally exorcise the food. Meanwhile poor little Ayana was whining and crying because she was hungry and tired. Damali knew exactly how the kid felt.

After five minutes she decided to abandon the fruitless wait by the window; all that was doing was making her stomach growl. A watched pot never boiled. She left the window with a heavy sigh of frustration and went to find the guys in the War Room. They'd all abandoned the Situation Room. Marlene and Inez were putting the kitchen back together with Mom Delores. Ayana was coloring at the kitchen counter. The senior male members of the team had each taken a quadrant to make sure the perimeter was secured and some were busy packing weapons, getting things ready for the inevitable road trip. Young bloods were hunkered down behind serious technology. The process made her tired.

It had taken two hours to decontaminate the house, going through the basic prayer litany with sea salt, white sage smudges, white light, and much holy water flinging and incense burning. Now Krissy was manning four HD screens and keeping track of bizarre news, while J.L. was charting a course trying to triangulate the origin of the contagion. Heather, Marj, and Juanita had gone into an intense divining session. The Neteru Councils had white-light blasted her and Carlos for extra measure, but they seemed to be as stumped on the origin of the plague as the team.

This had to be ferreted out on the ground. Everyone was in a holding pattern for at least twenty-four hours, lest they kick off the ultimate human disaster.

From what she could surmise, the contagion was coming from multiple dark vortexes. Yet, it was hard to tell for sure, because every time she tried to focus her inner vision on a source, several scenes would interchange as decoys. Her dragon pearl oracle was baffled, too, and Zehiradangra was working with the Heather trio, igniting the other stones in the Neteru platinum collar necklace, hoping to get impressions for the seers that could help.

The source of the struggle was obviously playing with her and Carlos, just as it was clearly getting twisted pleasure from confounding the Councils of Light. Damali knew that to be a fact the way she knew her own name. Hellholes had been opened up everywhere it seemed, and humans were carrying the black plague of shadows within them, simmering just beneath the surface of their spirits, waiting to emerge as a violent force. The clock was ticking, and human beings were a time bomb. One false move and there'd be mega collateral damage.

Humanity was, in effect, being held hostage. It was now a game of chicken; who would blink first—the darkside or the Light? If the Neterus did, then anything could happen and the casualties would be astronomical . . . the biblical proportions no one wanted on their watch. If they did nothing, the darkside would toy with them and make them twist.

As Damali walked into the tech section of the War Room, J.L.'s and Krissy's attention snapped toward her.

"Got anything?" she asked, glancing at J.L. and then Krissy.

"I've been searching for news anomalies and got plenty of really sick shit coming back at me, D," Krissy said in a horrified whisper. "Two fourteen-year-old kids on the same day in Pennsylvania tried a Columbine-type wipeout in their high schools—one of the kid's mothers actually bought him the assault rifle. Look, this comes on the heels of the Virginia Tech massacre. What mother in her right mind buys that for her kid, ya know? Another one . . . six hillbillies in West Virginia hold a woman hostage, abusing her, making her eat dog and rat feces. Who does that kind of twisted crap unless they're possessed?"

"Okay, okay, I've heard enough," Damali said quietly, her gaze leaving the tube, but her hand resting on Krissy's shoulder for support. "I get the picture. Take a break; this will jack up your head."

"These are *real* news reports," Krissy said, her voice holding repressed horror as her gaze became distant. "That's just one small segment of the eastern part of this nation . . . I went to Africa—"

"Baby, that's enough. Take a break," J.L. said quietly and firmly.

"Good idea, Kris," Damali said, trying to get the horrified young Guardian to stand and leave her post.

But Krissy shook her head, immobilized by what she'd witnessed. "I went all over Europe and the Middle East news sites, searching, but the most insane, senseless acts of violence were committed by young people right here where there's supposedly no war. Where there's abundance. The things that are happening," she added in a near whisper, "they're an abomination. I went all over and . . . and . . . it's all demonic. But somehow in the midst of the worldwide insanity you can make sense of that in a war-torn land—a lot of it is old news, the same craziness just continuing, not that it makes it any less chilling. Not that it makes me okay with it, or that it means those people's lives aren't as valuable or the suffering isn't worthy of worldwide outcry. But the stuff that's making me about to puke is happening in quiet suburban communities or in the cities where there's not supposed to be droughts and wars and land mines. I don't understand."

Damali held Krissy by the shoulders as J.L. turned around and then stood. The sound of his wife's panicked whisper drew him near and Damali squatted down to make Krissy's eyes meet hers.

"It *is* demonic, but that's why we've gotta find the source and find it fast. We cannot give up. If we do, this whole thing implodes, and everybody that's been infected will act on whatever violent, demonic messages are being thrust into their minds."

"We *really are* at the end of days, aren't we? It's just really sinking in, even after everything else I've seen." Krissy's pained gaze sought Damali's for comfort and understanding and then went to J.L.'s. "A twenty-year-old cop shot four teenagers for teasing him . . . for just calling him a name. Killed them at a pizza party in their house. They were about to graduate high school—just like me and Bobby would have a couple of years back—and they died screaming and then he killed himself. Four college kids were shot execution-style in Newark . . . they were just eating cheese steaks and hanging in a yard. It's not getting better, Damali—not even after all the demons we've been killing and killing and killing. The darkside is winning. The presence is going for the young people. I've separated out continuing tragedies from really new, bizarre incidents and spikes in new areas we haven't seen major patterns in. I don't know what to do—I feel so helpless."

"The future," Damali said, looking at J.L. and hugging Krissy. "Write me a program, dude. We went after Hell's future, the Antichrist, so they're retaliating by going after the kids—but with all the other madness that was already swirling around in the atmosphere, they banked on us never figuring out what they were targeting." She stroked Krissy's back as her Guardian sister silently wept from information trauma. "Keep the faith; it ain't over till it's over."

J.L. nodded. "Talk to me, D—I got you. What kind of

program, though? What part of this do you want me to focus on?" He caressed his wife's hair and kissed the crown of her head. "C'mon, baby . . . why don't you help your mom with the divinations. Enough for a while, all right?"

Damali handed Krissy off slowly to J.L. and waited while he hugged her and then watched her slip from the room in a traumatized daze.

"She'll be all right, D," J.L. said after a moment. "It's . . . she's never really focused on the horrors of the world, even while we battled. Seeing kids like herself, seeing how twisted normal people have become is scarier to her than seeing vampires jump out of alleys or werewolves howl at the moon."

"Tell me about it," Damali said, fingers combing her locks.

J.L. nodded. "I can cut this data a hundred ways from Sunday, but you've gotta tell me what you're looking for or it'll be an exercise in futility."

"What do kids have in common?" Damali began pacing to clear her head. "Cell phones, Internet community pages, and music—those are the three most common elements in America that cut across race, gender, religion, and class pretty much, right?"

"I'm on it, D . . . but . . . kids could be on places like My-Space and Facebook from anywhere in the world . . . phones could be—"

"Music!" Damali paced back and forth and then punched the wall. "Ringtones go into cell phones. Music gets put up on blogs, Internet community pages, goes over the radio waves, goes under commercial jingles on cable, you following me, J.L.? And what do we do? Music. They're rubbing our noses in it. But the world is so fouled already, so chaotic that this insanity just simply blends into all the rest of it."

"I can hack the online community pages of recent teen victims and perpetrators, isolate any music, see if there's common ground—find the record labels, see if those labels are getting primo airtime, see if they've done recent new jingles, try to do a search on the most popular ringtones and see if there's some matches . . . might take me a few, that's a lot of data to crunch, but I'm on it."

They both stopped speaking as Krissy came back into the room. Her normally creamy complexion was ashen and her gaze had a faraway look.

"I can't find them; I don't know where the others are. I don't wanna walk down the hallway by myself." Tears rose in Krissy's eyes. "I don't know what could come into our house."

"I know you got this," Damali said to J.L., taking Krissy's hand as she and J.L. exchanged a knowing look. "C'mon, kiddo. Been where you're at right now. You need some air."

"My wife hasn't eaten since she scarfed down a bag of barbecue Kettle Chips and I know she's starving—might slip up and taste something wrong by accident," Carlos fussed as Marlene stood over his tub. "The Covenant trucks are outside and I wanna make sure that nothing slithers over the doorsill with the food drop, Mar. Seriously."

Marlene stood in a wide-legged stance, grasping her walking stick in one hand horizontal to the tub, the other hand holding the huge black book of rituals, *The Temt Tchaas,* over his bath-water, as well as wearing an unyielding expression. She'd opened a violet energy pyramid over him and he watched it hover just above his head, causing a tingling sensation and mild ripples in the water. Shabazz kept his Glock 9 cocked at the ready, his gaze keen, with blue-white static crackling down his locks and arms until it spilled down the barrel of his favorite weapon, Black Beauty.

"You do you right now," Marlene snapped. "Mike, Rider, Jose, Yonnie, Bobby, and Berkfield are on the truck. 'Nez, Tara,

Valkyrie, and Jasmine got the prayer line I laid down on lock and are slinging white light as we speak. Right now, brother, my main concern is that after I douse you for the third time, nothing jumps up outta that white bath or tries to drown your stubborn ass. I'm following Aset's prescription to the letter."

Carlos let out a hard breath and looked at Shabazz. "Watch your aim, man. If you gotta shoot at least aim for my chest. You shoot where you're aiming right now and you might as well kill me."

Despite how hungry everybody was, and no matter how good the food smelled, no one moved toward it. The team simply held hands, said the collective prayers led by Marlene, which took a full fifteen minutes to complete, and then when they dropped their grasps, everyone went for a weapon. Multiple clicks echoed through the dining room. Mom Delores pressed Ayana's face to her hip, shielding the child's vision.

"The baby is gonna remember this craziness all her natural life!" Eyes wild, Delores sought Inez's gaze for comfort.

"Momma," Inez said quietly, holding a 9 sideways, pointed toward the broccoli. "We just trying to be sure everything is cool. I hate this as much as you do."

Three tense minutes passed. Damali stepped forward, ignoring Carlos's narrowed gaze. "It was trying to get one of the Neterus, so I'll be the guinea pig."

Carlos grabbed her forearm and drove his sword of Ausar into the table, rattling dishes. "Uh-uh. White light it to heat up the dishes, I'll see what we've got, then . . . if it's cool, we all bust a grub."

She nodded. "All right. Make it do what it do."

No sooner than she'd said it, a wave of white-light energy rippled off his blade over the tablecloth and down the floor. The heat swirled over the dishes, causing casseroles to bubble and steam to waft off cooled vegetables. Guardians redoubled their stances, holding weapons with two hands, waiting.

"This is a damned travesty," Rider argued, watching the salad with a frown. "So it has come to this—the blade of Ausar is a kitchen aid and we can't even have a glass of water in our own home without calling the freakin' Vatican for an exorcism. Well, dammit, I for one refuse to live like this! C'mon out of the romaine lettuce, you slimy little bastards! I am sick and fuckin—"

"Rider! C'mon, man!" Big Mike yelled. "Chill!"

"Chill? Is it me, or does it seem strange to anyone else but me that we're now worried that the bogey man might jump out from under the croutons?"

"Jack . . . the language," Tara said in a weary tone. "She's three. I'll wash your mouth out myself if you drop another f-bomb around her."

"Thank you, T," Mike said. "Don't make me shoot you, man. The kid don't need to see that, either."

"All right, all right, I'm sorry." Rider sighed and looked at Ayana's wide brown eyes. "Uncle Jack is having a real hard time because he's hungry, his blood sugar is low, and he's cranky. Don't say bad words like him. Okay? I'm sorry, sweetie."

"I don't say bad words 'cause Nana will whip my butt." The child looked up at her grandmother with a wide-eyed stare.

"Good looking out, Nana," Rider said with a smirk. "Oh, man . . ." He put his gun back in the holster. "All we need now is a visit from Child Protective Services, huh? Uncles curse, drink, and the whole family levels weapons at the dinner table, while Nana whips a little girl's butt. Lovely. I don't care if larvae as big as me come out of the mac and cheese, I'm eating dinner. They have protein in them anyway and grubs are a delicacy in the Philippines or some damned where—I saw it on the National Geographic Channel. Maybe it was Borneo?"

"Rider, man," Carlos warned, "you weren't in the kitchen with me and D this morning. It was nasty, bro. For real. You might wanna ease up."

With that Rider shrugged, pulled out a chair, and flopped down in it, and then dug a big serving spoon into the macaroni and cheese. No one moved as Rider flung a huge glob of the casserole onto his plate, poured brown gravy all over it, then picked up his fork. Jasmine cringed. Marjorie closed her eyes. Inez made a face. Val held her breath. Damali put her hands behind her back and rocked on her heels.

"If anything starts moving, I swear I'll barf," Jasmine said in a tense whisper.

Krissy covered her mouth and dry-heaved while Juanita and Heather hugged themselves. Tara chuckled. Marlene just shook her head. The male members of the team passed nervous glances, but for a moment, none of them moved.

"The answer to your question is, I don't know," Tara said, finally sitting down beside Rider.

"What question?" Rider mumbled through a mouthful of food.

"The question every woman in this room is silently asking, how do I live with you? Truthfully, I don't know."

It was back to a wartime drill. Shifts. Over the next twenty-four hours, the watch would be split up into thirds, eight-hour details so that each couple could get some rest and so that everyone would be fresh when they got the word that it was time to move out. Bellies were full and thank goodness nothing was wrong with the meal. Whatever grub was in the house was safe for now, and the bottled water and tea and coffee had also gotten a clean bill of health.

J.L. and Krissy would take first watch and keep the computers going, along with Heather and Dan, Jasmine and Bobby, and

Marj and Berkfield. That was the normal protocol; let the young bloods do the daylight and the less severe darkness with one senior couple. This time, Krissy would be on light duty and was only assigned so she could stay near J.L.

But during the heart of the night, those with serious combat skills, night vision, and old vamp assets were on call. That meant Jose and Juanita, Tara and Rider, and Yonnie and Val were up. Then in the dangerous transition period from darkness to dawn going into full daybreak, the Neterus were up with Mar and Shabazz and Inez and Mike, whose audio capability could pick up a phantom whisper anywhere in the house at that hour.

The worst part of it all, though, was the waiting . . . waiting for the Dark Realm to make a move, waiting for J.L.'s complex programs to make sense of the chaos . . . waiting for the Covenant to provide reinforcements and a recommendation . . . waiting on the Light to give them sure guidance . . . waiting on a strategy to gel in her and Carlos's minds. Right now she felt like she was about to leap out of her skin.

Sensing her tension, Carlos stripped his T-shirt over his head and flung it toward the bedroom hamper and missed. "Get some rest, boo. We ain't gonna figure it out tonight and the shift change is gonna kick our asses like it always does. We haven't done this drill in a while, and you definitely need your rest."

She watched the muscles move beneath his bronze skin as he unzipped his jeans and bent to unlace his Tims before stepping out of them. What seemed like steel cable made his shoulders and the width of his back expand as he moved to complete the simple task. Reflex caused her gaze to slide down his spine and over the steel-cut lobes of his ass and thighs. Her husband's body was like a piece of stone art, and she always enjoyed watching him change his clothes, even if nothing in particular was going on. It was like appreciating a finely crafted sculpture. Damn . . . they'd broken the mold when they made him.

"I can't turn off my mind, but at least I ate," Damali said after a distracted moment while drying her damp locks with a thick terry towel. She sat cross-legged in their huge king-sized bed in a pair of cut-off shorts and one of Carlos's wife-beater T-shirts, fending off the miscellaneous random thoughts that floated through her mind.

"Noticed you didn't touch the falafel they sent." He gave her a half smile as he stripped off his boxers and found a pair of gray sweats to put on.

"Ruined that dish for me for life, you know. Damn!" She coaxed her mind and line of vision away from his groin.

Carlos laughed. "I couldn't watch Rider eat the mac and cheese and forget brown rice or white rice, period, for a long-ass time."

"But I feel Rider, though," Damali said, flinging the towel away from the bed in a sudden rush of annoyance. "I feel violated by all of this. Like . . . WTF, ya know?"

"Right—and since Ayana's not in the room," Carlos said, sitting down heavily on the edge of the bed, "what *the fuck!*"

Damali stretched out her legs and fell back with her arms outstretched. "I know, I know, I know . . . and the team is gonna freak when we tell them—like I'm already freaked out that all this is happening while all this is happening, kiss my ass—what are we gonna do?" She didn't even want to say the word *pregnant* out loud now.

Carlos shrugged. "Make it up as we go along, like we always do. If you haven't noticed, I'm trying very hard to keep my head on straight, keep doing this by the numbers like we always did . . . that's why I'm going to sleep—will get up for our shift, just have to keep on the grind." He lay next to her on his side and leaned down to kiss her. "One thing I'm not gonna do, though, is stay up for eight hours and worry, then try to deal with this bullshit fried. Even vampires and whatever stop and regenerate, so you know we mere mortals need to. Get some rest, baby."

"We didn't used to roll like this," she said, giving him a sly smile as he fell back against the pillows.

"You didn't used to be pregnant."

"I take exception to that."

He closed his eyes. "That's just a statement of fact. I'm not trying to argue or get philosophical. It is what it is and I'm very happy that it is. Grateful. But after what we saw today, been through today, I just want to close my eyes and blot anything negative out for a few. Cool?"

She snuggled in closer to him and leaned up on one elbow. He glanced at the light and made it turn off with an agitated twist of his mind.

"I can see in the dark, you know."

"Baby . . . please. . . . For real."

"We used to think outside the box, get creative in solving anything they threw at us. We used to take risks, stay up all night, and figure out a solution—like you should have seen how horrified Krissy was today. That poor girl was watching the news reports getting overwhelmed to the point of tears—it's horrific what's happening. But I have a theory."

"Music, I know," he said in a weary tone and then slung his forearm over his eyes. "Makes sense, 'cause Fallon is seriously pissed off and his mate, Lucrezia, is the queen of poison. The way me and Yonnie figured from the old days, Fallon probably stepped up because he was the only one on the council that was really hip to Yonnie's potential double-cross . . . so it makes sense it would be coming from his old empire strength. Thing is, we've gotta isolate where he's rebounding from—and like I said, we ain't gonna figure it out tonight."

"But—"

Carlos leaned up and kissed her quickly and then flopped back against the pillows.

"We could make a reconnaissance run to—"

"Are you crazy?" Carlos removed his forearm from his eyes and stared at her in the dark.

"Well, yeah . . . you used to love that about me. Thought it was sexy."

For a moment the two of them stared at each other and Damali finally cracked a smile.

"You were just messing with me, right?"

"Okay, yeah . . . dang. You're so serious."

"Correct me if I'm wrong, but this *is* serious."

She traced his chest with one finger. "I know . . . but . . ."

"Baby, if I didn't know better, I'd swear you were high." Carlos sat up and looked at her hard, his brows knit.

Damali giggled and threw her head back, allowing the blue-white moonlight coming in through the skylight to wash over her. "I feel *fantastic* all of a sudden . . . just full of energy—bursting with it."

"I knew it . . . oh, shit, they got to you. Poisoned my wife!" Carlos started to get out of bed but she held his arm tightly.

"No . . . this is normal. The rush Aset said I'd get once I got past the first dicey month." She smiled widely and then hugged Carlos. "I never got my period. The baby's gonna hold. Endorphins are making me giddy and I feel like I could run a marathon!"

He held her back, searching her eyes in the dark with a silvery gaze. "You sure?"

"Yeah," she whispered and then kissed him slowly. "I miss you, too. The nausea is *soooo* gone."

"I love you right on back, baby," he said, gently but firmly pushing her away from him and trying to get her to lie down.

"Okay, now that we know what's going on, you get some rest. Tomorrow, we'll know more, J.L.'s programs should have more details . . . but for now, you know . . . chill."

"It's such a rush, Carlos," she whispered. "I feel like I'm buzzing and I wanna go hunting."

"*That* cannot happen," he said with no nonsense in his tone.

"Remember what we used to do before going into a big battle?" she said in a sexy murmur and then kissed his chest.

"Yeah, but *that* also cannot happen. Go to sleep."

She leaned back on her elbow, pouting. "Who says and why not? It was part of our whole thing as a couple."

"Listen," he said gently, moving damp locks away from her face, "it's still real early. Anything could happen. We just learned that there's a real bad contagion out in the world and I accidentally—once again—brought some of it into the house." He kissed the bridge of her nose and traced her cheek with one finger. "Bringing it into the house is one thing . . . possibly bringing it into my wife is something I just can't live with. I love you."

"I love you, too," she said cradling his face. "But it's been six weeks."

He chuckled. "Six weeks, three days"—he glanced at the digital clock on his nightstand—"and about five and a half hours, to be exact."

She laughed softly while doodling on his chest with her forefinger. "Do you still think I'm sexy, even though I'm carrying?"

"Completely," he murmured. "Please go to sleep."

"Well, uhmmm . . . when do you think you might not feel so worried?"

He let out his breath hard and forced a smile. "Nine months will go by before you know it, assuming we both live that long."

"What!"

"Baby, it's for the best, you know that. We have to take the long view and the high road . . . before there were issues and I can't be the reason—"

"Nine months, ohmigod, Carlos, you're serious, aren't you?"

"Well, yeah, I'm serious. Why wouldn't I be? I don't even know why we're talking about it in the midst of the freakin' Armageddon. I can never figure out the female mind, no matter how many so-called psychic powers—"

"*Nine* months," she said in a harsh whisper. "Carlos Rivera, listen to yourself. I'm not La Madonna."

"No disrespect to the genuine article, and definitely not trying to blaspheme or get us in trouble . . . I know there was and is only one . . . but, to me, you're my Madonna, okay?"

"No, no, no, no, no," Damali said quickly, waving her hands in front of her. "You can't think like that. I'm your wife. No. Better yet, I'm your lover—I was that before I became—"

"Baby," Carlos said quietly and peacefully, his voice dipping to a caressing octave, "you are carrying my child. I cannot process you as my lover and be able to think in terms of nine months without you . . . so work with me, here. Okay. Visualize . . . you are a vessel of the future, you are the one and only person who has ever had my back, walked through Hell with me, loved me to the bone. I'm not doing *anything* to hurt my son. I say this mantra at least three times a day and more at night. So, you just rest, eat right, I'll bring you whatever you need . . . will—"

"You said son," she shrieked. "How do you know this!"

Carlos smiled and pecked her forehead with a kiss. "You wanna go out hunting at night, got a kill-rush . . . *sheeit,* that's *my* boy."

"Oh, my God! What if it's a girl? Huh? Then what?"

He sat up in bed. "Shit, well if it's my baby girl, then you *definitely* ain't going out, slaughtering demons, carrying her out there at night—uh-uh . . . ain't having it."

Damali slapped her forehead and fell back against the pillows with a thud. "You are such a chauvinist, Carlos . . . you are *not* making sense! I'm a huntress till I die—a Neteru!" She popped up when he smiled and then shook him by his thick shoulders. "This entire conversation is insane. Tomorrow we go into battle, we might die. All of this could be moot. The Neteru credo is to live in the present, prepare for the future, and never turn your back on the past. I want to make love to my husband who is now treating me like I'm . . . I'm . . . I don't know what?"

She stopped trying to shake him, which had been an exercise in futility. He was practically made of stone and unmovable.

"You were sick for weeks and I didn't want to bother you," he said, gathering her into his arms. He placed a breathy kiss against her temple and inhaled the scent of her freshly shampooed hair. "Everything about you was new and fragile. No matter how much I want you, I'd never violate our future. What I wanna do and what I'm gonna do are two different things. Besides, I have just the outlet for all that pent-up energy . . . gonna seriously do some damage and hunt the bastards to the ends of—"

"Yeah, but I'm better now and I'm okay," she whispered against his chest, closing her eyes tightly. "And I'm so horny."

When he didn't immediately answer her, she looked up at him. A wide smile had slowly spread across his handsome face. Moonlight caught the brilliant white of his normally even teeth that were gradually changing as the slight crest of fang threatened his incisors.

"Go to sleep, boo. *Hot damn,* I *told you* it was a boy!"

# CHAPTER FIVE

She punched her pillows, tossed and turned, and finally conceded to grudgingly stare up at the skylight. How in the world could the man just nod off like that and sleep with everything going on? How did the male mind just go click, and turn off, and then once refreshed, merrily resume the problem solving anew in the morning? For her, things had to be settled, first. A clear path, a solution developed, then rest came from the release of worry.

Not to mention, hundreds of thoughts were attacking her brain. Curious questions like, why did the unexpected burst of energy make her so damned horny all of a sudden? *Nobody* had prepared her for all of that. Feeling like that clearly made no sense, given the fate of the world and what they were probably facing. Maybe Carlos was right . . . damn . . . maybe it was a boy, because she sure had something akin to a testosterone rush hitting her system real hard right about now.

Then, again, maybe she should just chill. For once in Carlos's life he was making perfect sense. They were supposed to keep the secret, according to the Neteru Councils. She had indeed been ill for weeks. Plus, what if something did happen . . . they'd both be devastated, and the last thing he needed was something else on his conscience to feel guilty about. Yeah . . . he was right this time. She needed to chill. Had to go to sleep. But, damn, he hadn't even looked at her sideways, let alone with any type of longing . . . not even before they found out about this new world crisis. That was definitely not Carlos.

But what if her carrying really did change the way he saw her? What if now that she was about to be a mother, he no longer found her sexy . . . like that would matter if the end of the world was at hand. She tried to make herself laugh, instead tears filled her eyes. Okay, she was tripping. It didn't matter. Besides, there was some prophecy out there that she hadn't asked Val about when she'd had the chance to and to do so now would tip her hand. She could ask Aset again, but the ancient Queens were being very cagey on the subject. Maybe it was bad news, that's why they didn't wanna say? Who knew?

Damali turned over on her side and spooned Carlos, bathing in the comforting warmth of his body heat. He stirred slightly and pulled her hand into his. It was an unconscious reaction, one developed over their years of sleeping together in the same bed.

She kissed his shoulder. "You asleep?"

"Uhmmm-hmmm," he mumbled absently.

She curled in closer to him and kissed his shoulder again. "You sure?"

"Uhmmm-hmmm," he murmured, but his breathing had changed. He was waking.

"Are you sure you're still attracted to me now?" she asked softly against his shoulder blade and then held her breath.

"Uhmmm-hmmm," he said in a low rumble. "Stop worrying and get some rest."

"What if after I have the baby, I don't snap back and my stomach and thighs get real heavy and my behind gets all . . . I don't know. Then, my breasts get all—"

"D . . . c'mon, go to sleep. I don't wanna talk about it right now."

"You can't even think about it, can you?" She swallowed hard, surprised to be tasting tears.

"No . . . I honestly can't," he said in a strained voice. "I can't allow myself to even go there, okay?"

"All right," she said in a dejected tone. "You were just being honest . . . straight no chaser . . . I just thought that you'd still find something about me that would be attractive if I got heavier."

"Help me, Father," he said quietly. "D—I cannot think about your behind, your thighs, or your breasts getting bigger right now because that'll give me the shakes. Can we just go to sleep and not discuss *anything* remotely sexual for the next nine months? In fact, that word is banned from our vocabulary." He sat up and wiped his palms down his face. "Like, okay—let's talk about the end of the world. That's a real erection killer. Let's talk about potential demon portals . . . anything, baby, that is off the subject, all right?"

She peered at the tent his body made beneath the sheet and swallowed a smile. "I'm sorry . . . I just thought you weren't interested in me because we always, you know, have a crazy, go-for-broke moment before we go into a big battle . . . just in case one of us doesn't come back—or if one of us gets injured so badly we can't do that anymore. I just missed you. I'm not used to this new lifestyle."

"I miss you, too," he said, briefly touching her face but then pulling his hand away as though she'd burned him. "Don't ever think I don't, all right." Before she could answer, he turned away from her and slid down, pulling the sheet up over his shoulder. "Get some rest. The hormone concentrations in your blood are spiking and that's what's sending you all over the map . . . they'll level off."

"You can smell that?" She leaned over and kissed his earlobe. "Do you know how long it's been since you actually—"

He held up one finger and she bit her lip. He didn't turn around and his voice came out on a hard rasp. "Stop."

"I'm sorry . . ."

"That's the other reason I don't need to be bothering you . . . you smell incredible. I don't wanna discuss it."

"All right. Good night," she whispered against his shoulder. "But I thought couples were never supposed to go to sleep angry . . . especially us . . . in dangerous professions."

"I'm not angry, just tired."

"Then why do you sound so pissy? Like, no good night kiss? My bad. Sorry I woke you."

He turned slowly, looking over his shoulder, eyes blazing silver in the darkness and presenting full fangs. "If you don't cut it out I will mess around and accidentally bite you. If you keep on baiting me, I'm out. I'll switch shifts with somebody; will do whatever I have to do to keep myself occupied. But I need you to meet me halfway."

Her palm slid over his cheek. "All right, I'm sorry. Yes, I admit it, I was teasing you . . . because I really wanted you to wake up and change your mind."

"I know," he said quietly and then kissed the inside of her palm. "But I can't . . . not after six weeks."

"Not even a little bit?"

For a moment, he just looked at her. "I don't tell myself those kinds of lies anymore." He smiled and turned to fully kiss her. "C'mon, D. If you just chill, let your mind drift, soon you'll go to sleep. Ask me how I know."

She deepened the kiss as she caressed the side of his face, loving how new beard stubble had begun to form on it. "I respect what you're telling me, you're making sense, I suppose . . . but damn."

"I know . . . damn." He swallowed hard and leaned his head back, closing his eyes.

She kissed his Adam's apple, making him inhale sharply through his nose. His warm palm slid down her arm and then covered her lower belly, resting there like a hot stone.

"In a little while, you'll be able to feel our kid move . . . and one night ain't worth potentially making you lose what we both dreamed of for so long."

His voice was so tender that hot tears quickly rose to her eyes again. "You're right," she said in a thick whisper. "I don't know why I'm being like this or even crazy enough to take the risk . . . maybe some of me is in denial. I'm even willing to admit to being hormonal—but will stab you if you ever throw that in my face." She chuckled sadly, and then wrapped her arms around herself and simply let the tears fall. "Maybe I wanted to just be the old us for a little while longer because I'm scared shitless about what's gonna happen the bigger I get and the more they come for me . . . if there's ever a day I can't draw my blade and back some demon SOB up. A major part of me is scared to feel the baby move, scared to get seriously pregnant, because if they do something once I know it's a baby—feel it, I'll die."

"Oh, damn," he whispered, gathering her into a hug and stroking her back. "I never knew you had all that going on in your head . . . I was just trying to G-up . . . be a solider about this thing. Wasn't looking at it like that." He began rocking her gently as she sniffed. "Was trying to deflect my basic instinct," he added, trying without success to make her smile.

They sat holding each other for a long time, just gently swaying.

"I ain't gonna let 'em take the baby—I swear, D."

"That's the other thing I'm scared of," she whispered against his chest. "If they come for you hard, like they will—the only other person on the planet other than you who can fight them as crazy as you would is me . . . and I'll be pregnant, not in top Neteru form. So, I'd have to choose between the love of my life and the love of my life, and I know you'd do something crazy like sacrifice yourself so that me and the baby could make it . . . but I'd just be existing if I survived. I wouldn't be *making it* at all. And I wouldn't want to hear about no prophecies, or why the angels came late, or the Kings and Queens couldn't do whatever. The darkside, if they get you, might as well cut out my heart . . . and if they get what I'm carrying, same thing."

She drew a deep, shuddering breath and looked up at him, tears streaming. "I've never had this much to lose in my life and I'm pretty fucked up right through here. I don't even know why I'm crying all over the place—I knew what was up going into this pregnancy. What the hell is wrong with me? Does being pregnant make you cry so much? I feel like I'm losing it . . . emotions going berserk. I *hate* being out of control."

He took her mouth slowly, tasting her tears as he laid her back ever so gently. Kissing away the hot streaks of moisture from her butter-smooth cheeks, he finally rested his forehead against hers, his third eye wide open while his eyes were shut. Words caught in his throat and failed him as he kept his weight off her, but blanketed her with protective heat from his soul. Never had a confession been so profound, so filled with the angst he knew so well . . . so simple, so eloquently put . . . so beautifully painful. Her sweet surrender made his hands tremble as they grazed her supple skin.

From her lips to her chin, his mouth found the cleft in her throat. Brushing the delicate concave with a tender kiss, he adored how it fluttered as her shallow breaths staggered in and out of her lungs and then hesitated. He knew . . . she didn't have to tell him. Her breasts were heavy and sore. Her nipples had already begun to change and get larger, yet they also ached for attention. He could feel it, could sense it in her slight arch . . . could smell it as her swollen valley spilled liquid heat.

His gentle kiss against her heart begged her to trust him. In his soul he knew she did when she gathered all the trust she had in her fists while they slowly balled the sheets within them. He understood—go easy but go, *por favor.* Her body was crying for release. She was his life-giver, his cup that runneth over, more than his rib . . . his vital organ, his heart, that blessed vessel that he'd never handle roughly until her contents were pushed into the world healthy and whole.

*"Corazón . . . te amo."* For a moment he had to rest his head against her stomach and simply breathe with his eyes closed.

Gently lifting his old T-shirt from her torso, he stared down at her beauty, making sure the rough cotton texture didn't irritate the overly sensitive skin beneath it. Her breasts bounced free and for what felt like endless seconds he took in every detail of change in their contour, how the areolas were slightly darker and wider . . . the lobes heavier. A rose tinge of irritation had spread along their underside. He ran his tongue over his incisors, sending them back up into his skull with a wince. Her light breaths quickened as he lowered his mouth to softly bring the tip of his tongue against the tight peaks.

Flesh against flesh contact released her trapped gasp; a soundless whistle of cool air over the angry surfaces produced her moan. A soft, sliding kiss down her torso caused her hard arch that sent a shudder through him. He hesitated, his will bending for a moment.

"Just a little bit," she whispered thickly.

He shook his head as he pulled her cut-off sweatpants over her hips and down her calves. "I can't." He stopped her pending argument by gently spreading her thighs and looking at her. He wanted to ride her so hard right now that he dared not chance it. She took a deep breath to begin her protest but his French kiss against her wetness transformed it into a seizing gasp.

The difference in her scent and the new density of her love essence made his eyes cross beneath his lids. Everything about her was becoming more lush, more sensual, thicker, more earthy. The new taste of her and her surprising texture drew a deep moan from inside his chest. Just a little bit . . . no, he couldn't chance it. Her bud was engorged, had become a meaty grape beneath his slow figure-eight attention to it, and yet she was straining, her mind single-focused. Just a little bit . . . he was dry-humping sheets and mattress. Just a little bit . . . he was losing his mind.

Contractions suckled at his tongue as her hips lifted and dipped, trying to capture his fingers and tongue, her voice a low, raw moan of frustration . . . but nothing needed to enter her, he refused to chance it. Refused to give himself permission to even think about it, regardless of the agony clawing at his scrotum.

Hands under her backside, then holding her hips, he devoured her completely until her voice hit the ceiling. Breathing hard, he stayed with her through the rough tide, hugging her torso until the shattering orgasm ended, and then slowly kissed up her belly, briefly took her mouth, and rolled onto his back panting.

She drew against him like he knew she would and he clenched his jaw so hard that he almost sent his fangs through his bottom lip. She moved to blanket him and all he could do was shake his head. Her body was used to him following through. He could feel her craving him, demanding that their standard not be violated with every slick pelvic rock of temptation. He held her hips firmly, considered insanity for a few seconds, and then breathed out the word, "No." She stopped struggling and kissed down his chest, capturing one of his nipples and making tears fill his eyes.

"I want to return the favor," she whispered, but he grabbed her by her shoulders, halting her slow descent down his body.

"You can't . . . or shouldn't," he said quietly. "Not right now. I'm too . . . just don't."

She cradled his face and he closed his eyes. "Why, baby?" she whispered. "You're not contagious, you haven't—"

"Last time I was supposed to be okay. Everybody thought they'd got whatever, that I was cool, but I was carrying around tainted seed from the Chairman's throne . . . shit. I was fucking possessed."

He sat up abruptly with his eyes closed and dropped his head back. "I don't want anything fucked up anywhere near you, understood? I'm not playing around this time, not pushing the edge of the envelope! This thing we've kicked off down there, this time, D, is much worse than fighting Dante, fucking with Cain, or even going up against Lilith—and Padre Lopez told me out of his own mouth that I'm still connected to them. That's how the Light is gonna use me. So, I'm really stressed right now, you gotta give me some space so I can deal."

"All right," she said gently, cupping his cheek with one hand. "I'm hearing you, okay?"

He nodded and winced, keeping his eyes tightly shut.

"But I don't want to leave you like this," she said quietly. "It's just not right . . . how can I do that as your wife? Had I really understood what you were trying to—"

"I'll be cool, just gotta leave it alone and it'll go down, okay."

The pain in his expression made her chew her bottom lip for a moment. "I could—"

"You'll catch a bicep cramp. Ask me how I know . . . go to sleep."

"Oh . . . baby."

"It's cool. For real. I just wanted you to get yours, ya know." He opened his eyes and his voice fractured as he spoke. "Sometimes, woman, I don't know what to do to show you how much I care about you."

"You trust me?"

He looked at her. "Absolutely not."

They both chuckled, temporarily relieving the tension, and he finally conceded to a kiss.

"I understand what you're worried about and I promise I won't do anything dangerous," she murmured into his ear and then allowed her hand to slide against his stomach. "Lie back."

"D . . . I'm weak, okay," he said, falling back onto his elbows. "I admit it."

"Close your eyes," she said, taking his mouth and leaning against him as much as she could without violating his request.

"Baby . . ."

"I know," she murmured before deepening the kiss, grasping him around his base, and then slowly beginning to stroke him. "It hurts like hell."

His hands sought her hair and his kiss became brutal. He pulled away from her mouth with a sharp gasp, his irises solid silver as her rhythm increased, her hand gliding over his love-slicked contours, honoring veins and upthrusts.

"I know what you want to do . . . same thing I want to do . . . wanna get it so good that my wings come out . . . wanna knock my head back and drop all in my jugular on the down-stroke. It's been so long, all you want is a little bit."

"Oh, God . . . 'Mali . . . you just don't know."

He turned his head away quickly as though she'd slapped him. She knew he was beyond trusting himself not to grab her, so she knocked his head back and bit him hard over his tattoo. His arch lifted them both off the bed and his deep moan ran all through her as he clutched her back, his thrusts now frenzied against her slippery palm.

"Let it go, baby . . . you ain't gotta hold it no more," she crooned against his tattoo as she released her wings. "I got mine; you took good care of me, *papi. Te amo.* You always take good care of me."

This time when she bit him, he held her so tightly he almost fractured a wing. His voice rent the air in halting, agonized jags just like the convulsions that spent him. She rode it out with him, suckling his tattoo, keeping pace with his upthrusts, her breaths synched with his, her vocal register raw from talking trash in hard pants for him. But she wouldn't let him go until seed crept over her fist like molten lava in a thick, white emulsion.

Dazed for a moment, and then panicked, he let her go and struggled to sit up, trying to peer around her wings. But she held him tightly and gazed into his eyes.

"It's normal," she murmured, her eyes sliding shut as she inhaled deeply. "I don't even have to look."

Just seeing her do that with the expression she had on her face sent another hard contraction through his cock, making it bounce in her fist.

"Told you you'd get a bicep cramp," he said in an embarrassed chuckle.

"That's because you didn't have all the special effects when you did it alone," she said with a sly smile, kissing him slowly and coming away with his bottom lip between her teeth. She let it go bit by bit and pulled back to allow her gaze to search his face. "Didn't have the audio to go with the visual . . . and the skin-on-skin, or the sense-around-shudders, or the sex-scent bank . . . or the body double," she added, nipping his jugular sweet spot. "Or the body heat to go with it."

"You ain't never lied," he murmured, breathing through his mouth as she stroked him slowly, using his own seed as a lubricant.

"You need to go again?" she whispered into his ear.

"You?" he murmured, nipping her neck.

"Uh-huh. . . ."

"Thought so." His voice was a low, subsonic rumble. "Me, too. Damn, girl, I missed you."

She released her hold on him and flopped onto her back. He covered her in a searing slide and took her mouth prisoner until he'd devastated it.

"But, I still don't think we should . . . at least not yet." He was panting hard, thrusting against her love-slicked thigh, grip tightening, fangs dropping. "You've gotta be strong, all right . . . 'cause, shit . . ."

"All right," she whispered, wrapping her legs around his waist, "but it's gonna be a *long* almost year."

He nodded, sweat rolling from his forehead, down the bridge of his nose and coursing down his temples. "I know," he murmured against her hairline, "the only way I'll be able to hang on is if you talk me through it."

# CHAPTER SIX

Damali opened her eyes with a yawn and stretched, then looked over at the vacant space in the bed beside her. Immediately she became aware that the sun was at its apex. It was too bright in the room! She'd never overslept her shift like this and never needed an alarm clock to rouse her. Damn!

She sat up quickly and rubbed her palms down her face and glanced at the clock on the nightstand. It had been turned around so that the digital display faced the wall.

"Oh, man . . . baby . . ."

Swinging her legs over the side of the bed, she stood and hurried to the bathroom. A note was folded in half to form a tent over the toothbrushes so that she wouldn't miss it. She smiled as she looked at the big hand-drawn heart on the front of it. The words inside were typical of Carlos—brief: *Relax. I got this.*

"Yeah, you do," she said with a pleased sigh. "I love you, too."

Philadelphia, Pennsylvania. . . .

Father Patrick stared up at the cardinal from his wheelchair as his Covenant-provided nurse-bodyguard bowed discreetly and left the room.

A heavy oak door closed behind him and the elderly priest listened hard for the turn of a lock, but detected no additional sounds beyond retreating footsteps echoing down the long corridor. Philadelphia had become the murder capital of the nation . . . primarily young people were committing the murders and were dying. His heart ached as he stared out of the large, leaded, beveled glass windows with failing eyesight. Why, God, did he have to be old and sick now when there was so much left to do?

Silence echoed loudly as the two clerics considered each other with no love lost or trust between them. There had always been strained tolerance between the secret activities of the Covenant and the mainstream diocese operations. One viewed the other as being akin to unregulated special ops with an unspeakable budget and very little accountability, while the other regarded the mainstream as the unflattering face of political debauchery.

Father Patrick stared at the man who'd called him out of his convalescence in New York. Pride had made him answer the call without an escort of his remaining Covenant brethren, rather than admit to being infirmed. Rage made him refuse to be a captive in a safe house afraid of the Devil. At this point, he didn't care if these personal attributes that had made him take leave were considered sins. He was a warrior to the end, and if he died en route to a meeting, so be it. But he would not be a hostage to a nursing facility! Perhaps that was arrogance or vanity, he couldn't be sure. But he was very clear on one thing, he was not about to allow the Unnamed One to make him bow down to his wishes. Ever.

Seeming unsure how to begin, the cardinal folded his hands behind his back. Father Patrick didn't make it easy on him. He kept his expression stern, brows knit, remembering the last cardinal that had betrayed him, his Covenant brethren, and the entire Neteru Guardian team. Suddenly becoming paranoid and feeling trapped, he glanced around.

The meeting room within the cathedral basilica of Saints Peter and Paul was deep and wide, cobbled out of huge gray stones that seemed more suited to an eleventh-century castle than any modern era edifice. Cool, damp air soaked into the elderly priest's bones, making him gather his blanket around him more snugly. He hated needing a wheelchair. Heavy brass lamps flanked the gleaming mahogany table from the vaulted ceiling above. Prisms of colored light poured into the chamber through exquisitely detailed stained-glass windows to coat the high-back, crimson velvet upholstered chairs. He watched his superior's troubled brows knit into one long, furry white caterpillar before he spoke.

"You have been well while on the mend, I take it?" the cardinal finally said, failing miserably at his attempt to make small talk. "That is a blessing."

Father Patrick sat up taller in his wheelchair, feeling old annoyances beginning to rise within him. "Given who I did battle with, I would have to agree."

The cardinal blanched and nervously clasped his hands before him. "Indeed. Indeed. You are one of our finest exorcists and we are glad that you did not succumb to the demon attack."

Fury made Father Patrick's hands tremble. He wanted nothing more at this moment than to be able to stand on his own and to propel himself out of his confinement.

"I am a warrior. A Knight Templar, one of the last of my kind and we would never bow to Satan. We are used to attacks from all quarters. It is we who held true to the cross when even our own papacy denied us and believed the lies of the debtor, King Phillip. We renounced nothing as we burned at the stake and died vindicated in our own souls, if not on paper. So, yes, I was *well* and am *blessed*. Thank you." A wheezing fit stopped his angry diatribe, but his burning gaze finished his point without words.

Hurrying to the center of the table, the cardinal took up the crystal pitcher and quickly poured a small tumbler of chilled ice water for Father Patrick. Bringing it to him, he held his hand firmly around the glass so the priest could sip from it, but did so in a way that allowed the infirmed man his dignity. Once he'd drunk his fill, the cardinal took the glass away and set it on the table. Still agitated, Father Patrick watched the cardinal's robes sway as he walked, regarding the man with open disdain.

"Please hear me this time, old friend," the cardinal said in a quiet, shame-filled voice. "I know much has transpired and there were times when you felt we'd abandoned you—"

"You did abandon me!" Father Patrick wheezed. "You abandoned those children. You attacked the Neterus with benign neglect and so much more! What you attempted to do to Damali is unforgivable. Were it not for the vast resources of the hidden Templar treasuries, that entire Guardian squad would have been at the mercy of the Darkness!"

"Yes, yes, we know. It was an unfortunate set of very political circumstances before . . . and we are now trying to make restitution."

Father Patrick sat back in his wheelchair and eyed the cardinal with a hard glare, causing the man to turn away to stare out the window. He followed the cardinal's line of vision, which had become fixed in the direction of the Masonic lodge only blocks away. There was an agenda, he could feel it. The very fact that they were meeting in Philadelphia was part of it, he could tell. But with his second-sight weakened from the ultimate demon attack, he couldn't be sure. Frustration riddled his being as he quietly acknowledged the loss of yet another part of himself.

"Why? Why now, after all these years?" Father Patrick lifted his chin indignantly, his tone more of an accusation than a question.

The cardinal blotted his brow with a neatly folded white

linen handkerchief that he'd extracted from the deep pockets of his robe. "Because we must . . . we need the Templars to return to restore order. We need this secret group that you all whispered of for centuries to be victorious."

Father Patrick leaned forward. "Are you saying that you are finally recognizing the existence of the Neterus?" His voice was an awed whisper.

"We were wrong," the cardinal said, coming in closer to speak to Father Patrick in a conspiratorial whisper. "The Vatican has released the scrolls of the Templar trials and has reversed the decree of heresy. After seven hundred years, the Templars will be exonerated. We need you as warriors in these, the end of days."

The senior cleric spoke quickly, fervently, bending so that his and Father Patrick's faces and eyes were on the same level, his hands clasped in a plea. "You Templars have secrets; have guarded even the Holy Grail. Your organization was the richest in all of Europe and the entire banking institution that we know of today is based upon the development of your treasury. Cathedrals, castles, and enduring monuments were built by your financing, and there are secret passageways and tunnels that could lead people to safety now as then. Our resources are strained from all the . . . litigation of late." The cardinal briefly closed his eyes as shame filled his voice. "We must change the way things have been done or lose all credibility in the eyes of humanity, but more important, within the eyes of God."

"Something *specific* has happened." Father Patrick stared at the cardinal. "It had to or you wouldn't have come to me. The Vatican never reverses itself."

"King Phillip was an animal . . . a debtor who was under the sway of dark forces and used the Templars to rob their treasuries—but he didn't get it all, only a small portion," the cardinal replied tensely, not directly answering Father Patrick's charge. "Back then we thought he was the Antichrist, but it was not time . . . there is one that has been made now."

"Yes. I'm well aware," Father Patrick said dryly. "I reported this to you and it was probably taken as seriously as any of my other reports. Now you want me to lead you to the Templars' hidden treasury because the mother church is falling on hard times for covering up the sins of her pedophile priests?"

"No! This is not about the money." The cardinal's hands trembled as he blotted his brow again. "This time the pope knows what you say is true."

Tense moments of silence passed as both men stared at each other. Father Patrick leaned forward, dropping some of his resistance and the shield of resentment he had toward his superior.

"What has changed?" Father Patrick placed a hand on the cardinal's forearm.

"The Beast has grown bold, confident, flagrant. It came to His Grace and made him an offer he was told not to refuse . . . and then laughed at him."

Father Patrick blinked twice, stunned.

"It threatened the pontiff's life and then cited all the abominations in the church's history . . . all the blood on the hands of so many popes and showed him a . . . a catalogue of souls from our ranks. From the Crusades to the Inquisition to even turning a blind eye to the holocausts of slavery and Hitler. Our treasuries have blood on the silver. And then it laughed and said that we could not even raise our mightiest warriors against him because we had even betrayed our Templars."

The cardinal dropped to his knees before a stunned Father Patrick and gathered up his hands within his. "Patrick, we must make amends and make our peace within our ranks. If the pontiff doesn't go along with this diabolical plan to endorse the Antichrist as a unifying world leader, he will be assassinated, a demon will replace his seat, and all that we know and love will cease. The human devastation will be quantum. We must reach out to all faiths, all denominations, and bring all people together who believe in the Almighty . . . join our treasuries to keep this disaster at bay. We can no longer have sects and remain fractured as a house divided."

"Who is the one the Beast asks him to endorse?"

"That's just it. We do not yet know. The Unnamed One is making his rounds, going to various senior political sectors within all the nations, striking his deals and positioning for the imminent ascension. The Catholic Church is a huge block of world opinion, hence we are in the crosshairs of this travesty. But we have word that he's going to all the other major religious leaders, too—if any accept this deal, there could be complete chaos."

"The pontiff cannot yield to this."

"No. He will not. He would give his life, he will die first for the love of God . . . but he is playing along for now, just as the others presumably are." The cardinal gripped Father Patrick's hands tighter. "He will wait until the last moment . . . until he gets a name. That name will come to you from us, only to the Knights Templar, so that it can be given to the Neterus. There has also been secret agreement by Muslim, Jewish, Buddhist, and Hindu religious world leaders . . . the pontiff has met with them all, the Dalai Lama among them, and each has vowed to give the name they receive to their warrior representative within the Covenant."

Father Patrick closed his eyes. "Finally." He let out a hard breath and then opened his eyes to stare at the cardinal. "It took the end of times for men to see that the angels preside over us all . . . how sad. Maybe the Devil serves a purpose after all."

"We have heard there are angels that have actually come to you . . . to your warriors." Nervous eyes stared back at Father Patrick.

"You are now reading my reports." Father Patrick's tone was even, years of struggle with the church hierarchy and all its bureaucracy making it tight and unsympathetic.

"Yes," the cardinal said, nodding fervently. "The angels have protected your warriors, true? They will hear your prayers in this most critical endeavor?"

"Yes." Father Patrick's eyes held his superior's, but now rather than being filled with rage, sudden compassion caused tears to rise within them. "You have gotten to this level and never been witness to a miracle, have you? It was all politics and positioning. Until this happened, you didn't truly believe that evil existed, did you?"

"We . . . we thought . . . people. . . . But this was an entity!"

Awed by the revelation, Father Patrick pressed on. "You knew men were evil. You knew people also did angelic things. Therefore there was no unseen for you, right? You believed in the deeds of mankind, but in your soul were very unsure of there being a real mystery of faith . . . so, in truth, you had lost the faith, had lost your way—you thought all this was theoretical, didn't you? Answer me, man!"

Agitated, Father Patrick fought off the cardinal's hands and unsuccessfully tried to stand. "You sent us out as exorcists really thinking human beings simply had psychological problems, and only kept the practice so that the so-called ignorant, common masses would stay with our church . . . but until Lucifer himself showed up in a chair facing the Pope and smiled at him, you didn't believe that the Devil existed, did you?" Father Patrick sat back in his chair, winded. "That old demon must have had quite a laugh . . . but I could have saved you and the pontiff the trouble of being surprised. *I saw him and fought him.* For *years* I tried to tell you this—for years, man, I tried to get through to you all but you treated me like a mental patient . . . or worse, like a child to be indulged and dismissed."

Two large tears rolled down the cardinal's cheeks without censure. "Forgive me, Father, for I have sinned . . . it has been years beyond your comprehension since my last honest confession. Do not forsake humanity because I, we, so many of us were arrogant and vain. Come back to us and protect us. Pray for us. Forgive us. Bring the angels into our company. We are afraid."

"That was all I ever wanted," Father Patrick said quietly. "The truth. I never got that from the Vatican hierarchy . . . just evasions and political equivocation."

"I'm sorry," the cardinal said, beginning to sob against Father Patrick's clasped hands. "We're all so sorry and know not where to turn."

Father Patrick made the sign of the cross on the cardinal's forehead. "I, as only a man, can grant you absolution and have, but the Father is the one you must commune with during these most difficult of times. I will not abandon you, nor will the Templars. God most assuredly will not, if you seek him with a true heart. We Knights took a vow, we have no right to dishonor that vow—because it was not a vow between the vagaries of men, but a vow between us and God. Beyond our prayers and attempts to ensure the safe passage of innocents and the pontiff, what would you have us do? Tell the pontiff that the Original Order of the Knights of Templar is at your service in the battle against the Antichrist." Father Patrick bowed his head slightly and then stared at the weeping cardinal.

"Once the Antichrist has been identified . . ." Mucus strangled the words in the cardinal's throat, halting his statement.

"You need us to be the church's assassins—like old times."

The cardinal closed his eyes. "Let us pray."


Every step she took felt like invisible springs were helping her walk as she bounced down the hall in search of her teammates.

The ever-present scent of fresh brewed coffee drew her toward the kitchen. Mike and Carlos had never succumbed to herbal tea, despite all of Marlene's and Shabazz's urging. Damali took another deep, satisfied inhalation as she walked. The scent of burning wood from the fireplace was everywhere and the comforting smell of it wrapped around her.

Practically giddy, she studied the air, noticing how she could now almost actually see subtle shifts in the molecules within it. She could nearly make out the variation between floating ash, sunshine, and the haze left behind by smoldering embers. Everything had an aura . . . but unlike when in serious battle or trying to do a divination, somehow her second-sight was on full blast without her even trying. As she entered the kitchen, she felt Carlos round the house and come up the deck stairs.

Damali looked down at her arms and stared at the goose-flesh the sensation had produced. "Whoa . . ." It was beyond profound. She could even hear him breathing and he hadn't opened the sliding-glass doors that led in from the deck yet. Her attention snapped up to look at him. It was too freaky. Carlos's normal panther-stealth footfalls against the wood outside had sent a minor vibration through the kitchen floor that she felt like an earthquake aftershock. Yeah, okay, she had normal heightened Neteru sensory capacity, but this was ridiculous.

"G'morning, sleepyhead," Carlos said with a wide grin, coming over to give her a quick kiss. "What?"

"I don't know," she said slowly. "Everything for a few seconds there was real intense."

He gave her a sly grin and went over to the stove without comment and flipped on the burner under the teakettle. She smiled and sucked her teeth. He didn't have to turn around for her to know he was smiling wider.

"You know what I mean . . . and not because of last night."

He shrugged and fished down a canister of loose chamomile tea. "See, I wasn't even going there."

"Uh-huh . . . okay," she said with a soft chuckle. "But you shouldn't have let me oversleep my shift," she said in a more serious tone. "Folks will really start to wonder, you know."

"No, they won't," he said with a broad grin. "Mar and 'Bazz already know the deal. Mike was like, 'Where's 'Mali?' I just pounded his fist and said, 'Still in bed.' He just gave me his most classic shit-eating grin, shook his head, and said, 'My brother.' Men keep things real simple. We ain't into conspiracy theory unless it directly affects us."

Damali folded her arms and had to laugh. "Outrageous as always. Now every time I see Mike he's gonna be giving me his famous my-name-is-Bennit-and-I-ain't-in-it-big cheesy grin. But you forgot about Inez. She'll be suspicious."

"Baby, relax," Carlos said with an easy sigh. "It's cool."

Damali chuckled. "Uhmmm-hmmm . . . everything is *real cool* this morning, isn't it?"

They both looked at each other for a moment and then burst out laughing.

"More cool than it was last night, right?" She came in close to him, but rather than hug her, he pounded her fist and made her laugh harder.

"Ya heard?" he said, avoiding body contact with her while filling the tea ball, still laughing. "But see, girl, you've gotta learn how to surrender."

"I thought I did that?"

He gave her a look that said puhlease, and kept fidgeting with the process of making her tea. "You kept pushing till you got what you wanted."

"Not fair," she said, cuffing his shoulder and then planting a kiss against it. "Like you didn't want to . . ."

He looked at his shoulder. "Not fair, but true—and exactly why I got up and got out of bed and left you there."

On that note she held up her hands and crossed the room to sit on a stool. "Guilty as charged."

"Completely." He took the kettle off the stove before it sounded and poured hot water over the tea ball, then hunted for the raw honey. "But I also wanted you to get some quality rest," he said, hesitating for a moment to look at her as he found a spoon.

"Thank you," she said quietly, holding his gaze. "I know this lull in the action won't last long . . . and it was nice to just have a little time to be normal, you know?"

Carlos nodded. "I hear you, baby." He brought her tea over to her and set it down carefully on the counter. "You feel up to some fruit . . . maybe some cereal?"

She studied his face. "What's wrong, Carlos? It's all in your eyes, the tone of your voice—something's happened, hasn't it?"

"I just want you to have a few to yourself. I want you to have your morning tea, some breakfast—"

"It's afternoon, I have a job to do, and—"

"So do I," he said, rounding on her. His tone was firm and all play had gone out of his expression. "My job is to protect my wife, *comprende*? It even says so in the Bible."

"Where?" she said, trying not to smile.

"I don't know, but it's in there, trust me."

She lifted up her mug of tea and blew on the surface of it to cool it, then said a quiet prayer over it before sipping it. "Thank you for the tea . . . for the sleep late coupon . . . for last night, and for loving me. I'll eat some oatmeal, too, even. But I want you to take the second-sight barrier off me, Carlos."

When he looked away, she knew she had him.

"I'm picking up strange distortions despite the shield you lowered over my senses—I'm seeing colors brighter, auras, hearing better than Mike, all sorts of stuff because my third eye obviously knew it was blocked even when I didn't. And even though I know we *swore* to each other that we'd never block each other from picking up environmental information . . . under the circumstances I'll let this *one time* pass because I know you did it from a loving standpoint." She paused and allowed her silence to challenge him. "But don't do that to me again without my permission. I wouldn't do it to you."

Carlos let out a hard breath. "Okay, all right. I'll admit it. I put you in a bubble. My bad."

"I'm not Ayana."

He turned to look at her, his eyes pained. "But you're carrying precious cargo."

"How bad is it?" she said quietly, setting down her tea.

He let his head hang back and closed his eyes for a moment. "Bad. You want a banana with the oatmeal?"

"Drop the barrier, Carlos."

"Eat, first." He walked over to the stove and pulled out a small pot.

"Talk to me," she said in a calm tone, studying the stress in his back.

"It's the perfect storm," he said, adding water and a pinch of sea salt to the pot before hunting for the canister of oatmeal. "Last night about two A.M., Yonnie shot me a jolt. The West Coast is on fire from Santa Barbara to San Diego. Even Malibu is in flames. Multimillion-dollar homes going up just like shacks. Fires sprung up outta nowhere—the National Weather Service is claiming La Nina and the Santa Ana winds blowing from east to west out of the mountains and valleys with no humidity . . . down to like a 4 percent factor, saying that after the drought in the region, the dry condition is what's caused the tinderbox. Now, this morning, they're saying arson may have started it—but we already coulda told 'em the darkside was behind this bull."

Damali looked out the window and covered her heart with her hand. It wasn't fireplaces . . . damn. "Drop the shield," she whispered. "Please."

"I'm begging you, D. Let me tell you what I know, and after you've had breakfast, I'll drop it. You trust me?"

Begrudgingly, she nodded, but she hated being treated as though she were so fragile she might break.

"Thank you," he said, his voice quiet and tense. "They've already evacuated two-hundred-and-fifty-thousand residents as of six o'clock this morning. I-15 is shut down, and by now more than half a million people have been evaced. Four hundred thousand acres have burned and it's still blazing out there. Meanwhile, New Orleans is getting hit with flash floods again—the Gulf is about to be targeted, it seems, for major flooding, while the central part of the country is getting beat to death by tornadoes and while the Southeast is getting hammered by a drought so bad that Atlanta . . . *Atlanta,* D, is rationing water. Their pipes might go dry within the next ninety days."

Her gaze remained fixed to the horizon beyond the sliding-glass doors. "The fires make sense. They know we're located somewhere in the region . . . somewhere close to our old stomping grounds."

"Yeah," Carlos said with disgust, shaking too much cereal into the heating water. "They know L.A. was my old favorite zone. Know we had a Beverly Hills joint at one time, might have even felt our vibrations down in San Diego—but because we're cloaked by prayer, and they can't find us, the Beast took a torch to the entire region. Firefighters are calling this the worst siege they've ever seen and as soon as they put out one fire, another one explodes. Just like in Athens."

"They thought we were gonna fall back to Athens after that last battle, our team thinking we were victorious . . . oh, shit," she murmured. "So he burned down the capital."

"That motherfucker knows no bounds, D," Carlos said, pointing at her with a wooden spoon, causing her to stare at him. "He's burned down an entire U.S. coastline! They've had to stop Hollywood productions, got almost a half a million acres of primo real estate up in flames, burning down the entire West Coast to get to one house of rats—us."

"They want us out of hiding, Carlos. We can't stay here. Our prayer barriers hold against evil, but not natural events like fire and floods. Brilliant move on their part. The house is gonna get consumed, sooner or later. All those people . . ."

"I know. I know." Carlos angrily stirred the bubbling slurry of cereal as though it had offended him. "But he's trying to herd us into his trap." Carlos jerked his attention up from the task of making cereal. "Check this, Damali. He burns out the West Coast to get us on the move. Makes the old areas we would have fallen back to, like the safe house in Arizona, unlivable with insane tornadoes. Floods out the Gulf, dries out crop country, and will no doubt be sending plagues there shortly . . . the only place to go is to the highly populated areas down the eastern seaboard where there are *serious* military installations and nuke plants, feel me? Where, if we take a stand like we did in Greece, a lot of human casualties will result. It ain't gonna be like that brief firefight we had in Harlem—naw. Next time they'll try to box us in where there's so many innocent civilians that the blood on our hands will haunt us till they get us. I know it like I know my name."

Damali nodded and sipped her tea. "Then we need a counterstrategy. Oughta do what they least expect."

"Been working on that," Carlos said, spooning globby, lumpy oatmeal into a bowl for her. "Hail Mary full of Grace!" He shouted the half prayer over her food and snatched a banana off the platter of fruit on the counter, peeled it like he wanted to fight it, and then yanked the drawer out to find a knife. Cutting the banana over the oatmeal like a sushi chef, he then flung the knife toward the sink and missed, only to have it mount into the wall to the hilt.

"Thank you, baby," she said calmly, accepting his furious attempt at breakfast. She didn't say another word as she sweetened the thick, sticky oatmeal with honey and made herself eat a good portion of it.

Damali forced peacefulness to ooze from her being. Her husband was so upset the man was practically levitating. By this point, she'd seen so many phases of Carlos that she should have been prepared for this one, too—but she wasn't. She was pregnant and halfway into the first trimester. That reality and the fact that the worst of Hell was chasing them had clearly sent him to a place of pure primal reaction. Yet, the best of who he was had always been his intellect under fire. If he divorced that, none of them would make it. But to reach that place that had retreated so far behind the panther was going to be a delicate process. Right now, the panther was feeling cornered, hunted, its mate and progeny at risk, and it was bearing fangs.

"The problem," she said in a nonjudgmental tone after a while, "is that you've been working on this alone." She covered his hand with hers as he sat across from her, staring out the sliding-glass doors. "Two heads are better than one, especially when there's this much heat in the system. I'm your better half, remember?" She smiled but knew it was bad when the offhanded comment didn't break through his stonewall expression. "Drop the veil around me, baby . . . seriously. I need to be able to see."

"Fine. I can't argue with you, Damali. Never could."

"I don't want to argue . . . I understand why you didn't want me to know—but in these end times, we have to have each other's backs . . . I have to have yours, if only as an extra pair of eyes and ears right now so you can do what you have to do. I also need to know as co-general of this team."

"I respect your position on the team, D, but how about respecting the fact that I don't want my wife and baby traumatized, all right?" He looked at her hard. "How about if I wanted you to get one good damned night of sleep. To let you eat one meal that ain't been tainted or poisoned."

"I know that," she said softly, trying to pour balm on his shattered nerves. "And I love you for that . . . respect the hell out of you for doing that. But the only thing that will truly traumatize me is having something happen to you while I am blindsided. Please don't shut me out of our future, Carlos." She'd made her voice as tender as she could, knowing that to fight him like she had in her old ways and days would just make the panther roar louder, when the objective was unity.

When he didn't immediately respond, she touched his arm and looked at him deeply. "I know the weight of the world is literally on your shoulders right now in a way that, as a woman, I probably can't imagine. But as your woman, let me have your back by helping you dissect this threat so we can come up with a serious strategy as one. Would you trust me, baby? I'm not demanding . . . I'm asking you, as your wife, to let me in."

He stood and walked over to the sliding-glass doors and stretched out both arms to brace himself against them. She heard him let out a hard breath and watched the thick muscles in his shoulder blades knot with tension.

"Damn, I loved this house, D . . . wasn't trying to move again. Not in this lifetime. Pisses me off!"

Within seconds she saw plumes of smoke and fire lines decimating the landscape. The relentless sound of chopper blades beating the air made it appear like a scene out of an old Vietnam War movie. Everything as far as she could see was being consumed by a fast-moving, glowing red carpet as though Hell had vomited itself topside like napalm. A quick, unimpeded scan sent the deafening roar of new fires exploding, gobbling up land like a moving freight train at her. That sudden, intense sound, followed by a blast-furnace of heat almost knocked her off her stool.

Fire planes crisscrossed the horizon, dropping plumes of ochre-colored flame retardant. Yet as she scanned she could feel the unnatural heat within the flames, could see the metal alloy in car hubcaps turn to molten, liquid amalgam as it leaked down blistered streets. A sickening awareness then hit her; the National Guard ranks were all deployed in Iraq—culled down in numbers so critically low at home that the local human population didn't stand a chance against natural disasters at home now.

It took everything in her not to yell at her husband for keeping this from her while she'd slept or to jump up and run hollering through the house for an emergency team meeting. Instead, she stared out at the surreal scene and took another bite of lumpy oatmeal from her spoon and then quickly shoved several pieces of cut banana into her mouth with it. Five more minutes wasn't going to change what was happening, and she needed to use that time to chill Carlos out.

Yeah . . . to keep him chilled out, she needed to remain chilled out. That was the only way they could pull it together and think. The third biblical seal had been broken on the beach in the Greek isles, breaking the economy with it. The black horse was riding hard, devastating industry, crops, tanking the insurance industry, screwing with jobs, thus the housing market— this fire, not unlike the billions being plowed into the war, would have a long-term economic impact that she couldn't even fathom.

Damali briefly closed her eyes. Revelations 6:6 entered her mind as a black scale flashed through her second-sight. *"A ration of corn for a day's wages, and three rations of barley for a day's wages."*

But the oil industry and the pharmaceutical industry, known then as *the wine,* would not be hurt.

Panic was unacceptable. Panic was deadly. Futile. But at the moment, there were simply no words.

# CHAPTER SEVEN

"Do what?"

A hard silver stare met her as Carlos turned away from the glass doors. Incredulous, he rubbed his palms down his face and began to walk away. She could tell he was going for distance before he said something that couldn't be taken back.

"You missed the obvious, that's why I said what I said." Damali knew the riddle would hook him and she smiled inwardly as she heard his footsteps stop. She casually got up from her kitchen stool and went to the sink to rinse out her bowl and then shook her head. Some things were simply reflex. Who cared if the dishes were done, given that the house was probably about a couple of hours from being ash.

"Love?" he said, indignant, and then folded his arms over his stone-carved chest. "Love them to death, D . . ."

"Check it out," she said calmly, pointing toward the horizon. "When I had my vision before, everything was being consumed by these dark entities entering people. No doubt there's been a lot of bodies snatched, but I'm still seeing choppers out there, planes . . . what did you tell me . . . there's like eighty eight hundred firefighters on the line, plus how many Red Cross shelters open and neighbors helping neighbors, right?"

"Yeah, all right," he said, dragging his fingers through his hair and coming more deeply into the kitchen.

"That means that the vision I had was skewed. Just like that food that came in and turned all maggoty, my vision was off. Maybe it was residual tainting from before J.L. installed the filters. But all of us in this house have been panicked out of our minds. Krissy wigged so hard that me and J.L. had to take her out of the War Room for air. The goal of this thing is to make people hopeless, make them panic, make them think that the end is finally here—when you and I both know it ain't over until the Creator says it's over . . . and we have to keep on keepin' on."

"All right, all right, I buy that part. Yeah, the illusion is to make everybody trip. I know I've been buggin'—with good cause, too. But how in the hell are we supposed to love this so-called shit to death?" Carlos threw his hands up in the air and began to pace. "I mean, what the fuck, D. What's to love?"

"People," she said flatly. "It can't win if we focus on loving and helping people, rather than going after the darkside directly. That we've never done before on this team." She walked to the glass doors that led out to the deck. "Normally, as soon as the blazes started, we would have kicked in a hellhole, sent in troops, and did a search-and-destroy operation. But we're messing with their heads right now—we haven't surfaced. So, they're going nuts blasting the whole country with everything they've got, trying to get a reaction."

She watched as her husband moved in closer and leaned against the sink. She had him where she wanted him—open and listening.

"Think about it, Carlos. We need to employ a judo move here, allowing the adversary to fall from the momentum of his own weight. They're aggressively attacking . . . we fall back and let their forward momentum roll them over our heads."

She turned and gave him a hard smile. "Yeah. We kick their asses with love. See, I'm figuring that the people who couldn't be taken over by the shadows had to have a love of humanity within them so hard . . . a love of the Creator, by whatever name they know, something sterling within their spirits that wouldn't allow the takeover. Not every kid got taken over. Not every doctor, not every policeman, or man, woman, chick, or child. Feel me? Something is causing a barrier to that, otherwise it would be anarchy out there. Like *Dawn of the Dead*. People would be looting, killing one another out in the streets right before everyone's eyes, cops and anyone with a gun would be up on rooftops and towers like snipers picking people off as we speak. When it goes there, baby, that's when we're at the last of days. That's *the prom*. This is just a midweek dance. Right now, this is bad, but not the worst."

Ever so slightly, she watched Carlos's shoulders begin to relax. By degrees the tense muscles in his biceps lengthened as his arms unfolded. She watched him glance out the window, brows knit, silver gaze on the flaming horizon. She could almost feel his razor-sharp intellect slice through all the illusions before him and engage like a gear that was back on track. Then he nodded.

"Yeah," he said, going to the glass. His tone was so low and distant that she knew he was really talking to himself.

"Still no sign of them?" Lilith screeched as she blew open the doors of the Vampire Council Chambers and sauntered forward.

Her council stood to greet her and she eyed each member with suspicion. Fury at a lack of results had her in a stranglehold, and she turned her bitter venom on her two injured councilwomen first. Their injuries were a reminder of her Dark Realm's heavy losses. Sebastian had lost an arm, his conjuring arm; Elizabeth Bathory was burned beyond recognition. Lucrezia was a wreck. Revolted by Lucrezia Borgia's condition, Lilith shook her head.

Gorgeous, fire-red hair framed Lucrezia's delicate, porcelain white skin. No wonder Fallon had been so taken with her, enough to make her his mate. A pair of sensual, smoky green eyes stared back at Lilith, silently begging for mercy. *There is no mercy in Hell, bitch.* Lilith shot her a telepathic message, taunting Lucrezia as she strode forward and waved away the little gargoyle creatures that scampered at her feet looking for blood bits. The vampires waited, none breathing, to see what vicious course her foul mood might take.

The councilwoman seemed trapped by Lilith's glare, and Lilith allowed her to twist with uncomfortable anticipation as she filled her goblet with blood from the pentagram-shaped council table's veins. Lucrezia's picture-perfect nose balanced her once pretty features . . . Lilith shrugged. Sad that her lower jaw had been ripped away by her own husband to save her life. Silver poison at the hands of the Neterus made it necessary for Fallon to tear at the substance, wrest Lucrezia's esophagus out of her once lovely throat down to the stomach before the silver-laced blood damaged her dead heart.

"Have you no dignity?" Lilith said in a quiet, lethal tone as she spun away from the table and took a sip of blood. It was a rhetorical question, really. Lucrezia's vocal cords were gone.

She'd never expected an answer from her as she ascended her high-back, black marble throne and angrily sat. If Lucrezia had finally summoned enough energy to cover the hideous results of the Neteru poisoning with illusion, surely she would have. That was the thing that so enraged her—Lucrezia didn't have the strength to do so yet and might never—none of them did, at a time when the dark empire needed strong warriors.

Lilith's gaze narrowed as Fallon Nuit flung out his arm and

covered his wife's face from the nose down with a heavily beaded veil. "Such a waste," she hissed and then glanced at Elizabeth, who had turned away to cover her burned face with gnarled hands.

"You were once Count Dracula's wife!" Lilith shrieked, suddenly standing. In a rage she sent her golden goblet crashing to the black marble floor, but even the ever-hungry Harpies dared not go near the spill now. "Look at you! How could you be so stupid to take a bloodbath topside in the gray-zone, or to feed, and not check for treason? It was arrogance and stupidity that allowed you to drop your guard."

There was no response to the diatribe as Lilith's searing gaze raked her subordinates. "You never depend on a man to save your carcass . . . had I depended solely on Lucifer all these millennia, where would I be? Exterminated! Where is your guile, your personal brand of treachery, your me-or-them survival instinct as a *goddamned* queen of the night! I am ashamed to call you mine. There's not even a coherent plot against the female Neteru to return the favor."

Lilith waved out her arm toward Fallon Nuit and Sebastian. "Fuck them! You two councilwomen should have come together to develop a foolproof plan to not only avenge yourselves and restore your honor, but to exterminate these two worthless bastards who were more interested in screwing you than ensuring your longevity and welfare! What has become of Hell?" Her gaze narrowed on both councilmen. "They would *rue* the day that something so horrific ever befell me . . . but you whimper for me to fix this travesty. It is your right and choice to do so—I don't have to sleep with them."

"He couldn't repair me, Madame Councilwoman," Elizabeth said in a piteous murmur. "He lost his conjuring arm and the prosthetic one he casts in illusion is powerless. His left is building strength now, but—"

"Did you have balls enough to ask my husband to repair your arm? Nuit was cut with a Neteru blade and lost a leg, and it was repaired! Did you even bargain for your conjuring limb?" Lilith shrieked, whirling on Sebastian, who ducked a black blast.

"No, milady. I suspected that you were both too busy attending to the more important matter of the heir's survival. My arm is nothing. I felt it best to wait until a more auspicious time to approach him . . . as I'm sure his level of frustration is high now." Sebastian kept his head low like his simpering tone, cringing on his throne.

"Get your fucking arm repaired by the only one who can! I need your spells, not excuses." Lilith hissed and then spit black blood. It sizzled on the hot floor and she folded her arms over her voluptuous chest, now speaking through battle-length fangs as she returned her withering gaze to her councilwomen.

"You two bitches are worthless to me while you cower in the darkness of Chambers and convalesce. Sebastian . . . look at your wife, who was once the beloved of Vlad the Impaler. She was a Hungarian queen, a goddess of beauty and refinement, but look at her now. An old hag! Vampire females never succumb to the loss of beauty at any cost—and most assuredly it is unbefitting a councilwoman!"

Trembling with fury, Lilith spun on Sebastian again and offered him an evil smile. "Necromancer . . . shall I raise Dracula and see what he thinks of Elizabeth's once lily-white skin charred and twisted so that her dark hair and eyes are all that is left of what he once remembered? I am so tempted—"

"No! I will go to the Dark Lord and get my limb restored!" Sebastian shouted, coming around the table to genuflect before Lilith. "Madame Chairwoman, please, that won't be necessary— I will redress this injustice, like Fallon will—"

"Do not *dare* speak my name in this transaction," Fallon Nuit said coolly in *Dananu*. He strode around the table, uttering in the bargaining language of his kind. "The question of whether or not to raise Dracula should be Elizabeth's, not yours, since you allowed her to be harmed."

"And you have not allowed your wife to be! Look at Lucrezia's face!"

Nuit bowed but took no offense. "My senses were duped by the Neterus, just like yours, my friend—but I cuckolded no one's wife. Vlad was a monstrous general in his prime . . . and one of Lucrezia's relatives, who was adept in debauchery and deception, was a pope. We must begin to look at the long list of resources we have yet to employ, *n'est-ce pas?* If your actions stand on their own then what have you to fear?"

"I don't fear making the necessary request, it was simply the timing." Sebastian's eyes glittered with hatred as Nuit glared at him with contempt.

"I've had a limb restored down on Level Seven," Nuit said coolly, "and if that process doesn't make a man out of you, nothing else will, *mon ami.* Although, from the look in your eyes, my bet is that you'll put off the inevitable as long as possible . . . maybe Elizabeth would be better off if the Count were back in his full glory, hmm?"

"Raise him," Elizabeth whispered, her voice strained. She turned her disfigured face toward Lilith, tears rising in her large, brown eyes. "We are linked, and Vlad would be strong enough to heal me."

"I will take that under consideration," Lilith said dismissively while studying her French manicure. "My only concern is that Vlad is impulsive and would make a run at my throne . . . which would mean I'd have to exterminate him permanently."

"You have the power to heal them both . . . and me," Sebastian offered quietly.

Lilith stared at him for a moment and then laughed cruelly. "Yes, I do, don't I? But what have you assumed I've been doing all this time?" From her peripheral vision she saw Fallon, Lucrezia, and Elizabeth draw away ever so slightly as she approached Sebastian.

"You were healing the heir," Sebastian said quickly. "That was the sum total of your focus, milady."

"Good answer," Lilith said in a hissing whisper. "Could it be that I was also waiting to see what *you* could do on your own?" Her voice rose on a powerful crescendo that sent the transporter cloud of bats in the vaulted ceiling into a screeching frenzy. "My husband has been making world leaders offers they cannot refuse, positioning. The Unnamed One, our Dark Lord, has been fucking with the weather, crashing economies, bringing humankind to the brink of world war and nuclear destruction— thus sending you dark cover to aid an ambush . . . what have you done with this time!"

"Built a media empire that assaults the human spirit with shadow elementals and demon principalities that will later make them susceptible to the plagues wrought when the pale horse is released with the breakage of the next biblical seal," Nuit said with unwavering resolve. "I have driven humankind mad, simply put. Leveraging the natural disasters with human insanity shall surely drive the Neterus out of hiding."

"Explain," Lilith screeched, sweeping away from a cowering Sebastian. She stood before Nuit and studied his expression for signs of fraud.

"I've bonded the phantom realms to the airwaves, riding that into the human psyche through their technological toys. The message is decadence," he said in a sensual whisper. "Lack of hope," he murmured, beginning to circle her. "Hatred and human horrors. Their sense of survival is already being compromised with the economic plummets . . . loss of jobs, housing foreclosures, identity theft, and tightening credit restrictions, and of course the thing that drives them from their creature comforts—

so-called natural disasters," he whispered, clenching his fists and motioning in the air as though he were wringing out a wet towel.

"We will ride the black horse of economic distress, showing them decadent celebrities living like kings and queens while they can barely afford to keep their lights on. They will covet and greed will spiral—they will sell their souls for the price of silver under these auspices," Nuit murmured. "It is a part of the shadows. Many humans will break under the strain. Those with dim lights within cannot fight off the toxin."

He smiled as he watched Lilith's fangs adjust to mating length. "Lucrezia's specialty is poison . . . mine, guile and empire-building." He leaned in close enough to whisper in Lilith's ear. "I let her poison the airwaves in the music and entertainment industries . . . including the news. We are bringing you dark recruits twenty-four hours a day, seven days a week, globally . . . and given Lucrezia's unfortunate convalescence and the condition of her throat . . . I have been making master vampires for you, by the dozens."

A slow smile formed on Lilith's lush mouth. She caressed Nuit's jawline and nodded. "Well done, Fallon. *Very* well done. Abstinence from your wife becomes you and I bet that has also improved the quality of her venom, yes?"

Fallon chuckled as his wife released a nasal-created hiss. *"Oui."*

Lilith cast a bored gaze at Lucrezia and issued her a warning in *Dananu* as she repaired the councilwoman's damaged jaw, throat, and torso. "You both have earned my respect and therefore this reprieve. Know that I can only do these types of healings in spaced increments, then must feed and rest. Grafting over silver is as dangerous for me as it is for you . . . and until the heir was healed, I could not waste my energy like this. However, Lucrezia, when I come to you for the old pope in your line, I expect results."

Lucrezia dropped to her knees, sobbing and nodding as the beaded veil disintegrated and new skin began to crawl up her throat and mangled jaw.

"Feed your wife and go fuck her somewhere, Fallon . . . and be ready to report topside within the next twenty-four hours. I want a strategy in place. Better yet, the Neterus' heads on a pike."

Lilith's gaze hardened as it left Nuit and she glanced at Sebastian. "Go to Lucifer and cower at his hooves that he might repair you to do our empire's bidding. The results are uncertain, as you are correct—he is in the worst mood I have *ever* seen him in since the original fall. But that is your only option. I refuse to waste my energy on you. And *if* you survive the ordeal of my husband's healing, do be sure to bring me something equally as devastating as what Fallon has offered this council . . . raise something from the extermination pools—or I may grow bored with you and your wife."

Marlene walked into the kitchen with Shabazz. Both older Guardians stared at the young couple and an awkward silence briefly paralyzed the foursome. Damali was the first to break the tense standoff with the simple statement of good morning.

"We didn't want to interrupt," Marlene said. She glanced at Shabazz nervously. "But we're gonna have to evacuate the house soon."

Shabazz nodded. "Everything tactical in me is feeling like something's about to blow. We might have a half hour." He looked at Carlos. "You up for a full transport out—and you know where we're going?"

"Where's Ayana and Mom Delores?" Damali said, interjecting quickly. She knew Carlos didn't have a clue where he could put them down safely yet, and going into the middle of a hot-zone with a three-year-old and a civilian grandmother was out of the question.

"In a safe house in Philly. While you were still resting, Inez and Mike agreed early this morning, and Mom Delores was grateful to be leaving here when she saw the smoke. In Philly they just raised ten thousand men to stop the violence and Father Pat went there for a meeting at the cathedral basilica . . . plus we got a serious Guardian crew back east, so . . . it's all good. I spoke to him, he's cool." Carlos hesitated, worry straining his expression. "He's still weak, though, and said he had something to tell us when he could be sure his info wouldn't be hijacked out of the air."

"Yo."

Everyone in the kitchen turned quickly around to meet Yonnie's voice. He stood in the doorway, having moved so silently that it unnerved the frayed senior team.

"I should have heard you coming, man," Carlos said, as he pounded Yonnie's fist.

"All of y'all shoulda heard me coming, but your focus is elsewhere. Not good. I coulda snuck you as a daywalker . . . shit—y'all better tighten it up."

"It ain't your shift," Shabazz said, his gaze hardening with frustration.

"With the world up in smoke, do it have to be?" Yonnie leaned against the sink and folded his arms over his chest. Palpable tension coiled around him. His sinewy form seemed like he was ready to spring into action to meet Shabazz's challenge, if it went there. Defiance blazed in Yonnie's dark brown eyes and his wild Afro seemed to add to the visual affect of an indignant, young man. Wearing a wife-beater T-shirt, a pair of gray sweats, and no shoes, Yonnie looked like he'd just rolled out of bed but was ready to rumble.

Carlos rubbed the stubble on his jaw. "Aw'ight, y'all . . . look, we gotta—"

"Git the fuck outta here, is what we gotta do, man," Yonnie

said, scowling. "You of all people know how the other side rolls. Can't be no dillydallying."

"We were having a team meeting with senior Guardian staff trying to determine the best course of action, Yolando," Marlene said bluntly. One hand went to her hip. "You're new, and there's a way we do things to ensure the safety of the team and any humans we decide to go near."

Yonnie pushed off the sink and materialized a toothpick in his mouth in agitation. "Sis, I might be new, but I ain't stupid—and me and C go way back."

"Call my wife sis one more time and I'ma bust your new ass," Shabazz said, moving forward.

Carlos flat-palmed Shabazz in midchest. "C'mon, man, that's just Yonnie when he's tripping." He glared at Yonnie. "Respect, man—Mar is housemother, you feel me?"

Yonnie held up both hands in front of his chest. "My bad, Miss Marlene, but, like . . . I'm getting all kinds of funky vibes, yo. The shit is making a brother jumpy."

"He's tapped in," Damali said, diffusing the contest of wills with raw truth. She looked at the group. "He's new, just out of Hell. If anybody can feel movement"—she turned to Yonnie—"talk to us."

"See," Yonnie said, pointing at Damali and walking to the other side of the kitchen. "That's why I always liked your woman, C. She listens. She hears. Aw'ight. I'ma tell you what I'm picking up." He wiped his palms down his face and let out a weary breath. "Nuit has been making master bitches—'scuze my French—like there's no tomorrow. It's like brotherman is on steroids, or something. Don't even ask me how I know. Then, I'm trying to chill, flipping channels in the bedroom, 'cause if I didn't leave Val alone she was probably gonna stab me . . . and I'm listening to a report that I know a lot about. They said that cocaine did better than the freakin' Dow Jones this year." He went over to Carlos and pounded his fist. "But we coulda told 'em that, man."

"What's any of that got to do with the plan to get out of here?" Shabazz said, growing agitated. "We already knew they'd be making new vamps and drugs ain't new, so what?"

"It's got to do with territory and a councilman getting stronger, 'Bazz," Carlos said, pounding Yonnie's fist again. He looked at his old friend from his old life. "Expansion. Nuit is in full favor if he's slammin' vamps like you say he is, *hombre.*"

"He got da hoes working day and night, and in a minute, they'll be on the street with fangs and real strong." Yonnie nodded and smiled, flipping the toothpick in his mouth with his tongue. "Mr. Chairman."

"I really wish you wouldn't call Carlos that," Marlene said, tension making her begin to pace. "He's not that anymore. Can't even think like that anymore."

"He *better* think like that," Yonnie said, losing his smile as he stared at both Marlene and Shabazz. "He better remember *all* that shit from his old life." Yonnie cocked his head to the side and looked at Damali. "You know I ain't lying. . . . C was one of the baddest mofos in the valley, and that's what we need right now—not some politically correct—"

"Right," Damali said, intentionally cutting off Yonnie's statement before the word *bitch* could come out of his mouth. "We need the truth, straight no chaser."

Carlos gave Yonnie a hard glare, the edges of his irises beginning to flicker silver. Yonnie was crazy, but wasn't *that* crazy—Damali hoped. After all, everybody was hyped.

But if Yonnie said the b word in reference to Carlos, there'd be no telling what could erupt in the kitchen. There wasn't time for that. Right now it was imperative for her to agree with the plan to go old-school gangsta so that Carlos wouldn't sit the fence. Decisions were going to have to be swift and possibly reckless, and her husband was so worried about her that he was erring on the side of caution.

"No disrespect, Mr. Chairman," Yonnie said after a moment, calming down a little but lifting his chin with pride. "I'm just used to seeing the old you, man . . . that cock-diesel, crazy motherfucker who would go for broke without hesitation. I know you been playing it safe on account of the kid—"

"Ayana ain't got nothing to do with this shit," Carlos said, his voice escalating as he pointed at Yonnie.

Yonnie rolled his shoulders. "I ain't talking about Ayana, aw'ight. I'm talkin' 'bout yours, bro." He motioned toward his nose and glared at Carlos. "What, you think I ain't know? You think my senses is that off since I crossed over? That's why I'm telling you I got your back. Fuck all this seniority shit, we gotta go for broke. I'm planning on being an uncle—ain't got no blood relatives, but y'all, man. So let's do this shit."

"Oh . . . my . . . God. . . ." Marlene began walking in a circle.

Shabazz just closed his eyes. Damali opened and closed her mouth as Yonnie gave Carlos a warrior hug and nodded.

"You *da man,* motherfucker," Yonnie said, laughing as Carlos let him go. "How you pull that off during the Armageddon and half dead, sheeit, I'lln't know!"

A huge smile broke out on Carlos's face. "You gotta keep it on the low, man. For real. Orders from On High."

"I ain't messin' with them," Yonnie said, waving his hands in front of his chest. "If *they* said keep it on the low, shit, my lips are sealed." He made the sign of a key turning a lock in front of his mouth with his fingers and then threw away the imaginary key.

Carlos glimpsed at Damali and then gave his attention to Yonnie. "Just like they ain't trying to blow up oil fields and are fighting to keep all the bombs away from those resources, the darkside ain't burning South America or Turkey, they . . . ain't directly going to war in the cash crop breadbasket zone. Cocaine *is* their Dow Jones."

"That's what I've been waiting to hear, man," Yonnie said, wiping his forehead. "The old you back in action." He looked at Damali. "I know you got a lot riding on every decision being right this time, yo . . . I feel you. But we can't afford to have you playing it so conservative that they get us because we didn't do something buck wild."

"And do not damage the oil and the wine," Marlene murmured. "Seal three."

"Since that third seal is broken, you gotta get 'em with love this time, Yonnie," Damali said, and folded her arms over her chest. "We've gotta stop this thing with the most powerful energy on the planet—love."

Shabazz and Yonnie both reacted instantly, their voices blending into a single outraged question. "What?"

"That's right," Marlene said with both hands on her hips. "Noetic science—combination of quantum physics, spiritualism, and psychometrics . . . bet you gentlemen didn't read the Internet pages I copied for you?"

Three sets of male eyes sought the kitchen floor and then the horizon.

"Ten bucks says J.L. read it, though," Damali muttered.

"I'll raise Shabazz twenty, who're you telling—don't even get me started," Marlene fussed, cutting a glare at Shabazz as she answered Damali. "It's real simple," she added in a huff. "Damali is talking about shifting energies on the planet, tapping into the fifth force of psi, which is on the order of photons, gravitons, leptons, and quarks. Psi is a river of energy with currents all around us—like the river of life that never stops flowing—and if as little as 11 percent of the population shifts perspective, we can create a paradigm shift . . . hence why music is so dangerous and used for every major revolution. It's a universal language." Marlene shook her head as the men in the group gaped at her. "*Hello* . . . quantum physics, quantum mechanics. . . . Y'all need to read, I swear!"

Damali let out a heavy sigh. It was always a clash between yin and yang, male and female energy in the house and battle tactics. She couldn't even begin to deal with the shock of Yonnie knowing her condition. That reality had spiked a panic rush within her that she just had to suck up and let go, because if Yonnie knew then it wouldn't be long before the darkside figured it out. Her only hope was that the Light had somehow silver-shielded her. Not knowing for sure, though, was the terrifying part. Unfortunately, she didn't have time to address that right now.

"We're fighting on multiple fronts," Damali said, moving to the kitchen counter. "They're using natural disasters to flush us out, sending fire, floods, twisters, whatever they can through our old stomping grounds. They know we have to move to avoid all that, and if they see a miraculous reversal of nature—like a fire going out on its own, or whatever, they'll know where to target more pressure. So, I'm guessing, Heaven wouldn't blow our cover like that—but has given us the means to help ourselves outta that type of jam." She used her fingers to count off the points, sporadically moving tabletop items around to visually make her case.

"Then they went after human capital—people's psyche's and spirits, and are breaking people's backs with the economy," she added. "They figured if the disasters don't drive us out into the open, clusters of really horrific human behaviors might send our team in on a reconnaissance mission to investigate or to try a direct intervention. But I say let's use our resources to flood the airwaves with messages of hope and love and get people helping their neighbors more . . . let's move that psi around and start chipping away at the 11 percent we need to sway the balance, because that's the only thing that's gonna inoculate people from the darkside taking up residence in their spirits."

Damali folded her arms again and gave the men around her a slight smile. "My condition hasn't made me all wishy-washy. Once we narrow down the target, we kick their asses. I'm just trying to be efficient and minimize human casualties."

"Damn," Yonnie said, smiling. "Your woman is still gangsta, man. I love it!"

"That's why I love her," Carlos said with a half smile. He looked at Damali, his smile fading as he tried to comprehend her strategy. "So, we get the underground Guardian teams to start blowing up the Internet and guerilla radio waves and all that with what . . . like stories of victories?"

"Yeah," she said flatly. "I'm not saying we ask people to put their heads in the sand or to try to convince them that bad things aren't happening out there, or that the economy doesn't suck. But we want to remind them that there's still more good than bad overall. And we get our rebels to start playing cuts from every positive artist we can, even if it's old music. Get the Covenant in the loop, too, in order to get word out to the houses of worship to stop talking about everything that's going wrong, but start claiming victory about all the good that is happening, despite the seeming odds. That ought to begin to create a reversal of some of those possessions."

"I'm down with that," Shabazz said. "Makes sense from a manifesting energy standpoint . . . what you think is what you attract—but get to the part where we hunt their asses down."

"Follow the money," Carlos said, stepping closer to the counter.

Damali backed up and watched, loving how his former confidence clicked into place like a loaded Glock the moment he knew his boy Yonnie had his back. It was amazing to witness and they hadn't violated any rules . . . Yonnie knew because Yonnie was Yonnie. She watched Carlos begin to talk with his hands over the surface of the countertop, the heat beginning to cast hologramlike, shimmering images just above it.

"The West Coast is, for all intents and purposes, gone," Carlos said.

J.L.'s presence in the doorway made everyone look up. His eyes were bloodshot with dark shadows beneath.

"I got something here," he said, entering the room with a bucket filled with oddly cut copper piping. "Was up all night. Blood Music got gobbled up by a Canadian firm because the dollar is stronger abroad now . . . Council Group Entertainment. You have two guesses what the reference to Council Group means, and one doesn't count. They have a building in L.A., but their main headquarters is in Toronto."

"That's still North American territory, bro," Yonnie said, glancing at Carlos.

"No doubt," Carlos said, rubbing his chin as he and Yonnie exchanged a knowing look. "Nuit called your bluff, so I guess that SOB made the come up. Would explain the power rush you've felt coming off him, since you were linked more directly to him than I was."

"Same board of directors as Blood Music had, but now he's a multimedia conglomerate bigger than Time Warner," J.L. said, glancing between Yonnie and Carlos. "The link that led me to them was that every one of their artists' hits was on the MySpace pages of the teens who'd committed the most recent sicko violent crimes. Ten dollars on red says CGE is Fallon's new playground."

"You's a bad man, J.L.," Shabazz said, going over to pound his fist. "What's up with the bucket, though?"

J.L. looked at the small assembly of Guardians around him. "Krissy was bad off. Her mind and spirit took a hit from all the negativity. When we went off shift, she couldn't stop crying and she had balled up into a fetal position in the bed."

"You should have come to get me," Marlene said quietly.

"Before you put in the filters, that girl downloaded everything off the Net and listened to it all day long—"

"I know, Mar, but I had to do this myself," J.L. said with a frown. "She'd only stop crying when I'd remind her of all the good that was in the world . . . she was looking at the fires, panicking, going into a cold sweat. So I built something, because I figured if it was affecting her like this, what about a regular average person . . . that's why I didn't come to you, Mar. I knew it was something I had to figure out on my own."

"You read the article I'd put under your door last week?" Marlene said, scowling at Shabazz.

"Yeah, of course, Mar," J.L. said. "I always read the cool stuff you give me. That's how I learned to build this . . . the psi around Krissy was all jacked up."

"You owe me money," Marlene muttered to Shabazz. He didn't say a word, just went in his wallet and handed her a twenty.

"What's in the bucket, man?" Carlos said, surveying J.L. from an uneasy distance.

"Prayer-infused, catalyzed resin with copper, silver, and aluminum shavings for conductivity. Then to stand the copper pipes up in the solution till it hardened I used a form board, just a piece of plywood with holes cut into it so the pipes wouldn't fall over. Then I took seven copper pipes, inserted rutilated crystals in them and capped them off. What you then have is a homemade energy transponder. A white-light superconductor. I'm a tactical, right?"

J.L. looked at the group who only returned blank stares. "Okay, so I set my intention on positive white light and read positive info out loud while touching the copper piping, sending a tactical charge into it . . . and then took my hand off it, put Krissy's hands on it, and I watched dark static get sucked out of her body and get trapped in the resin. She chilled right out after that." J.L. smiled when everyone's eyes widened. "Don't touch the bucket, though. That black slop in the bottom caught in the sticky resin is what was making my wife sick—she got it from the airwaves. I figured I can set it in the yard and just let it burn since we're gonna be out soon. Right?"

"Right," Marlene said slowly. "Any other reason why you might not have wanted me to do a standard purge, J.L.—even though your invention is awesome and something we might need in the future? I'm just saying?"

Marlene gave him a sideways glance. Everyone watched J.L. shift nervously from foot to foot.

"I had to be sure I got everything out of her my way, Marlene," he said after a moment. He went to the sliding-glass doors, opened them, and then bounded down the steps.

"She's pregnant," Marlene said flatly. "I'm taking full paycheck bets."

"Lotta that going around," Shabazz muttered. "And hell no, I ain't betting no senior seer."

They all looked at Yonnie.

"Not a word," Carlos warned. "Not one word, man."

"Peace," Yonnie said with a shrug and waited until J.L. rejoined them at the counter.

Damali and Carlos shared a private glance, but said nothing.

"What's the plan?" J.L. asked, seeming so nervous he looked like he was about to leap out of his skin.

Carlos clapped his hands together and rubbed them hard, drawing friction-produced sparks before spreading them out on the table. "Old-school," he said, placing his hands flat on the tiled surface and causing the map of the world to begin to appear in a shimmering glaze on top of it. "They don't give a rat's ass about a building in downtown L.A. if it burns. They probably dangled that CGE building in front of us as the first lure, hoping we'd charge in there and bust the place up—but we didn't."

He moved his finger down the shimmering replica of the coastline and then wiped it away. "Fires, primarily focused here in San Diego where they sensed us, but they couldn't get an accurate bead on us because we haven't come out for weeks. But when I took that drive to get Damali some grub, they were all over my trail like flies on shit. That's why the worst of the wildfires are down here in San Diego. Just like in Athens, these were started by arson, aka the darkside."

As Carlos went through each geographical barrier, he made a section of the country disappear. "The Gulf—flooded out before the San Diego fires, 'cause they were still looking for us, not sure where we were. Droughts, twisters . . . but what hasn't been hit?" Carlos looked up with a hard smile. "Motown, Motor City. Otherwise known as Detroit. Why?

"Strategic location to quickly fall back to Canada from the United States, if you've got a music label in the States, plus that area's got the whole music legacy thing going on . . . besides, what was the most positive music influence talking about love?" Carlos looked at Damali and smiled.

"Rhythm and blues," Damali said. "The last castle. You take R&B, jazz, neo-soul, and turn those positive genres negative, hey . . . you affect a lot of people. We already saw what the effects of negative hip-hop did—the positive artists are fighting to hold their own. But Detroit has a lot of history, a lot of psi in the plus column that would be hard to overwrite."

"The Underground Railroad history alone would be hard to track over," Marlene said, glancing around the group. "Blacks, whites, and Native Americans came together up there—they'd have to blot out the energies of Sojourner Truth and Frederick Douglass . . . naw. Wouldn't happen that fast up there. Plus all the love songs that came out of the Motown empire, it would take them some time to wear that down."

"But the economic crash hit Detroit hard," Yonnie argued.

"Had a lot of depressed mugs up there. Murder rate through the roof. Be real. Detroit has issues, all love train music aside."

"Right," Carlos said, adding continents to the shimmering mosaic on the countertop. "But it's bigger than that . . . if you follow the money." Yonnie pounded his fist. "Negative music lyrics, movies, and news broadcasts coming out of CGE are just the conduit to create depression, lowered resistance to negative vibes, loss of hope, and to let the shadows in—but they started with music because music is so pervasive and is the universal language. But this bigger picture is all about the Benjamins and world domination."

Satisfied when the team nodded with understanding, Carlos pressed on. "First of all, a weak dollar internationally means that foreign countries can easily gobble up real estate in the United States, especially places compromised by natural disaster. So, Canada, Britain, Ireland, France, Japan . . . Dubai, anywhere their currency is stronger than ours at the moment, can start to make a serious down payment on America. And what will that do?"

Carlos looked around the group and then answered his own question. "Start a national panic. Americans, already feeling stressed by wars, natural disasters, hate crimes, breaches in justice and national conscience, conspiracy theories, unchecked government wrongdoing, whatever, will fall back into some serious hateration of other nations. Look at what happened when oil prices shot up more than three dollars a gallon; Americans lost their minds. When people panic, they don't think. We've seen that happen time and time again—that's how the Patriot Act got passed and now everybody's civil liberties are in jeopardy. Fear is just another dark entity that breeds mob thought, coaxes out insanity. This whole game is being levered by oil and drugs— the wine, yo."

"You ain't never lied, man," Shabazz said, looking at Carlos.

Carlos nodded. "This bullshit is about to be a house of cards, economically—and yet, our allies can't really afford to have us as a superpower fall. We're the army for half of the so-called civilized world. But sooner or later manipulating interest rates won't fix what's broke. Meanwhile, those on the darkside with an agenda are already invested in war. Oil, drugs, and everything that goes with that—and getting paid, lovely. C'mon, Blackwater is just one example—they ain't even being coy with the names anymore!"

"Just in your face, *blat-ow,*" Yonnie said, opening his arms. "Like letting dirty motherfuckers off the hook in broad daylight that woulda got you and me triple life, slim."

"Then they'll be a call for unified currencies and a collective world leader," Shabazz said, rubbing his chin, "just like prophesied."

"So this takeover of people's minds is more than about just getting us out of hiding," J.L. said, his eyes roving over the faces around the island counter.

"It serves multiple purposes, like I keep saying," Damali said flatly.

"Yeah, and since coke is doing better than the Dow Jones, like oil is king, and we know who runs that," Yonnie said, pointing at the shimmering map, "then whoever controls those product lines is who buys up most of the shit and leverages the hell out of this war game, causing market crashes and panics at will—herding people worldwide like sheep to get 'em to do whatever."

"Correct," Marlene said, leaning in. "So, South America just has people-madness happen, but is spared most of the natural disasters in its coca-producing and oil-generating regions. Africa is already plugged into the oil game from Nigeria, but is riddled continentwide with the blood-diamond wars, AIDS, drought, starvation, and every kind of disease known to humankind—"

"But like Asia," Damali said emphatically, "it has enough bodies to feed off of. Look at the water crisis in India—the Ganges is a cesspool and human disease is about to ravage that region if it doesn't get the situation under control. Things are so crazy there that the macaque monkeys in New Delhi are going mad, getting aggressive enough that they killed a high-level government official—made the man fall off a freaking balcony at his home! Monks are getting clubbed to death in Burma . . . and look what happened in Pakistan—they assassinated the former prime minister over there and innocent people are dying. That region is being hit hard, like Africa, to keep it from being a dissenting voice with any real strength behind its massive populations."

"Feeding grounds, sis. That's all it is," Yonnie said in a weary tone. "None of those nations and continents you listed, including South America, are contenders to run the world because of their chaos. Unfortunately, they're the breadbaskets for the world, but are also ripe feeding grounds for the Apocalypse troops."

"So, think about it," Carlos said, using his finger against the shimmering surfaces. "If South America, Africa, Pakistan, and India and developing nations are political noncontenders for world domination, but can fuel it like a resource bank for blood, oil, and drug cash crops, and bodies . . . with the Caribbean only a tidal wave away from being gone if they dissent, and Australia not being militarily strong enough to get in the mix, then that leaves the United States to polarize with Western Europe and Canada against Asia, Eastern Europe, and Russia—with the catalyst to kick all this off being the good ole Middle East."

"Book of Daniel, chapter seven," Marlene said, shaking her head. "Remember his vision. . . . The lion-bodied eagle—which we know can only be the newly aggressive U.S. and Europe alignment, versus the four-headed leopard dragon—which I'm sure are the four main nations in Asia—North Korea, South Korea, Japan, and China, versus the bear—which is nothing but Russia and the old Eastern bloc. Then comes the fourth one with iron teeth—guess who that belongs to? The New World Order leader, which crushes them all . . . and we don't need to say *his* name in this house."

J.L. nodded and looked up from the counter at Carlos. "Dude, I stay on the news watch, right. How about the United States and Europe just came together over Iran as a rallying point in a meeting in Tokyo . . . but Russia disputed their findings and doesn't want them to put U.S. missile defenses in Poland or radar base stations in the old Czech Republic areas."

"My point exactly. It's already under way. I know chessboard moves, bro," Carlos said, nodding. "It's all coming down to the big three zones, with the United States, Canada, and Europe banding together as a singular superpower against the others— watch. Then you-know-who defeats each of the three weakened, bickering blocs of nations and creates the fourth one . . . which is *the* New World Order ruled by the darkside."

Damali traced her finger down the eastern seaboard of Carlos's shimmering map. "All right, so that's the big picture. But for now, we've gotta focus on whatever little bit we can do to stem the tide. So look at this move . . . Detroit to Toronto, then come down to Rochester, then Buffalo, to New York City, past Philly, to Washington D.C., Chicago and Ohio are in there, too, but the way I traced is a more direct route."

She stared up at the team. "With all the disasters, look at what hasn't totally burned yet or completely flooded out . . . human madness is what has those areas in their grip all the way down the East Coast to Florida. But notice how they aren't jacking it up? The darkside is shifting the psi in the heavily populated, but strategic, areas of the strongest contender for the new world order—here."

"Proverbs eight," Marlene said, nodding, and then high-fived Damali. "Wisdom is personified as a woman in the Good Book . . . that was based on Ma'at, check it out, fellas. Our girl is on."

"No lie. D is on and poppin'. The Pentagon is on that route, so is Cape fucking Canaveral, yo," Yonnie said, folding his arms. "If you're gonna take over the world and be a potential host nation for the Antichrist, you ain't messing with your key locations."

"And the Kennedy Space Center—where missiles could be launched—is on that route, too," J.L. added, glancing at Carlos.

"This Detroit to Canada thing makes sense," Marlene said after a moment of contemplation. "It's still Nuit's North American province if he moves into Canada . . . much more wilderness with direct access for all the new vamps he's made to retreat back to a hemisphere that literally goes into darkness for six months a year."

"Great place for the Antichrist to deliver the daylight bite to the minions of new supervamps they're making, too," Shabazz said in a disgusted mutter.

"Yeah, we need to keep our eye on Canada. You ain't gotta worry about Mexico on the southern border," Yonnie said. "They ain't a contender. But they, like South America and Central America, are where Nuit's drug cash comes in. As head topside mofo, Nuit is going to be an acting general we have to get past first . . . then when we kick his ass, no doubt Lilith and her ole man will be the serious battle—but they ain't gonna risk bringing their heir out in the open yet. That's my two-cent bet on the thing. And, if they decide Mexico is becoming politically problematic, or if they need a diversion, we already know they can blow that big ass volcano that's sitting near Mexico City, and Central America can get swept away in a tsunami like the Caribbean and Polynesia could."

"So, how about if we show up in Nuit's backyard for the Detroit International Jazz Festival and scout his minions, send him a little message that we ain't slow by getting real close to his new headquarters? Let's be bold, take it to him rather than being on the run," Damali said with a smile. "Let's throw the bastard a curveball—and since I was locked in the house all of August and couldn't go out and party for my birthday, why not? They hold it every Labor Day weekend, which is only a coupla days away. I personally wanna show the brother some love."

Carlos just looked at her and she smiled wider.

"We know the route they don't want blown up—namely the eastern seaboard . . . but I'll bet they don't think we're crazy enough to take the party over the border into Canada now that we know the Anti—" Damali shrugged. "Chances are they're banking on us trying to run to where we have a strong Guardian presence."

Shabazz cut Marlene a look. "Detroit . . . I haven't been back there since I was a kid and did time for a crime I didn't commit." He dragged his fingers through his locks and stared at Damali for a moment. "You sure, baby girl? I mean, Detroit used to be the murder capital before Philly, and some of the places we might have to roll . . ."

Damali hugged Shabazz and a silent understanding passed between them. She knew what he was saying without words. Concern for the baby was making him edgy, just like Carlos. "It'll be fine. We've already played Hell—so Motor City ain't half that bad."

Shabazz hugged her tighter and forced a smile. "Since it was the last stop to Canada, Mar is right. There's a lot of Underground Railroad routes that go right through the city. We can use them and I know we've got a decent Guardian presence up there, no doubt."

"I'll do a divination," Marlene said, her gaze holding Carlos's.

"Don't worry. Where you put us down will be on hallowed ground." She closed her eyes and reached out to hold Carlos's and Damali's hands. "There's a Catholic church in Detroit that's standing out like a white-light beacon in my mind . . . that has symbols of the Akan cut into the archways . . . Our Lady . . . something of . . ." She opened her eyes abruptly, clearly frustrated. "I can't get more than that—the new church's name is blotting it out for me. Fountain of Life Church of God in Christ—it's now Baptist or A.M.E. or maybe Seventh-Day Adventist. The old energy dissipated on me because the new energy there is very strong, very good. There's old living quarters in the back behind the rectory and the church."

Marlene shook her head as though trying to clear a haze from her mind. "How can they have Akan symbols in the stone masonry, though? The structure is hundreds of years old, goes back to slavery days. Why would priests in that era commission—"

"Where, exact location?" Carlos said quickly, glancing out the window at the approaching flames. "I've still gotta rally the team, sweep us all into a transport with gear."

"It's in the nine-hundred block of St. Mary's Street between West Chicago and Greenfield on the west side of Detroit about a mile away from I-96."

"If it is that old, and a *Catholic* church, with *African* symbols in the stonework . . . then, Mar . . . it has to be a secret Templar hideout." Damali's gaze tore between Marlene's and Carlos's faces. "Only the Templars would have been looking for a Neteru with Akan markings here in North America, and would have been invested in making sure that the Guardian birth line to the Neterus would have been brought out of slavery into free Canada—we have to talk to Father Pat. That has *got to be* an old Templar safe house, if not a citadel . . . and who knows what kind of tunnel system, secret passageways, or whatever, are in that building?"

Yonnie glanced out the kitchen's glass deck doors and then back to the group. "Not to rush y'all or break up this impromptu war meeting . . . but, uh, we need to make a decision about that location in Detroit we can fall back to with quickness. If you haven't noticed, the bottom of the deck's on fire."

# CHAPTER EIGHT

Carlos glanced around the small courtyard behind the centuries-old Catholic church that had been taken over by a new denomination. He hated moving the team like this—just a wild-ass shot in the dark to land hard without a prior environmental sweep. But it was what it was. Time had run out.

His worst fears were realized. The rectory in the back was a host to occupied administrative offices; he could see church staff milling about behind the windows and could hear children in the basement . . . had to be a day care center. Schools flanked the front of the church and the back of it, and his team was standing there looking like a guerrilla army, strapped to the nines with grenades, automatics, and a trunk of supplies.

"Anybody feeling like if we don't take cover, in, say . . . maybe five minutes, popo is gonna be all over us?" Yonnie stashed his 9mm in the back of his sweatpants and then looked down at his bare feet. "And, bro, can we get some decent clothes? It was bad enough that the house burned to the ground with all my best Italian leathers in it, but I don't go out in public like this. You know how we used to do the damned thing, homeboy."

"Yonnie . . . man," Jose said in a near growl, "chill. C is working on it. Ain't you, C?"

"Yeah, I'm working on it," Carlos said, glancing around. "Shit."

Heather tossed Damali the divination necklace she'd lent the seers during their watch shifts. "Before some kids or civilians see us, ask Pearl."

"I said I'm working on it," Carlos muttered, taking offense.

"Well," Rider said with a sarcastic sigh, "this is cozy, while we wait." He nodded and began walking around the small courtyard looking for potential hiding places big enough for the entire team that were not to be found. "Our Lady Gates of Heaven—fitting for the last gate we'll probably see this side of freedom the moment the cops get here. I don't figure they'll buy that we work for Homeland Security in these just-out-of-bed outfits toting heavy artillery—you think?"

"Rider, I've got a lot on my mind, man . . . you ain't making my job any easier," Carlos said in a low, threatening rumble. "So fall back and give me space to think."

Rider's gaze hardened to meet Carlos's challenge. "I'm not into high fashion, but the whole look screams terrorists or drug gang to me. That's the only reason I'm agreeing with Yolando here that time is of the essence—all right. So don't get your boxers in a bunch."

Carlos shot Damali a quick look that dared her to intervene. She rifled her fingers through her locks and walked away, scanning the area before she said anything irrevocable.

"What about the sanctuary?" Juanita offered, glancing at Carlos with empathy.

Carlos motioned toward the placard near the door with his chin. "We jettisoned out of San Diego at almost one in the afternoon . . . that means it's near four, central time—and they have vespers prayer. Somebody will probably be in there setting up and we'll give 'em a heart attack if we roll in there like this."

"Garages," Berkfield said with a quick nod. "You pull us some SWAT uniforms from the local precinct and let me be your lead bullshit talker. I know the police drill from my old days on the force. The rest of you just look mean and say nothing if we're seen or stopped . . . but I know where Carlos is going with this thing—not around any kids. Can't have a shoot-out here and we've gotta clear the area in case something is already tracking us."

Damali nodded as she stared up at the vaulted archways that led from the rectory to the church. Adinkra symbols had been cut directly into the stones in the oddest of all places, a Catholic church, just as Marlene had said. "Yeah, Berkfield . . . good plan," she said in a faraway voice. "We can change in the garages."

She rubbed the surface of the pearl that was set in her platinum-collar necklace with the other six stones she'd collected during her awakening, feeling them heat in her hand. "What are you trying to tell me, Pearl?" she murmured to her oracle as the team trudged toward the bank of garages behind the courtyard.

"Look to the one-hundred-and-eight volumes of the Book of Enoch," the pearl said quietly. "Enoch was three hundred and sixty-five years old . . . his words were left out of the traditional Bible and were found by a *Scotsman,* James Bruce, who brought it back from Axum . . . Ethiopia, in the 1800s. These books were found among the Dead Sea Scrolls. . . . The angel, Uriel, was his guide. . . . Follow *Uriel,* that angel's name will shelter you while here in Detroit, Damali. . . . Ask Marlene to look up Genesis 5:21–24."

The pearl fell silent as the group gathered in one of the church garages that didn't have vehicles and storage boxes in it. Damali looked at Carlos.

"Okay, now that was the strangest divination Pearl has given me to date."

"Sounds like girlfriend was speaking in code . . . put emphasis on the word *Scotsman,*" Carlos said, pulling in SWAT uniforms and hurriedly passing them around the team.

"Seal the area with prayer," Damali whispered. She glanced at Carlos. "And silver-box it, too. We need to talk."

The team quickly changed without modesty as Marlene set up a barrier and Carlos followed up by closing off the area with a translucent silver seal. As soon as all precautions had been taken, Damali went to the center of the group.

"Zehiradangra is sensitive to anomalies in vibrations . . . so she's not going to just tell us where to go in an open, potentially toxic airspace. Who knows, she might be feeling the same bouts of anxiety and paranoia we felt before J.L. put the filters on our technology, and Heather was leading the seers in the house on a divination where Pearl could have picked up something that freaked her out."

A slight pink blush glowed within the pearl to confirm Damali's suspicions and she nodded. "Z didn't feel comfortable— but this is a Templar safe house . . . it's just occupied so heavily by civilians, we can't use it."

"Okay, quick deconstruction of the code," Carlos said, rubbing his jaw. "The Scotsman reference has to be Father Pat— he's been trying to get a message to me, but he doesn't dare chance telepathy while he's still so weak. Pearl kept slinging a bunch of facts that were just a jumble of rhetoric, even if true. So each one has to be a part of the code."

"Father Pat is the Scotsman," Damali said. "But Enoch's age . . . three hundred and sixty-five is a year." She looked at Carlos. "Something's about to jump off within a year, maybe?"

"Okay, and something important was brought out of Ethiopia to here, or knowledge from Ethiopia is something we need to use. One or the other, or both." Carlos rubbed the tension out of his neck. "I hate riddles, I swear I do."

"The name Uriel means God is my light to the east," Valkyrie offered. "I know the names of all the major angels . . . we were taught them in Nod. So this must mean that if we get trapped, try to head east?"

"Maybe," Jasmine said, working a headache away from her temples with graceful fingers. "But it could also mean to call upon that angel at the very end." She glanced at Bobby, who looked pale. "If we are to die here in a last stand, it is good to know which angel will collect our souls."

"We ain't dying down here," Bobby said, growing agitated and walking in a circle.

"Then what the fuck are we doing here in Detroit?" Dan spat. "I don't get it!" He looked around the group, his blue eyes wild. "There's no way I can get you in on the jazz fest docket this late—the group doesn't do jazz, and this thing is being billed as the Rumble in the Great Lakes, okaaay. Some show-down between Chicago and Detroit jazz legends, of which we are neither. But the name of the event gives me the creeps un-der the circumstances. *The Rumble in the Great Lakes!* So, right there, I've got a bad feeling about it, and if we're trying to keep a firefight from civilians, this isn't the place to be! Six frickin' stages over four days, out in the open with thousands and thou-sands of civilians . . . is it just me, or is anybody else con-cerned?"

"We're not here to play music," Damali said calmly, "so you don't have to get us on the docket. But we know that this is one of the last bastions of positive music, as well as a great fallback city for CGE . . . so their agents of turmoil will no doubt be in-filtrating the crowd, trying to get something to pop off, infect-ing people, whatever. Our goal is to tag one of the little bastards and see if it runs home so we can follow it back to its power center. That strategy worked before when we used it to locate the darkside's heir. But we're not trying to put innocent people in harm's way. However, the crowd also gives us cover to maneuver in day and night. Might take 'em a minute to spot us."

"You don't have to explain shit, D," Carlos said, glaring at the team. "Last I checked this wasn't a democracy. We are functioning military-style. You got a problem with Damali's game plan, then you got a problem with me. No dissention in the ranks, right now. We ain't got time for it."

Marlene stared at Carlos. "Can you bring me a Bible out of the sanctuary pews?"

He nodded and made one materialize in her hands.

She opened the text carefully and found the Scripture Pearl had suggested she read. The group leaned in, but Marlene's eyes filled with tears and she walked to Carlos and hugged him.

"Baby . . . listen to me, no matter what, you can't lose your faith or turn back."

"What, Mar?" Carlos said, breaking her hold on him. "Tell me straight-up. I don't need no surprises right through here."

The older woman sighed heavily and touched his face before going back to the text. "When Enoch had lived sixty-five years, he became father to Methuselah. And after he became father to Methuselah, Enoch walked with God three hundred years and had other sons and daughters. Altogether, Enoch lived three hundred and sixty-five years. Enoch walked with God, then he was no more, because God took him away." Marlene closed the book.

"Talk to me, Mar," Carlos whispered, swallowing hard. "You're the elder seer on the team . . . you know what you feel in your gut, like I know it in mine—but I need you to say it."

"In the beginning—like Genesis is the beginning—when Father Pat was sixty-five, he met you . . . became like a father to you, baby . . . and you were immortal then . . . like Methuselah would live untold years—and now as a Neteru will live longer than the average human." Marlene let out a hard breath.

"My dear, dear friend, Father Pat, really became like a grandfather to this team of sons and daughters, and has the wisdom of a man who has walked with God for three hundred years . . . as a Templar, a warrior . . . he has walked with God a very long time, Carlos. He was badly injured and never fully recovered from that last attack. And, soon . . . God will take him away."

Marlene briefly closed her eyes as the rest of the team members' shoulders slumped. "Do the numerology. One hundred and eight volumes or chapters condenses down to the number nine . . . nine is the end number. Pearl was trying to tell us about beginnings and endings. The Book of Enoch is primarily about the battle between good angels and bad angels, and it also deals with when angels mingled with humankind to produce Titans . . . and the banishment of the fallen angel. We already know who she was referencing there."

Carlos nodded as Damali touched his arm, noting that the pearl in her hand had blushed a pink affirmation again. "It's cool," he said, lifting his chin and sending his gaze out of the garage windows. "I knew that. Felt it. We got a reprieve. It's the cycle of life, and shit."

"We'll go talk to Father Patrick soon," Damali said quietly.

Carlos didn't answer, just turned his focus to Shabazz.

"We've gotta get out of here. This is your old turf, man . . . where to?"

"We're like a half mile from Second Baptist," Shabazz said, raking his locks. "Solid energy up in that joint. . . . It's over on Monroe Street in the Greektown historic district, but was the first African American congregation here. Sojourner Truth, John Brown, Douglass, you know . . . everybody pulled people through the system using that church as a way station."

J.L. punched in the name of the church on his iPhone and then put the address of the current location in to get directions.

"It's 441 Monroe. Two minutes' jog—head east on Cadillac Square toward Bates, left on Randolph, right on Monroe."

"Dressed like this, though, holmes?" Jose said, opening his arms. "And strapped? Gonna cause a stir. We gotta find somewhere we can drop this gear and go camouflage, yo, to blend in with normal civilians."

"Set us down in the mouth of an alley, C," Mike said, "and we'll do like we always do—make it up as we go along."

Too disgusted to debate anything, Carlos simply whirled the team in an energy fold-away to the address. But when they stepped out of it, they were looking out of a small gap between buildings and scaffolding toward a busy intersection, and the church was gone.

"Oh, shit," Shabazz said, turning around in a circle. "They demolished Second Baptist for a freaking casino? A historic landmark? Now that's sacrilege if ever I saw it!"

J.L. glanced up, confused. "Dude," he said to Carlos, his brows knit. "This isn't 441 Monroe."

"Whatduya mean, this ain't Monroe!" Shabazz shouted, practically stuttering as fury lifted his locks off his shoulders with static charge.

"I homed to the damned location you had in your mind, man," Carlos said defensively, glaring at Shabazz. He rubbed his palms down his face, tension making him ready to drop fang.

"Bigger problem," Mike said, positioning his rocket-propelled grenade launcher higher onto his shoulder. "People is walking by staring, we causing a scene, we in the middle of a doggone shopping district looking like a bomb squad, and we needs to be real cool . . . like fall back deeper into this alley so C can get us inside somewhere. This is real uncool."

"Ya think?" Rider said, glaring at Carlos. "Later me and you need to talk about you getting your head together, but now isn't the time."

"Just be cool, look at the building foundation, and follow me back into the alley," Berkfield said, leading the way.

Dan glimpsed Carlos. "You okay, man?"

"I'm fine," Carlos snarled. "We cool."

"Good. Just checking. No disrespect intended, back at the other location." Dan held Carlos's arm as the others caught up with Berkfield. "It's just that Heather can't take a lot of energy jostling right now . . . you know what I'm saying?"

Carlos blinked twice. Dan nodded and looked away.

"She can't go through another loss. I know the timing is really bad . . . but I just wanted you to know, if anything happens in a firefight, let me go, make sure she makes it."

Carlos rubbed his hands down his face again. "Oh . . . shit."

"I'm sorry, man," Dan said, and then lifted his chin. "But regardless of how fucked up the timing is, be happy for me, man."

"Yeah, yeah, I gotchure back. Congrats, we'll smoke a cigar later," Carlos said, moving out. The alley wasn't big enough. It felt like all the air was being forced out of his lungs by a hard blow. He glanced at Shabazz, now getting a clearer image of Second Baptist Church. "We couldn't go to the sanctuary on Monroe, anyway," he muttered. "It's crawling with tourists right about now—so I need a solid church, temple, mosque, whatever, in your old zone, 'Bazz . . . a joint without major population issues."

The team gathered around Shabazz for a moment, everyone seeming disoriented. "The only place I know of that is real cool that can feed us, house us, has clothes on the rack, and has the Black Holocaust Museum up in there, is the Shrine."

"What Shrine, man?" Yonnie asked, nervously chewing on a toothpick. " 'Cause we're batting a thousand on churches right now."

"Where I'm feeling we should go has platinum ancestor energy and every obscure text you can want . . . plus meeting space and serious real estate . . . where if we're legit we can also go in there packing like revolutionaries—'cause they used to it." Shabazz folded his arms over his chest. "They were around back in the day before I could really appreciate them for being a community treasure."

"No offense, 'Bazz," Jose said. "But you were away for ten years, then add another twenty or so . . . like, all I'm saying is, a lot can change in thirty years, brother."

"If the Shrine is gone, then black Detroit might as well be gone," Shabazz said in a surly tone. "It's still here—I can feel it in my bones."

"Then let's do the damned thing," Carlos said, looking at Shabazz and waiting for a location. "Where?"

"The Shrine of the Black Madonna is over on Livernois Avenue. Ex-Panthers, Angela Davis . . . the who's who of countermainstream rolled through there and the energy is solid." Shabazz glared at Jose and then Carlos. *It's there.*

" 'Bazz, not trying to be funny but, Second Baptist was supposed to be solid," Rider argued. "So don't get all salty, as you call it, with Jose and Carlos, man."

"Carlos missed the drop, not me—don't get it twisted. So I ain't salty, period." Shabazz relaxed a little and gave Rider a hard half smile when his Guardian brother held up his hands and gave him a quizzical "what's up" look. "Rider, if the Shrine ain't where I say it is—then my bad. But if the great lady is still there, then I'll have you in a dashiki and wearing a kufi before it's all over, brother—which is perfect for the jazz festival . . . also better than SWAT riot gear for stashing weapons."

"Is it hallowed ground?" Marjorie asked, looking at Bobby and then Krissy with concern.

"They pour so many libations up in there and have that place so blessed out that anything foul will torch on impact." Marlene gave Shabazz a nod of appreciation. "The Shrine is still there."

Carlos wiped his hands down his face. He didn't say a word, just moved the team in a fold-away on his next deep inhalation.

Her plan was perfect.

Elizabeth crept deeper into the shadows of Hell's complete darkness, gathering up the elements of evil she would need. Lilith was preoccupied, tending to the slowly healing heir's every whim, no different than her fellow councilman and woman who were busily working on the front lines—now that they'd unfairly gained Lilith's favor. Sebastian had finally been shamed into going on the foolhardy mission to meet with Lucifer himself, and might never return. Good riddance! Yet they all thought she was supposedly too weak to be of immediate use or concern. . . . There'd never be another time like this. The hour was nigh.

Overconfidence had made them all forget that she'd seen Sebastian raise Vlad's army from the skeletal remains of shattered bones and rotted flesh. A shrewd sorceress in her own right with a powerful protectress near, she'd witnessed his spells cast for Lilith's demands. While the council was unaware, her witches would live again . . . her tragedy avenged. The first kill she would offer her husband would be Sebastian's weak throat!

There could be no other more auspicious time to pilfer Sebastian's spell treasures than while he was bargaining for his life with the Dark Lord and begging for the return of his conjuring hand. That negotiation would consume his complete focus. If he discovered her treachery through spies, she could always claim to have been looking for a way to bring him back from the brink of extermination, given that Satan was in such a foul mood. It would be so easy to make Sebastian believe she'd thought he'd been executed on Level Seven and was thus attempting his resurrection. He would never suspect that she would attempt the futile—risking her life to steal from him, an older, stronger entity, for the purpose of reanimating a beheaded vampire. But by all the evil in her dark heart, the Carpathian ruler would ride again!

Elizabeth released a soft, mad chuckle as she entered Sebastian's normally guarded spell chamber unafraid. The massive gargoyle sentries had fled the moment he'd gone to Level Seven, obviously aware of the odds of his return. Only Sebastian's faithful serpents remained.

As she swept into the forbidden vault, his black adders uncoiled from their slumber and protectively swayed over his dark tome of evil incantations. Eyes narrowed, they hissed at her intrusion and she gave as good as she got until they slithered away. She smiled as she found the right page, instantly memorizing every line of the spell, and then her red glowing gaze went to the rows of apothecary jars filled with every gore imaginable . . . it was all there, the exotic ingredients she would need. His cauldron spit acid at her and she laughed shrilly, her madness now in full bloom.

"I'm already burned beyond recognition. Take your best shot . . . but beware; you could be scrap iron. Sebastian is meeting with the Dark Lord and is as good as dead. If you do not make friends with me, *his wife,* and refuse to do my bidding . . . who shall protect you from the molestation of Hell?"

The cauldron belched its assent and settled down to a slow, rhythmic bubble, ceasing its protest. What had never been openly discussed in council was the fact that Vlad had been beheaded by a blessed blade while still human. That bitch, Lilith, knew the secret . . . fear of a coup had kept her silent. But *she knew.* Vlad, in life, had made a pact with the Devil that, should he be defeated in battle and executed, his remains could always be reanimated unless slain in death by a Neteru.

Soon, the enemy of her enemy would be her friend. Sebastian would never know what hit him.

"Let me and Marlene go in easy first," Shabazz warned as the group gathered in the small alley behind the store. "We'll go in the front and see if we can get them to open up the back door. Too many of us going in with riot gear on will be problematic."

"We feel you," Jose said, "just hurry, bro."

Shabazz and Marlene handed off their weapons, but Marlene kept her carved African walking stick. She smiled at Shabazz as they rounded the row of stores on the block.

"This SWAT uniform with dreadlocks and my walking stick is gonna cause some poor soul up in the Shrine serious cognitive dissonance."

"I know, but it's probably the only thing that's gonna help them believe we're not 'the man,'" he replied, making small quotes with his fingers in the air as she opened the door and slipped in.

Shabazz stopped for a moment and looked around. The place hadn't changed in all those years. There was still a long entryway with racks and racks of nonmainstream books. No one was in that section, as the heavier volumes were toward the back. Titles called out about revolution, the foundation of democracy, the spiritual essence of humankind, every conceivable eclectic mix; it was a thinking person's paradise. Thick incense residue hung in the air, frankincense and myrrh. The store needed a paint job and the rug was well worn, but it welcomed like a grandmother's house, nonetheless. Shabazz inhaled deeply as Marlene turned to look at him.

"Feels good to be back home, doesn't it?"

He nodded and swallowed hard. "I never got a chance to come back after I got locked up." He stared at her and she came close to hug him. "Back there with the others, I didn't know if this place would still be here . . . but it was. Allah is merciful."

Marlene stroked his back and looked up. "C'mon, baby . . . let's learn these young folks some old-school ways, huh?"

Her comment made him smile and he stepped around her to take the lead, walking them through a passageway that led into the main section of the store. But he stopped to take in the grandeur of it all that was hidden within a seemingly humble community structure. Majestically carved masks and statues from the motherland graced the walls, and ornately carved statues from West Africa created a stunning gallery. Glass cases filled with silver jewelry and beautiful ethnic beadwork dotted the store, and a full section of clothing made of gorgeous silks, embroidered cottons, and the most exquisite hand-loomed textiles made his breath catch. Aisles and aisles of books and a large meeting space caught his eye, until he was forced to blink back moisture.

"I'd forgotten," he said quietly and reverently to Marlene. "The old corner philosophers and revolutionaries used to try to tell me about *the people* and *the culture* when I was slinging on the corner . . . they couldn't tell me shit, though, because I knew it all." He glanced around at the masks and then touched the edge of a tall giraffe carving that was made from one solid piece of mahogany. "This is why they want to destroy the motherland . . . the cradle of civilization. Don't you see how beautiful she is?" He turned to Marlene, eyes pained. "We can't let Africa, or the diaspora, or any land be made into cannon fodder . . . can't let them overrun food-producing nations and people in the so-called underdeveloped areas for greed and blood sport."

"Can I help you?" an older woman challenged.

Her glare was keen as she flung mixed, gray dreadlocks over her shoulder with much attitude. She wore royal purple African robes covering her thick build and her many silver bangles sounded as she promptly folded her arms over her ample chest.

She had swept out of the back room with a customer, handing the man his order before taking a challenging pose. With open hostility, she looked Marlene and Shabazz up and down and sucked her teeth.

The few straggling customers had edged away from Marlene and Shabazz, and one of them had obviously gone in the back to alert the disgruntled manager that cops were in the house. One look at the manager's expression told them that everyone in the store was hostile.

"Yes, ma'am," Shabazz said after a moment. "You can definitely help us."

"Why you people come in here harassing us, huh? You think jus' 'cause they got new laws that let's y'all run amuck on people's rights you can come into our place and just do anything you want? This is a *house of worship,* if you haven't noticed. This here downstairs is our bookstore and Shrine shop—but we're legal, legit, and our holocaust museum is listed—"

"We're not five-o," Shabazz said.

"Cops, Homeland Security, FBI, what I care?" the woman said in a huff. "You think you can come in the community and treat folk any ole kinda way—and you oughta be shame wearing dreadlocks . . . whatchu do, use that while you were undercover and then—"

"Ma'am . . . can we talk to you without an audience?"

The woman looked at the patrons around her. "Oh, hell no you can't! Just 'cause you my color don't mean you my kind! This New World Order got folks hoodwinked, bamboozled, scallywagged, and lied to, my so-called brutha! I know my rights. I ain't gotta say nothing to you without an attorney—or you planning on kidnapping me like you do all those folks and throw me in some prison offshore? These people seen me—tell my grandbabies *the man* came after they grandma, you hear me! But I ain't dead! No justice, no peace!"

"You can't be rolling up in the Shrine and taking this sister out of here. We'll be in touch with Reverend Sharpton and anybody else we gotta call, believe that!" a patron shouted from the sidelines. "We know what you trying to do."

"Come check our pockets," Marlene finally said, throwing down her walking stick and opening her arms and legs in a to-be-frisked stance. "We ain't *the man,* far from it. We're running from *the man* . . . and, these uniforms came in handy from our last situation."

Shabazz followed Marlene's stance, opening his arms and legs. "Sis, we need sanctuary and got our people out back who need to be hidden in your upstairs meeting area . . . plus a change of clothes, if you can spare it. We'll pay . . . but we don't need no static from the authorities."

*Carlos is gonna have to mind-stun all these folks real good,* Marlene mentally shot to Shabazz as he glanced at her. *TMI, they don't need to be in all our business, but there's no other way to get them to chill out but to tell them the truth—folks can sense bull versus fact, if they get calm enough. Let me keep working on this sister.*

Skeptical patrons glanced at each other, but offered no further commentary. The woman unfolded her arms and moved forward a bit.

"We've been running all the way from California, and need sanctuary from being hunted," Marlene said carefully. "You know how we used to do, back in the day . . . sometimes we had to follow the drinking gourd, blend in with Native Americans, look for signs in quilts, feel for the moss at night on the north side of tree trunks . . . do whatever it took, including disguise ourselves however we had to in order to make it on through—shoot, some of us even passed till we got where we was going. It was all about survival. That's all we trying to do now. Survive, sis. What kinda sense would it make for us to show up here in riot gear, unarmed, asking for clothes, me and my husband wearing locks—which can't be grown overnight—and me carrying an African walking stick, if we intended to bum-rush your store like the authorities? Stop and think about it."

"How I know you ain't lying?"

Marlene's gaze locked with the woman's. "Because I'm a seer and so are you, sis," Marlene said flatly. She sent a hard assessment over the woman's body. "Your mother just passed—I'm sorry," she said quietly.

"They coulda been watching you, sis. Coulda put a satellite on you or bugged your house . . . mighta been tailing you 'cause you from the Shrine and seen you at the funeral, at the cemetery. Don't believe the hype," a female patron said. "They be wiretapping people's lives!"

"All that's true," Shabazz said calmly. "But we didn't."

"She used to call you Bebe," Marlene said gently, ignoring the conspiracy theorist's valid claims. "Before you changed your name to Owatunde . . . but she said to you, "Bebe, don't you worry none, I'm going to glory in peace.' No one was in the hospital room but you and her, sis, when she passed. You leaned close and she whispered that in your ear . . . no bug could pick that up, she said it so softly at the end. She died holding your hand. I swear to you, we're not authorities. And I promise you, your momma is all right."

The older woman relaxed her stance and drew in a shuddering breath, then swallowed hard.

Marlene turned to Shabazz. "Let her in, stop blocking her and drop your protective tactical charge . . . she's a seer so let her see me."

Shabazz nodded, but looked at the store manager hard. "You about to get a privileged look into some really deep realities, sis. But it's only fair, 'cause we need some really deep help."

"Be careful," a male patron warned. "How they know you was gifted? Maybe that's why they here—to kidnap you into a secret government project for people with ESP . . . they did that before, you know. Took folks into them programs during the Cold War and be experimenting on 'em. *I know.*"

"Then if she's a seer, she'd see that about us," Marlene said in a dismissive but gentle tone, keeping her gaze on the store manager. "I'm open. Bring it."

It seemed as though the entire store had become paralyzed by silence as the woman stepped a little closer and regarded Marlene and Shabazz with quiet curiosity. Then suddenly as though a bee had stung her, she stepped back and covered her mouth for a few seconds.

"Yeah, like I said," Shabazz muttered, relaxing his stance.

Marlene dropped her arms. "What did Divine Spirit tell you about us?"

"My name is Owa, for short. . . . We'll help you." The manager pressed her hand to her heart and then yanked out a huge ring of keys from her robe pocket. "Brother Muata—lock the front door and put the Closed sign up, then drop the gates. Sister Sylvia and Miss Mary, go 'round the back and open the door for those folks—don't say nothing, just wave 'em in and get 'em up in the sanctuary, quick. Then bring 'em down one by one to pick whatever they want for clothes off the racks." She was breathing hard as she barked orders and the few patrons in the store scattered to carry out her commands.

"Hidden Guardian camp?" Shabazz said to Marlene.

"Yep, you called this one on the money," Marlene said with a proud smile and then began laughing. "Even though we didn't have time to let J.L. do a formal computer search for Detroit safe houses, instinct worked like a charm and Jack Rider's gonna have to wear a dashiki to the jazz fest *in Detroit.*"

Shabazz chuckled and relaxed, nodding.

"We been hiding in plain sight for more than thirty years," Owa said, rushing over to Marlene and Shabazz to reverently shake their hands and then hug them. With tears in her eyes, she fanned her face. "You know we got a Shrine in Atlanta and another one in Houston. Wait till I tell them who's here!"

"Just not over the phone . . . lines are compromised, so are the airwaves," Marlene said.

Owa smiled. "We don't *ever* mess with regular technology . . . we send this through the divinations altar to altar, chile."

"My sister," Marlene said, embracing Owa with affection. "Thank you."

"No . . . Queen Mother, Marlene . . . bless you for coming to us in these end days." Owa turned and looked at Shabazz and offered him a slight bow before turning back to Marlene. "And thank you for letting my heart rest easy about my momma. For the record, nobody knew she called me Bebe but family."

# CHAPTER NINE

The team followed Sister Owa through a labyrinth of racks to the museum area. She stopped and outstretched her arm, her eyes holding a fusion of excitement and reverence.

"This is why we're here," she said proudly. "We went through all of this and still we found goodness in the world worth surviving for."

Marlene nodded and looked around the team, her gaze settling on Shabazz. "And I'm now oh soooo clear that this is why we were shunted from pillar to post today. We were supposed to come here to remember what Sister Owa said, as well as to probably get used to that feeling of being on the run again—but not to give into the group dissension or the fear."

The team's senior seer allowed her gaze to rake each member slowly with compassion. "We've *all* still been trying to process the poison out of our minds, even our Neterus, white baths notwithstanding. Look at how we've been acting, talking to each other on the team, going over old mess and vibrations that we'd already learned not to do from the school of hard knocks. We got infected, people, and had to shake it off to unify—once again . . . it's not a learn-it-one-time-and-you're-done type of thing. Unity requires ongoing maintenance, just like marriages and relationships are ongoing work. If we had gotten into those other locations, maybe we would have missed the lesson . . . the Creator makes no mistakes—Ashe."

"Ashe," Owa said quietly. "And maybe we needed you all to come to let us know that the thirty-plus years we've been at the struggle have not been in vain . . . there really is hope on the horizon—some light in this dark tunnel we've been in."

Quiet affirmations rippled through the group as Owa began walking. The team fanned out slowly as members peered at the horrific scenes of bondage on the walls, mute as they passed each exhibit, reading placards with hands pressed to hearts, some shaking their heads, not even realizing their bodies were moving in such a manner.

Oppressive silence, except for the recorded sounds of the museum, kept Guardian voices at bay . . . those eerie sounds were reminiscent of human captivity and the daring attempts of escape against all odds, reenacted in a cacophony of barking bloodhounds, the sounds of wailing, some spiritual hymns, an auctioneer's rabble. But as the team gathered around some of the artifacts, murmurs of sheer disbelief finally spawned a sudden ricochet of conversation.

"Oh, my God," Krissy whispered, her fingers grazing an iron collar. "We'd been told about this in high school and read it in the books we had to read for class . . . but they actually put this on a human being's neck."

"This is barbaric," Bobby said, his eyes wild. "They really did this to people . . . I mean, I read it, but . . ."

"It was never a part of your reality," Inez said, no judgment in her tone. "Unless it affects you directly, most people don't think twice about the things that have happened here or anywhere else in the world. In some parts of the word, things like this are still happening. Check Darfur."

"It ain't about continuing to fight among ourselves, though,"

Shabazz said, looking around the group and making sure that old cultural wounds didn't bubble up and simmer over within the team itself. "That's evil's old con—to get otherwise decent people to act like animals toward each other for greed, gain, lust, power . . . y'all know the deal. Then get people to justify it by calling another group primitive, or heretics, or somehow making them the scapegoats. This is one holocaust among many." He shook his head and walked deeper into the exhibit.

Owa nodded, her voice patient and firm, as she picked up very tiny manacles. "This was for the babies, the children. Look inside. There are spikes so that if you turn your head it will hurt. These are bits used for mouthpieces, like you'd bridle a beast of burden."

A collective gasp cut through the group. Heather rushed over to touch the small iron shackles and then stooped to let her fingers trace a small burlap sack that had been worn by a child.

"How could anyone . . ." Heather whispered, her eyes filled with horror and pain. "Me father was from Ghana . . . a hundred years ago they might have captured him and put this on him. Me Scottish mother could have been flogged and driven from 'er home for simply loving him and making me? They would have put these shackles on me as a baby . . . sold me away from her." She peered up at the group, bewildered. "Babies? Children as young as our Ayana?"

Jasmine was right by Heather's side and she squeezed her shoulder. She looked over at her sister-in-law, Krissy, and opened her arms to invite the embrace. "This is why we came here, Marlene is right. We needed to remember what we're fighting for and to never bring the fight between us as a team, no matter what. It's so easy to forget, to slip back into old patterns and old ways and to shut the grim world out—like that's over there and I can't do anything about it . . . but we have to do a little bit, any way we can."

Dan squeezed his wife's hand as he squatted down beside her. He gazed at Heather and then glanced up at Jasmine, agreeing. "My people have a saying, Never again. As long as this type of atrocity is allowed to happen to any people, then all people are at risk."

Tara nodded and quietly threaded her arm around Rider's waist. "My Cherokee people were in this, as well as my African American ancestors . . . it is all a bloody trail of tears."

"But the babies," Marj whispered thickly. "If what's coming next is more evil than this . . . we must all come together and take a stand. Don't people get it?"

"I read about it, knew about it, but this is just . . ." Berkfield shook his head and wiped his palm over his scalp. "I had buddies back on the force who were as ignorant as me. If people saw, were educated, they couldn't hide from the truth. If they didn't think that's *those* people, but thought in terms of—holy Christ, that's *any* people, ya know?" He looked around the group with a pained expression. "I used to hear guys say, 'Well, shit, that was way back then and I personally didn't have anything to do with it.' But I'm like, yeah, you didn't, directly . . . but you need to recognize that it happened, that you maybe got a leg up because it did, and be respectful of the people who lived this or any other horror like it. I wasn't popular in a lot of places. Then I'd get to thinking about a lot of stuff I saw in the criminal justice system that I'll go to my grave unable to reconcile. When I see stuff like this I wonder why God didn't just send a thunderbolt a long time ago to be done with it. I bet He wanted to just nuke this joint, seeing this kinda thing."

"Yeah, well," Carlos muttered. "The jury's still out on that end-it-by-the-fire-next-time prophecy. The Man Upstairs might just have had His fill, who knows?"

Carlos rubbed his jaw and landed a hand on Berkfield's shoulder. "Regardless, you can't take the guilt on for every person who can't see—just like none of us can. Prejudice comes in all colors, man . . . I'm from L.A. . . . ask me how I know. You got *hombres* poppin' homeboys, who smokin' whites, who flat-blasting Asians, who can't stand East Indians, who at war with Pakistanis, who hate being mistaken for Middle Eastern, who battling Russians, who can't stand skinheads, who hate Jews and gays and everybody pretty much, and cops gunnin' for everybody who don't look like them, feel me. It's insane. You didn't start the madness and you're out here with your life on the line trying to fix it. So stop lacerating yourself as you do this walk through, bro. That's not why we're here." He motioned to Krissy and Bobby with his chin. "Same goes for you young bucks. Ain't about that." He glanced at Rider next, and let his gaze settle on Marj and Richard Berkfield. "We all fam and this exhibit is just an example we're supposed to learn from. But we ain't casting aspersions."

"Definitely not," Damali said, watching quiet relief edge through the team. "We're supposed to learn from every culture, every shred of human history, and to pass this one by in our own backyards after going around the world learning, is crazy. We have to be honest and ultimately face our own inner demons right here before we try to step to whatever global conscience. Last stop, charity and healing begin at home . . . and there's a lot of drama we need to atone for here in the good ole U. S. of A."

"True dat," J.L. said, raking his hair with his fingers. "Especially if this joint is one of the big three superpowers in the last days and times, man . . . and you-know-who might make it number one and only . . . *all* of this bull gotta get accounted for and redressed. Can't sweep it under the rug and then wonder why we've got bad karma bubbling to the surface."

"True, young brother. Every ethnic group represented here," Owa said, "and many more that we do not see, have been abused at the hands of evil . . . but as you look at this exhibit, the one thing that evil cannot abide is healing. If the common people from every land stopped believing the lies and joined together to help each other and to believe in the fundamental good of all, we could stop this thing." She held up the small shackles and rattled them like Shaker beads. "It is time for people to wake up and unite! This isn't a black thing, a white thing, a Native American thing, an Asian thing, or a Latino thing, or whatever . . . this is a human issue. Fundamental human rights. That's why we're here."

"Ashe," Damali murmured as she stood before a mock tree that was laced with a disheveled mannequin hanging by a noose. "Enough. When I see this, I say *enough*. How many inquisitions, wars, despotic leaders, or oppressive regimes until the planet wakes up and says, enough?" She ruffled her locks up off her neck. "How do we get people to just wake the hell up?"

"We got a saying down South, baby girl . . . ev'ry shut eye ain't sleep. People know, but they scared and ain't steppin' up 'cause the mess is hittin' 'em five ways from Sunday. Lotsa folks is in churches, temples, and mosques—folks be praying, trying to figure out what to do, because they feel it closing in on 'em. But *they know* time is short and bad change is coming . . . feel it in they gut, they bones, can't get no peace. Everybody ain't crazy. Uh-uh. We jus' don't hear about them, 'cause you-know-who got the propaganda machine going." Big Mike smoothed a huge palm over his bald scalp. "I'm from Mississippi, and I know, D. A noose ain't no joke." He turned and pointed to the speaker system. "The sound of them dogs got the hair standing up on the back of my neck."

"DNA-level memory, baby," Inez said quietly before she turned to Dan. "I've been to the holocaust museum in D.C. . . . the room of baby shoes." She closed her eyes. "All those little shoes . . . they actually put people in ovens. We have to remind people that this world is worth fighting for—there are children that have to inherit something worth living for . . . we can't let the darkside just take it without a fight."

"We're gonna help 'em remember, 'Nez," Carlos said, rolling his shoulders. "Because, I for one have had enough, too, like D said—and hell no, we ain't going down without a fight."

Marlene looked at Owa and smiled a sad, weary smile. "I think this was the battle pep talk our team needed. Much better than a sermon—'cause you can show folks better than you can tell 'em." She glanced around the team again and spoke matter-of-factly and with no judgment in her tone. "Even before the airwave poison, we were getting frayed, people. Fractured in our mission. Self-absorbed due to our own individual issues. But that's not why we're here as Guardians and Warriors of the Light."

After receiving nods of agreement, Marlene waved her hand out toward the exhibit. "Plenty of good people laid down their lives so we could even be here. We stand on their shoulders. Most who made the ultimate sacrifice knew they wouldn't make it to see the change they'd died for—but that didn't matter, the change was worth it to them anyway. It was a matter of principle. We've been blessed, but we've also gotten comfortable . . . and frightened that our comforts will be taken away, which destroys our fearlessness . . . which makes us conservative and wanting to play it safe. I stand here guilty as charged. Once I got my Shabazz back, I've practically been scared to leave the house."

Carlos looked at Marlene squarely. "Me, too. Guilty as charged, Mar. Now more than ever before, the thought of losing my wife, our home, or a single member of this team has jacked my head up—I ain't gonna lie." He glanced at Rider. "Yeah, I was off today . . . slow on the decision making, ain't gonna front. You said you wanted to talk to me about it, let's go right now." Carlos opened his arms wide and cocked his head to the side. "I ain't ashamed to admit it. I feel like I've got more to lose now than ever before and that makes it hard to just bust a crazy move that could get any of us smoked . . . when it was just me, hey"—he pointed at Rider with a hard snap—"but it ain't just me. It's a whole lot more than that—so, yeah, I'm struggling with my new reality, brother. My bad."

Rider nodded. "I'm sorry, man . . . you're right. Guess whatever peppered this team got me, too, and as usual my mouth was the first portal." He turned to Marlene after Carlos relaxed and let out a weary breath. "Guilty as sin, Mar." Rider dragged his fingers through his hair. "Shamed to say it, but . . . as a Guardian, once I got Tara back, I didn't give a rat's ass what was happening out there if I could keep it away from our doorstep." He glanced back at Carlos. "Might not be politically correct, but it's honest."

Jose pounded Rider's fist. "We ain't hating, man . . . we all right with what you talkin' about."

Dan rubbed a hand across his forehead. "I think I'm first in line in that politically incorrect category—and that would have shamed my parents if they knew. They were big into remembering the sacrifices people made so that we could be where we are today." He waved his arm toward the exhibit. "I've shamed those who made the ultimate sacrifice here, or in Nazi Germany, because deep in my heart I don't want anything to happen to my family while the world's going to hell in a handbasket. I don't even want us to do that concert in a couple of months . . . and only half-ass booked it because I just wanted us to not be on the road in the line of fire."

"It's cool, man . . . we all understand where you at," Mike said. "Ain't nobody mad at nobody up in here. I ain't trying to be on the road, either, if we don't have to—problem is, we have to. But, still in all, who don't wanna look after their own peeps?

I got my wife, a baby daughter, and a mother-in-law, who's like my momma, to worry about, and it's eating a hole in my stomach, too, young bro. You ain't shamed nobody with the truth—it's the Devil who's a liar."

Damali's and Marlene's gazes met as they caught Yonnie hanging back behind the group. He'd been unusually quiet throughout the tour, almost detached, and his body language rigid.

"Hey, man," Yonnie said to Dan after a moment, glancing around the exhibits. "Don't be so hard on yourself. You here, ain't you? In fact, we all here, ain't we? Nobody wants to be the ones to have to do what has to be done. I bet if you go back in history, plenty of people that stepped up didn't want to . . . when you get into the quiet corner of their souls. Yeah, I can promise you they didn't wanna step up, but had to and did . . . like you have to and are right now." He looked at Owa and then glanced at Marlene. "Is this sister cool enough for the real truth? Or should I stay in my civilian game face?"

"Owa," Marlene said calmly. "Sister . . . like most Guardian teams, we have members on our squad that have . . . unique gifts—but our folks' skills are a little more exotic than the run-of-the-mill sixth sense capabilities. What you are probably about to hear may blow your mind, but just know you ain't crazy."

Owa nodded and looked at Yonnie. "Speak, brother. Tell us the story."

"Ain't no story—it's plain fact," Yonnie said, breaking away from Val's attempt to soothe him with a touch at his back. "All this in here," he said waving his arms about. "Sheeit—this is the Disney, sanitized version . . . I was *there*. All right. Seen it."

"He's a past life seer?" Owa murmured, her confused gaze seeking Marlene's.

"No! I was *there*! In the flesh," Yonnie suddenly yelled, "and I need to get out of here, okay. Now. Pronto. *Immédiatement!*" He walked in a circle for a moment and then wiped his brow. "This is all good, learning about the past—but it's still textbook until you been through it. Don't even *try* to comprehend what they did to the children—I refuse to discuss it. And what they did to men and women is not for polite convo." He pointed at a noose and then a whipping post, his arm shaking as he spoke. "That will take your soul. That right there will turn you into an animal, a beast, will steal your humanity." He pulled his arm back in a hard snap. "But the funny thing is," he said, growing eerily quiet and then staring at Carlos. "That was the best that humans possessed by demons could come up with—let's call that *Hell-light*. You ain't seen nuthin' till real Hell bubbles up this time."

He walked away and back out of the exhibit into the bookstore area. Carlos held up both hands, motioning to the group not to follow.

"Give me a minute alone with my brother," Carlos said, leaving the exhibit to find Yonnie.

When Carlos approached, Yonnie was doubled over in the bookshelves, breathing in hard inhalations through his mouth, dry-heaving.

"You all right, man?"

Yonnie glanced up, eyes blazing red with battle-length fangs presented.

Carlos held up both hands in front of his chest. "Easy, man . . . it's gonna be all right. Breathe."

"I can't read about that shit, can't think about that shit, can't walk through that shit and not remember, man . . . and you chained my ass to a tree and bullwhipped—"

"No!" Carlos shouted. "You know what that was, and it wasn't me! That was some shit that came off that throne, man!"

Tears of rage shimmered in Yonnie's eyes as his voice fractured to a pained murmur. "You were *my boy* . . ."

"I'm still your boy. Let the flashback work its way out on the next swing," Carlos said, stepping forward, " 'Cause it wasn't me."

Yonnie swung so hard that when the feral punch connected with Carlos's jaw it made both men lose their balance. Shelves fell with a hard crash and books scattered everywhere. Carlos and Yonnie hit the floor at the same time. Up on his feet in seconds, Carlos grabbed Yonnie around his upper arms the moment he lunged at him again, and he hugged Yonnie hard.

"Get it out, man. I didn't do that to you. That's the poison talking. Get it out."

"Why!" Yonnie hollered, his voice fracturing as he struggled to break free from Carlos's hold. "Get the fuck off me! Why you do that to me, man?"

"*They* did it to you—Hell's best. *I* got your back, *always* got your back . . . ain't let even my wife take your head when you was a daywalker, 'cause you my brother, man—we gonna get through this. It was fucked-up what they did to you in life and death—but I got you . . . just let it out—just me and you, here, aw'ight?"

Yonnie's struggles slowly gave way to a returned embrace. Mournful sobs tore through the store and Carlos quietly black-boxed the area to preserve his Guardian brother's privacy. There was so much pain riddling Yonnie's body that he could barely hold them both up. Man pain stabbed into his chest. Broken pride. Decimated dreams. Indignity upon indignity for two hundred years poured out of Yonnie's battered soul until the weight of it nearly buckled Carlos's knees. Then slowly, without warning, the storm passed, leaving both Guardian brothers in a warrior's embrace drawing short breaths, not sure what had transpired.

"You been holding that for two centuries," Carlos said in a thick rumble, finally letting Yonnie go.

Both men stared at each other. Yonnie turned away, ashamed, but Carlos landed a supportive hand on his shoulder.

"Confession." Carlos waited until Yonnie's now normal, but bloodshot, brown eyes met his. "I'm scared to fucking death this time out, bro. Nerves are so damned bad I couldn't get a sanctuary address in a fold-away right, and could've gotten the team butchered from that stupid shit I just did, missing Monroe Street. But I've got shit cooking my brain. My wife is pregnant and this ain't a drill . . . and I know, like you do, how bad Hell really can be. The fucking Devil himself is pissed off at both of us, man . . . he called me out *mano a mano* and is coming for mine like I came for his—so this right here that just happened, so you could get your head right, stays between me and you. Nothing but respect," Carlos said, pounding Yonnie's fist. "You ain't no punk just because you let out what most motherfuckers couldn't carry for a day, let alone two hundred years, aw'ight."

Yonnie nodded. "Yeah . . . I hear you," he said in a gravelly tone.

"If I come to you like this . . . if anything happens to D, I'ma be right here, too . . . totally fucked-up. You just ain't see me go to the rock before—Marlene took me there in front of the whole team—I'm sparing you that embarrassing shit."

"Get out of here." Yonnie gaped at Carlos and then wiped his face. "*You*, Mr. Chairman?"

Carlos nodded. "Yeah. Last I checked, I was part human . . . you are, too, now, man."

"Fucked-up, ain't it?" Yonnie said with a half smile. "The being human part."

"Completely . . . but whatchu gonna do?" Carlos let out a hard breath on a shrug.

"Suck it up and deal." Yonnie pounded his fist.

"As brothers," Carlos said.

"As brothers," Yonnie confirmed, and then wiped his face.

"Take a walk to the men's room . . . splash some water," Carlos said. "I'll tell the team whatever. Ain't a man been in battle that hasn't gone here . . . either that or they lose their damned minds. If they tell you otherwise they're crazy or lying."

"Or both," Yonnie said with a sad chuckle.

"Yeah, man," Carlos replied, walking away. "Or both."

She'd waited for this opportunity—for Sebastian's fear of Lilith and his venomous jealousy of Fallon Nuit to make him desperate for a win. He'd even made a deal with the Dark Lord, and amazingly returned whole with his conjuring arm intact. Such desperation in a man besieged by fear and guilt and hatred was bound to make him sloppy. But that he was the more adept necromancer was something she could use to her advantage. He hadn't even noticed the invasion to his spell chambers; he'd been too preoccupied with obtaining results and keeping his groveling carcass alive. Sycophant. And the gall that he'd made her wait . . . refused to waste his restored powers on healing her before doing Lilith's bidding. For that injustice, he'd surely pay.

Elizabeth held her charred hands firmly clasped together, only glimpsing her faithful sorceress, Dorka, from the corner of her eye. Luring Sebastian to the depths of the Hungarian forest had been mere child's play. His ego would allow him to believe that now that she was so badly burned, he could play Dark Lord and master over her . . . that she would remain an emotional cripple—her beauty in ruins and grateful for his attentions until he got around to making her lovely again.

She watched him arrogantly promenade around the clearing, preparing to raise any beast or demon that had not died by a Neteru blade. The haughty glee practically resonated off his sallow skin. Rage gnawed at her insides as he waved his arms and pranced along the vectors of the bloody pentagram he'd drawn with human blood under the blue wash of the full moon.

Oh, yes, he was in his element . . . she seethed as he craned his long fingers until they'd become talons, calling up the unholy legions that had been vanquished by mortal men. The display was theatric, all hellfire and brimstone, drawing forth swirling winds that lashed their faces and billowed his council robes in an attempt to demonstrate prowess that he never owned.

But she waited, patiently, for the lines drawn in blood around the butchered goat's head to begin to bubble. She waited until the dead human female carcass began to blister with maggots. She waited until black blood sweat ran down Sebastian's gaunt face and he closed his eyes, shouting the last necromancer command for the dead to arise—and that's when she did it.

A black charge left her hands as Dorka jettisoned the skull of Vlad the Impaler with his burial ashes into the center of the ceremonial perimeter. Slashing at her wrists, Elizabeth added her Council-level blood to the offering, along with all of her hatred and the black magic she'd collected throughout the realms. The words she shouted scorched her throat till she sputtered black blood. Her hair was on fire, her robes engulfed in blue-black flames. Searing pain ripped a shriek from her, but she held out her arms, calling forth the greatest vampire that had ever existed.

Screeching and twisting, the lesser shadows that had already risen drew away to the woods for safety. Sebastian turned to her in slow motion, his mouth opening in horror as he screamed the word, "No!"

Before he could inhale the next breath, the ground splintered open, toppling trees and sending black lightning in reverse up toward the sky.

A huge black stallion's skeletal head lunged out of the ground, its massive barrel chest and cloven hooves heaving forward to escape the Hell furnaces. Its rider carried a long pike in one black armored fist. He turned slowly, tossing back his face shield to reveal his regal heritage, eyes blazing black fire and fangs fully extended. Fury rippled down his left arm to engulf his hand as it released his horse's reins and reached toward Sebastian. A war cry rent the air as the magnetic snatch-force dragged Sebastian off his feet.

"My wife and my castle? Interloper, you die!"

Hundreds of warhorses followed their leader from the pit, each vampire rider holding up a pike, skewering badly decomposed human remains impaled through the rectum, along the entire length of the body, exiting the mouth. The moment Dracula's horse reared on its haunches, his soldiers lifted their pikes in a deafening cheer, waving mutilated human remains like gray-green flags.

Limbs and entrails flopped against raised pikes as their horses charged forward and headed toward the feeding grounds in the Carpathian Mountains. Elizabeth dropped to her knees and sobbed, overcome, as she watched Sebastian held aloft in Vlad's black charge.

Strangling from the death grip, Sebastian could offer no defense. She stood slowly as her former husband regarded her condition. His expression was unreadable, and for tense seconds she wondered if her maimed condition would make him turn away from her. Tears glittered in her eyes as she waited and pure contempt overtook his countenance. The spell had backfired . . . Elizabeth covered her face and spun away.

"He has let this fate befall my beloved?"

Elizabeth stopped at Vlad's words and cautiously nodded, slowly turning back to face him.

"Then determine his fate now," Dracula growled.

"Impale him," she hissed, pressing her hands to her heart. "But do not let him die . . . the Chairwoman forbids a loss of resources at this time. Just make him suffer."

"No, please," Sebastian croaked.

Dracula threw his head back and released a primal bellow

that shook the night. Instantly, Sebastian was in his grasp, his head savagely yanked to the side as his jugular was assaulted by massive fangs.

"Yes, drink," Elizabeth crooned, excitement thrumming through her. "Drain him of his daylight essence and leave him like he left me, trembling and weak, near extinction."

She watched the stronger male entity fill himself as the weaker one struggled and twisted to no avail. Desire flogged her entire being as she witnessed the erotic scene, loving every moment of how Vlad greedily heaved in deep gulps of black blood till it ran from the corners of his mouth. Then he threw back his head, sated, stronger, more alive—the color reviving beneath his skin, his fangs now white and glistening instead of yellow and gnarled. Gone were his skeletal features as healthy-looking human skin began to cover his bones, fashioning him back into the handsome warrior of old that he'd been.

Time seemed to stand still as he looked at Sebastian and smiled, eyes meeting in a silent exchange of bitter understanding. Two large tears slipped from the corners of Sebastian's eyes as he closed them to his fate and Dracula released the pike he'd been holding.

A black current of force sent the pike flying in a goring spiral that moved faster than Sebastian's vocal cords, entering his body through one orifice and coming out his mouth with blood and guts. A hard flick of Vlad's right hand caused the slicked pike to descend into Hell like a flaming arrow, carrying a burning Sebastian. With a heat-seeking missile's voracity, the pike dove into Hell to penetrate Sebastian's throne in Vampire Council Chambers.

Dracula slid off his mount, outrage still glistening in his eyes. "Come to me, my love. You have given me *daylight*—a conquest I never achieved before my unfortunate demise. Feed from my veins and heal your abominable condition. Bring me bodies while my army replenishes itself for battle."

"Then what would you have me do," she murmured, moving toward him cautiously.

He smiled wickedly and fully removed his helmet, then shook out his shoulder-length brunet tresses. "I have impaled your imposter husband—marriage cancelled. After hundreds of years away . . . it is only fitting that I also impale you."

Emotionally spent, but with a new spirit of determination, the team trudged upstairs to the spacious meeting rooms and private living quarters.

"Sister Sylvia and Brother Muata are bringing you all some vegan platters . . . and we'll gather up the clothing and sandals and silver you selected," Owa said with a calm, satisfied smile. "We'll put each outfit in an individual mud cloth bag for you so you can use the facilities to freshen up and have a place to keep your fatigues when you go to the jazz fest tomorrow."

"Tomorrow?" Marlene said, drawing the group's focus.

"Yes . . . it runs Friday through Labor Day."

Damali glanced at Dan and then Owa. "We thought it was Saturday through . . . never mind. I guess I was just hoping the team could adjust before . . . that we'd have some time to get our bearings and do a little more research before . . ." Damali threw up her hands. "Marlene said it right. We were getting comfortable, sloppy—guilty as charged."

"Oh, no!" Marlene said quickly, spinning around and then cringing. "Speaking of sloppy—my black mud cloth bag . . . all these years, how stupid! *The Temt Tchaas!* Talk about the pot calling the kettle black—I left it in the house in San Diego!"

"No, you didn't," Carlos said, pulling it through the ether for her. "That's one of the first things I always jettison to a safe house, then I move everything else. I always got your back, Mar."

Marlene walked over and hugged him. "For a man with a lot on his mind, you sure keep a lot on your mind. Thank you."

"*De nada,* Mom," Carlos replied and hugged her hard. "It's cool. We're all off."

They both smiled and a silent thought leapt from Carlos's mind into Marlene's. *Gotta know what's gonna happen next with Damali and our kid, you know.*

Marlene just patted the side of his face and nodded.

"This great hall room," Owa said with flourish, "has seen Nelson Mandela, Malcolm X, so many greats I cannot begin to recount . . . and now the Neteru Guardian squad?" She fanned her face and a bright smile graced her lips. "The Detroit team is going to be here bringing water, blankets and sleeping bags, air mattresses . . . we have VIPs in the house and most of us have been waiting all our lives for this moment. You all can use this room as your war room and weapons area. I'll get some pallets readied for you so you can rest. It's been a long time, since Panther days, that we've had a visitation like this. . . . We have some couches and pullouts, some old bedrolls. But we never have visitors like this anymore. We gonna pour libations and eat plenty and tell stories and keep the watch."

Carlos and Damali forced smiles and shared a private glance. Rapid-fire telepathic communication whizzed back and forth between them in a split second as Damali approached their kind hostess.

*Damali, maybe I'm wrong, but . . . I'm getting the distinct impression that this particular Guardian team has been primarily focused on the civil rights front and the free the Diaspora struggle, not the demon-hunting front.*

*Oh, God, Carlos, I know. They've been dealing with human atrocities and keeping the spirit of justice alive, pouring libations for that and whatnot . . . but I haven't seen nary a weapon up in this joint.*

*Shit, D, what have we gotten these innocents into? They're getting Guardians to come, the house is gonna fill up—and I think they think we're gonna be telling old revolutionary tales while we sing "Kumbiyah." They're doing a heads of state thing, not a hunker down and get ready to rumble kinda thing. She probably thought Yonnie was speaking in the abstract as a seer or from some past life memory, not the real deal.*

*If it gets hot, we abandon this building to save it and everyone in here and take the fight to the streets.*

*Sounds like a plan,* Carlos said in a mental jettison, wiping his his face with his fist.

*Maybe they just do things differently in Detroit? We gotta ask 'Bazz when the coast is clear.*

Before any hint of a mental conversation could be detected or a lack of response taken for rudeness, Damali went to Owa and hugged her. "Thank you for the sanctuary. We're both honored and humbled by it."

# CHAPTER TEN

"Oh, now it gets *truly* interesting," Lilith said as she walked away from the dark vision mist within the pentagram-shaped table. The fanged crest immediately closed down over it as she coolly regarded the flaming pike that had careened through the vaulted ceiling, disturbing screeching bats, to lodge in Sebastian's throne.

Billowing smoke and the stench of burning vampire flesh filled Vampire Council Chambers, causing the Harpies that hunkered near the hem of Lilith's gown to squeal in discontent. Gray-green little gargoyle bodies fought with one another to hide under tables and behind thrones, agitated at the intrusion, while transporter bats began to take diving swipes at crackling skin, hoping to snag a tasty morsel.

"Away, you little thieves," Lilith admonished, going up to Sebastian. "Sad but true, he is still a councilman and you may not feed on his remains—even though he does look like a spitted barbecue pig."

She dispassionately watched Sebastian scrabble at his throat with blackened, skeletal fingers, and then slow amusement made her chuckle until she outright belly laughed the moment she realized what had happened.

"Oh, this is priceless!" she screeched, walking in a circle. "Elizabeth is truly a woman after my own heart. I didn't know that royal bitch had it in her!" Pressing her hand to her stomach, Lilith howled and then finally blew Sebastian's flames out. She clucked her tongue in amusement. "No . . . not a barbecued suckling. I was wrong. You look more like a roasted marshmallow . . . all gooey and icky and sticky . . . and, ugh—crusty."

She shook her head and walked around him. "The females are always the best at exacting revenge, we are so much more creative than you, darling. This is what I was after. I needed them to rise to the occasion . . . to stretch and grow into their full fury." Lilith tapped a tapered finger against her lips and sighed. "I so hope Lucrezia deals with Fallon and puts his arrogant ass in its place. Then we will have true balance of power on this council."

Sweeping away with a flourish she collected a goblet of blood to sip while she studied Sebastian, trying to decide what to do. "So . . . Vlad is back. Interesting. You accidentally allowed Elizabeth to get ambushed and to burn, thus screwing her; for the favor, she had her husband shove a pike up your ass and then let you burn . . . exquisite. Ahhhh . . . balance. And were we not so resource-bound, I'd leave you here for at least a hundred years, but I cannot afford to let a decent necromancer get exterminated all due to a domestic dispute. How fortunate for you . . . but maybe not, since Vlad will now take Yonnie's vacant throne at council."

Lilith chuckled when Sebastian's body twitched in protest and she waved her goblet under Sebastian's nose with a shrug, teasing him mercilessly. "How can I not invite him when he's sent me such a powerful request—and I take it that Liz is probably installing him now? Council sessions should be delightful going forward. And we *all* must be at his coronation."

She leaned in and flicked a serpent tongue into Sebastian's

vacant eye sockets, tasting where his eyeballs had liquefied from the heat and had run down his cheeks. "Definitely leaning toward marshmallow." The moment the gore touched the back of her palate, Lilith shrieked and began laughing all over again.

"You stupid bastard—you actually allowed Vlad to suck the daylight out of you, too!"

Owa beamed as Sister Sylvia came up the stairs with a large aluminum pan filled with savory stir-fry vegetables, followed by several team members bringing in warm breads, brown rice, jerk-style seitan, vegan pasta dishes, salads, succulent fruits, fresh squeezed juices, raw honey-sweetened homemade lemonade, and an array of all natural ingredient desserts.

Even though the Neteru team tried to assist, they were met with jovial protests from the hospitable Detroit squad. Long meeting tables had been pushed together in the general-purpose room and covered with brightly hued African tie-dyed cloths, and meeting-room chairs were added to create banquet seating. A huge potted fern with wide, low fronds temporarily graced the center of the table, and Owa gave explicit instructions to the Detroit crew about making sure all the food to be blessed was on the table before they began. This included any utensils, paper or otherwise, that were to be used. Damali and Carlos nodded with Marlene and Shabazz, taking note that they might have unwittingly misjudged the due diligence of their hosts.

Lifting a large drinking gourd filled with water, Owa smiled and looked around the table. "We ask the ancestors for permission to proceed." She poured a healthy splash of water on the plant and uttered "Ashe" with Marlene, enjoining the standing group to do likewise after each recited line. "We ask the Most High and all the angels in Heaven to bless this family while on their mission. We ask for their continued protection, and the protection of any children they have or bear . . . for their elders and loved ones outside the circle of their compound . . . for their travel mercy and deliverance . . . may their Light be ever bright. Bless them, this food, this offering, their lives. Keep them whole and sustained through the darkest of time till there is light."

"Ashe" rumbled through the spacious hall. Bodies began to truly relax. Tension gave way to fatigue as breaths that had been held slowly released. By the time Owa finished her ministrations and the plant had been removed from the table to make more room for the food, the Neteru team looked like they were ready to fall down if they didn't sit down.

"Warriors . . . friends . . . family, please let us tend to you for now." She waved a gracious hand before the table like a queen mother and bade everyone to sit. "I know you think you all gotta be on guard because we just some old revolutionaries." She winked at Damali and Carlos, causing them to blanch and Marlene to chuckle. "But we gonna show you how we do up here in Detroit."

"Folks are still at work," Sister Sylvia said as the curious Neteru team began taking seats. "See . . . this here place is the fallback position . . . can't have a lot of firepower that human workers can find. But our folks who work up in them plants . . . whooo-wee, y'all. They coming before it gets dark."

Owa laughed as the team's gazes shot from one to another. "No, we ain't been up here singing 'Kumbiyah' all these years— but I ain't mad at ya . . . just means *our* disguises worked."

"Oh, Miss Owa," Damali said, covering her face with her hands. "We meant no disrespect—just didn't want anything to ruin your lovely space here or to get anybody hurt."

Owa laughed in good nature and hoisted a layer of her African robes to reveal a handheld Uzi and a cell phone. "I don't know what you said to your husband, but the young bucks was thinking all sortsa mess that was so easy to pick up." She shook her head and clucked her tongue, then ruffled Bobby's hair. "Young wizard, I'ma hafta learn you how to *be cool*."

With that, the team broke out into pure laughter. Plates got passed, dishes dug into with huge spoons and suddenly all formality fled. However, no matter what they said, they couldn't get Owa to sit. She'd eat a little, then hop up with Sylvia, constantly orchestrating the utmost of hospitality. Soon, her cell phone began to sound and a big smile crossed her face.

"They here. They got a key," she said, glancing at her watch. Hurrying to the steps she waved the incoming team up to the multipurpose room and then turned to address the long banquet tables with pride. "*Dese* be my people!"

A pretty-faced, athletically built Guardian with a short Afro and the deepest set of dimples one ever could encounter beamed a perfect white smile as she came to the top of the steps. Coca butter and inner light gave her flawless walnut-hued skin extra luminance as she moved past the window. Carrying a sidearm and a Glock in a shoulder holster and wearing just a simple T-shirt and a pair of boot-cut jeans, everything about her solid frame said no-nonsense.

"Yo, family," the first Guardian said. "My name's Alicia, but my tights call me Trouble. You met my sister in New York up at Monsta Burgers—Adrienne—we call her Mo' Trouble."

"Hey!" Damali instantly replied, jumping up with Carlos. "Fought with your sister on the roof, she covered me with a handheld. Tall sister with awesome braids?"

"Yeah," Alicia said, laughing, and pounded Damali's fist. "That'd be her."

"Girl, gimme some love!" Damali laughed and opened her arms. "We bled together, so we family now." She hugged Alicia warmly and passed her off to Carlos. "My other half—I know your sister told you about my version of trouble."

Alicia gave Carlos a quick warrior's embrace. "You know she

did. I'm glad she told me about the silver eyes and fangs—or I'd hot this brother in a heartbeat in a firefight."

"Don't shoot. It's all family," Carlos said, laughing.

"You best be telling my folks about any special issues y'all got," Owa said, chuckling nervously. "They're a little trigger-happy—this is Detroit."

"I got the fangs, too, ma," Yonnie said, waving at Alicia from where he sat at the long table. "My boo got wings—plus, our grand master shogun," he added, wolfing down corn bread and pointing toward Shabazz, "he goes panther in a smooth shape-shift. The rest are general regulation seers, tactical squad, audio—that's Big Mike. But, yeah, we got some family that got a little extra somethin' somethin'."

"Cool," Alicia said with a casual shrug while more Guardians came up the steps. "As long as we know up front, it's all good." She turned and waved her arm out, making quick introductions. "This here is my homegirl, Candace . . . bad momma on technology and got the juice—tactical. You met Sylvia, Mary, and Brother Muata already . . . seers like Mom Owa, and Muata got the ears. But Gus is our strongman, another tactical, and Craig is our team sharpshooter and explosives man—a tactical. Warren, we call him Navajo, he's our nose—a bad tracker and he's got a lock on the Canadian side real good. Then, Barbara and Earl . . . they're from Chi-town's team, but are visiting for the jazz fest, so I figured you'd wanna meet them, too—because they definitely wanted to meet you all."

The team stood and handshakes and fellowship broke out in earnest. The team went down the row, first greeting the tiny five-foot-two powerhouse, Candace, who had the most wonderful laugh that sounded like tinkling bells and big brown eyes that drew you in. Her size, however, was deceiving—the sister carried a switchblade; a bowie knife; a serrated-edge hunting sickle; and a Beretta—even though she looked like butter wouldn't melt in her mouth at ten paces. Standing beside the dark-haired Greek giant, Gus, she looked like a little girl with a very womanly body.

Next to the huge Greek was the solidly built, clean-shaven, young African American executive look-alike, Craig, who seemed like he'd just come out of a business meeting. He wore a navy blue pin-striped suit and an Oxford blue shirt with a starched white collar, French cuffs, paisley tie, Cole Hann shoes, the works—but Craig's pecan-hued eyes held a depth of knowledge that only fellow soldiers could understand. It wasn't until one hugged him that it became clear that the man was thoroughly strapped.

Navajo could have been Jose's brother, built lanky, sporting a ponytail. Wearing urban corner-boy baggy pants, an oversized T-shirt with Tims, and a black-and-white bandana tied around his head, he just leaned back and smiled, pounding fists. Damali and Carlos shared a look and smiled, approving of the team that greeted them.

"I got da cars, yo—*borrowed* from the plants . . . built Ford tough and Dodge rough, wit Hemis under da hoods, extra exhaust systems, da whole nine . . . since you gonna need to ride or die, yo." Navajo folded his arms over his chest, beaming with obvious pride.

"Aw, Navajo," Alicia said, shaking her head. "You didn't jack the plant again, man . . . you were supposed to get those rides off the street from our stash—not fresh off the lines."

He shrugged and shot her a dashing smile as the greeting commotion became quiet. "They VIPs, sis—show some hospitality and some love."

"It's stealing," Alicia shot back.

"Nope—it's *borrowing,* and we'll get the rides back to the body shop, detail 'em, take out the extras when we all done and roll back the odometers like we used to do on the street . . . ya know, ya know."

Jose laughed and shook his head, but pounded Navajo's fist. "Back in the day, me and you woulda been road dawgs."

Carlos had to laugh, too. But before he could add his two cents to the debate, a loud female voice and a pair of heavy footfalls came up the staircase.

"Chicago in da house," a petite woman shouted, her booming voice surprising for her tiny frame. She was followed by a rock-solidly built male Guardian with a gleaming bald head. "Hey, family!" she said with a wide grin, excitedly looking around the group.

"Hey," everyone said in unison, as her infectious grin and warm personality bathed them.

"I'm Barbara," she announced, not waiting to be introduced, "straight pimp gangsta from Chi-town, and this here is my partner, my road dawg, Earl."

"I don't know her," the man beside her said, laughing. "She crazy, drives like a lunatic, and—"

"Don't you get me started, Earl," she fussed. "See, I used to drive a bus for Chicago Metro, and I told him we had to get here on time. But my brother there, he gotsta be stylish—wearing gators to a possible shoot-out with the darkside . . . you know how the men from Chicago be *sharp* . . . anyway, he was making us late, and I don't play that. Where my gun at, Earl?"

"First of all, I told you I wasn't coming up to no jazz fest where there was gonna be fine women without having my rags right— you know I don't roll like that. And, why you need firearms up in the Shrine? I told you I left that pump in the danged car—you can't jus' be walking down the street with a shotgun in broad daylight, Barbara, no matter how pimp gangsta you is."

"See, this was why I wasn't trying to come to the fest wit his ass—'scuze me Mom Owa."

"You wasn't gonna come with me?" Earl said, feigning shock. "Girl, you lucky I rode witchu! Then you had me calling on Jesus the whole drive—just putting on your turn signal and moving over into a lane that already got a car in it—"

"Negro, that's how I learned to drive a bus. They told us, put the signal on and just move over and they'll get the hell outta your way! They did, too, didn't they?"

"But you wasn't drivin' no danged bus, girl! You was in a Kia! That was an eighteen-wheeler you was moving on."

"Well you the damned tactical that's supposed to have my back and clear the road—that's why they call it riding shotgun, okaaay. Don't get me started."

"Who? Get started? Barbara, don't make me tell on you, 'cause—"

"Oh, oh, so it's like that, huh?" Barbara whipped out her cell phone and began a text message. "I'ma tell my girl, Dyanne and her husband—uh-huh, and she gonna put you on Guardian network blast up on her station. . . . Yeah, when she does her vampire info show for training—"

"You ain't have to go there . . . how'd I know that girl up in that club was a vampire, with her fine ass? And even if you put me on blast to Dy, that still don't mean you can drive! Plus, it ain't got nothing to do with nothing, because I didn't get bit."

"That's 'cause I had your back—but now you trying to talk about me and my driving up here in fronta *Neterus* . . . man, you know I'll take my earrings out over that mess!" She pushed Send and stuck out her tongue at Earl. "Now. Dyanne got the update about what happened in that stepper's club."

"So! Dy and me real cool on the team. She's our communications czar, and ain't putting me on blast like that."

Barbara flashed him a brilliant grin. "I know, but she's laughing her ass off—you ain't gonna never live it down."

"You ain't right, girl."

"They're always like this," Alicia murmured to Damali, trying hard not to smile, but her dimples gave away the restrained mirth. "My apologies, but the girl can drive a tank in a firefight though."

"Hotep!" A woman yelled coming up the steps, her footfalls quick as lightning. When she got to the top of the stairs she shrieked and ran over to Barbara, hugging her profusely. Slightly taller than Barbara and much stronger than she appeared, she hugged her Guardian sister off her feet, laughing. The new-comer's almond-hued skin was tattooed with gorgeous spiraling dragons and Adinkra symbols across her shoulder blades that framed the edges of her olive-green tank top. Her beautiful brown eyes were merry, and her pretty mouth was set in a pout as she dropped Barbara down and flung her russet-toned dread-locks over her shoulders. "Me and Lissa oughta not even speak to you, heifer. How you gonna come to the jazz fest and not tell the Chicago team and meet the Neterus!"

"Girl . . . see, what had happened was," Barbara said, laugh-ing. "Aw, Jackie, don't be mad, for real—"

"No, for real, Lissa is coming up here to kick yo skinny little ass." Jackie put one hand on her hip, but her smile was wide as she wagged a finger at Barbara.

At the sound of the keys in the door, both Guardian sisters temporarily stopped arguing and raced to the steps as a six-foot-tall, black-linen-suited, statuesque brown beauty barreled into the multipurpose room, braids and M-16 swaying.

"Oh, shit, my *glamazon* sister is here!" Earl hollered. "Lee Lee, whassup, boo?"

"Earl," she fussed with a big smile. "The onliest thing keeping you from getting your asses kicked for leaving me in Chicago when the Neterus was in the area is you giving me my props."

"You are glamorous and an Amazon, boo—you know I had to coin a phrase just for you, baby. Glamazon!"

She sucked her teeth and rolled her eyes at him, but then laughed as she flipped Barbara the bird. "So, where they at?"

The Neteru team looked from one to the other, trying not to laugh as Barbara hid behind Jackie, playing around. Using Jackie as a body-shield, the tiny, curvaceous woman with the Halle Berry–style short haircut, white linen suit, and designer shades pointed at her six-foot, muscular brother who was just as fly. Earl was rocking tan linen and matching gators, and didn't look like he was ready in the least to go round-for-round or pound-for-pound with Lissa.

"It was all Earl's fault," Barbara said, laughing harder as Lissa lowered a weapon at her with a wide grin.

The moment Earl took a breath, Barbara, Alicia, Lissa, and Candace jumped on him, verbally pelting him. It was clear who had the verbal advantage, and after a while he simply gave up, smoothed a palm over his gleaming bald head with a sigh and shrugged.

"I can't do nothing with 'em, can't take 'em nowhere. I'm putting out a plea for a transfer with the Neteru team. Need some more male Guardians up in Chicago to have my back, feel me?"

"Humph," Barbara said, and finally turned her attention to the Neteru team. "It didn't have to be all that, Earl."

For two seconds the room was still and then suddenly it erupted into booming laughter.

"Okay," Owa said. "You have now met Detroit and some of the Chicago team. Initial looks mighta been deceiving, but you think we can handle some vampires up in the house?"

"Most definitely," Carlos said, pounding Shabazz's fist.

The transporter bats didn't screech, they shrieked as they whirred Vlad the Impaler with his newly reclaimed wife into Vampire Council Chambers. Nuit was already sitting in his throne, tense, with Lucrezia at his side, her expression unreadable. Sebastian drew back within his as Vlad surveyed the environment with an air of familiarity, ignoring him to stride closer to the table.

Elizabeth hung back as Vlad approached Lilith and dropped to one knee before their councilwoman, not sure if her presumptuous actions to bring back her late husband would draw Lilith's approval or her wrath.

"Milady," Vlad said with old-world charm, "it has been eons."

"Indeed," Lilith said coolly. "But have you forgotten that entering chambers requires the protocol of a blood check at the doors?" She took a sip of blood from her goblet and motioned toward the massive, black marble doors. "The golden-fanged knockers need a bite . . . if you pass inspection, then we know you're the genuine article."

He looked up into her eyes, his burning black with lust. "I will endure the bite, as you wish . . . but I assure you, Madame Councilwoman, I am the genuine article."

"Then rather than trouble yourself with crossing so far from me to complete such a rudimentary task . . . perhaps I could sample and see? Or are you afraid that the Dark Lord's wife might smell a coup and rip your lungs out?"

"With daylight in my veins, the love of my life by my side . . . my army replenished and war at hand?" He dropped his voice to a gravelly rumble. "Lilith, tell me why I would be so impetuous?"

They both smiled and Elizabeth relaxed. Vlad tore away his breastplate and turned his head to the side to give Lilith access to his jugular. She slowly leaned forward and traced the pulsing surface of it with her index finger.

"Beautiful," Lilith murmured. "I don't know why we didn't do this earlier." Her strike was cobra-fast and brutal. Vlad released a groan of pleasure that made all witnessing councilmen swallow hard. When she came away from Vlad's throat, she wiped her lush mouth with the back of her hand and retracted her fangs, seeming almost pleasure-drunk. "You've gotten stronger while in the Sea of Perpetual Agony," she said, awed. "I think I'm in love." Then she laughed as she stood and offered him a goblet. "Your old throne awaits . . . you've yet to be properly installed in it."

"Welcome," Nuit said cautiously, finally finding his voice.

"Welcome," Lucrezia said in a nervous whisper.

Vlad nodded and walked over to the pentagram-shaped table, not immediately going to his throne. He downed his goblet and submitted to a fang strike by the crest to open it, and then began reading the minutes.

"Good," Vlad said, looking at Nuit. "You are on record as having no part in reanimating my wife without me. . . . Nor had your bride." He shot a threatening glare at Sebastian. "Not even the traitor, Yolando, was so foolish. For that, I will kill him swiftly rather than prolong his agony."

"You have exacted your revenge, Vlad," Lilith said evenly. "We cannot afford strife among us. Sebastian didn't have her that long, and trust me, there was assuredly no lasting impression. Therefore, by edict of Level Seven, there will be no more intracouncil assassinations, torture attempts, et al. Just for the record."

"As milady so desires," Vlad said with a sneer toward Sebastian, who looked positively white with shell shock. "And, as it appears in the record, her installation and coronation was dismal."

"Shockingly so," Nuit said, sitting forward and making a tent with his fingers before his mouth. "Twenty minutes or thereabouts, I'm told."

"Twenty minutes?" Vlad snarled and walked over to where Elizabeth stood immobile.

"Tragic, but true," she said, delicately placing her hand within his.

"Not fit for a countess of pain."

"No," she murmured as his hands found her alabaster shoulders. "I yearned for you until even my tears bled."

She closed her eyes as his fingers found the edge of her black lace gown, toying with the fabric. He bent and kissed the crimson satin ribbon that was tied around her throat and then led her by the elbow to stand before Lilith's throne.

"Allow me to properly install my wife at my own coronation, milady."

Lilith crossed her long, shapely legs and nodded with a droll smile. "I would have been disappointed had you not requested to do so."

Vlad smiled and turned Elizabeth toward him, so that her back faced the council thrones. Lucrezia's quiet gasp seemed to add to his pleasure as he slowly removed Elizabeth's gown and allowed the yards of black fabric to pool at her feet on the floor.

The council's eyes studied the intricate back piercing that left a row of six golden rings on each side of her spinal column, with a tiny ring at the nape of her neck. A scarlet ribbon was crisscrossed through the loop work, designed almost like a pulley, and the ends of it hung free like kite tails that flanked her sides. Red, angry marks surrounded each ring where tender skin had been freshly pierced. Elizabeth's narrow hips swayed in anticipation as Vlad slowly removed his armor, and her smooth, flawless buttocks trembled ever so slightly as she waited for him to near her.

"If you so much as blink during the coronation," Vlad warned Sebastian, "I will take my chances with Madame Councilwoman's edict."

Vlad closed the gap between him and Elizabeth and took up the edges of the ribbon, slowly winding it around his fists. The moment she leaned in to take his mouth, which was just a hairsbreadth from his, he yanked hard on the ribbon, causing her to shut her eyes tightly with a wince and her back to bleed.

"Tell me you need an assistant," Lucrezia murmured and then smiled triumphantly as Nuit eased back in his throne, his expression suddenly unreadable. "You see, my husband has been very busy making new master vampires while I've been convalescing . . . therefore, I've been bored. Now, since there can be no objection—given that fair exchange is no robbery here, I should like to help properly welcome you and the countess to court." She offered Vlad a charming bow from where she sat. "Your prowess is legendary . . . and our hospitality has been lacking of late." She glared at her husband and then gave Lilith a knowing glance, arching her eyebrow.

"My, my, my," Lilith crooned in a seductive tone, "just when I thought Liz was the only bitch in here but me." She raised her goblet to Lucrezia. "I like your style. Timing of the revenge is just as important as the elements it contains."

"I so agree, Madame Councilwoman," Lucrezia said, and then lifted her goblet toward Lilith before taking a sip.

Vlad stared at Lucrezia, his eyes filled with lust as she ran a ruby-red, manicured nail down the front of her crimson satin gown, opening it to expose her perfect, petite breasts. A red glow began to overtake her cat-green irises and she seductively shrugged her mane of scarlet hair over her creamy shoulder. He glanced at Elizabeth, who swallowed hard and subtly nodded, the yearning standing between them as though it were another entity.

"I could use an assistant to help bind her," Vlad murmured, and then smiled at Nuit evilly. "Unless your husband objects?"

For a moment, Nuit didn't answer, but thinking better of a challenge, he lifted his chin. "*Non*. . . . I do not object."

"Good," Vlad said. "You have an empire that can deliver messages of our conquest quickly—that can inspire fear . . . I have an army that is worthy of worldwide terror . . . we should be allies." Not waiting for Nuit's response, he turned his focus to Lucrezia and offered her the ribbons.

Elizabeth's head dropped back as soon as Lucrezia stood before her, their taut nipples grazing each other's, each woman's soft skin becoming goose-pebbled with anticipation. Vlad rounded Elizabeth and kissed her bleeding piercing sites one by one, causing her to groan. But rather than strike her, he took both nude women's hands and led them to his throne.

Securing Elizabeth's wrists at the top skeleton posts on either side of it with shackles, he gently opened her legs to make her stand spread-eagle while he caressed her damp inner thighs and bound her ankles to the base of the throne. Then he bade Lucrezia to stand before Elizabeth and motioned for Lucrezia to return the ribbons to his palms.

"Welcome her to Council properly," he said in a thick murmur, his dark gaze holding Lucrezia for ransom. "Please, Baroness."

"I shall do my very best," Lucrezia promised him in a breathy murmur and then turned her attention to Elizabeth.

Lucrezia touched Elizabeth's mouth with trembling fingers, slowly bringing the pad of her thumb across her bottom lip, then she kissed her gently, tangling tongues. Pulling back, she watched as Elizabeth's eyes began to glow and she allowed her hands to trace her shoulders, then her collarbone, and to flow over Elizabeth's breasts. Elizabeth briefly closed her eyes, but a sharp tug at the ribbons by Vlad made her open them wide again.

He stood behind Lucrezia, staring over her shoulder at Elizabeth as Lucrezia lowered her mouth to Elizabeth's delicate skin, her tongue painting a path of pleasure between Elizabeth's breasts, suckling under the petite lobes until she moaned. Drawing a tight pink nipple into her mouth, Lucrezia sent a saliva-slicked finger to caress the tip of the other one, and then swayed her breasts against Elizabeth's, coaxing a gasp from them both.

But a hard yank kept Elizabeth's hungry mouth from seeking solace against Lucrezia's. In frustration, Lucrezia licked at Elizabeth's tightening nipples while massaging her own until Elizabeth began to writhe. Vlad wound the ribbon tighter around his fist and pulled hard with a wicked smile, making Elizabeth cry out, but grow deadly still again.

Lucrezia smiled against her breasts and slowly kissed down Elizabeth's torso, her tiny pink tongue causing the bound woman to tremble. Finally Elizabeth's uncontrollable shudders gave way to openmouthed pants as Lucrezia neared her mound, looked up for a moment, and began to slowly consume her.

Although she remained stock-still, Elizabeth's husky moans reverberated off the council walls, creating an echo chamber that aroused transporter bats and sent Harpies into mating frenzies. But Vlad wouldn't allow her to move. He stood behind Lucrezia, naked, breathing hard with need, watching her limber spine dip and sway as her tongue tunneled into his wife's canal. Lucrezia's graceful hands cupped his wife's thighs, her thumbs holding her lips open as she suckled Elizabeth to tears.

Wet sounds of tongue lapping against swollen, hot skin made Nuit swallow hard as quietly as possible while Lilith uncrossed her legs and opened them wide, allowing several of her Harpies to slip beneath her gown hem. Sebastian didn't move, his distress shown only by his slightly flared nostrils on each inhalation and exhalation.

But as Lucrezia drove two fingers deep within Elizabeth and suckled her clit, Elizabeth made the fatal error of arching. A hard yank made her voice rent the air. Lucrezia looked up over her shoulder at Vlad, unsure. His eyes were hard, but his voice was filled with thick desire.

"Go to her. Comfort her . . . and I will comfort you."

Immediately Lucrezia slid up Elizabeth's body and took her mouth, cradling her skull between her hands. Her mound urgently mated with Elizabeth's, causing more hot tears to slip from Elizabeth's eyes, and then suddenly Lucrezia arched with a thunderous moan as Vlad entered her from behind. Unable to help herself, Lucrezia bucked against his slow steady thrusts, rubbing herself against Elizabeth at the same time. But each time Vlad's wife would become overwrought with passion and begin to move, he would punish her with the ribbons until she finally sobbed.

Nuit squirmed uncomfortably in his throne as Lilith hissed with pleasure from her Harpies' attention. Sebastian simply looked forward, gripping his armrests, barely able to breathe. Then Elizabeth's voice rent the air in a murderous scream as Lucrezia came against her and yet Vlad still would not allow her to move.

Quickly, his breaths now hard pants, he unfurled the ribbons in his grasp and tied them around Lucrezia's waist, binding both women together, belly to belly. Kissing Lucrezia deeply, he stared at her for a moment and then took Elizabeth's mouth as he unsheathed himself from Lucrezia. Moving with deliberate speed, he slid under Elizabeth so that her back pressed against his stomach, wrapping his arms around both her and Lucrezia.

The moment his body touched the throne seat, all of the knowledge within it up to his reign and beyond it fused with his spine, causing him to arch and cry out. Black current ran over his skin and the power of the charge made his fangs lengthen against his will. Frenzied, he lifted his hips in a violent upthrust and entered Elizabeth, pumping wildly, then leaving her body to seek Lucrezia's, making both women writhe and moan and compete for his penetration. Then the second the black charge drew back into the marble, the Council Chambers went dark, torches blew out, the throne became a four-posted bed under a blanket of Carpathian stars.

Still bound, both female vampires clawed at each other, trying to get more of their body surfaces to rub against the other as he serviced them with alternating thrusts. Wails of passionate discontent bounced off thrones and the cavern walls, as his deep, growling responses bottomed out their pleas.

Suddenly, he left Elizabeth's body, focused on Lucrezia until she heaved and climaxed, holding Elizabeth's ribbons, making her shriek with need. As soon as Lucrezia's body slumped, he released Elizabeth's ribbons, mounted her savagely, and tore into her throat with massive fangs. Her orgasm eclipsed his in force and voracity, knocking Lilith's head back and making both Nuit and Sebastian shudder where they sat.

"Bravo," Lilith whispered, too dazed to even clap. "*Bravo*. Nuit . . . your coronation takes second place; there is simply no way to top a standard-bearer."

"He is the Count," Nuit admitted begrudgingly, his gaze riveted to Lucrezia's naked body with longing. He then smirked at Sebastian and glanced down at his fellow councilman's erection. "The Harpies will oblige, but I don't suggest you even do that in Vlad's presence."

Sebastian closed his eyes, trying without success to shut out Nuit's humor noir. The violent episode on the chamber floor passed slowly, and Vlad made each star slowly fade with it, bringing the threesome back onto his throne nude and exhausted. He took up Lucrezia's hand and kissed the back of it.

"Thank you, fair lady," he said, breathing hard as he helped Lucrezia off of his lap. "I couldn't have done this installation properly without you."

Lucrezia blew him a kiss. "The pleasure was all mine, Count Dracula."

Elizabeth's fingers sought Vlad's now wild profusion of brunet hair and his tangled in hers, blood staining the corners of their mouths. Her gaze sought his, searching his face with deep passion. He kissed his wife gently, not watching Lucrezia return to Nuit.

"And thank you, beloved," Vlad murmured against his wife's bloodied throat. "After we feed, I will bring you justice as my fair exchange gift for another lifetime gift that you've given me . . . this time under the sun. The Neterus will die."

# CHAPTER ELEVEN

Stories got told, more food got passed, and war strategies were discussed between much-needed camaraderie. At points the laughter became so infectious that Guardians were waving one another's comments away while wiping their eyes. But as the sun began to set, the group's composure changed. Damali and Carlos shared a glance that wasn't lost on the group.

"So, family," Carlos said, hating to destroy the cool vibe, "me and my boy, Yonnie, need to drape some truth on y'all tonight. This morning and this afternoon, we got lucky." Carlos shot Yonnie a meaningful glance.

"Sho' you right, bro," Yonnie said, chewing on a toothpick. "Want me to school 'em on what I used to be?"

"I ain't gotta tell you twice," Carlos said, leaning back in his chair to yield the floor to Yonnie.

Yonnie simply nodded and leaned forward at the table on his elbows. "Daywalker. Ex-aficionado."

Barbara and Candace were on their feet and drew so fast that all Yonnie could do was smile.

"Glad you ladies got the reflexes," Yonnie said coolly. "If one of 'em comes by day, you're gonna need 'em."

"It's peace," Carlos said, monitoring the bristling new tension in the group.

Navajo had calmly stood and drew what looked like a long pipe out of his baggy pants and tossed it to Alicia, who caught it with one hand. As though she were simply putting together a thousand-piece puzzle, she kept one eye on Yonnie while she began taking sections of a weapon out of her boots until it became clear that she was assembling a custom-made rifle at the table.

"Don't mind me. You were saying?" Alicia's gaze was set hard in her pretty face as she screwed the long barrel on and began loading in shells.

"He's our bird dog to the other side, right through here," Carlos said, his gaze raking the group. "Don't get it twisted. He's on our side, but fresh out of the darkside. I used to be like him once not too long ago."

Shoulders relaxed and gazes widened as expressions begged for clarity.

"A Neteru?" Lissa asked, leaning forward as she slowly lowered her Glock. "We'd heard all sorts of rumors . . . but . . ."

Damali turned her head to the side with a smile. "Light 'em up, baby . . . show this team your work. I had Neteru antitoxin running through my veins, which is the only reason I'm still standing. But you all need to see what a councilman can do."

"Don't be sexist," Yonnie said with a half smile. "Them bitches—I mean, females on council, 'scuze me—ain't no joke, either."

"Yonnie ain't never lied," Carlos muttered, staring at Damali's jugular vein until every pulse point he'd bitten in the past flared red and then raised into two angry puncture wounds.

"Dayum," Yonnie said with true admiration in his tone, shaking his head. "You da man."

The Detroit and Chicago teams were on their feet.

"Talk to me," Earl said, a Glock cocked first at Yonnie, then Carlos and Damali.

"I'ma say this once," Carlos muttered in a deep rumble. "Take that gun outta my wife's face or this is gonna be a real short training session."

Earl snapped the gun up to a safety position, but his gaze remained on Damali's wound sites. "You did that to her . . . or, or something got to her? What da hell . . ."

"Precisely," Carlos said in a flat tone, returning Damali's skin to its former unmarked beauty as he spoke. "*What the hell.* This is what we're trying to tell you. When I was on the other side, not biting her wasn't an option . . . but I cared about her. That right there you see are love nicks. Rider can tell you all about it, too. But trust me, if I didn't love her, you woulda been staring at cartilage." He smiled and pushed back in his chair as the color drained from the local team's faces. "Any of you all got a deep bond with anything coming up from the pit? If so, then we don't need to tell you nothing. If not, take a seat and go to school."

Nuit slowly strolled up to his key human don, a careful smile on his face as his human helpers angrily surveyed the veritable army that surrounded the drug czar at la casa. Nervous energy kept gazes steely and fingers flexed over automatic weapon triggers. Trust had never existed on either side of the border, but the latest incident made it completely evaporate.

"They seized *twenty-six tons* of my cocaine in Manzanillo?" Nuit said in a lethal murmur, beginning to circle the sweating don. "That would be twenty one thousand, carefully cut, and processed packets that made it safely all the way here from our friends in Colombia to arrive in Mexico in a cargo container." He neared the man and wiped a finger down the side of his ruddy, pockmarked face, and then tasted the oily residue with flourish. "How?"

The man bowed and backed away from Nuit. "Señor, I sincerely do not know where the human leak came from, but we will—"

"No," Nuit hissed between his lengthening fangs. "I will tell you where the leak came from." He spat out each word, eyes beginning to glow red with fury as the don's army backed into the muzzles of Nuit's bodyguards' Uzis. Drawing in a deep, nasal hock, he spit in the don's face, his narrowed gaze daring the man to wipe away the offense. "You stupid, superstitious bastard—you were the fucking leak!"

"No, señor! I have *never* betrayed the family and have never—"

"It's in your goddamned sweat!" Nuit bellowed, bat wings ripping though the seams of his black Armani suit. "My palate is many things, but wrong . . . never." With an iron grip he held the man by his jaw, watching terror leak from his eyes. "You went into a church for your godson's christening, *oui*?"

Nuit tightened his grip when no answer was forthcoming. "Frankincense and myrrh—the bullshit incense of cathedrals pollutes you—then as you said the prayers over that baby, you stupid fuck, you thought of one to say about this shipment . . . hoping that it arrived without incident." He flung the man away from him, leaned back, and roared with frustration. "Weak, sniveling, human flesh, how could you be so stupid in the end of days to take our business in your soul into a house of worship where angels there for the sake of the child could hijack our fucking intent!"

Before the man could gain his footing after stumbling away from Nuit, a black current snatched him back into Nuit's grasp. "The Cosa Nostra was just hit for this same type of idiotic bullshit!" Nuit yelled, making the blood vessels burst in the man's eyes as he raged on. "He typed a Ten Commandments of their rules—a *Ten Commandments*—as though angels wouldn't read something like that over his shoulder and out him," he added, laughing cruelly as the don wept blood. "Putting things on there like, respect your wife, do not take another man's wife, do not take money that isn't yours, do not frequent bars—my partner who runs Europe will suck the goddamned marrow from his bones and feed him to the Harpies for this travesty! The fucking Mafia is now writing down rules of engagement like they're chivalrous Templars . . . oh, *mon ami,* we are indeed in the end of days. But you have cost me *twenty-six tons* of product with a street value that I am currently at a loss to even estimate." He shook his head and released a weary sigh. "What should I do?"

"For all the years I've served you, been loyal . . . mercy, *por favor.*"

Nuit looked at the man with blasé detachment. "Mercy?" He shook his head as the man began bleeding from every orifice. "I do not even know the definition of the word."

Yonnie pounded Carlos's fist, leaning past a few members of the Neteru team to reach him. For the next hour, the Neteru team updated the local squad about the phenomena of daywalkers, the differences in strength between master vampires and those of the Ultimate Darkness, Council-level. Sparing no details, the Neteru team went over the last battle, as well as fully deconstructing what happened with the New York squad.

Carlos looked around at the stunned faces and jumped in as soon as there was a lull in commentary by his teammates.

"Yeah, like I said, your sister, with Phat G and them in Harlem, were fighting some of Vlad's old army plus two Council-level vamps. The only reason the squad made out like they did was because the two council vamps were punks . . . wanted to use Vlad's army as cannon fodder and not get in the mix. But I guarantee you next time, it ain't gonna go like that."

"My sister said the things they fought were different, stronger . . . the numbers of them was crazy," Alicia said, her gaze tense, but in full command.

"She was right," Damali said flatly. "Here's the thing—don't think we're coming up here trying to act like we've never been where you are right now." She glanced around the table. "When our team first started out, we were doing what you all have no doubt been doing . . . battling local, strong, second- and third-generation vamps, the occasional werewolf, beating back the tide. But we lost almost half a squad in Mexico, body count-wise . . . plus the entire Brazilian team."

Alicia crossed herself. "We heard about the losses in Mexico . . . and you know, stories been running rampant in the underground—but you know how that goes. People been in battle with the Neterus, heavy casualties, and the whole nine yards, means that stories get embellished. I'm not hating, just telling you how I know human nature can be."

"I feel you," Damali said, ruffling her locks up off her neck to relieve tension. "But whatever they told you about Cain's crazy ass was true . . . whatever they told you about Fallon Nuit was mild—he's stronger now."

"Fact," Carlos said abruptly, standing and beginning to pace. "So, it's almost like, when we come to town, expect to lose squad. Seeing us on your doorstep ain't no happy occasion. That shit stresses me, and I don't mind telling you." He waved his arm out to indicate his squad. "Stresses the whole Net squad . . . especially after breaking bread, laughing, chillin' . . . in wartime, people get to be your family real quick, which means leaving them on the asphalt with a stake in their chest ain't easy."

Silence sliced through the room, swirling with the dull hum of the fan blades as all eyes remained fixed on Carlos.

"I wanna develop a new protocol," Carlos said, turning away

from the team and looking at Damali. "It just came to my mind . . . might be stupid . . . I don't know. But, I've got a bad feeling that's giving me the creeps."

"Talk to us," Shabazz said, leaning forward with one hand resting on the other fist. "Something giving you the willies is making the hair stand up on the back of my neck."

Carlos nodded and shot a glance around the somber faces in the room. "If it gets too hot, situation critical—I jettison anybody I can to a sanctuary. Period," he said, waving his hands as protests began to erupt.

"Naw, man—we ride or die," Navajo said, standing again.

"Detroit was the murder capital before Philly took it, brother," Alicia said, checking her clip. "We go down as one."

"Let me say this again, with clarity," Carlos said, gaining a subtle nod from Damali. "We got folks on this team, me included, that still can't half sleep at night because of what happened in Cuernavaca. Ain't trying to go that way again."

"Morelos wasn't no joke," Big Mike said, adding to Carlos's argument. He glanced at Marlene and then Shabazz and briefly closed his eyes. "You ain't seen what they do at the lower levels of Hell . . . y'all lost a few to vamp bites, no disrespect and not minimizing those losses, but when they come like they did out there and you ain't got no fallback position . . ."

"The One Who Remains Nameless walked into a sanctuary— a cathedral—and attacked a seasoned priest who is a freakin' Knight of Templar from the Covenant," Rider said very slowly, his gaze roving. "The bastard was able to get to that old warrior simply because the fallback position Father Patrick had was shaky. Mind you, the man himself wasn't shaky, but the particular house of worship he was in when the entity came to him was devoid of the Almighty."

Alicia was on her feet. "Right here is safe, so is Second Ebenezer—you can't miss it, huge white edifice right off the highway and is consecrated to the max, you feel me. So, any of our junior members that gotta get saved, no problem . . . but I'm straight in my spirit. Ready to do what I gotta do. Just like New York had your back, Detroit and Chi-town are ready."

Berkfield nodded and laced his fingers together across his bald head, then looked at Damali and Carlos. "They're warriors. It'd be like telling young Marines or Green Berets to fall back just before the big one. Never happen. They've been waiting all their lives for this. They got battle lust, mission, purpose . . . and they want in on this fight." He shrugged and let his breath out hard and closed his eyes. "I'm old 'Nam . . . like my man, Big Mike. Can't tell the new jacks—they have to get in the hole, smell the rounds going off, feel the mortars and claymores blowing up, feel that shell shock compression hit— taste dirt, then get that first splash of a buddy's blood across their faces . . . then they've gotta puke up their guts and live with the bullshit in their minds for eternity. Only then will they know what you tried to save them from." He opened his eyes and simply stared at Carlos. "You warned them, your heart was in the right place, but it's their decision to ride or die."

Again, tense silence had snuck into the room like a thief to steal voices. Verbal protest was absent, but the defiant stares said everything; this team would not be moved.

"Psalm Sixty-five," Alicia said in a philosophical tone, "or Ninety-one, then strap up and the rest is up to God."

"What you gonna do with that?" Marlene said, her tone weary as she stood slowly. "Sixty-five it is, then?"

A slight vibration disturbed water glasses and drinks at the table before anyone could draw a breath. Instantly every tactical Guardian on the combined teams turned to the seers, their shout singular: "Incoming!"

Combined effort sent a blue-white charge around the building as chairs toppled and African statues began to fall. Seers locked in to a singular vision and then they began shouting coordinates in rapid-fire succession.

"We've gotta clear the building!" Marlene yelled, dashing toward the stairs.

Owa was right on her heels. "Gas main under it won't hold much longer—but they want us out."

"Then let's give 'em what they want!" Alicia shouted, as Guardians scrambled for weapons.

"Take it to the street!" Barbara yelled with Earl.

"Shields up!" Carlos shouted, throwing a disc in front of the local team that was exiting the building the traditional way, while he and Damali halved the Neteru squad in a simultaneous fold-away transport to the street.

Cars bounced, civilians ran screaming, car alarms sounded, traffic lights and utility poles violently swayed. Moving away from the Shrine to protect it as a fallback position, the teams fanned out, taking cover, their eyes keened on the huge boulevard that suddenly began to buckle.

"Point of entry!" Damali yelled, leveling her Madame Isis blade toward the first crack in the asphalt to release a blue-white nova charge. But the second it hit the blacktop, everything around them went still.

Carlos turned around in circles with the rest of the seers, confused as their second-sight lost track of the huge mental shadow. Damali shot the ground with white light in several more places, testing in the eerie stillness as pedestrians tried to stand and then fled, hollering that an earthquake had hit Detroit. Then, as though a train was coming right at the team from underground, asphalt buckled, slamming slabs one into another in split-second intervals. For a moment, the stunned teams couldn't move as they watched Livernois Avenue turn into what seemed like giant dominoes slamming into each other, eating up time and space between them, and then it belched open, sending flames and sulfuric embers everywhere.

What came out of the hole was instant death. Stumbling Guardians at the ready began firing. Brother Muata lifted his Glock, but was impaled before the shot rang out. The pike that tore through him whirled in a bloody, burning spiral, his youthful face frozen in torment as the pike stabbed into the bricks of a nearby building, carrying his body with it. Massive midnight stallions heaved from the open street mounted by skeletal demon warriors that raised pikes, all following the lead black horse that could have dwarfed a small dragon. Then its black-armored rider appeared from a black mist, sitting high on the creature held firm between his thickly muscled legs.

Snorting hellfire and brimstone with his mount, the cavalry's lead rider brandished a steel pike like a sword, pulling back on the reins as his horse reared wildly and released a war screech. He glanced around with a searing black gaze and snarled before bellowing out to the Guardian squads.

"Neterus!" the black-armored rider shouted. "Meet your fate at the hands of the Impaler!"

"Oh, shit," Yonnie whispered in the alley crouched beside Big Mike. "Liz raised Drac, man! I told you this wasn't no bullshit." He caught Carlos's attention in the adjacent alley and received a nod as Big Mike took aim with a shoulder launcher.

"Fuck you!" Yonnie shouted, making a mad dash along the side of a building to create a diversion.

Vlad's entire army jerked their attention to the alley just as Mike's shell released. A hail of pikes followed Yonnie and missed as he dove behind an overturned vehicle. But as Mike's shell rocketed toward the demon battalions, Vlad's horse opened its mouth, breathing fire, and detonated the hallowed earth explosive before it made it halfway across the street—sending Mike, Inez, and Rider diving for cover. A black charge to the buildings that shielded them was Vlad's answer as his steed then pawed the broken sidewalk. Patient, Vlad waited, holding up his metal-gloved fist for his army not to advance, watching the building rubble cascade down on the trapped Guardians, and the instant a shield covered them, he reversed his charge— sending Carlos sprawling.

Pandemonium broke out in the streets. Barbara and Earl commandeered an abandoned city bus, and using Earl's tactical charge, they white lighted the skin of it and then put the pedal to the floor. Alicia was riding on top of the sidewalk-careening vehicle, her rifle picking off demons that tried to send pikes through the windows.

"They're going kamikaze!" Damali shouted, entering the street behind the bus that was playing chicken with Vlad's war-horses. "Suicide explosion! No! Get those people outta there!"

"You get outta the street, D!" Carlos shouted, jumping up and missing a pike by seconds. "Take cover!"

But the bus kept going. It had reached eighty miles an hour, and sheer momentum, along with tactical charge assistance from Earl, pushed the speedometer higher.

Every so often a pike would break out a bus window, sending glass flying like shrapnel. Navajo was right behind it in a souped-up Olds convertible, white lighted, driving insane with Candace standing and firing silver automatic rounds, blasting demon guts and sending embers into the air. But a flaming pike hit the hood of the Olds, impaled the engine, and flipped the vehicle end over end. While Carlos covered Damali, Shabazz's quick tactical snatch pulled both younger Guardians to safety before the hurling car could crush them and explode in the gas station twenty yards away.

Lissa's sure shot got a pike-wielding demon before it launched a flaming brimstone missile at Shabazz. Splattered with burning slime, they both scrambled to a new alleyway for protection, while the teams covered them. Owa, Sylvia, and Mary kept the pressure on from the south end of the boulevard, while Neteru team Guardians repositioned. But Damali and Carlos were wide open, heading down the street trying to stop the bus.

One mind—J.L., Dan, and Bobby reached out simultaneously and pulled Barbara, Earl, and Alicia to them just as the bus bomb slammed into the front line of Vlad's cavalry and detonated like a deadly roadside explosive. Demon body parts littered the ground and fell like flaming fuselage. Earl, Barbara, and Alicia hit the ground with a thud, rolling to safety behind parked cars and avoiding pikes, but within seconds were back up firing.

Craig and Gus had given up their sniper posts to run into the street daredevil-style, cranking the engines on twin detailed red and canary-yellow Mustangs, hollering to Damali and Carlos as they doubled back to avoid Vlad's heat-seeking pikes.

"Get in!" Craig shouted as the red Mustang passed Carlos. The moment it did, Craig bailed, leaving the vehicle unmanned, to drop down on the street, then turned to hit three demons in hot pursuit of him with pump shotgun shells, blowing off their heads.

Carlos was over the side of the convertible Mustang's door in a one-handed leap, falling into the seat, and then he spun out to go back for Damali.

Gus was already in motion, heading directly toward her with the yellow car eating up pavement, one hand firing a Glock, the other steering as he crossed Damali's body plane. But what happened next was a slow-motion horror. Vlad's pike whizzed by Damali's head by millimeters, caught Gus in the center of his forehead, splattering her face and shirt with Gus's brains and blood. Gus never made it out of the car. The split second of hesitation that Damali took in not simply shoving Gus's dead body aside cost her precious moments.

The yellow Mustang listed with the driver's body weight, spinning the wheel at a perilous angle. The car instantly banged her hard, slamming into her pelvis, knocking her back, sending her flying toward raised demon pikes. Every tactical on the squad sent a charge in to get her out of the road and to keep the car from running her over, as Carlos stood, driving while standing, reaching out to also move her.

It all happened so fast. Flying shells from well-meaning team members were already discharged and airborne in the demonic army's direction . . . the same direction Damali's semiconscious body was hurtling.

Bullets spiraled past her in slow motion as Carlos's hands emitted a blinding white-light carpet to burn away anything that could harm her. Shells incinerated with the flash. A third of the army melted with a screech. Vlad raised his forearm to cover his face. Bobby and Krissy sent a razor-wire of electric current like a bullwhip from utility poles and downed lines to back off a secondary wave of demon onslaught, while their parents and the rest of the Guardian team prepared for hand-to-hand combat.

Fully fanged, Yonnie and Tara had jumped out front with J.L., who had grabbed two demon pikes as he flipped into a martial arts stance. Covered by the team's sharpshooter, Rider, along with Juanita, Heather, and Jasmine, Shabazz shifted into instant jaguar, cutting a line between Vlad's army and Damali's free-falling body with a menacing roar. Candace brandished two bowie knives at Inez's flank as she unsheathed switchblades in each hand. Marlene was already running forward, magic walking stick glowing white-hot like a pike. Val was down on one knee, sending whirring silver arrows to pick off demons one by one, her targets frying on impact as Heather and Jasmine dropped to the concrete with the other Neteru seers and super-charged the ground around the squads Stonehenge-style.

For Carlos, five seconds might as well have been five minutes, it all seemed so fast, so short, so insane, so slow as his wife's body fell while he forced his car beyond the limits of its capacity by sheer will—his arms out, trying to catch Damali before another intelligent missile sought her. The moment her body thudded against his, all breath left his lungs with a hard, guttural sound. Encased in a golden shield of Heru, he secured her in the seat with the vehicle still careening forward on a collision course with a huge, spiraling pike sent from Vlad.

The entity sneered. Insanity fractured Carlos's skull. A Neteru war cry left his lungs and the next thing he knew he was on the hood of the car, traveling a hundred and twenty miles per hour, Damali unconscious . . . they had hurt his wife! A moment of hesitation filled Vlad's pitch-black eyes and just as quickly burned away. Battle bulked and too crazy to think, fangs fully extended, Carlos's arms opened wide and he slapped the center of his chest to invite the pike—which suddenly melted to black amalgam beneath his silver glare.

A black steel blade filled Vlad's hand as he roared and his horse reared. Every demon sentry behind him followed with a war cry, and began charging. A golden shield covered the car, the teams kept the pressure on, decimating Vlad's army—but the demons kept replenishing themselves from the crevices in the broken asphalt. Then all of a sudden, Vlad turned his attention away from Carlos and looked at the battling Guardian squads. Shadows suddenly filled the air and dove down into human bodies in an aerial attack. Guardians screamed out in agony.

Carlos could feel it all, see it all inside his head. He turned in slow motion to look to his flanks, between buildings, at the cars he passed in a blur, then he glimpsed behind him at Guardians writhing on the ground. Seconds ticked away. Tactical Guardians had been hit with the sensation of Hellfire burning them—

using their gift in an evil twist against them. Seers were going blind from horrific Hell scenes so powerful that they actually caused physical pain. Audio sensors were suddenly deafened by screeches at earsplitting decibels that made them puke up their guts on the street, incapacitating them and rendering them vulnerable. Anyone with a human body simply shrieked at the knifelike agony that riddled their skins.

The first image that came to Carlos's mind was the giant, white highway edifice Alicia had spoken of. There was no democracy. He jettisoned the local team there within seconds, praying that the hallowed ground would reverse their pain . . . Marlene glanced up—the agony in her mind so severe that he could barely see her face. Something in the shadows had her by the leg. Shabazz tried to get to her, roaring, naked, feral, in a twisted mid-shape-shift to save her.

"Raven's father!" Shabazz hollered through his distended jaw, as Yonnie struggled with his own pain to lend assistance.

"Follow Uriel," Damali's pearl shrieked from her necklace. "God is my light to the east! Seven miles away!"

"It's 33 East Forest," Shabazz cried out, writhing and then collapsing. "Only church with Uriel and headed east from here!"

Searing heat filled Carlos as the car slowed and he felt the life pulses of the entire Neteru team enter his palms at once. The image lit his mind like it had been stabbed with a poker. His mind became united with his destination: A one-hundred-and-twenty-foot, freestanding bell tower flash-blinded his brain for a second, then another image of an eight-foot, two-hundred-pound copper statue of the Archangel Uriel pierced his third eye. The door to the Cathedral of Pisa in Italy fused with the campanile of this church. Europe's Venice wonders became one with his fold-away destination. Rose windows swirled into carved wood, huge domes, and ceiling portraits. Organ music made his head pound. The great halls of England stared back at him as he tumbled forward with the team, Damali in his arms, to land in the sanctuary of First Congregational Church of Detroit.

Marlene was the first to recover, sputtering out her words as she held her locks in her fists, tears streaming down her face. "How could that have been Jerome? I killed him myself when he turned and went after our daughter to give her to Nuit!"

"Baby . . . he went dark," Shabazz said. "You have to accept—"

"No! I prayed over him. His soul was supposed to go into the Light. He was a Guardian!" A sob caught in Marlene's throat and broke free.

Shabazz pulled her near as Guardians slowly recovered. "Then, maybe it was just an illusion—"

"Wasn't illusion," Yonnie snapped, walking over to Carlos and peering at Damali. "He was a Guardian in name, but hated the fact that Marlene was more gifted . . . that she would have been the team's leader, the mother-seer until it was time. He wanted the role of head honcho, couldn't deal with the way things were playing out, even though it wasn't Mar's fault or intent. Jealousy got him. Pride, too. He was done before she iced him."

"How do you know?" Juanita snapped. "Mar don't need ta hear a buncha speculation right now."

"I *know* because it registers real big at dark throne level when Guardians go dark—that's why they wanted my man here, Carlos, so bad." Yonnie folded his arms. "You need to chill, sis, and check the attitude. We're all on the same squad, remember? But Marlene's man wasn't as gifted as she was, so he couldn't deal with hers, that's how he got jacked . . . didn't like being a father so soon, wasn't down with the service-to-mankind deal he got—wanted some cash, some flash . . . and one night while his dumb ass was crying in his beer, he got that. So don't tell me I don't know what happened—ain't that right, Marlene?"

Marlene nodded and wiped her face. "Don't curse in the House of God after all we've been through," she added, looking at Yonnie. "Especially all you've been through."

"It's cool, baby . . . just chill," Jose said quietly to Juanita as she snatched away from him.

"It's *not* cool, and don't tell me to chill!" Juanita shouted. "I know how he felt, then. Who wants to go through what we just went through, trying to raise a family . . . what's gonna happen months from now, Jose—tell me that?" Tears leaked from Juanita's eyes as glances of new awareness passed around the team.

But the argument sounded so far away to Carlos as he stared at his battered wife. Fury mixed with fear mixed with adrenaline mixed with outrage to create a crazy cocktail in his system as he slowly laid Damali on a pew.

"I don't care about whatever," Carlos muttered quietly, staring at Damali. "Just wake up is all I'm asking."

She was breathing; he could feel her breaths rise and fall, could see it. She wasn't bleeding, he would have known immediately, if she was. Her eyelids fluttered as he wiped off her gook-splattered face, trying to remove some of the carnage. He could also feel the ground beyond the sanctuary trembling. The dark shadows couldn't breach the fortress, but they could blow a subterranean gas main and essentially nuke the joint.

Carlos looked up with the team, watching brass chandeliers sway in the arched ceiling and altarpieces begin to slightly vibrate. Berkfield and Marlene moved in with Marjorie, prepared to begin the healing, regardless.

"Everybody pull themselves together and somebody call the Queens for my wife. Heal her." Carlos looked around, seething. "I'll be back."

PART III

SHOWDOWN

"Vlad, you mutha*fucker*!" Carlos shouted, the moment he cleared the church steps.

"Likewise!" Vlad hollered from his position across the street. "You attack my wife and expect no redress? Arrogant, young fool!"

"And there's no fool like an old fool, but I'ma teach you some new era shit tonight!" Carlos shouted, bringing the Mustang around the corner using the sheer rage that was blistering his mind.

He ducked a flaming pike as it whirred by his temple, grazing it before it disintegrated the moment it crossed the threshold of hallowed ground. Carlos punched the dashboard as he leapt over to the side of the vehicle, too furious to even sit behind the wheel. Instead he stood wide-legged, one foot on each bucket seat, a blade in one hand, shield in the other, revving the engine with his mind, and then allowed the tires to spin until they smoked against the blacktop. "You are gonna so wish you had stayed your ass up in the Carpathians—"

In a snap, both combatants charged each other, moving forward in headlong, breakneck velocities—Carlos rocketing forward in a car, Vlad on his nightmare. The blade of Ausar was clenched in Carlos's right grip as a huge burning pike filled Vlad's. At the moment of sure impact, both combatants left their mounts—the car slamming into the steed, sending the warriors airborne, twisting, as they slashed their weapons at each other, missed, and then hit the ground in a hard roll, only to jump up more enraged.

Lilith brought her head up with an angry jerk as she spied Sebastian skulking around Council Chambers. Her gaze narrowed on him, leaving the black vision mist of the pentagram-shaped table to concentrate on him for a moment. Absently she stroked the golden-fanged crest so that it would pause its replay of the action occurring topside while she studied Sebastian. A slow, annoyed growl filled her throat.

"What is it?"

"I have something for you, Madame Chairwoman."

She stared at him. He'd engaged her in *Dananu,* the bargaining language. But what, at this juncture, would Sebastian have to bargain with? Curiosity tugged at her, despite the fact that she had little time for games.

"Be swift," she commanded. "A pivotal battle rages topside."

"Indeed it does," Sebastian said, his voice oily with triumph. "I have raised the ultimate information."

"Oh, please!" Lilith said, waving him away and returning her focus to the table. "Your ex-wife raised Vlad. Every scheme you've launched has been a debacle."

"Raising Elizabeth and Lucrezia was not a debacle."

Lilith looked up and glared at him. "Speak to me, you toad, or become one!"

"I have located the Neteru prophecy child . . . the one that can avert the loss of one-third of the earth's population during the Armageddon, as told in their holy Kemetian scrolls of Sebek and in the lost books of their Bible."

When Lilith became stone-still and stopped breathing, Sebastian nodded and smiled.

"You lie," Lilith whispered.

"No . . . not this time," Sebastian said with triumph. "It was so easy and I must thank Vlad and Elizabeth for creating the perfect diversion."

"How?" Lilith said, her excitement barely concealed as she swept toward Sebastian, rounding the black bargaining table.

"The female mother-seer had an Achilles' heel. The father of her only child was a Guardian but became one of ours . . . and on that day she slew him with her walking stick to his chest in a domestic dispute. But his head was never severed by a Neteru blade." Sebastian circled Lilith, rubbing his hands as he spoke in rapid bursts of excitement. "I knew something was amiss when the entire team went into hiding. The stench of human pregnancies filled the air as Vlad battled and it was hard to tell which one . . . so many of the female Guardians gave off the aroma." He closed his eyes and leaned his head back, inhaling deeply. "Decoys. Instinct said if that many were surrounding the female, and the males had gone into complete suicide attack mode . . . then they were protecting something extremely precious."

He swept away from her and rushed to the table, causing her to nearly run behind him to keep up as he pointed to the black mist. "Look at him, Lilith. There's your evidence! The male Neteru left his wife inside a white-hot cathedral that is impenetrable with an entire team to take on Vlad and his entire army alone!"

"Unbelievable . . . Mr. Rivera, where did you find the time?" Lilith murmured, her hand over her dead heart as she stared at Sebastian and then into the mist. "But we must know for sure, before I report mission-critical news like this to our Dark Lord."

"My raised essence of soul-stolen Guardian, in demon form, touched the mother-seer . . . felt her panic over the loss of her potential grandchild," Sebastian said, making small quotes in the air as he said the word *grandchild*. "My demon siphoned it all from the Guardian, Marlene Stone—every single panicked thought that she telegraphed. The moment Damali hit the ground and didn't immediately get back up, the older woman sent out SOS radiating prayers of white heat. Go back in the mist's record," he ordered, causing the captured scenes to reverse to the point where Damali's body collided with the runaway vehicle.

"Look at the blue-white heat waves radiating from the mother-seer who was on the ground already . . . watch them wash over the female Neteru." Using his long index finger, he craned it toward the dark, vaporous mist. "Look at the charge that explodes from the male Neteru to wash over her and to keep all falling debris from her. Then look at the murderous response in his eyes that gave even Vlad a second of pause."

Lilith leaned in and studied the slow-motion, frame-by-frame image of Vlad's expression. "Absolutely amazing."

"Does Carlos Rivera seem the least bit afraid of his fate at that moment?" Sebastian paced as he spoke, counting off evidence on his fingers. "Also look at the male Guardians. There's no human sense of self-preservation within them. They are functioning from the purely reptilian segment of their brains, down to the R-complex . . . which is a very dangerous thing, but also a very advantageous thing to exploit."

Lilith nodded. "Dangerous indeed." She stroked the tension away from her temples. "This means angels will be involved." Her gaze shot toward the table. "But if this is true, then why haven't the ancestral Neterus come to her aid or the angels simply shown up to protect her?"

"Could it be they're deployed in a search-and-destroy mission seeking your heir?"

"Or," Lilith murmured, lost in thought as she stroked her chin, "they must know that a premature, heavy-handed show of force by their side would tip us off. It is still human, this prophecy child, and as such must navigate the vagaries of fate on the earth plane in order to be born. It doesn't get a free ride. Interesting."

"While Elizabeth is fighting the Neterus with Vlad . . . and Lucrezia and Nuit are raising the Antichrist's war chest, replacing the recent incalculable losses that their territories just sustained, we could raise the pale horse of the Apocalypse. We could do this while no one, not even the Neterus, would be aware."

For a moment, Lilith simply stared at Sebastian.

"At the end of the battle in the Greek isles to protect the heir," Sebastian said coolly, "their side raised the black stallion that shall harm not the oil or the wine . . . but that is the last one that they can alone raise—the next one is our pawn . . . remember that for balance, in a sense of Divine equity and just after the Dark Lord's fall during the Big Bargain we were given access to two horses at the end of days to use to tip the scales, true?"

"Yes . . . it is true," Lilith said in a faraway voice.

"Ah, but you have rightly been focused on the healing and development of the heir in his hidden North American caverns beneath Washington, D.C. However, I beg you not to overlook this opportunity, Lilith. We get to raise the pale horse, then their side can break the fifth biblical seal . . . which will give them access to bring back the souls of all those slain and martyred— even those stolen from Dante's infernal Book of the Damned."

"Hence the reason the release of the pale horse is not to be taken lightly by our side. That would give the Light the edge to possibly annihilate us with all those—"

"Think of it though, Lilith," Sebastian said quickly, cutting her off in his excitement. "We have a chance that allows our Dark Lord to raise the pale horse of human plagues. It is what we've been waiting for. And if there is a plague upon the land, after Lucrezia's and Nuit's shadows poisoning through the airwaves, the babies will die. Even the Neteru Guardian team, and even the Neterus, had been weakened by sustaining the poison for a time . . . their females, if carrying, will not be able to fight off the pandemic outbreak wielded by the pale horse."

"We must be careful with that one, though," Lilith warned. "The heir is still healing and has human code in his DNA . . . it came through the pollution of Cain's seed merged with my husband's . . . and while I'm sure my ova and the Dark Lord's seed cast a dominant darkness around his immune system, we must still take care."

"Understood," Sebastian offered, but undaunted, pressed on. "Do remember, however, what it says in the texts; *the rider was named Death, and Hades was following close behind him*." Sebastian spun and clasped his hands together. "We *are* Death. That is *our* rider. Our province. Hades *is* Hell . . . our armies. The pale horse, as it states even in their tomes, was given power over one-fourth of the earth to kill by sword, famine, plague, and by wild beasts of the earth. No child will escape the plagues, death, Hell, and destruction that our fallen angels of the Apocalypse release. Our heir will be a fully matured male when he finally awakens from his chrysalis state. That compared to a human Neteru baby that will take twenty-one years to come into its own. If our plagues don't get it, how long can they run? How long can they hide? Even if we kill the Guardians' progeny, missing the Neteru child, it would decimate their team's morale, make them sloppy . . . and from there it is only a matter of time."

Sebastian opened his arms in an impassioned plea. "Lilith,

even after the Light breaks that next seal to release their saints in a retaliatory strike, the chess move comes back to us again to break the sixth seal. We still retain the upper hand. The great earthquake—"

"Where the sun turned black like sackcloth made of goat hair, the whole moon turned bloodred, and the stars in the sky fell to earth," Lilith murmured, warming to the idea and finishing Sebastian's scriptural quote.

"A fitting coronation for your heir."

The two demons stared at each other once more.

Lilith inclined her head ever so slightly, her eyes glowing black. "Your proposal has significant merit. Let me think about it."

Hand-to-hand combat met black magic steel against Neteru blade. An elbow to Carlos's jaw opened him up to swing range as he stumbled back for a second, but then he severed Vlad's pike in half with a double-handed blow from his sword. Pikes coming at his back from Vlad's demon forces made Carlos duck and pivot to avoid being fatally impaled. Vlad had to quickly throw up a black-box to avoid fire from his own troops.

"Siege the citadel!" Vlad ordered, pointing to the cathedral. "Leave him to me!"

"We can't, milord! It is impossible to get near the gas and power lines under it," one of his demon captains shouted back. "Everything below the fortress is white-hot."

Clearly fearing retaliation for being unable to fulfill the command, the demon pointed a human-draped pike toward the large copper statue of the archangel that guarded the bell tower. "This is Uriel's—"

A lightning bolt cut through the sky before the archangel's name had left the demon's lips, simultaneously smiting the demon to ash as it lit the huge copper statue. The statue's eyes glowed with white fury, and from that unflinching glare, a crackling white envelope of protection sealed the cathedral.

"Seize the infidel to our dark empire!"

In the three seconds it took for Vlad to bark out his command, Carlos had fallen back to his vehicle and begun sending white-light pulses from the tip of his blade to the holdout position Vlad's army had taken on top of neighboring buildings, exploding demons everywhere he could see. Vlad called his injured stallion to him, pulled three innocents through the glass of an office building, and flung them to his nightmare creature.

"Feed!" Vlad ordered, watching Carlos grapple with trying to keep his demon army away from the perimeter of office buildings, while also trying to fight against his black shield to get to the screaming humans being cannibalized by his stallion. Vlad threw his head back and laughed as the horse disemboweled a man that was still alive, and then snapped off the head of a terror-stricken, shrieking woman. "That is what my army will do to your Guardians the moment we find a weakness in that fortress—and know that all human domains, even those perched upon hallowed ground, have a weakness in the end of days!"

Choices contracted within Carlos's mind. Something very fragile within him snapped as he looked at the three dead bodies on the ground being consumed. Demons had begun sacking the buildings around them to feed and replenish their fallen warriors. The images of human carnage haunted him in the tense few seconds as windows exploded out to the street, the sounds of screams pierced the air, and bat-winged, skeletal creatures began to feast. It was the battle of Nod happening all over again, but this time on the earth plane.

Sickened by what he witnessed, a charge filled Carlos's hands, but when he released it, what came from his fingertips was a fury-filled black charge that sliced through Vlad's shields and knocked him off his mount.

"I *told you* that *tonight* I'd had e-*fucking*-nuff!" Carlos yelled, and then sent his vehicle forward, standing on the seats and riding it like a surfboard up the side of the building in a crazed zigzag pattern, heading for Vlad. Plate-glass windows exploded under the screeching tires; demons lifted their heads from their victims and temporarily stopped feeding. Carlos threw his head back and released another Neteru battle cry, but this time as a blinding white-light charge left the tip of the blade he held in his right hand, a pure black charge of dark power tore from his left hand.

"They used to call *me* the Chairman, bitch!" Carlos shouted, sending alternating black and white pulse mortars at Vlad, whose shields wouldn't hold against the onslaught.

In a rare display of uncertainty, Vlad glanced around at his thinned troops and called them to safety.

"Retreat!"

But no sooner than the word had left Vlad's fanged mouth, Carlos sent a combined black-and-white charge to blanket the ground around them for a mile.

"If you're gonna go to Hell tonight, then let's go together, motherfucker!"

Vlad leapt toward his crippled stallion, which had not yet regenerated from the Mustang collision. A white-light charge from the tip of Carlos's blade instantly entered through the creature's eyes and exploded its head, leaving flaming reins in Vlad's hands. Demons that surrounded him immediately paid the ultimate price, melting and bursting into flames from Carlos's silver glare as he dashed toward Vlad like a man possessed.

Through a splinter of night, a thick black cloud of transporter bats emerged and swarmed, forming a hissing, screeching tornadolike funnel to collect Vlad. Hurling debris, cars, street signs, and anything not firmly secured into Carlos's path, the swirling manifestation surrounded Vlad and then took off, heading deeper into the heavily populated area of downtown Detroit.

Beyond fury or sanity, Carlos became a white-light blur behind the dark funnel cloud, closing in on it as it ate up asphalt and flung debris in its wake. Attempting to knock Carlos off course when the debris didn't deter him, a retinue of brave but foolish bats defected from the cloud and dove at Carlos, only to fall to the ground screeching and burning from his silver sight.

Gaining momentum, the dark twister lifted above street level, moving like a horizontal cone along the People Mover monorail—the wide top end of the funnel sucking in power from the rails, siphoning in bodies from the train cars to strengthen and feed the demons, and then jettisoning metal and gore behind it.

Clarity came to Carlos in the form of a quiet place in the midst of the fury . . . a place that he'd never found before. There was no noise, no time, no forward thrusting velocity, even though his body was traveling almost at the speed of light. He could see another train car in harm's way just ahead of the ravenous funnel.

Carlos reached out his hands, abandoning his blade. The blade of Ausar fell between the fabric of the universe and the power from it leapt into both palms. A ball of black light fused with the white light that shot from his hands, creating a thick energy rope that instantly wound around the bottom tip of the funnel cloud. Then the time-space differential snapped back into real time the moment he yanked on the cord.

Demon bats fell out of the funnel's centrifugal orbit. Vlad crashed hard on the People Mover rails in a sliding collision as the combatants entered Cobo Center Station. Battle-frenzied, disoriented bats screeched and flew at humans, smashing the plate-glass windows leading into the convention center while

Vlad and Carlos began a low altitude flight chase through the glass-and-chrome structure.

Vendors dove for cover, workers and tourists scattered, as the two missilelike forms rocketed past them, ripping up carpet, scorching the air, busting out glass panels, and upending furniture from the sonic boom shock waves of their energy signatures.

But concern for collateral damage slowed Carlos's roll. It also tapped his dwindling energy reserves as he soft-flung people out of harm's way, and shielded the innocent from exploding glass and twisted metal as he passed civilians while trying to stay on Vlad's tail.

Reality warred with his conscience; he had to get Vlad out of the building before there was enough structural damage to bring it crashing down on thousands of innocent people.

In a partial ruse, Carlos momentarily slowed enough to come out of an energy whirl, panting, wiping silver sweat from his silver-soaked body. The hint of vulnerability was all he needed to reverse the chase and to get Vlad to come after him.

Bursting through the glass-and-chrome doors, Carlos allowed himself to be pursued by the enraged entity, crossing the pristine white concrete that led to Hart Plaza. A wide circular fountain on one side of him and with the Detroit River in sight, he knew he could battle away from the population density of office buildings and possibly pull Vlad into the water while chanting a blessing to holy water fry him. But the moment he swerved his course toward the riverbank, Vlad veered off, blowing away traffic along Woodward Avenue then careening toward the Detroit-Windsor tunnel that would take him into Canada.

Carlos didn't need to see more; he knew where Vlad was headed. If he got to Nuit's Toronto offices, another refreshed army awaited. But in Vlad's immediate path were motorists who'd be trapped in an inferno as black Hellfire scorched the tunnel entrance. It would take all of his power to send instant cooling and fire retardant into the opening behind Vlad, who was using the innocent as body-shields.

In a quick fold-away, Carlos came out on the other side of the tunnel and hovered right in Vlad's path. The sounds of car accidents, multiple collisions set his teeth on edge and jarred his skeleton, but he had to stop this threat.

The impact of Vlad slamming into Carlos almost flattened him. But fury and old street ball made the contact flip into a tackle, ending with Carlos's hands around Vlad's throat in the middle of the highway.

Black charge cracked down Vlad's arms as his hands also found Carlos's neck. But the silver glare that raked Vlad's face made him cry out and cover the burns with his palms. Both warriors struggled to knock the other off balance, using their legs as weapons in the vicious dance. Razor-sharp, talon-edged bat wings exploded through Vlad's armor to stab into Carlos's shoulders and a spaded tail whipped out from Vlad's spine to drive itself into one of Carlos's kidneys. Carlos bellowed from the pain and arched, but didn't let go of Vlad's throat, reveling in triumph as his silver-saturated blood began to incinerate any appendage that molested him.

"How you like me now, bitch?" Carlos said through his teeth as Vlad scrabbled at his throat. "Go ahead, put your thumbs in my eyes, open up a jugular with your fangs, get all up in my silver shit and watch your ass get neutered one appendage at a time!"

Battle-length fangs filled Carlos's mouth as he turned Vlad's head to the side to deliver the ultimate vampire indignity—dethroated by an adversary with longer fangs.

"After I rip out your throat, Count, your head by the Neteru blade is mine."

The chime of his sword filled the air at the same time Carlos released his right hand to have the searing heat of the weapon fill it. Injured and exhausted from the battle and chase, Vlad struggled—but a millisecond movement of his eyes made Carlos drop him, spin away, and allow Elizabeth to gore him with a black blade.

A black charge hit both Vlad and Elizabeth, hurtling them backward before Carlos could think. It was instinct sparked by fury. Nuit opened a section of night with Lucrezia and quickly dragged the injured couple through it. However, before he could completely shut the dark portal, Carlos sent several combined mortars into it.

The earth belched out huge international messenger demons with barrel chests, straight from the Vampire Council on Level Six. Blade swinging, crazier than crazy, Carlos took the rush as he took heads, the new onslaught actually giving him energy rather than depleting it.

But the sudden urge to feed from the gore sobered him. He was getting lost in the memory, had to follow the fast-moving red-glowing pulse point on the ground. Carlos spun and took off, his eyes on the ground as his body again became a blur with scythe-wielding messenger demons in hot pursuit. Suddenly he was in a tunnel, underground, but not in Hell. Disoriented he slowed, looked around, and to his horror he was in an underground mall beneath the city of Toronto!

Humans were everywhere. The potential for catastrophic losses made him surface, breathing hard, dirty, sweating, injured, and gore-stained. Carlos turned and simply looked at the few straggling demons that had chased him this far, incinerating them, and finally began to feel the deep stabs to his shoulders along with the kidney injury.

His palm went to the wound site on his back, and came away with thick, silvery-red warmth. But the beacon had stopped.

Carlos smiled and stared up at the massive building. He was

standing in front of CGE's Toronto headquarters . . . a gorgeous modern glass structure that he was so tempted to implode, were it not for the very real loss of human life that would occur. Instead, with his last ounce of energy and before Nuit's forces rallied to attack, he simply white lighted it from the roof down to the gas mains beneath the street, chuckling as demons fried while bailing out of windows . . . then dropped from sheer exhaustion.

Damali opened her eyes and sat up with a gasp, toppling Marlene and Berkfield. "I have to go get him!"

"He said—"

"He's in an enemy hot-zone, Marlene! I don't care what he said!"

"You were just out for twenty frickin' minutes, D," Berkfield argued. "And in your condition—"

Damali pointed at Berkfield to say no more, but didn't speak. Her eyes said everything. She took a breath and composed herself. "I'm going to get him."

"No need," Carlos said, staggering into the sanctuary, "Seth and Abel gave me a lift."

"You look terrible!" Damali said quickly, going to him. "What happened?"

"I'm all right," Carlos replied, weaving a bit and catching himself against a pew. "Better question is, what happened to you?" He looked at her hard, studying her eyes and then let his voice drop to a tone of gentle concern. "Tell me you're all right, boo?"

"She is," Marlene said, jerking Carlos's focus to her. "Open a channel to me while Berkfield works on you—you look like Hell."

Carlos nodded and half fell, half sat on a pew. Berkfield simply shook his head as he studied the wounds for a moment. But when Damali came close, Carlos yelled at her with a wince.

"Back up—you know better than that! I don't even want the Caduceus near me if you're touching it."

"But you've got a serious kidney wound, Carlos," Damali shot back. "You broke team protocol, left out on a suicide mission—what if you'd been gored out there or are bleeding to death! What if the ancient Neterus were battling darkside forces and couldn't get to you in time? Obviously, they and the angels were elsewhere while we were scraping over on Livernois Avenue."

The need to feed was almost as excruciating as the wounds. He couldn't answer her immediately, had to breathe through the agony, suddenly realizing that by allowing his dark side to surface for added strength, that bonus dividend came with a severe price in the recovery process.

"Just back up," Carlos muttered, not wanting her to know about the black charges his hands had unloaded on Vlad. "No Caduceus or Neteru angel wing healings. I'm cool. It ain't that bad. I got two kidneys and they only got one . . . wasn't like it was my heart—which it would have been if something had happened to you. So, we do this old-school healing method, 'cause I've just been in a demon free-for-all. What's the matter with you?"

Carlos closed his eyes as Marlene laid a palm on his forehead.

"You ready to open a channel?" Marlene asked as the rest of the team glanced between both Neterus with curiosity.

"Yeah," Carlos breathed out in pain as Damali began to walk in a circle, biting her lip as her fingers laced on top of her head.

*I immediately called Aset for a healing and to send me the Caduceus to help her. Berkfield was scanning, but he couldn't find anything wrong. There were no internal injuries, no hemorrhages. Aset finally answered and said Damali didn't need the healing staff of Imhotep—the fetus shut her down. Right now she's got a newly formed silver-and-platinum layer shielding her entire pelvic region.*

"What!" Carlos struggled to sit up, but Berkfield flat-palmed him.

"Easy, buddy. You gotta get better . . . so lemme work while Mar informs, deal?"

Marlene looked around the team, making up a flimsy excuse for such a rude and blatant telepathic exchange. "We're in a cathedral, brother needs to tell me stuff to flash to the other seers, but we don't need to take chances by saying any forbidden names."

Begrudgingly, Carlos leaned back down, his gaze riveted to Marlene's. She'd told the team the truth, but with some serious omissions along with it. But it worked. Bodies around him began to slowly relax, even though no one took their eyes off Marlene's stoic expression.

*When the black charge sent the car into her . . . oh, yeah, it slammed her hard, all right.* Marlene never blinked as her mind sent off a rapid-fire flurry of information that made Carlos's eyelids flutter. *But the jolt, along with the adrenaline, made the baby spike something within its system that flooded hers. That effectively shut her down . . . made her stop battling this early in her first trimester— which both Aset and Ausar said would make you go nuts. You are the one at this early stage, they said, who needs to draw the heat. Later, she'll be back in business . . . but for now, you've got some kinda crazy thing time-releasing in your body that's ridiculous.*

"Tell me about it," Carlos said, too weary to respond telepathically. He glanced around the rapt team and then tried to focus on Marlene, while ignoring the pain shooting through him from Berkfield's ministrations. But his attention kept drifting to Damali.

"I'm all right," she said softly. "Just a little scared, but I'm cool."

Again, teammates shared confused glances that Marlene tried to body-block from Carlos's view as she redirected his focus.

*We've got three definite pregnancies on this team, in addition to your wife's.* Marlene closed her eyes for a moment and let out a hard breath. *Eve said these aren't decoys . . . so before you go there in your mind like I did . . . given what happened to my own daughter, know that it's a sacred number. This situation we're in now is different than what happened years and years ago.* Marlene paused. *Your child will have three Guardian protectors from birth . . . with a fourth mother-seer . . . little Ayana.*

"Seriously . . ." Pure awe filled Carlos's voice as it trailed off and his jaw went slack.

*Yeah,* Marlene said in a quick mental whisper. *Seriously. Your kid has a serious burden to carry in the future . . . I'll tell you about the prophecy in a bit. But the ancients didn't want Berkfield to know, on account that he has a grandchild on the way and he could have started to think negative thoughts about his daughter's baby being sacrificed for yours—when it's not like that.*

*Oh, man, Mar . . . this could get really twisted . . . really set the team back years in healing and cohesive strength. Can't be no dissention at this point, Mar. One team, one mind, we've gotta stand strong to face what's out there.*

*Precisely . . . if not handled right we could revert to old, unproductive behaviors that will indeed be the end of us if we do. But now that the cat is halfway out of the bag, who knows what the Queens will say about telling everybody else? But truth be told, this secret is wearing me out.* Marlene let out another hard exhalation and glanced at Berkfield. "How you doing, buddy?" Marlene asked, trying to cover for the sigh.

"Working on the man," Berkfield said, sweating and panting through a surge. "But I sure wish he wouldn't get so busted up then come to me."

Marlene returned her gaze to Carlos. *He found out when he scanned Damali to help her . . . his hands felt another pulse, felt another energy as he touched her pelvic area to try to stop whatever internal bleeding she might have had. There was nothing I could do. But the Queens didn't want anyone prematurely told because the information could have been siphoned and used by the darkside . . . and the others who are carrying on the team might also panic, thinking their child would be an expendable decoy.* Marlene shook her head. *In these end of days, our side will not be using babies as cannon fodder, Carlos, believe that.*

"That's good to know," Carlos said, releasing a weary breath and finally relaxing for the first time since they'd left San Diego. *But it's still a lot on everybody's head . . . I mean, aren't most Guardian teams made up of seven warriors around a Neteru?*

*Yeah,* Marlene said again, this time giving Carlos a quizzical glance before she looked at Damali.

*Do the math,* Carlos mentally replied with his eyes closed. *If 'Nita, Krissy, and Heather make three, plus we got 'Nez's little girl, making four . . . it's only a matter of time before we're looking at Val and Jasmine.*

"Oh, my God," Marlene accidentally whispered aloud. "You are so right."

Marlene's statement made Guardians look from her to Carlos then toward Damali as though observing a fast-paced pickup basketball game in the park.

*But that's only six,* Damali mentally shouted, butting into the conversation she'd been listening to so far without comment.

*Don't count Tara out,* Carlos said flatly, turning his head to look at Damali squarely. *She might be in her forties, but what dat mean? Stranger things have happened. Yonnie and me are alive, so's Tara, for that matter. If the Great Divine wants something to go a certain way, you know that's the way it's gonna go.*

"Oh, my God . . ." Damali murmured, her hand going to her mouth.

"Yeah," Carlos said, vindicated as he felt his body beginning to heal. "So gimme a break for going after Dracula solo. *That's* why I was out there like a madman. End of story."

Lilith never looked up from the black mist in the center of the council table as Nuit and Lucrezia helped a badly beaten Vlad to his throne. Nuit caught Elizabeth by her waist as she stumbled forward, trying to make it to a goblet of blood. Thick bruises covered Elizabeth's torso from the hard white-light charge that Carlos had hurled at her. Had it not been for Nuit's shield, her heart would have exploded out of her back onto the highway.

Lucrezia hurriedly filled a goblet and then rushed over to bring it to Vlad's lips. Nuit materialized one in his fist and lifted Elizabeth's head so she could feed.

Both councilmen regarded each other warily—weakness in the dark empire was a direct threat to one's existence.

"He is not so easy to kill, after all . . . *oui, mon ami?*"

Vlad snarled at Nuit, but didn't answer as he regarded Elizabeth's bruised upper body.

"You were fortunate," Nuit chided in *Dananu*. "But we respected your decision to war under the incentive of passion. But I have lost more than a limb to the man . . . therefore, next time, let us be more strategic in our approach. We should combine forces."

Vlad's gaze narrowed. "So be it," he replied in gravelly *Dananu*.

"Where is Sebastian?" Lucrezia asked, her gaze on Lilith's back.

"He had a proposal for my husband," Lilith said without looking up from the mist.

Silence strangled the members of council for long minutes, then Lilith lifted her intense gaze from the black mist and smiled. She surveyed Vlad's ragged condition and chuckled.

"Oh, yeah . . . Sebastian was right this time. The male Neteru flipped out and kicked your ass."

"I will avenge this dishonor!" Vlad slammed his goblet down on the arm of his throne and struggled to stand.

"No, you won't," Lilith said coolly. "At least not right away."

"I will have my vengeance. As soon as I have regenerated I will seek them out and exterminate them all! Why will you refuse my request for the dispatch of immediately replenished resources?"

Lilith wagged her finger at him, making a little tsking sound with her tongue. "Because it's bigger than you being pissed off and your ego being bruised. Simply said, the female Neteru is pregnant."

# CHAPTER THIRTEEN

He had to get out of the wheelchair. He *would* get out of the wheelchair! There was just too much to do before he simply gave in to the Devil, rolled over, and died. Not as long as there was breath left in his body. He would spit in the entity's eye with his last gasp if it came to that, and it was now, more so than ever, his life goal to thwart Lucifer at every turn. He just needed more information, the right clues to locate his unholy heir . . .

Of the fourteen books of the Septuagint, eleven were accepted in the Roman Catholic canon. Some of the clues to where the Antichrist would next appear had to thus be in the books of the Apocrypha. At this juncture, none of the faiths on the planet could afford to neglect the works of the ancient texts simply for political reasons. Why weren't the books he needed, the research materials that were vital to assisting the cardinal and ultimately the pontiff he'd been asked to protect, here then? He needed a decent library that housed obscure texts!

The fact that each faith was still feuding over semantics and whose doctrine came first or was more valid rankled him no end . . . and why his own hierarchy still refused to recognize the basis of it all coming from Kemet was beyond his comprehension. Moses even studied in Egypt where the forty-two laws of

Ma'at were in force prior to the Ten Commandments. Why did the truth threaten people? The Darkness could only be defeated by the Light of the truth—and the truth was knowledge in its purest form, which was in turn power. The darkside had mastered burying the truth with lies and illusion and human infighting . . . didn't people understand!

The elderly cleric briefly closed his eyes; the urge to yell out was so compelling. Tools, guidance, help from the angels . . . Divine intervention had been given to humankind in many forms since the beginning. Even the stars foretold truths, and Kemet's science of the stars, along with that of the Chinese and Mayans, was accurate down to predicting when Pluto—the planet of death and endings—would collide with the galactic center, spelling unparalleled change. Last year, it hit . . . and since then, the end of days spiral had begun.

And, yet, with all that he knew as a Templar, he was bound to a damned wheelchair! If the angels wanted him to help avert the crisis that was quickly bearing down on humanity, then why would they leave him disabled? It didn't make sense. There was no logic to this at all.

He couldn't get to his secret Templar locations where unabridged texts and invaluable, original scrolls were hidden, because that would divulge and endanger centuries-old secrets—that would require breaking his vows. At his age, after all he'd endured throughout his life without wavering from his commitment to the brotherhood, death was a better option than such forfeiture. Yet it was also impossible to even access the abridged Masonic lodge libraries because they weren't on sacred ground . . . and his personal safety was an issue with those who so-called nursed him. Adding insult to injury, his requests for certain texts were met with skeptical optimism.

That's why there was no other way. He would walk again, would be self-reliant, would get what he needed for himself, and *would not* remain a captive of frightened men! Time was evaporating while his shortsighted clerical brethren quibbled about where he should search for information!

Father Patrick stared out of the leaded, beveled glass windows of the seminary, pure outrage causing tears of frustration to fill his eyes. The night had become his enemy, too, holding him hostage inside a diocesan facility like a child. Yes, he was an old man—but he was still a warrior! The doctors could find no true physical cause for his sudden infirmity. Therefore, it was purely spiritual in nature and he refused to be confined at this important hour. His mission was clear.

Once strong hands, turned feeble by the ultimate demon attack, gripped the arms of the wheelchair. Trembling biceps gave out under his unsuccessful attempt to stand. His mind was so able and yet his body now bitterly betrayed him. But he would not give up, not ever.

Didn't those in the healing profession who surrounded him understand how maddening it was to be like this now after all his years of personal independence? Each day had been the same; the seemingly endless passage of time that folded into the nights that he'd only recently learned to fear. But this night would be different. He'd decided that as he'd opened his eyes in the morning and, as usual, it had been necessary to call a nurse to help him with something as profoundly private as maneuvering to use the bathroom.

He no longer wanted to hear platitudes regarding his past accomplishments from Rabbi Zeitloff or Imam Asula, no matter how much he loved them or they him. Couldn't his fellow Covenant brethren understand how it felt to have critical work to do, but to be trapped in a body that didn't function?

Monk Lin's patient counsel suddenly came into focus as fatigue got the better of him. Just like he had to stop struggling in the wheelchair right now, Lin had said that he had to stop warring with his condition, stop the rage, and use it to his advantage. How was that possible? If God would simply grant him the wisdom . . .

A prayer of humility found its way inside Father Patrick's embattled mind. *Oh, Lord, use me as your vessel in whatever way You deem fit . . . I surrender to Your will. What, Lord, would you have me do to protect your people?*

As the words filled his mind, sudden peace followed, consuming all the questions and doubts that had plagued him for months. Rage gave way to clear discernment, and from that grew a strategy that made him smile.

"The darkside thinks I am an old man and an easy link to siphon," the cleric said aloud to the Divine presence he felt. "Then let them take a dose of poison from me."

"Yes, let them drink from your vessel a bitter elixir," a gentle, disembodied voice said. "Just as I led Enoch and promised him, they may hide your stories, disguise your witness, but your truth will be known in time. There are many ways to fight the unholy."

Tears streamed down Father Patrick's face. "Uriel?" he whispered, bowing where he sat and crossing himself.

"Yes," the voice said, growing in strength as a warm golden light surrounded the priest. "The children's most precious of secrets have been divulged. . . . Templar, you above all your brethren know the power of secrets and when such tender shoots of a new harvest in the garden of men must be protected. Tuck these knowings back into hiding by not hiding yourself. Let the Darkness move within you, claiming victory and knowledge, but we will plant that which they seek within you, corrupted, and shall take back that knowledge from the unclean, which we must reclaim through our clean vessel and servant—you. Have faith in this final hour, knowing that you have provided our side with the most profound of gifts . . . you have been a warrior to the end and you have not failed your mission."

The angelic presence was gone as quickly as it had spoken, but the warmth and peace it emanated remained. Father Patrick smiled as he looked out of the window, staring across the street from the huge Gothic building made of stone to the more modern Lankanau Hospital just across the busy road. His hands found new strength, but this time he didn't fight his wheelchair to escape it. Steady palms moved his wheels forward and he discovered the surprising ability to open his private room door. The long corridor didn't dissuade him, nor did navigating the eerily vacant environs to find the elevator make him turn back.

There was no fear as he silently waited for the lit button to signal and the elevator doors to open. He was a warrior and would be till the end. There was no second-guessing the archangel's request for him to have faith. The personal visitation was an honor of a lifetime. No matter the outcome, he'd been told to stop hiding so the angels could use him as a vessel. His path had been cleared—the normal security guards, nursing staff, and seminary personnel were divinely nowhere to be found.

Giddy with awe, Father Patrick chuckled to himself at the so-called coincidence . . . there was no such thing as coincidence, everything in Heaven and earth was divinely orchestrated by a master plan.

Blind faith propelled him from the sanctuary of hallowed ground down the handicapped access ramps and along the extensive network of driveways on the moonless night. The humid air felt good on his face, just as the vision of his long-dead wife opening her arms made him weep with joy. He'd missed her so . . . she and his son had been the cornerstone of his previous life before his vows, and she'd come back. *She understood.* She was proud of him; her gentle smile said all had been forgiven.

Although his son's suicide had scarred them all, the two people he'd loved most in the world waved at him from just across Lancaster Avenue. His beloved wife and son had come to see him. His hands were steady on his wheels, propelling him forward, off the pavement, and over the curb as his heart burst with indescribable joy.

He never even felt the impact of the bus.

"No!" Carlos shouted, leaping up off the pew and almost toppling Berkfield.

"I'm sorry, I'm sorry," Berkfield said quickly, pulling back his hands. "I was trying to do the healing without hurting you, man."

"Forget the damned healing!" Carlos shouted. "Just get off me!"

"It's his third eye," Damali said gently to Berkfield. "It's not what you did; it's what he just saw."

Guardians rushed over, panicked, literally holding their breaths as they waited for Carlos to reveal what had stabbed into his third eye. But Damali knew. The team watched in horror as she covered her face with her hands and doubled over as though she'd been punched in the gut.

"*Madre d' Dios,* they finally did it!" Carlos walked in circles for several seconds, holding his skull as silver tears glittered in his eyes, unable to even put words to the tragedy.

"What's up, man?" Shabazz said, rushing forward even closer with the others as the Guardians pummeled Carlos for answers with rapid-fire questions.

"Talk to us, man," Yonnie said, beginning to pace. "What's the deal?"

Jose briefly glanced at J.L. before looking at Carlos. "Is it incoming? We gotta leave the church? You got another sanctuary on lock?"

"How bad, dude?" Rider asked, checking the magazine on his weapon.

"Whatever it is, bro . . . you know how we do. Spit it out," Big Mike barked, his nerves snapping under the pressure of anticipation.

Damali and Marlene hung back. Marlene closed her eyes and Damali hugged herself.

"Give the man some space," Damali said, her quiet voice strangely cutting through the din.

All eyes went to Damali as Carlos strode down the center aisle toward the altar, battle bulking as he went.

"*He* had a reason," Damali shouted behind Carlos. "Baby, don't you go up to that altar and reverse your entire life in a fit of rage—you hear me! Not now! I need you, this team needs you! If the Light let it happen, the Almighty had a reason. Have faith."

"What reason could be good enough to allow a Philadelphia city bus to crush an old man—a priest!" Carlos yelled, becoming hysterical as he spun on Damali and pointed toward her and then slapped the center of his chest. "My father-seer! *Compasión,* Jesus!"

"Oh, God, no," Juanita murmured as team members all slumped, hung their heads, and wept.

"This is why I *never* make snap decisions in a fit of panic or passion," Lucifer said with a smug, dangerous half smile as he regarded Sebastian.

Sebastian watched blood and gore drip from his Dark Lord's hands as he palmed a small replica of the earth for a moment and then tossed it to Sebastian.

"It . . . it . . . was irrefutable information, milord," Sebastian said nervously, and then quickly caught the energy globe as it slammed against his chest, cracking bone. "We siphoned her mother-seer . . . and—"

"And *forgot* that during the end of days," Lucifer said evenly, "angels are particularly afoot, trying to throw us off the trail of their heirs, using devious and diabolical ruses that I must confess often rival my own. If you had walked the earth to and fro as long as I have, you would have known."

The Unnamed One's eyes burned with black Hellfire, but his form remained normalized. Rather than the huge beast that he could turn into when thoroughly enraged, he was still just majestically tall and athletically proportioned by human dimensions and standards. There were no bat wings, cloven hooves, horns, or spaded tail yet. He was still wearing a business suit as he slowly rose from his throne.

Sebastian dropped to his knees with a plea for mercy in his eyes. His Dark Lord's response was to walk over and grab a fistful of Sebastian's sweaty hair to yank his head back.

"The only reason I have not given in to my first impulse to rip out your spine and feed it to my favorite Hellhound, Cerberus, for coming down here and attempting a bargain with me for power enough to match Vlad—by trying to pawn off faulty information as your wager—is because this was the treachery of an archangel. Had it been a normal angel, your ignorance would have offended me . . . but Uriel and I go way back in our disputes. I should have known his hand was involved in this when I first granted you an audience."

"Master of all that is evil . . . I meant no disrespect," Sebastian whispered, trembling, his knees frying on the searing cavern floor.

"Of course you didn't. But as we are all well aware, the road to *my door* was paved by good intentions. Didn't they teach you that the moment you came to Hell!"

"Yes, and I'm so—"

"Don't say the word *sorry* . . . it will tempt me to peel your flesh away from your bones, very, very slowly. But I cannot give in to such diversions of pleasure during this time in the empire . . . as well as the fact that losing a good necromancer is a blatant waste of resources, regardless of how worthless, otherwise, your sniveling carcass may be." He slapped Sebastian's face hard enough to splinter his jaw as he released Sebastian's hair from his grasp and paced back to his throne, and then knit back Sebastian's jaw with a glare. "And you can thank me for your life and your healed jaw now. I need you to be able to speak in order to cast your spells, so even that I have returned . . . am I not merciful?"

"Oh, most merciful . . . thank you, thank you, a thousand times thank you."

"Then get the hell up and stand like a man and a true councilman and taste the sample I left on your face."

Sebastian scrambled to his feet and touched the bloody print his master had splattered against his cheek, unsure of what to make of it.

"Separate the parts of the blood signature of the old priest for me! Whatever does Lilith teach you on council? It contains the memories; DNA of generations, anything you want to know about a human is in the blood!"

"Yes, sire!" Sebastian said, bowing, but clearly still not understanding.

"So that your ignorant condition does not get the better of my rage, I am going to simply assume that you are too overwhelmed by my presence to properly think," the Devil said coolly. "Take this information back to Lilith. Tell her that had I listened to your foolish proposition to release the pale horse early in this battle, I would have played right into the hands of our adversaries—thereby effectively making it possible for them to replenish their armies by it being their turn to break the fifth seal so that their martyrs and saints could return." He leaned closer to Sebastian as he spoke through lengthening fangs. "And be *very* sure to tell that bitch that I said to never send one of her minions to me so ill-informed or I will have to come to her council to conduct basic training . . . something that I do not have time for at present. Something that none of you would want."

Terror-stricken, Sebastian's gaze sought the blazing floor. "A mistake like this will never happen again, I assure you. I thought I had taken every precaution and that every potential loophole had been sealed . . ."

"But you were battling an archangel," Lucifer said coolly, sitting back in his throne and regarding his manicure of threatening talons. "Didn't you notice which sanctuary they chose to retreat to? They fled to a house of Uriel, and that sanctuary was like a citadel to Vlad's army . . . you must watch not only where our enemies advance, but to where they retreat. That is *basic* war strategy, *Sebastian*."

Furious but introspective, Lucifer leaned his head back for a moment and closed his eyes, making a tent with his fingers before his mouth. "It was a perfect ruse, if I do give credit where credit is due . . . sending multiple pregnancy fragrances to perfume the air and to confuse our troops . . . putting a false vision into the mother-seer so that our demon siphon of her human mind would collect the wrong data—in the event that their side was irreparably breached—fully knowing that our demons could not siphon the silver-reinforced minds of the Neterus."

He nodded and stood, beginning to pace as he ripped the energy globe from Sebastian's grasp with a black charge and reset it in its normal hovering position in the air just before his throne. With a quick flick of his index finger, he made it begin to spin slowly on its axis again.

"*This* is why I stay so busy," he said with a weary sigh, glaring at Sebastian. "I must *always* double-back and do my own research. Had I not gone topside to lure the old priest out of hiding to finish off the job I'd begun, I would have thought the Neteru female was pregnant and given you my pale mare."

He studied Sebastian for a moment. "You see, they always leave a back door . . . they always forget one variable. The old man was the variable, one that I beautifully exploited tonight. They thought he was safe from me, therefore they didn't recode the information in his mind. He was a priest, a pure vessel, and had the truth—*there is no Neteru child incubating yet.* None of the females on her Guardian team are pregnant. The male Neteru was given extra power by them, undoubtedly, to fight Vlad like a madman to make it all appear plausible. But that was all complete bullshit to get me to send the majority of my forces after the Neterus, to the possible delinquency of protecting my own heir. Very shrewd and it almost worked, had I not done my own follow-up research . . . something that I'm sure they assumed I'd be too busy to do at this time in the dark empire."

"Forgive me . . . please forgive the entire Vampire Council for such a potential oversight of the obvious," Sebastian whispered, his eyes still wide with terror. "We didn't know how involved the angels were with this . . . with minor border skirmishes with the Neterus. We thought their angelic forces were solely focused on seeking the dark heir—which was why they'd come out in force in Greece—or, or, or which was why they fought our side at the second Masada . . . but who knew they'd show up in Detroit?"

"There are more than *two hundred million* of them," Lucifer snarled. "Haven't you ever read the Bible?"

"Only key excerpts, sir," Sebastian said, quickly lowering his head in a submissive bow.

"Then let me enlighten you. Angels can bring life through the wombs of human women and can therefore trick our side into believing that they had! But as a Vampire Council General, Sebastian—you imbecile, do you honestly believe that at this time of escalated war, the Light would be so foolish or careless as to literally allow one-half of their elite fighting squadron of Neteru Guardians to be weakened by the physical state of multiple pregnancies?"

"No . . . no, Your Greatness—that was a foolish assumption on my part. Forgive me for even coming to you with such a ridiculous concept. It will never happen again, this I assure you."

"Foolish? It was stupid!" The Dark Lord propelled himself from his throne and began to pace again as flames swept through his chambers. "Why I ought to strangle Lilith with my own bare hands for sending you down here like this with such bogus information! That bitch is so needy . . . like a child, always wanting attention!"

After the potentially destructive moment passed, Lucifer released a long, weary breath of flames. "Unbeknownst to the Light, I'd had a beacon on that old man. He and I shared unfinished business, and I never allow myself to be cheated—*no one* cheats the Devil. I knew one day or night he'd leave hallowed ground . . . and the moment he did, he'd be mine. It was a good way to kill two birds, maybe three, with one stone . . . in this transaction that delightfully bloodied my hands. Tonight, for the effort, I got the old cleric who'd defied me, fucked-up his male Neteru, and broke the heart of the female Neteru . . . since she's one with her husband and his pain is her pain. Who knows, the male used to belong to me . . . this might piss him off enough to make him recant the Light."

The Devil looked at Sebastian for a moment and then laughed. "Now *that* would be a truly interesting reversal of fortune."

Carlos sat down on the polished stone steps of the altar with a thud. "They massacred him, D," he said in a gravelly voice.

"I know," she murmured. "Baby, I know . . ."

"I should have been there . . . they got him while I was fighting up here. If I'd been on my game, had been focused, I woulda been able to send him a message, woulda maybe picked up a vibe that they were coming for him."

"Carlos, you *cannot* blame yourself. You were in the battle of your life—the entire squad could have been massacred—you simply can't blame yourself."

For a moment he just looked at her. "Then who else is there to blame, D? He was my father-seer. That would be like you not picking up when something was about to happen to Marlene and not moving Heaven and earth to make sure that it didn't. He'd been reduced to a helpless old man and he needed me . . . but I wasn't there. Baby, I just *wasn't there*." Carlos closed his eyes and slumped forward, leaning his forearms on his thighs. "Oh, God, what am I supposed to do with forever knowing that I just wasn't there for Father Pat like I shoulda been, Damali?"

Her hand caressed his back. "We'll go get him . . . we'll go to Philly . . . we'll bury him righteous and—"

"There's nothing left to hardly bury, D," Carlos said in a ragged murmur, his pained gaze holding hers as he looked up. "The Covenant clerics and the Templar brothers will have to cremate him."

She closed her eyes and hung her head. "Let me check on the Detroit team you jettisoned . . . just five minutes, then we'll leave for Philly. All right?"

"Yeah," Carlos said, his gaze drifting toward empty space in the nave.

"I've got a sight-link with Owa," Marlene said in a gentle voice. "They're all good . . . mourning their losses of Gus and Muata like we're mourning our own."

Carlos nodded. "Good to know I did at least one thing right tonight . . . sent 'em somewhere they didn't get smoked."

Damali's hand sought his back again as she spoke to Marlene.

"Ask her what the public spin is on all the destruction, Mar . . . we've gotta get some prayers for damage control in place before we leave here—otherwise, there'll be a panic. Who knows, it might already be too late."

Marlene became still to send the question to Owa at the sanctuary where the local team had been jettisoned for safety. The Neteru squad remained so quiet within the church they were holed up in that the very silence around them seemed like a gong.

"There is no general public panic. Events from earlier this evening have been spun on the evening news as a massive and unusual earthquake coupled with a fast-moving tornado that crippled downtown Detroit and reached as far as Toronto," Marlene said in short bursts of information, translating Owa's vision into her sight, and then into a verbal format that the entire Neteru team could immediately hear. "But Motor City's officials say their town is tough. They're still having the jazz festival, just moving stages to different locations."

"Good," Damali said in a faraway voice. She turned her attention to Carlos and stroked his hair for a moment. "Let's go to Philly. . . . Baby, do you want to take us, or I can do the fold-away?"

He didn't even look at her as he spoke. Defeat claimed his being as he sat slumped with his back to the altar and his gaze seeing nothing on the floor.

"You take the team, D. I ain't got it in me . . . and need to just roll solo for a little while."

# CHAPTER FOURTEEN

For reasons he'd probably never fathom, but thoroughly appreciated, when he'd said that he needed to roll solo for a few, his wife didn't argue. Unlike every other time in the past, she'd simply said one word to him that spoke volumes, "Okay." Her tone, her eyes, the gentle touch at his jaw with that one single word said more than anything. He knew she was asking him to make her a promise and her requests were reasonable: Baby, come back to me alive. Baby, don't do nothing crazy that'll break my heart. Baby, remember that I love you . . . and know that I respect and trust you enough, even at this hour, to give you some room for your head.

Carlos walked through the main marble hallway of Philadelphia's Masonic Temple at One Broad Street. He had to get word to the Knights Templar that one of theirs had fallen, but didn't begin to know where to start looking for a contact. Father Pat deserved to be buried with full Scottish honors, Templar honors, Guardian honors, clerical honors; the man was a VIP as far as he was concerned. But how to get in touch with the elusive Templars was anybody's guess.

All he knew for sure was that Damali had come here for part of her Neteru education, and that Father Pat had come to

Philly, which had the oldest lodge in the United States that re-
sembled the original at Westminster Abbey. Putting the two facts
together from there, he'd have to make it up as he went along . . .
even though it probably wasn't safe to roll without a serious plan.
But deep inside he wished like hell something would try to fuck
with him right now.

The peaceful vibrations within the darkened superstructure
had a calming effect, however, as he silently strode beneath the
twenty-two-foot vaulted ceilings, gazing up at the star patterns
cut into the skylights. The feeling of being in a sanctuary swept
through him, even though he was well aware that the building
wasn't formally considered hallowed ground.

As he walked past gorgeous stained-glass windows and white
marble statues of angels, he told himself maybe there were real
angels standing guard as silent sentries. Maybe the Light knew
he was on a fool's errand. Maybe that was all just wishful thinking so he could justify the insanity of leaving the safety of the
team to be walking inside a practically deserted building that had
what seemed like hundreds of rooms, looming halls, and dark corners where he could get smoked in the blink of an eye with no
one the wiser. Even the human security guard was asleep and not
doing rounds. Given who was after him, what good would that
one poor soul do anyway?

But as Carlos continued walking through the quiet, abandoned space, his thoughts roamed freely and collided one upon
the other until he felt hot moisture streaming down his face.

*They had taken his father-seer* . . . the one man who'd sat with
him while he was at his worst—a brand-new vampire—but had
faith in his best, that he could become a Neteru. That insane,
brave, outrageous elderly priest had found him in the desert in a
cave at daybreak, but had sheltered him in the darkness, had
even sheltered him from his own clerical brothers. Father Pat
had broken every canonical law, tossing blood packs to a known

vampire to revive him, had thrown away the exorcism rites and simply talked to him like he was a human being with a soul. Had loved him. Had believed in him. Had hung with him till he got out of the prison he'd been in. Was the only one beside Damali who really visited him while he was on the inside of the Darkness. Had said he was worth something greater than he was showing himself to be then—said he wasn't giving up on him, and didn't. Had never broken that promise to him; had made it a vow.

*They had taken his father-seer* . . . when it was Father Pat that had stayed Imam Asula's machete on more than one occasion in the early days of his becoming. It had been Father Pat who'd brought him, a predator, a carnivore, into a clerical safe house and had sat facing him in that spartan cleric's chamber, talking to him about his life and death and decisions and the love of his life and his mission and purpose and every single damned thing his biological father had not.

*They had taken his father-seer* . . . Jesus wept! Father Pat was the one who had prepared him to be man enough to stand before Ausar and Adam and to have the strength of conviction to trade in a Vampire Council throne for a seat at the Neteru Kings' archon table. The man had literally been his lifeline back from the Darkness into the Light, even before the ancients in rarified air came to stand at his flank. And no disrespect to his Neteru brothers, the Kings, but Father Pat *was human* and here on this earth—a man who understood all about the flesh being weak and hard choices . . . was a man who bled red blood and had risked his human life to give him a word. That's what no one except maybe his wife could get; Father Pat had been his rehab, had helped him beat the blood hunger; taught him more things so subtly that he probably couldn't even remember them.

Perhaps most important, the man had even taught him that it

was futile to raise one's fist at God and cry out, "Why!" But that's just what he wanted to do right now.

*They had taken his father-seer* . . . the last of his old family. Everyone else that could crush his heart if they died had already been taken, except Damali. And while he was beyond grateful for that, the one man that he would have wanted to be there to hold his son, to christen his firstborn, had died horribly at a demon's hands. It wasn't the fact that the old man had passed; it was the way the darkside had done it. He understood the seasons of life and wasn't railing against the inevitable. If Father Pat had simply died in his sleep as an old man, he would have been hurt, but not felt like this.

Yeah, yeah, yeah, he knew philosophically . . . intellectually . . . that once God put His topspin on it, matter could not be created or destroyed . . . that life was eternal . . . that on the other side was Heaven, had even glimpsed it. Whatever. But that didn't change the fact that losing Father Pat hurt like hell or that there was something stabbing into his chest like a blade so sharp that he couldn't breathe . . . because fact was, Neteru or not, he was still human.

He had questions, so many very real human questions for the Light—like why would a man who'd given his entire life to the service of the Almighty have to die so tragically?

*They'd taken his father-seer,* they'd taken his father-seer, dear God in Heaven, *compasión,* they'd taken his father, his seer, his second set of eyes, his friend, his counselor, his *father-seer,* and he wanted to shout at Heaven and demand a response that made sense. But he was too far gone under the tutelage of Father Patrick to raise his fist at that source anymore. Oh, Jesus, they had taken his father-seer . . . not just taken him, but tortured the man while Carlos wasn't there.

That fact alone left a burning, shouting, hollering question in his mind, asking anyone who would listen On High, "Why, dammit!" But for the life of him, the fight was gone . . . this shit hurt so badly there were no words.

Instead of lobbing an angry complaint toward Heaven, he found himself sliding down a thick white column to sit on the floor defeated. The original question that had filled his chest so hard and fast that it threatened to burst his lungs if he didn't yell it out in the church in Detroit had lost its force and simply came out as a garbled, pain-filled whisper, "Why?"

Fingers in his hair, elbows on his knees, the dam broke. If he couldn't protect an old man on hallowed ground, how in God's name was he gonna protect his wife and kid during the fucking Armageddon—let alone his pregnant Guardian sisters and little Ayana? They said God wasn't supposed to put anything more on a man's shoulders than he could bear . . . maybe that was a human-inspired lie, at this point what the fuck did he know?

The only thing that was clear was they'd taken his father-seer and the Devil had truly kicked his ass with that move.

"Lu said what?" Lilith backhand bitch-slapped Sebastian and then pointed at the dark mist in the center Vampire Council table with a long talon. "My own eagerness for a win allowed me to even entertain your insanity. Look at him!" she screeched through massive fangs. "He's alone, broken—does he seem like a man who has a pregnant wife to protect and a bunch of pregnant female Guardians weighing down his team?"

Bat wings tore from her shoulder blades as her spaded tail violently ejected from her spine to stab into the pulsing veins of the black marble table, shredding her black gown and splashing black blood. "In trying to barter for the release of the pale mare into your inept care, you have unnecessarily cost this council, *and me,* credibility with the Dark Lord! You will *never* have such an opportunity to do so again!"

"You went to Lucifer with *that* bullshit, *mon ami?* Trying to get the pale horse of the Apocalypse?" Fallon Nuit stood and walked to the far side of chambers with his goblet of blood and flamboyantly raised it in a toast to Sebastian. "You are now the most insane sonofabitch I know, the most courageous, and the most soon-to-be extinct. May the Darkness have mercy on you."

Wounded but quickly recovering, Vlad struggled to stand with a vicious snarl as he stared at Sebastian. "I can feel your attempt to bargain against me just radiating off your sickly skin . . . but that your scheme has backfired on you is enough for now. Later, you and I shall settle a score."

"Think what you like," Sebastian said, lifting his chin and glancing around at his fellow council members. "I had what I thought was solid information at the time, but apparently there were variables I hadn't considered—such as archangel support to our adversaries. Don't think that any of you at this council could not be fooled by those entities!"

"Rather than quibble about who was right or wrong," Lucrezia said with a dangerous smile, "might we not seize the opportunity to attack the male Neteru now while he's grieving . . . and alone?"

Elizabeth shook her head. "No. It could be a trap. Our Dark Lord just smote a clean priest—the Neteru's father-seer. While I may hate them, I respect their side's shrewdness in battle, having witnessed it on more than one occasion firsthand. The Light will retaliate, and probably has invisible reinforcements around him as we speak. Why would they allow Rivera to be out and alone and bitterly grieving during the end of days? He's *bait,* Lucrezia. We struck down one of theirs, now they will use that to make their side seem vulnerable, in order to make us grow lax and overly confident . . . and when we rush in to assassinate the male Neteru who seemingly sits alone now, we'll be ambushed."

"I agree," Lilith said, giving Elizabeth a nod of approval before issuing Sebastian another withering glare. "We need to monitor them for a while, see where they go, what their next move will be, and wait for a real vulnerability when *they* aren't prepared—not the other way around."

There was nothing she could say to him. Carlos was emotionally beyond reach at the moment, and the only thing she could do was pray that he was protected . . . but more important, she prayed that the Creator would grant him some peace. That thought remained in the back of Damali's mind like a quiet dirge as she brought the team to a key Philly safe house in the Germantown section of the city.

The team came out of the fold-away across the street from their destination on the hallowed ground of an old stone Methodist church. At that hour in the morning, Germantown Avenue's cobblestoned streets were quiet, the old streetlamps glowing off masonry that was laid down at the birth of the nation. Across from the church grounds, a huge, urban, public school loomed, its massive structure sending long, ominous shadows to spill onto smaller adjacent buildings.

Guardians looked at her for the order to move out and leave hallowed ground. Damali nodded. She needed to get her team quickly inside the Nile Bookstore and Café. Everyone was strung so tightly that if a stray cat had scurried across the street it would have probably set off a chain reaction of RPG-launched explosives and automatic weapon report.

She held up two fingers, pointing at Shabazz and Rider so they'd flank and cover her as she jogged across the street to gain safe house entry. But she held up her fist to the rest of the team so they'd stay put and on safe ground until she could determine if everything was still cool. The silent transaction took only seconds, yet the logistics of moving that many people, safely, weighed heavily on her shoulders. Her thoughts immediately went to Carlos with every footfall as she crossed the cobble-stoned street. The man had so much on his head . . . if God would just *please* give him a break.

As expected, the metal grates were pulled down over the Nile's large storefront plate-glass windows, but she peered between the steel bars to search for any signs of movement within. Everything was still, and yet she knew Guardians were watching her from some vantage point between the brightly hued African ensembles and books that decorated the left bank of windows or from the vegan café side of the shop that flaunted menus and flyers in the other windows on the right.

"Hotep. Enen-a Neter, ita em kheperaungkh. I submit to God who comes in the form of transformation and life," Damali said, standing at the front door.

Locks and tumblers turned and a rack of steel grating lifted. A thick-bodied, mahogany-toned warrior answered the door wearing only white meditation pantaloons.

"Praise be to Neter," he said with a big smile. "I'm Mehki, the seer-healer you mind-locked with. *"Herukhuti tua en pashet a Set hur Apep.* I overthrow Satan's intelligent and animal evil." He paused for a moment and then glanced over Damali's shoulder, suddenly seeming worried that her team might have been harmed. "Where are the others?"

Damali waved her squad in from across the street. "We are all fine—no one from our Neteru squad was lost. Tua-k, Tua-tu, brother. Thank you so much."

Mehki waited until Damali's team was safely inside and then turned the series of bolts to secure the building. Moving swiftly, he went to a ceremonial altar that was arrayed with eucalyptus branches, sacred water, anointed candles, pinecones, garlic, fresh ginger, and spices laid out on a long red-and-purple tie-dyed cloth, and gathered an incense holder and a cylinder of clear water. He lit the incense and, within seconds, heavy plumes of pungent smoke filled the air. Without apology or permission, he splashed Guardians and the door and then swung the incensor toward them until the team was nearly choking. Appearing satisfied that no one had burst into embers, he beamed as he returned his ceremonial items to the entrance altar.

"Mehki greets you warmly, brothers and sisters—welcome to our house. All is in the hands of the Divine and it is our honor to host you," he said, his eyes taking in the large group before him. "I teach Qi Gong body energy systems, martial arts, and am part of the Herukhuti brotherhood," he said proudly.

"Good to meet you, brother," Shabazz said, giving Mehki a Kemetian traditional embrace. "We are honored that you opened your home."

Mike and Inez stepped forward as Damali went around the team introducing Guardians and describing each person's gift.

"You took in my baby girl and my momma," Inez said, offering Mehki a deep Kemetian bow. "Thank you, bless you."

"We are blessed, sister," Mehki said. "You know it is African tradition to add to one's compound—there is always room at the table for one more. Neter blesses a full house. You do know that the baby has sight, a future Guardian in the making . . . every child belongs to the entire village; every elder is to be revered and their wisdom gleaned from." He glanced around excitedly. "The child is strong."

"Yes . . . Ayana is special and I bet Delores is having a good time here," Marlene said with a knowing smile, giving Inez a wink.

"I bet she is," Inez said with a slight chuckle. "And my momma needed somewhere she could hold court."

"We can wake them, if you'd like?" Mehki said, searching the faces around him.

"No, no," Inez said. "If I can just peek in on her and give her a kiss. . . ."

"This must be hard," Mehki said, looking first at Inez and then slowly sending his deep, compassionate gaze around the team. "That's why we had to open the school. We decided we just needed to create a bridge to the future, no matter what happened. Before, in the early days, like when we all got the call to step up, we had lived our entire lives feeling different, not knowing who we were. But have you noticed," he added, his eyes shimmering in the street lamplight that pierced the shop's darkness, "the children are coming faster, stronger, with the gifts—not just to Guardian parents, but to regular parents as well. It's as though the Light is paving the way . . . and somewhere there must be schools that guide these gifted children. We all cannot be warriors forever, and yet, this is also a way to fight the Darkness. Light up one mind and you have cast out an army of demons and affected potential generations."

"That is so true," Damali said in a reverent tone, glancing around the shop. "But where . . . how do you secure the space?"

Mehki nodded, waving his hand toward the left side of the long, rectangular facility. "The bookstore doubles as our library and it has room enough for community classroom space—gotta educate the masses, too. Must give the people small sips of water until they learn how to take a big gulp." He turned to his right and indicated toward the café. "But for them to retain the knowledge, they have to eat right. This café doubles as our kitchen for the Guardian team and the children's school. We feed the public, but also our own . . . and you have to cook your own and not lean on the toxic poison out there that pollutes the mind, body, and spirit."

"Say it again loudly, brother," Marlene said with a wide smile, looking around the team. "I am still working on these people, trust me."

"Getting off the fried chicken wings is like breaking a drug addiction," Mehki said, laughing. "You know I'm from Philly where the basic saying is, 'Ain't no thing but a chicken wing,' and we were raised on cheese steaks, hoagies, and mustard pretzels served by old men who vended, didn't wash their hands, and seemed like they hadn't bathed in a week. So, if I can change, *a Neteru team* can—c'mon, now, people."

Tension-relieving laughter filled the sacred space and Big Mike rubbed a palm over his scalp with a wide grin.

"Brother, you killin' me. I'm trying to get off the ribs . . . but you know, every time I think I'm safe, they keep pulling me back in."

"I'm not killing you, man, that pork is," Mehki said, laughing harder.

"I keep telling the brother," Shabazz said, shaking his head. "But I can't do nuthin' with him."

"Yeah, well, wait until Aquila and Urhra get on him. Our team mother and father do *not* play with the food thing at *all*. Just warning you . . . and Miss Delores got, uhm . . . things explained to her on day one. It's all good."

"Praise be!" Marlene said, shaking her head as Inez covered her mouth and laughed into her hands. "Now when I see Delores it won't be no mess, if another whole team got on her about her kitchen ways."

Mehki held up his hands, his infectious grin still making members of the Neteru squad chuckle. "I wasn't in it. Now through the center doors in the middle of the facility is where the courtyard is. We've poured enough libations to fry anything that might try to bubble up to the surface . . . and overhead, we have mosquito nets cast from the tops of one building to another, but have spun silver going through it, and then we purified it with incense and prayers, and our tacticals put a serious charge on it. That way our little ones can play out there unmolested."

With a proud nod, Mehki bade the team to follow him out the large center doors. "When we get across the courtyard, you've gotta take off your shoes when you go inside . . . we've got paper slippers at the door. Cool?"

"Cool," Marlene said, eyeing the group hard.

"Brother Mehki, you just have to forgive them," Damali said with a sigh as bodies bristled. "They just came out of a firefight in Detroit and don't wanna drop weapons or do anything that can make them feel vulnerable."

"We understand," he said calmly, "but it's house policy."

"I know," Shabazz said, glancing around at the team. "*We* know."

Although no one agreed, the squad followed Mehki through the double doors that led out to the open-air courtyard. Despite all his assurances of security measures, the battle-fatigued Neteru squad went on instant alert, entering the yard like a Delta Force on two-by-two detail, hugging the perimeter, weapons raised, and hand signals the only form of communication. By the time they got the short hundred yards across to the other building, Mehki's former mirth had dissipated.

"What have you guys just been through?" he asked quietly, his expression completely sobered.

"The darkside raised Dracula, blew up half of Detroit, and had us under heavy fire, holed up in a cathedral . . . and that was just this afternoon," Jose said, wiping adrenaline sweat off his brow with his forearm.

"Uhm . . . listen, the vibe is really not good for the children," Mehki said apologetically. "Wait in the entranceway and let me get the elders."

"That's cool; we'll wait," Damali said, rubbing the tension away from her neck. She gazed up at the huge, city block, square footprint of the school and the Guardian-student dormitory that was created out of an old abandoned textile warehouse. Chalk hopscotch grids and a small jungle gym graced the yard along with a basketball hoop. This was a home where babies lived.

"No offense," Mehki said in a quiet voice. "I . . . just have to check."

"No offense taken," Damali said softly as she absorbed images from Mehki's mind. Brightly colored classrooms filled with green plants, life, laughter . . . children learning. Khepera School of Transformation was a lighthouse, the future—while her squad was like a group of commandos bringing the energy of destruction near the tender shoots of new, growing life. To come here was wrong; she just didn't know where else they could have gone. The fact that there were children here had been thoroughly masked and all she'd had to go on was old team information.

"Let us wait outside, good brother, and maybe just let Inez go in and see her baby girl, then come out. We're used to the night and being in it. We've made it this far, so, hey," Damali finally said, gaining nods from her team, which was apparently on the same page. "Nothing, not even us, should jeopardize what you've got inside those walls. Our job is to protect you, your job is to be sure that everything here stays harmonious . . . and trouble, unfortunately, always seems to have a way of finding us."

When Carlos finally looked up, Ausar sat beside him to his right, Adam at his left.

"Go to your wife, young brother," Ausar said quietly. "She is navigating in the dark with a whole team in her arms."

Carlos nodded. "Yeah. I know. I just needed a minute."

"But she needs to build a lighthouse for the children," Adam said quietly. "She's being guided to see how."

"The world is blowing up all around us," Carlos said in a gravelly voice. "Every house we build gets torched. I'm done building . . . we're just trying to survive, man."

Ausar nodded and stood, his ancient Kemetian robes flowed as he offered Carlos his hand to hoist him up off the floor. Clasping it like a man drowning, Carlos felt the strength ripple through Ausar's arm into his.

"Your father-seer did not die in vain. The darkside did not prevail," Adam murmured and then held his hands in the Kemetian telepathic pose—left palm up, right palm down, both hands extended toward the receiver. "Let us tell you a glorious secret."

"I'm sorry," Mehki said, his gaze pained as he slipped back out into the courtyard.

Damali landed a supportive hand on his shoulder. "No, brother, don't be. This is how it should be. Seeing this gave me hope. Thank you for that."

Mehki smiled sadly. "It's just because of the children . . . you understand?"

"We do," Marlene said, bowing to him, and then the entire team followed suit. "You are a living womb and must be protected."

"I have put you all on our altars . . . especially your three Guardian sisters," Mehki said softly, indicating Jasmine, Valkyrie, and Tara. The seer's eyes glazed over for a moment and then he came back to the group. "They need to be a part of the Hetheru women's healing circle ceremony so that the true desire of their hearts comes true." He stared at them and spoke in a far-off tone. "You will be filled with the spirit, if it is the will of Neter—we will pray extra prayers for you in that regard."

"Thank you," Tara said quietly. "But I've already experienced my quota of miracles . . . just the fact that I'm here, alive, and still human is enough."

The cardinal spoke in quavering jags and hushed tones as Carlos stood in the foyer of the seminary surrounded by priests. The service for Father Patrick would be swift as the man had no living relatives other than those who loved him on the Neteru team. His squad plus the last remaining Covenant brothers would stand shoulder-to-shoulder and remember a life well-lived.

Despite all that Adam had told him, it still hurt his soul that his father-seer had been IDed through his dental records, and barely at that. When the cardinal had shared that bit of information he'd wished he hadn't heard, Carlos had simply closed his eyes and nodded.

It was important to focus on the larger picture—that the man's life had not been in vain, nor had his death, and that his last act of living had been to christen Carlos's unborn child with a chance to make it into the world. He would not let any more tears stain his face. It was time to go meet his wife and team at the safe house on Germantown Avenue. The service would be in three days, and there would be bagpipes there . . . courtesy of Philadelphia's finest.

"Thank you, Fathers," Carlos said and bowed, then turned, prepared to leave.

But the cardinal glanced around nervously in a way that made the other priests withdraw.

"Son . . . did Father Patrick speak to you before his unfortunate demise?"

Carlos shook his head, staring at the clearly terrified man before him. "No. That was probably one of the worst parts of all of this."

The cardinal nodded quickly and then looked around as

though he was being chased. "I don't claim to know about seers and Neterus and many of the things our good brother, Father Patrick, knew . . . but he loved you—said you were his secret weapon . . . in all the reports . . ." He wrung his hands and then dabbed at the sweat on his brow. "All is lost now, all is lost," he whispered in a frightened burst. "What shall we do?"

"What happened?" Carlos said quietly, also glancing around as he stepped closer to the cardinal.

"It is so horrific that I can't even speak it."

Carlos nodded. "You don't have to," he murmured, opening his gaze to the cleric. "I got it."

# CHAPTER FIFTEEN

Carlos immediately picked up Damali's energy signature at the Methodist church on Germantown Avenue and Haines Street, and then followed it across the cobblestoned road to a new white-light enclosure that had to be the safe house she'd taken the team to for sanctuary. As soon as he stood in front of the storefront, he opened a direct telepathic channel to her to be sure it was cool for him to enter. Neteru or not, one didn't just whirl into a Guardian encampment unannounced; it was too easy to be mistaken for a demon entity and get smoked by friendly fire.

Oddly, it took him several minutes to get Damali's attention because it seemed that every seer on the team was blowing her head up with a private instant message. Her mental capacity to manage the incoming was nearly fried.

Carlos stared at the front door of the Nile Bookstore and Café, wondering whether or not it would be just easier to ring the bell. The way rapid-fired questions were coming at Damali reminded him of watching kids in the street playing hard-core double Dutch jump rope—but this was championship level.

Sometimes there were two or three Guardian seers in her head at the same time, then one would quickly exit only for another one to hop in before he could, and then that person set a new tempo. Getting her to be able to acknowledge and recognize his signature pulse was going to require a spousal override, but he didn't want to panic her with an SOS.

After a few moments longer without success, he simply rang the bell. The chatter in Damali's head went still. Beaded drapes got moved to the side with a 9mm muzzle. Carlos let his breath out hard.

"I'm looking for my wife, man," he said loudly, losing patience.

Locks quickly got turned and he could hear heavy tumblers engaging. In a few seconds the door opened and he and Damali's entire squad could be seen behind a young Guardian male wearing white pantaloons and no shirt.

"Why didn't you call me, baby?" Damali said, slipping around the sentry at the door. She glanced at the local Guardian, who didn't appear to be ready to stand down. "Mehki, he's cool. It's him. I scanned him."

"All right, then. Cool," Mehki said, unsure. "Welcome."

"I tried to third-eye call but couldn't get through," Carlos said, stepping inside and pounding the local Guardian's fist. "Rivera. Carlos Rivera."

"Brother Mehki," the local Guardian replied and then glanced back at the team. "I'm so sorry, there's been . . . some issues."

"What issues?" Carlos said, glancing around at the faces that blankly stared back at him.

"We have children here," Mehki said. "I know this is new for Guardian compounds, but we're getting children sent to us like never before. The house elders over in the dormitory section are concerned . . . given all the weapons, the war vibrations, the recent extreme violence in your auras. Don't get us wrong, our local team elders *know* your team is above reproach and we're honored to have a visitation from the Neterus in this era . . . and we most assuredly don't think you all would do anything intentionally to jeopardize our precious futures, the children—but rather that if something's hunting you or stalking your team, it might track it back to this place where the children are. This is our dilemma. We want to support you, but . . ."

"This place is a lighthouse, Carlos," Damali interjected quickly, her gaze going between Carlos and Mehki. "We don't want Mehki or the mother-seer or father-seer of this compound to feel some type of way or to think we don't understand their position. They just started taking in children because the need in the neighborhood was so great . . . and they opened a school—but, Carlos, if something follows our team here and were to hurt any of their students, nobody on this team would be able to sleep at night."

"She's got that right," Marlene said, wiping her hands down her face to stave off fatigue. "That's why you couldn't get a mental word in with her, because all of us were blowing up her head with that same sentiment."

"I'd rather go up the street to a doggone hotel and take my chances with an Uzi under my pillow, C—rather than think we led Vlad's army up here to these kids, or worse. Feel me?" Big Mike said, running his palm over his bald head.

"I feel you, man," Carlos said, rubbing the back of his neck.

"Then, we be out, man," Yonnie said, shaking his head. "Ain't trying to have what I saw in Detroit come for no little kids. I never even went there while I was on the other side . . . but seeing hopscotch chalk lines and jungle gyms . . . *maaan*. That would make us no better than those stupid, punk-ass, young boy, drug thugs who ain't got cojones enough to step to their problem directly—but who do those Wild West school yard shoot-outs, spraying everybody, even kids that didn't have nuthin' to do with the bull. Naw. Ain't worth it, C, no matter what."

"We are glad you understand," a tall, regal man said as he parted the gathering of Guardians. "Hotep," he murmured, surveying Carlos and Damali, then their team.

All eyes went to the elder gentleman who spoke in a calm, but firm tone, as Mehki stepped back with a slight bow of respect.

"This is our house father-seer, Urhra," Mehki said with deference, motioning with another bow. "This is the legendary, new millennium Neteru team."

"Good to meet you," Carlos said, inclining his head with respect.

"Hotep," Damali said with a slight bow.

The man lifted his chin, his bronze hue set off by intensely dark eyes and a thicket of jet-black hair. His white-and-gold embroidered African robes crackled quietly with tactical static charge as he moved, gesticulating slowly with his hands as he spoke.

"Amen tua en hetep—peace. Ausar tua en aungkh—life. Tehuti tua en Tchaas—wisdom. Seker tua en aungkh hen—life eternal. Ma'at tua en aungkh en Ma'at—truth. Geb tua en khab—strength. All this I pray for you in the name of Neter," he said with an unblinking gaze. "Aquila and her sister are with the children and must remain as their sentinels, but send their deepest love to you. But I wanted to greet you myself and to confer the fact that there was no slight intended by our painful decision . . . yet, we cannot grant you lodging here."

"We understand, brother," Carlos said, clasping the local team's father-seer by the forearm in a warrior's grip.

"But we will not abandon our own," Urhra said, staring Carlos directly in the eyes. "We have made provisions for visiting teams—this is, after all, the City of Brotherly Love and Sisterly Affection, no matter the current murder rate. Philadelphia's tactical warrior Guardians will cover you while here."

"We keep a location for visiting dignitaries, based on the Qi Gong principles of men being electric and women being magnetic . . . this space is very, very safe," Mehki added with hope in his voice. "We would never just turn you away from our doors without an alternative."

Urhra landed a solid hand on Carlos's shoulder. "Mehki speaks the truth of Ma'at. To leave our family out-of-doors in the path of certain danger would be unjust and would violate all that we stand for. There are three houses on a small street. Share the vision with me, brother. They look like normal row houses just off Haines around the corner, but the insides have been gutted, the walls between them knocked out so that the houses are conjoined like Siamese twins."

The elder Guardian glanced around at the Neteru team, his voice filled with confidence. "You cannot tell this fact from the outside, but there is unity between the structures on the inside. Libations have been mightily poured and security measures taken . . . a full larder of revitalizing vegan food awaits in the adjoined kitchens, and there are enough bedrooms and linens for each of you to rest well. Hallowed earth and silver sealant have been spread across the basement floors before the concrete was again poured. All windows have been charged and anointed, as well as the vents. We have asked members from the Rowdee Black Giants squad in north-central Philadelphia to serve as sentries while your team rests."

"We fought with them before," Carlos said, nodding. "Good squad."

"No doubt," Damali said, nodding with agreement.

"We even have two very serious female warriors who will watch your backs here," Mehki said proudly. "Zulma and Kenyetta are the best seer-tacticals we have."

"Works for me," Carlos said, nodding.

"Excellent," Urhra said with a warm smile, finally relaxing

now that his alternative offer of hospitality had been graciously accepted. "Inscribed in the door knockers of each house you will see a cross surrounded by a circle—this is the angel Sebek's symbol, as you must know, and these houses are guarded by the Light."

As they passed a black Escalade on the street, a large, bald, ebony-hued brother that could have passed as Big Mike's body double gave the Neteru team a nod and flashed them a nickel-plated Glock 9mm. Another tall, lean brother with dreadlocks meandered down the opposite side of the street and then stopped to give the team a nod as he opened his army fatigue jacket and gave them a glimpse of a handheld semiautomatic. Two more Guardians discreetly saluted the Neteru team from the street as the squad mounted the steps to the row house compound. Two attractive, ebony-skinned women with blue static crackling through their locks stepped out of the shadows with a nod, then seemed to vanish back into the nothingness that had surrounded them.

"This is beautiful," Rider murmured with rare awe in his voice. "In plain sight if ever I saw it."

"I'm gonna stop talking bad about Philly," Jose agreed quietly as Carlos managed the door locks. "This is all that—right in the 'hood and who would know."

Everyone else withheld comment until the full team was inside and the space was double-checked for security. Once the full squad reconvened in the massive central portion of the house, only then did gazes wander to begin to take in their environment.

Gleaming hardwood floors washed with ceremonial bluing peeked out around the edges of hand-loomed Moroccan rugs. After the widened foyer, large, sandstone-hued sectional furniture draped in African fabrics created a comfortable seating

gallery in the middle of the house. Silver-framed photos of visiting dignitaries from other nations, each bearing their Sharpie
signature, graced the eggshell white walls. Lush plants soaked
in stained-glass prisms from the huge bay windows that were
flanked by heavily cushioned window seats.

The team looked around at the tasteful yet spartan display of
African art, handcrafted stools, intricately carved buffets, china
cabinet, and the long dining-room table that was draped in ceremonial white—complete with a thick spray of white roses in a
heavy crystal vase of water.

"They keep the joint at the ready like this?" Yonnie said in
amazement, finally breaking the group's silent thrall.

"I know," J.L. murmured, studying pictures of national fig-
ures in old black-and-white photos posing with Urhra.

"Just like our team," Damali said quietly, "a lot of teams have
been holding the line for years . . . but we've gotta take away a
serious lesson from the way these folks have just blended right
into the scenery of the community."

"You ain't never lied," Inez said, walking into the kitchen
with the group following her. "Look at this."

Stainless-steel appliances gleamed at them from a fully
loaded, three house-wide, renovated commercial kitchen. Cast-
iron and copper pots hung over the center stove galley. Huge
industrial sinks took in slivers of moonlight beneath the wide
windows.

Inez peeked out the miniblinds. "Three house-wide decks
and carports under them."

"Security hazard," Shabazz said, his gaze quickly locking
with J.L.'s.

"I'm on it. We'll get a tactical charge to reinforce those back
windows, the doors, and bay windows up front," J.L. said.

"Yeah, we'll get on it," Mike said, opening the refrigerator
and then sighing. "Fully loaded with all fruits and veggies . . .

gonna be a long three days." He turned to glance at Dan and Bobby. "See if there's any real food in the cabinets."

Dan and Bobby immediately complied, sacking cabinets, but after a few moments looked at Mike, shaking their heads.

"All whole grains," Dan said with a lopsided grin. "But there's some gluten-free cookies up there," he said, tossing a pack of oatmeal raisin bars to Mike, who caught it with one hand.

Marjorie yawned. "I don't know how you guys can be hungry. All I want is a hot shower and a place to drop."

"You can do that, honey," Berkfield said, going back to the UV-lit basement entrance. "They've installed commercial-sized hot-water tanks down there, same deal with washers and dryers. We could take turns covering for team members who were in the shower getting cleaned up, do cold-water laundry loads in between, this way folks can sorta get back to feeling normal . . . get some of the battle grime off of us." He looked around. "I don't mind doing the first laundry load and watch—they've got a big-screen TV down there, plus a coupla pool tables. I'm in Heaven. Whaduya say, Bobby, Dan . . . can you kick this old man's ass?"

"Rack 'em up, Pop," Bobby said with a grin, looking at his father.

"Me, Tara, and Heather can cover for the first crew to hit the showers," Juanita offered, checking her clip. "We can sit on the closed toilet seat, weapon at the ready, like old times down in Arizona, or wait outside in the hall—makes me no never mind." She shrugged when her Guardian sisters nodded their agreement. "Then we can switch."

"Works for me," Tara said as Inez started rummaging in the fridge.

"I take it you're on food detail with me?" Marlene said with a smirk, glancing at Inez's back.

"You know it," Inez said with a chuckle. "If folks are cleaning up—gotta feed 'em and fix some grub before they wanna start trying to order in Philly cheese steaks."

"Baby . . . dang—that is so cold," Mike muttered. "Guess I'm on first perimeter watch then, because I can't fall asleep till I eat."

"Good man," Carlos said with a weary smile, landing a hand on Big Mike's shoulder as he passed him. "Just like old times."

"Do you think we could ever have something like this?" Jasmine said quietly, making the entire team stop moving about to look at her. She glanced around, her eyes large and sad. "I mean, a place where kids can run and play in the street and you have neighbors and can walk around the corner to the store?"

"Would be nice," Tara murmured, touching the sheer tie-dyed yellow-and-white curtains at the window. "To me, strange as it may sound, this is nicer than what we had in San Diego . . . environmentally. This reminds me of home—how I grew up. San Diego was such a fantasy . . . but this . . ."

"I know what you mean," Juanita said softly, glancing at Jose before her gaze sought the floor.

"Maybe if the local Guardians figured out how to do such a thing, we could?" Val said, hope weighting each word. "Do we dare pray for something like this?"

"Walking up the ave," Shabazz said in a faraway tone, "kicking it in the corner bar. Going to the barbershop up the street . . . all that regular stuff is something for normal people—a gift, that as a Neteru team, we don't have the luxury to even fantasize about. Because, in the end, folks, when it's all said and done, we're like the plague . . . anywhere we stay for too long gets blown up. We've gotta keep moving to keep civilians from being caught in the crossfire between good and evil."

"Yeah, but isn't humanity in the crossfire of all that anyway?" Krissy said in a tear-thickened murmur. Moisture glistened in her big blue eyes as she stared at Shabazz and challenged him. "Even the Neteru team has to have hope, has to have a prayer, 'Bazz . . . otherwise, how can we, as humans, go on?"

"I, for one, can't go on without the hope that one day this will all be over," Juanita said, closing her eyes against a fresh on-slaught of tears. "Even if I'm just temporarily lying to myself."

Jasmine nodded. "Then, tonight, I'm going to lie to myself and just go take a shower."

Marjorie slung an arm over her daughter-in-law's shoulder. "Good idea, Jas . . . then for a little while, let's not think about any of this."

Eerie silence filled the kitchen, pain and trauma laden in the air.

Dan raked his fingers through his hair and let out a hard breath of frustration. "Carlos, man . . . do you think you can bring in those duds they gave us up at the Shrine in Detroit? We'd all picked out sizes and everything, and they'd packed them in individual bags, but we left the whole lot of it when we had that immediate call to arms. Might be nice to walk the streets tomorrow looking like a normal person rather than a soldier, know what I mean? Then we can go to those stores we saw on Germantown Avenue, maybe, and get some regular gear—like jeans, T-shirts, and sneakers, and whatever."

The team remained very still waiting on Carlos to respond; Dan's eyes held a silent plea as he stared at Carlos. "I know you're probably energy-tapped to the max, but if you think it's safe to drag in some fresh clothes, I think all the ladies could use 'em."

"Hell," Berkfield said, folding his arms and releasing a weary sigh. "All of us could use getting out of these damned demon-gook-splattered fatigues and into some casual cultural gear. Woulda been nice to just do something normal like go to the jazz fest . . . but *nooo,* it never works like that."

"Yeah," Carlos said quietly, his gaze seeking the window. "That's a good idea. Pick your rooms, I'll drop your bags, and people can get cleaned up, eat, and crash. Tomorrow is another day; we can hit the street and buy whatever. Two days from tomorrow will be the funeral—and I've gotta get a dark suit, anyway."

Damali watched the team's collective body language seem to instantly remember the loss of Father Pat. She knew they'd meant no harm. It was just that the things affecting their survival had come so fast and so furiously that even the death of a beloved team member had temporarily taken a backseat to the immediacy of security. Logistics were always paramount— where to go, how to hide, how to secure the new location, how to camouflage themselves amid civilians, how to get in clean food, water, supplies, and more artillery, how to steal a necessary few moments of regenerative sleep . . . all of that took precedence so they could live to fight another day. All of that was wearing. Living under constantly traumatic conditions didn't even begin to describe it.

Further demoralized by the renewed awareness that Father Pat hadn't made it through the siege, shoulders slumped, heads lowered, and bodies thudded against the walls, appliances, and countertop edges. Her hand sought Carlos's back, but he didn't move or look at her for a moment, just stiffened against her touch.

"All right, let's move out," Carlos said flatly, not looking at any one Guardian in particular. "Everybody knows the drill and has picked their watch. Those of you who are gonna take the first shift of showers and shut-eye, do it. Whoever's hungry, I suggest you bust a grub now, before some more bullshit jumps off. This house has been cleared."

No one said a word as Carlos walked out of the kitchen. All eyes sought his back and then Damali. The team listened as his footfalls crossed the floor and then went up the stairs to the second floor. No one had to tell her to go to him. She just silently left the room and followed the sounds of his movements through the house.

She found him in a room down the long west end of the hallway. The door was open, he was sprawled in a chair, head back against the wall with his eyes closed, breathing slowly. Two mud cloth satchels of clothing from the Shrine in Detroit sat on the floor beside him, evidence that he'd already dragged in each team member's previously abandoned gear. Carlos's pain was indeed her pain as she watched him fight against fatigue, trauma, heartbreak, and defeat.

Damali glanced around the pleasantly minimalist space before she shut the door behind her. She understood why Carlos had taken to the chair—besides just being utterly done, the pristine white cotton linens on the queen-sized bed would have been ruined by battle grime and the heavy, carved mahogany bureau and dresser from the motherland had the clean scent of lemon oil on it that defied one to sully it with dirty hands.

The poor man didn't appear to have the energy to move a limb, much less do more than pass out in a chair. It was as though he'd confined himself to a single place in the room where his grubby condition wouldn't leave as bad of a trail. Even the walls were white and the windows were flanked by ivory sheers. Just looking at the glistening floors she knew that the team should have removed their boots before entering the sacred enclosures, but it was too late for that now. They probably would have initially balked about doing that, anyway; they were all still wired.

Kneeling between Carlos's legs, she began working on his bootlaces, speaking in a gentle tone. "I'll cover you while you're in the bathroom. You take first shower and shut-eye this time."

He shook his head, but his body didn't resist as she began to slide off his grime-encrusted boots. "Uh-uh, I'm cool. You go ahead . . . you're the one who needs the rest and recovery."

She laid her cheek against his dirty pants leg for a moment. "No, baby . . . this time you give yourself a break. I'm all right." She pushed herself to stand before he could argue, bent to kiss the crown of his head, and then deftly unbuttoned his SWAT fatigue shirt. When he didn't resist, she slipped it off his shoulders, and then tugged at his T-shirt until it gave way, sliding it up his torso and over his head. She stopped his protest with a thumb pressed softly against his lips the moment she felt him inhale to release an objection. "Just do it for me, then, if you don't need the break," she murmured, cupping his cheek. She took him by the hand and made him stand, then unhooked his pants and unzipped them. "Get in the shower. I'll bring you a towel."

Extracting a 9mm from the back waistband of her jeans where she'd stashed it, Damali carefully set the gun on the dresser, her gaze holding Carlos's. Without a word she went back to him and slid off his pants and boxers, and made him step out of them.

"Let me find you a towel," she said in a gentle tone, hugging him for a moment. She laid her head on his shoulder, trying to send waves of empathy into his body through her touch, through her palms, through her soft nuzzle.

"You should be getting in and relaxing first with me covering you," he said in a pained voice with his eyes closed, and then slowly released her. He bent with a wince to sweep up his dirty clothes when she stepped away from him.

She stared at the multiple contusions and bruises on his body that were now beginning to angrily show. But she didn't say a word; it was that way with them. As long as they'd be in battles, one or the other of them—or both—would be coming home with wounds, if they were lucky. She was just glad that he didn't further protest as she handed him a fluffy white towel that she'd found in a hallway closet . . . his body would heal, that she could fix. Only, this time, the thing that the darkside had injured most was his heart.

Yonnie sat on the toilet seat lid with a gun dangling from his fingers. His shoulders were hunched forward, his head hung low, as he leaned his forearms on his thighs and stared at the white bathroom floor tiles that were slowly disappearing in the steam.

"I'm worried about my boy," he said quietly to Val as she turned off the shower spray and stepped onto a small white rug beside the tub.

"I know," she replied gently, twisting excess water out of her platinum locks and then beginning to dry off her wings. "Maybe you can talk to him in the morning . . . maybe after he has rested a while . . . after Damali has tried to heal his heart?"

Yonnie looked up, his gaze holding hers. "I love to watch you do that . . . dry your wings and then spread them."

She glanced away shyly and covered her nakedness with them. "You'll have to make them invisible again so I can go out amongst the humans later."

"Yeah . . . but later," he said, allowing his gaze to take in her smooth, dark, ebony skin that damply glistened beneath her walnut-hued feathers. "They're beautiful. You shouldn't have to hide them."

"People wouldn't understand," she said quietly, looking down at the floor.

"None of us should have to hide what we are," Yonnie said quietly. "I wish I could give you this—somewhere permanent to be . . . somewhere safe. But I can't."

"That doesn't matter," she whispered, swallowing hard. "You tried. The gift is that you cared to even try."

He stared at her and set his 9mm down carefully on the sink. "You're the gift," he whispered. "You make this whole ugly war of the world go away when I see you like this. I take that image with me on the battlefield every time."

Yonnie stood and slowly walked over to her and then traced her cheek with his thumb, careful not to brush her body with his dirty SWAT fatigues. "Figure, if I die, if the darkside comes for me and the Light can't get to me fast enough . . . I'll have an angel in my mind's eye. Will see her, my woman, naked, and beautiful, and clean, and pure with her big, beautiful, sad eyes holding only me in them. I could die like that, Val . . . with that image, and not care."

"Don't die on me, Yolando," she said in a quiet, urgent tone. "Please, for the love of God, don't you die on me."

She tried to close the space between them, but he held her away with a gentle grasp of her upper arms and yielded only to take her mouth.

"I'm dirty," he whispered into her mouth. "Just touching your arms put smudges on you again. Let me hit the shower."

She held his face between her palms. "I don't care if you've showered or not when you hold me . . . I'm just thankful that you're still alive to do that—don't you understand?"

He rested his forehead against hers. "Do you remember the one thing you said to me after we'd first met . . . the thing that destroyed a brother?"

"No," she murmured, lifting her head to look into his eyes.

His gaze drank her in, noticing that gooseflesh pebbled her arms. Trembling slightly he also noticed her breaths had become shallow like his. The sound of intermittently dripping water echoed in the small, warm confines of misted space. Suddenly, as though her cleanliness could wash away the stain of every human and inhuman horror he'd witnessed, he wanted to wash himself with the totality of her.

"You told me to be valiant, be victorious," he replied in a gravelly voice. "No one had ever asked me to be that in my two hundred years of existing. I want to always be that for you, baby . . . at least that."

"Then be valiant, be victorious now," she whispered, unbuttoning his shirt slowly, and sealing the moist space between them. "Dirty or not, conquer me."

# CHAPTER SIXTEEN

Two uneventful days and uneventful nights had the danger of lulling the team into a false sense of normalcy. Floors had been bluing washed and blessed again. Rugs had been cleaned and anointed to make up for the team's initial invasion of the house while wearing battle boots. Shoes now came off respectfully at the door. Clothing had been purchased the old-fashioned way. Guardians ate on the back deck and front porch, playing cards and kicking it with the north-central team.

But the overall mood remained somber. A funeral was looming and the loss was visceral. The cardinal had sent black funeral limousines, which everyone agreed was best—there was no need to make a fold-away entrance that would completely freak out the unaware powers that be.

Damali looked at her husband, who had barely said two words during the uneventful wait for the funeral. She watched him deliberately fold his white, pressed handkerchief into the breast pocket of his black Armani suit so that only a quarter-inch hint of it showed. He'd worked on polishing his shoes himself, laboring over every detail until they shone like glass. And now he stood there in the mirror adjusting his tie, his expression stone, only the muscle in his jaw pulsing.

Although she wanted to reach out to him, she also knew that now was just not the time. Hurt radiated off his aura in waves so profound that she could almost see them suffocating him. Yet she also knew that if she went to him right now, he'd shatter— and that would wound him even more deeply.

Right now, he needed to keep his game face on. Needed that steel grit to get through whatever he had to endure today. So she gave him his man-space, and had refused to wear black, knowing there was life on the other side of the earth plane.

Later she'd remind him that this was a homecoming. Later she'd explain why every female on the team had intuitively chosen a chakra color to wear, rather than black . . . and why she'd chosen green—the color of healing, of new life, and the heart bridge chakra. Later. All of that could be discussed later.

Right now, they needed to all go outside and get into the limos. Because, right now as he turned his back to her and walked out of the room, she could feel the black-box in his head quavering, melting, accidentally allowing her to see inside the pain he'd sworn to himself he'd never allow her to witness . . . letting her see the sacrifice that Father Patrick had made for them to hide their child.

Damali hugged herself for a moment and closed her eyes. Carlos yelling her name up the steps in a harsh tone jerked her attention to the door.

"The limo is here!" he yelled up the steps. "We gotta go, D."

She walked out of the room quickly and stopped at the top of the landing. Guardians were filtering out of the door, but she held Carlos's gaze as she descended the stairs. Silvery tears glittered in his eyes, wetting his lashes, but they wouldn't fall. His Adam's apple bobbed in his throat like a man drowning, but his mouth was tightly sealed against the urge to gasp and set hard like his knit brows.

"I'm coming," she said softly, allowing her tears to fall for Father Patrick, to fall instead of Carlos's for him. "I'm sorry."

He wiped her face with his thumbs and gave her a salty kiss when she reached the bottom of the steps. "Me, too—I didn't mean to yell at you." He then gave her a quick hug, lifting his chin high above her head. "It'll be all right," he said, giving her back a quick pat. "We gotta go."

She just nodded and swallowed hard, letting him pretend to himself that he was comforting her, was being the rock . . . she would be his shock absorber, would channel his pain, would wail and cry for him so that he didn't have to, so that he could pull her away from the grave site, could be the one to remain stoic—whatever it took to release the burden from his heart while protecting his dignity as head of household, because as neighbors came out on porches and Guardians climbed into the long, black vehicles that was the greatest gift she could give her husband right now.

"Ashes to ashes . . . dust to dust . . ."

Damali heard the final words of the service being spoken in a very remote part of her mind as she stared out over the rolling green hills of Westminster Cemetery that overlooked Belmont Avenue and the peaceful valley beyond where the Schuylkill River flowed. Members of the seminary stepped forward and handed Carlos a silver urn. She wanted to tell them so badly that the angels had come to collect his father-seer at the moment of impact and that his body was just a shell that had housed a bright, shining spirit that the darkside never got to claim. The man had been consecrated by the Light and what had been burned to ash and bits of bone was the least of who Father Patrick had been.

But bagpipes interrupted those thoughts.

Her hand went to Carlos's back. He glanced at Rabbi Zeitloff, who was shaking with grief and had begun to wail. Imam Asula, Monk Lin, and Dan went to the elderly cleric's aid as he beat his chest yelling, "Why!" She felt Carlos take a deep, laboring breath and she knew what was next.

Carlos simply opened the urn as he stared out at the horizon. His voice was quiet and gravelly, but contained inner strength. "Thank you for being my father for as long as you did. Enjoy going home."

Ashes funneled out of the urn in a furious spiral away from the small assembly. The cardinal seemed like he was about to pass out, but no one challenged Carlos for disposing of the ashes on hallowed ground without a permit. He then dropped the urn without even looking at it, and it bounced and rolled near the small grave marker that gave Father Patrick's birth and death dates. Damali stooped and placed a single red rose on the marker, but left the urn where it lay as Carlos walked off. Guardian eyes sought hers with a silent question in them, but she shook her head. The man still needed his space.

He couldn't breathe. Rabbi Zeitloff's wails rang in his ears. No matter what Adam had told him, the loss still burned like a hot poker through his chest. But he'd done all the mourning he was gonna do, had shed tears. Now it was time to redress this bullshit, even if it had purpose—even if it had duped the darkside.

A quiet presence that stepped out from behind a mausoleum vault made him start and take a fighter's stance to face it.

"I come with a message," a slightly built, now very pale priest said. His dark eyes held fear as he made the sign of the cross over his chest. "Please, in the name of God, don't hurt me."

Carlos studied the man hard and then realized he'd accidentally dropped fang on a civilian. Running his tongue over his incisors, he also willed his eyes to normalize. Only fangs and a silver glare could have stricken the baby-faced priest so badly.

"Are you a . . . the demon assassin we seek?"

"Depends on which side is seeking, but yeah, I'm definitely an assassin."

The cleric nervously raked his fingers through his mussed brunet hair. "The Templars told me to give you this on consecrated ground and nowhere else. I didn't know how to find you again—not even the cardinal did. But we prayed you'd come to the service."

Carlos waited as the cleric extracted a piece of folded-up paper from his vestment pocket and offered it to him with a shaking hand. The moment Carlos touched it, the man snatched his hand back and crossed himself again.

"Your eyes . . . your teeth . . . I saw your size change right before my eyes."

Carlos rubbed his palm over his jaw and glanced up at the priest as he opened the paper. "I'm not the undead—anymore."

"Anymore," the young cleric whispered in a strangled squeak.

"I got a reprieve from the Light, so I'm definitely the man for this job."

The cleric stepped back and crossed himself again when Carlos looked up with a frown from the paper he held.

"What the hell is this?" Carlos said, brandishing the paper. "What side do you work for!"

"The church, of course," the priest said, backing away.

"Then what's the church doing handing me a map of Washington, D.C., with a pentagram on it? You know who uses this symbol—and in the end of days that rat bastard is able to walk on befouled sacred ground! You better talk to me and talk to me fast, priest. Today is the last day you want to get on my bad side, playing games."

"I'm not playing games. This came from the Templar who left it under my door. I'm an empath . . . he sent a mental dart that pierced my mind and then I got a vision of Father Patrick." The young cleric backed up until his thighs collided with a headstone, and he covered his face and throat with his forearms as he began to weep. "Save me, Christ, from this abomination!"

"Oh, put your arms down," Carlos muttered. "I'm not about to rip your throat out. I just needed to know you weren't an agent for the darkside." He studied the map as the hysterical cleric slowly lowered his arms, panting. "What message did Father Patrick bring from the other side?"

"He showed me the Scottish Rite Temple," the priest said, winded and now leaning on a headstone.

"Why didn't he come to me directly?" Carlos said, eyeing the priest with suspicion.

"Because you were in too much pain," the priest said quietly. "I can still feel it . . . and I am sorry for your loss."

*"De nada,"* Carlos muttered, returning his attention to the map, somewhat mollified by the priest's explanation. "But, I don't understand." He looked at the map that seemed as though it had been printed off an Internet driving directions Web site, containing local streets of Washington, D.C., yet with a thick, hand-drawn pen line creating a pentagram on it.

"Look carefully," the priest said. "Massachusetts Avenue intersects with Rhode Island Avenue, Connecticut Avenue, Vermont Avenue, and K Street to form the five-pointed star immediately north of the White House . . . and remember the prophecy—they will come from the north to conquer." The cleric wiped a new sheen of sweat from his brow. "Then look at the positioning of the Capitol, Jefferson Memorial, and Washington Monument, which form a Mason's compass and a pyramid to the left of that. Even Metatron's Cube can be seen in all this. I'm not a Templar; I don't know what any of this means to your quest. This is all I know, I swear to you. But our dearly departed brother seemed urgent in the vision that he wanted you to push forward to Washington, D.C. Maybe there is more for you at the Scottish Rite Temple?"

"Metatron's Cube?" Carlos said, studying the map with new eyes. He suddenly jerked his head up. "Where's Rabbi Zeitloff?"

"Somewhat overcome and waiting in the cars."

"Thanks."

Carlos took off in a dash across the cemetery grass. He could see the cars and people milling about in the distance. The rabbi sat in the backseat of one of the black sedans with his head leaned back against the headrest. His eyes were closed and tears stained his cheeks, but he had considerably calmed. Dan moved aside as Carlos approached the vehicle as did Imam Asula and Monk Lin.

"He took it really hard," Dan said quietly as Carlos slowed to a trot and then finally stopped beside him. "We sent Bobby and J.L. to go get him some water."

Monk Lin bowed slightly and let out a weary breath. "These are hard times for us all."

"Persevere, young brother," Imam Asula said, and then swallowed hard as he stepped away from the car.

Carlos bent and peered in the door, and then slid into the backseat with the elderly rabbi.

"Hey . . . Rabbi," Carlos said in a gentle tone. "I know how you feel."

"Carlos, Carlos, Carlos," the rabbi said, shaking his head and slowly pounding on his chest with his fist. He opened his bloodshot eyes and stared at Carlos. "He was like my own brother. That crotchety old priest and I would debate till the wee hours . . . he was my friend. I have lost my dear friend. I am an old man; friends don't come easy now . . . who will I fight with?" He released a sad chuckle as new tears filled his eyes. "I should complain to Patrick for allowing this to happen to himself."

"I know," Carlos said, a sad smile tugging at his mouth. "He used to give me the blues and stayed on my case. I'm gonna miss that tough old man, too. So, maybe you and I can fight about philosophy sometimes, huh? How about it? I give as good as I get."

Zeitloff wiped his eyes with a shaking hand and then patted Carlos's cheek. "I should love to argue with you." He fell quiet and stared at Carlos, new tears rising. "I see now why he loved you so."

Carlos glanced away and took in a deep breath, needing a moment to regain his voice. He slowly extracted the map from his pocket and held it for a moment before showing it to the rabbi.

"The young priest said a Templar gave him this . . . our team has to go to D.C. It's part of a clue as to where we might be able to get a jump on the enemy. But he also said Metatron's Cube can be seen in this map. My Kabbalah facts are rusty, I admit, but I do know that Metatron is an archangel."

Rabbi Zeitloff sat forward quickly, adjusting his glasses on his nose with agitation. He spoke in short, excited bursts in hushed tones, constantly looking around him as he did so. "Enoch was swept away to Heaven and for his loyal service he sits at the right hand of Jehovah, Yahveh, *as the archangel, Metatron*—who was the one that transmitted the secrets of the Kabbalah to humanity to use to protect themselves from evil. Kabbalah by definition means, transmission and preservation of knowledge . . . to receive. A Kabbalistic message is one coming from the highest realms of On High, Carlos."

"Enoch also became an archangel?" Carlos said, eyes growing wide. "Damali's oracle used Enoch's name in the first metaphor—the first clue she gave us about things to come—when we got to Detroit."

"Then the pearl was giving you much more than you know," Rabbi Zeitloff said, leaning even closer.

"We thought it was a link to the Archangel Uriel," Carlos whispered. "So there were two of them guarding us. . . . Whoa."

"It was linked to Uriel . . . but look deeper, and understand the Enoch connection to your mission," the rabbi said in a conspiratorial murmur. "Enoch was the grandfather of Noah, and Yahveh forewarned him of the great flood. Yahveh told Enoch to inscribe all that is known on two huge pillars—the sum total of all human knowledge—so it would be preserved. Therefore," he added, pointing to the map, "Enoch is also our metaphor for symbolic architecture—messages hidden in the stone—just as the pyramids are Egypt's stone libraries. Something you seek or need to know is in the stones . . . in Metatron's Cube, that surrounds this deadly pentagram . . . perhaps only Templars or Masons that founded this country would know?"

The two men stared at each other for a moment.

"When Damali first went through her Neteru enlightening, part of her journey took her through a Masonic temple in Philadelphia," Carlos said, intermittently staring at the map and then Rabbi Zeitloff.

"Our friend, Father Patrick, was killed trying to get information from his Templar brotherhood for the cardinal," the rabbi said, now gazing out of the sedan window. "It's gotta be in the stone. The pentagram has always been there in the street layout, but someone also came behind it and encased it in Metatron's Cube, and that sits to the left of the Masonic compass and pyramid that is in the street grid, too . . . somebody knew. Somebody wanted to seal in whatever could emerge from that pentagram in the future."

"Yeah, and we've now got a pretty good idea how bad that thing is." Carlos stared at Rabbi Zeitloff for a moment. "What if something disturbed the lines on Metatron's Cube . . . wouldn't that allow the unspeakable to get out of the pentagram?"

"Yes," the rabbi whispered. "And it's right in front of the White House, in direct alignment."

"Then we've definitely gotta head to D.C. now."

The rabbi held Carlos's arm to stay his leave. "Ride the train. Preserve your strength. You must be careful and save your energy for emergency escapes from human and supernatural predators alike . . . you could be accidentally hunted down and shot by human forces who think you're a national threat carrying concealed weapons into the nation's capital. One false move and you could be caught and land in prison where they'll throw away the key, or worse, you could impugn your soul by having to kill a human lest you be killed—then what?"

His grip tightened on Carlos's arm, beseeching Carlos to listen. "Both you and Damali, as well as your team, are battle weary—if not in body, then in spirit—especially you, son. The stress that prevails upon your spirit is incalculable."

"What else is new?" Carlos said with a sad smile. "Stress is our way of life."

"Take the train. Dress like normal people on tour . . . and visit where you must, but looking like civilians."

"We'll take the train," Carlos promised him. "Maybe you guys from the Covenant could arrange for us to ride a small tour bus, get us some brochures and cameras, and maybe have some ammo hidden in the floorboards of the vehicle and taped under the seats that I can transport in fast if we get in a firefight?"

"I think we could do something of that nature," Rabbi Zeitloff said with a droll smile. "And maybe an old rabbi could come to help avenge the death of his dear friend?"

Carlos patted the elderly cleric on his shoulder, gently declining the offer of a suicide mission. "Maybe a good rabbi might best help this go-round by sending up prayers with his remaining dear friends, Monk Lin and Imam Asula—because this battle might get messy. We might need someone alive on the outside to post bail or to send lawyers, or maybe raise a protest march to free the Neterus and their team. We could definitely use a safe house location down in the District." Carlos smiled as Rabbi Zeitloff clucked his tongue in annoyance. "And we might need someone to come home to, if we make it." His last statement mellowed the old man considerably.

"I hadn't thought of that." Rabbi Zeitloff let out a weary breath. "We have a house for you in Georgetown."

"I don't wanna come home to nobody being there from the old original family," Carlos said quietly, looking Rabbi Zeitloff in the eyes.

"I understand, son," the rabbi said with a gentle tone. "We old men will stay alive to give you young ones something to hope for."

"You've gotta be here to bless babies in the future and to do Bas Mitzvahs and Bar Mitzvahs and to make sure we're doing what we should . . . you know?"

Rabbi Zeitloff nodded. "We'll do our part—you just make sure you do yours." He looked at Carlos and then suddenly hugged him. "You come home so you don't break an old man's heart. All of you. Not a single loss. You promise me."

When they got into the limo, Carlos turned to her. She'd watched everything transpire at a distance, but wasn't sure what all was happening. He didn't say a word, just cradled the sides of her face with his hands and slowly allowed his fingers to slide up and into her hair. He closed his eyes, and then gently rested his forehead against hers and simply opened up his mind's eye to her. It all poured into her brain so quickly and with such haunting thrust that at moments she gasped. When he was done, he was winded, she was panting. Without telling him, she'd pulled as much of the pain away from him as she could with the information. She touched his cheek with trembling fingers, never divulging that small detail. To battle this ultimate evil, he needed to be whole.

"How will we keep the public from recognizing us if we get on the Acela train?" she asked quietly. "To the general public, we're still the Warriors of Light band . . . and autograph seekers and whatnot could be an issue. Just sitting on the porch back on Haines Street got us enough looks to almost blow our cover."

"We're gonna have to slightly mind-stun 'em and hope for the best."

# CHAPTER SEVENTEEN

Damali peered around the huge, marble-ensconced edifice of the Thirtieth Street train station, her gaze roving up toward the glass and brass pathways of the ancient, majestic structure that linked north to south sections of the building along the western wall. The last time she'd been even near the place, thousands of demon bats and Harpies had shattered plate glass to whirl after her squad in a deadly funnel cloud. That night, they'd lost Padre Lopez. She could tell every Guardian on the team was revisiting the memory, and she was just glad that the building had been repaired so there was no outward memory trigger of that very bad night when Lilith was on their asses.

As she watched the central information board intermittently flip down small black panels to update train arrivals and departures, she wondered if going by rail was a good idea. Fold-away was best, but Rabbi Zeitloff was right—she and Carlos needed to preserve their strength. Going by car was just as perilous, maybe more so. An eighteen-wheeler could be sent to squash them like a bug, and the poor human driver that would have been temporarily possessed would be collateral damage. Then again, riding the rails meant putting hundreds of innocent passengers at risk, if evil decided to rear its ugly head while they were on board. But that was also true of highway motorists. A crazy chain-reaction pileup was no less dangerous.

Damali closed her eyes as her stomach growled. Auntie Anne's pretzels were calling her name, along with all the luscious, forbidden butter they were drizzled with. She could practically taste the tangy, pungent flavor of honey mustard sauce on her tongue . . . that and a lemonade.

Carlos stood up from the long, gleaming wooden bench. She looked up at him with a slight frown of concern.

"Everything all right?"

"Be right back," he said with a half smile.

Big Mike was right behind him. "Anybody else want anything?"

Dan headed to the Au Bon Pain. "Speak now, or forever hold your peace."

"Toffee cookies," Heather said with a grin. "Lots. And milk."

"Done," he said, pointing at her, and then whirling around to jog toward the store.

That was it, the team scattered to whichever food emporium was calling their names. Even Marlene was up on her feet with Shabazz checking out the Amazon Cafe smoothie bar. Resistance was futile. The team needed to eat, get a good base on before whatever kicked off—because who knew when something so basic as eating a decent meal might happen again.

Carlos was back before the others and he handed her a greasy bag loaded with pretzels and dip, along with an extra large tumbler of lemonade. "Already blessed," he said, sitting beside her.

She took a deep swig of the very sweet lemonade and her eyes crossed with ecstasy. "Thank you. How'd you know?"

"Same way you knew to put a pain siphon in that mental convo we had on the way back from the funeral."

For a moment she just looked at him.

"Thank you, baby," he said quietly. "I needed that . . . just like you need to put something in your stomach. Want a salad or fruit?" He glanced around the train station and then back at her.

Damali just shook her head. "Thanks, maybe later . . . wrong as it is, this was what I had a taste for."

Carlos took the huge plastic tumbler from her so that she could ferociously dig into the bag of buttery pretzels and he chuckled as she popped a large piece of sesame pretzel into her mouth with a moan.

"I should have gotten you something to eat," she mumbled. "You haven't eaten in days."

"Oh, don't worry—I always get mine," he said with a sly grin and sipped her lemonade.

She smiled as he dug into the bag and opened up one of the little mustard dip containers and then sat there holding her lemonade with one hand and a dip in the other as though he were a human tray. She broke off a piece of pretzel and fed him and they went on that way in companionable silence, both eating and coordinating the meal so that the butter from the bag didn't soil their clothes.

Before long, Big Mike was back with Inez carrying large Styrofoam trays. The aroma that wafted off them screamed great soul food. Damali and Carlos looked up and had to laugh.

"I don't know what's in the containers, and it isn't my business, but you know Shabazz and Marlene are gonna get on your cases," Damali warned.

"That place over there called Delilah's is off the chain, D," Mike said with a wide smile as he plopped down on the bench and opened his meal.

"You let him go to a place called Delilah's?" Carlos said, teasing Inez. "You know what happened to Samson, right?"

Inez smoothed a palm over Big Mike's bald head as he hungrily bit into a crispy piece of fried chicken. "He's got the jump on Samson—no hair . . . so what could I do?"

"Greens, mac and cheese, candied yams, corn bread, fried chicken, humph, humph, humph!" Mike declared, shaking his head as he devoured his platter. "Three days and three nights of vegan food and a brother just got broke down when I passed the place."

"I'm jealous," Inez said with a smile as she tore into a golden fried wing. "Might have to step to that sister who owns the joint for making my husband get that look on his face."

Much-needed laughter filtered between the couples as they waited for the rest of the team to return. In those short minutes the tension temporarily abated. It was a tiny sliver of normalcy that found its way into their lives in a very mundane place. But each person took it for the gift it was—just a few moments where one could laugh, break bread together, and just be like every other human being on the planet.

Carlos kissed her cheek as she dug into the bag to begin tearing apart the last pretzel.

"Rabbi was right," he said with a sad smile, glancing around the train station as Guardians made their way back to the benches.

"Yeah," Damali murmured. "This was just what the doctor ordered."

It was the strangest of post-funeral repasts that he'd ever experienced, but truthfully it was one of the best. Momentary peace claimed him as the old team banter went into full effect.

Limousines had returned people to the safe house on Haines Street so they could change into comfortable gear. Gone were the suits and dresses. Jeans, sneakers, tank tops, and T-shirts replaced all of that. There was time enough to pack a change of clothing in their mud cloth bags, and to stash a weapon in them for the road. The squad knew what time it was, but they also knew that living in the present, laughing in the moment when one could, was the key to life. Who knew what was next, or if tomorrow would even come. So you buried the pain, cried hard and deep and true, and then walked forward—embracing love and laughter with no less force than you'd embraced the pain. Monk Lin would have been proud, if he'd known they'd finally figured it out.

Carlos let his gaze drift to the large train information board as his wife's buttery hand slid into his. It was time to catch the bullet.

"Lilith! What is your plan?"

The double, black marble doors to the Vampire Council blew off their hinges at the bellowed question. Flames roared across the floor and encircled thrones, making the blood veins in the black marble blister and pop. Tiny, bony, little bat-winged demons fled the sea of flames baring jagged teeth and brandishing miniature pitchforks and daggers, hissing and spitting at Lilith's protective Harpies, causing them to flee. Vampires cringed where they'd previously been sitting in regenerative repose, their stricken gazes on their chairwoman as hooves sounded in ominous footfalls.

"I have only been away for three days and three nights and all you have done is monitored the Neteru team, who is now en route to be ever nearer to my heir?" an incredulous, disembodied voice roared.

"Yes," Lilith said calmly, leaving her throne and stepping through the swirling flames at the base of it. "That was prudent."

"Prudent?"

An invisible backhanded slap connected with her cheek, sending her stumbling against the bargaining table. She straightened herself with care and dabbed at the bleeding, open gash on her face with the back of her wrist.

"Yes, prudent," she repeated with no hint of tremor or

submissiveness in her voice. "Archangels had shielded them, had inserted themselves into this conflict. If we had acted prematurely to block them from their travel plans, attacked them directly, then that would have been an immediate red flag that our heir was nearby."

The flames that licked at the hem of her gown receded.

"Fallon and Lucrezia will use human forces in the media to attack and discredit them," Lilith said proudly, waving her hand toward her council members. "Elizabeth and Vlad will use the army of politicians and decision makers at our behest within the nation's political cesspools to send out legions of human law-enforcers. It is beautiful . . . higher-ranking evil men that belong to us can send lower-ranking men who are pure of heart on a fool's errand—and those who are sent to capture and detain the Neteru team will be human, therefore it will be against the angelic laws to kill them. We no longer have to use our own demons as cannon fodder and can conserve our resources for the larger military campaign we will wage at the very end. Sebastian will be my right hand of black magic to bend human wills and twist minds in the gray-zone of choice, earth, where even the angels cannot prevail against the will of a human. Trust me, there will be no justice. There will be no peace."

She released a sinister chuckle and stared out into the black void of nothingness just beyond the destroyed doors as the Council Chambers slowly cooled. "So let them go down to Washington, D.C.—where they will learn of our treachery at levels they've never conceived were humanly possible. There, for once and for all, they will get more than they've bargained for!"

"Is it me, or did this trip seem a little too uneventful?" Rider said quietly, leaning over the seat to speak to Carlos and Damali.

"Don't look a gift horse in the mouth," Shabazz muttered before either Damali or Carlos could answer.

"I'm feeling Rider, though," Marlene countered, giving Shabazz a sideways glance as the Neterus nodded.

Damali looked out of the window at the Baltimore-Washington corridor scenery whizzing by. "I know we've been covered by angelic grace, but still . . ."

"Why don't we wait to discuss this on hallowed ground and not while we're flying down the rails on a bullet train doing better than a hundred-and-fifty miles per hour?" Carlos said coolly, glancing at the small posse that had gathered near.

"Say no more; I'm convinced." Rider held up his hands and walked back down the aisle to his seat.

As they exited the Amtrak train at Union Station in Washington D.C., Rider's question niggled the back of her mind. Damali kept her gaze sweeping as the team walked down the concrete ramp to exit into the lively, grand old structure that defined eastern seaboard rail stations.

Bustling food emporiums teemed with activity. Small, expensive boutiques flaunted the latest in fashion temptations. Art deco black-and-white marble floors echoed with thousands of footfalls beneath massive, vaulted cathedral-like ceilings that were studded with breathtaking chandeliers above a brass rail spiral staircase. Unlike the boring modern architecture of an airport, the old train stations were artistic expressions of grandeur from a bygone era. It had been so long since she and the team had traveled by normal conveyance that Damali slowed her gait to simply appreciate it all and take it in.

Bright sun and balmy early September temperatures met them as they exited the station and hesitated for a moment at the cab stand. Then just across from the long, snaking line of cab commuters, in the next small cut-out they saw a white light-duty van marked CLERICAL WORLD TOURS AND TRAVEL.

Words weren't even necessary. The group's seers all exchanged a look and the team proceeded across the pavement divides to approach the van.

A chubby African American driver with a graying, scruffy beard and wearing a yarmulke opened the door and hopped down, followed out of the tour van by a younger man who could have passed for Bobby's older brother.

"Cordell," the driver said with a smile, shaking Carlos's and Damali's hands. "Glad you found us. I'm gonna navigate you around this city . . . since I *see* good," he said with implied emphasis. "And this young man here is Doug—your tour guide and my mechanic . . . *tactically* speaking," he added with a wink. "Plus we've got some tour support coming in from Philadelphia, our locals in D.C., and some folks are also comin' up from Georgia and the ATL . . . just to be on the safe side."

"Cool," Carlos said, making swift introductions as the team piled onto the bus.

Once the doors were shut and Cordell hefted his rotund frame into the driver's seat, Doug stood and began walking down the aisle, handing out brochures.

"Under the central floorboard," their tour guide said, pointedly holding each person's gaze for a moment as he gave them a brochure, "is enough ammo to send this vehicle into orbit. Seven handheld Uzis, three pumps, an RPG and shells, and ten 9s, plus three M-16s. Under each seat is a 9 and three clips, duct-taped. If we get in a corner and have to leave the van, we'll have to blow it—because what your team needs to understand about the local environment in D.C. is this—we've got CIA, FBI, Homeland Security, Black Ops, local cops, and every branch of the military down here at the Pentagon . . . Langley is a stone's throw down the road and they have enough satellites in the air to pick up the license plate on this vehicle, scramble F-16 fighter jets, and torch us before we ever turn onto Pennsylvania Avenue. We clear?"

"Clear as a frickin' bell," Rider said, running his fingers through his hair. "I knew I had a bad feeling about this tour."

"Yeah, well, we've been on pins and needles our entire Guardianhood, waiting for the day the firefight might come this way . . . just seemed like it was due. We thought the hit on the Pentagon during 9/11 was the big one, but it turned out to be human-inspired insanity." Doug looked away for a moment as a call came into his Bluetooth earpiece. "Put on the news," he said to Cordell, reaching to his hip for an iPhone.

Immediately J.L. whipped out his unit, too, as Cordell fiddled with the van radio. "They're saying that in going through the rubble after the West Coast fires, they found the house registered to some cult organization that the Warriors of Light were supposed to be living in . . . and they found weapons and drugs. They're looking for us for questioning. Said there's significant concern that we might be supporting terrorist groups."

"Let the games begin," Yonnie said to Carlos as the group went completely still.

"You people have a fallback position?" Doug asked, looking at Damali and Carlos. "This is a bad town to be wanted in for terrorism."

"We feel you," Shabazz said, glancing out the window.

"Our fallback position is a fold-away to a safe house," Carlos said, looking at Doug hard. "Just get us inside this," he added, pulling the map out of his back jeans pocket and opening it for Doug. "Then you can drop us off so you don't draw heat to your team that has to live here."

"Yeah, well, we've got a safe house for you over in George-town on M Street, but the problem is in the pentagram zone—we found out the hard way that unless you're outside of it on one of the Metatron Cube's axises, everything we've got shuts down."

"Talk to me," Carlos said quickly, glancing at Damali.

"That," Doug said, pointing at the satanic symbol, "is built into the stones. Therefore, while inside it, it works like a negative force field . . . seers can't see, audios can't hear, tacticals have no charge. Maybe as a Neteru you have more juice, but it's been our experience that we go back to being like a human Joe-regular inside that thing. So we hug the perimeter, and don't screw around inside it—ever. If you're going in there, you need to have a plan that's purely based on human engineering stuff . . . because I swear to you, if you get trapped in there, it's *ball game*. We lost half a squad over there in the early days."

"I can rig something maybe," J.L. said unsurely, glancing at the team.

"What about that copper pipe bucket thing you did just before we left San Diego?" Damali asked, glancing between Doug and J.L.

"I don't know," J.L. said honestly, dragging his fingers through his hair. "Might not know till we're in a firefight, which isn't a good time to figure out the thing is flawed."

"I'm in a 100 percent agreement with you, brother," Big Mike said.

"Here's the thing, too," Berkfield said, glancing around the team as he leaned over the seat. "I'm listening to what Doug is saying about the human factor . . . like the authorities. The darkside could sic human police on us and we can't walk down the street with a bucket of copper pipes, what amounts to shrapnel and resin. That just screams shoot me and call the bomb squad, anybody feeling what I'm saying here?"

"Loud and clear," Yonnie said, shaking his head. "You pop a decent human cop that's just doing his job, or we send a shell to hit a Black Hawk chopper that's on our asses, accidentally taking out some military good guy who mistook us for bad guys, and we might be dealing with a court date with the darkside, after all."

"I'm feeling you on *that,*" Jose said, leaning forward to pound Yonnie's fist over a seat.

"Now you see what our parameters have been down here," Doug said, nodding.

"Yeah, but we could have our stoneworkers stand on the perimeter of the Metatron's Cube and draw power from that," Heather offered, glancing around the group nervously. "If they can bend power negatively, we can pull out their lines by standing on the outer rim in our own formation."

"Qi Gong . . . women are magnetic, men are electric," Damali said, slapping Heather five. "Okay, so we keep the team on the outer perimeter—me and Carlos go into the hot-zone. If we get screwed, tacticals send an electrical pulse to hit us at the same time our evenly balanced female squad does a magnetic extraction."

"I don't like the plan," Carlos said, "but it's the only rational plan we've got."

"If something jumps off, we blur the license plates—immediately," Doug said, standing in the center aisle. "Otherwise they'll immediately decode it as a phony and rush the truck. Although we've taken great measures to have underground safe houses and vehicles, passports and IDs, there's always human error and the supernatural that can sometimes break our barriers. However, our biggest problem at the moment is, you guys are highly recognizable as a known celeb band."

"That part we can fix," Carlos said. "A lil' mind-stun never hurt anybody."

"Yeah, but in the hot-zone, that won't work," Damali said, touching his arm. "We're gonna have to go with human disguises when we go in there."

"All right, we can hook that up," Doug said, leaning down to look out the window.

"We got a problem at our first tour stop," Cordell said, slowing the van as police crime scene tape and a horizontal, black-and-white police cruiser blocked the boulevard that led to the Scottish Rite Temple. He stared at the helmeted officer that waved for him to turn and keep going, then followed directions. "Sixteenth Street is blocked and it looks like the two arteries, Columbia Road and Harvard Street are, too. We can't get to All Souls Church, National Baptist Memorial, the Unitarian Church across from that, or the Scottish Rite Temple, where we was headed."

"That is so not a good sign to be blocked out of four sanctuaries this early in the day," Juanita said, flopping back into her seat with a groan.

"You sound like me, sister," Rider said, his gaze narrowed as he peered out of the window.

"We could possibly get to the temple on foot," Bobby offered.

"No need," Carlos said quickly, looking in the direction of the inaccessible building. "The Templar I was supposed to meet inside the Scottish Rite Temple is dead."

## @ CHAPTER EIGHTEEN

"Okay," Damali said, dragging her fingers through her hair as the van aimlessly maneuvered through Washington's gridlocked streets. "If the information Enoch had was in the architecture, and Masons built D.C. . . . it's in the stones, and the map shows that it's in the actual concrete street patterns . . . there's gotta be another lodge or something we can do research on to find out what was in the Scottish Rite Temple."

"Try the mother temple," Cordell said blithely with a shrug.

"Where?" Carlos said.

Cordell looked in the rearview mirror and beamed. "The past is prologue, my friend. This old black Israelite knows a little bit. Right, Doug?"

Doug nodded. "Cordell is brilliant, but doesn't like to let people know. I learned the streets from him." Doug winked at Cordell.

"Hey, I'm just an old black man driving a bus . . . but I do know that thirteen blocks north of the White House and thirteen blocks south of the temple we was trying to get to, right on the corner of Sixteenth and S Streets, is one of the most important Masonic temples in the world. House of the Temple—headquarters of the Mother Supreme Council of the World . . . and the Supreme Council of the Third Degree of Scottish Rite Masons of the Southern Jurisdiction. Steps are set up in three, five, seven, nine groupings that lead to a doorway with a two-to-one proportion, just like the smaller Scottish Rite Temple on Sixteenth and Harvard. It's based on Kemetic architecture, and has one of the most impressive Masonic libraries in the world. Got 'Knowledge Is Power' etched in brass on two sphinxes of wisdom-knowledge and power-action."

Damali and Carlos shared a look, and Yonnie leaned forward.

"Cordell said knowledge is power is on that building?" Yonnie's gaze held Carlos's. "That's right off the old thrones, man—basic."

"I feel you, man," Carlos said in a low murmur, giving Yonnie the vibe to be cool and let Cordell talk.

"The Temple Room got thirty-three columns that's thirty-three-feet high . . . with thirty-three seats for the highest level of Masons—thirty-three degree Masons inducted into the Mystic Shrine," Cordell continued proudly. "So, if there's something in the stones that was in the Scottish Rites Temple, the mother temple would have it, too—they're mirror images."

"You said your contact was dead," Doug interjected, looking at Carlos and cutting off Cordell's spiel. "If bodies are dropping already, then you need an exit strategy."

"How'd it happen?" Berkfield said, glancing around the team.

"Man got his throat cut and so-called robbed trying to get up the steps to the temple so he could meet y'all," Cordell said, all mirth leaving his tone as he relayed the information he'd heard earlier on his police scanner. "Dougie is right. All y'all seers open up a channel so I can show you our network. If the house on M is under siege, then we gotta take you through the 'hood over in southeast and either out into Virginia or Maryland, depending on whether you wanna hide heading north or south. Worse case, we can get you out into the Chesapeake Bay and head you toward Bermuda, if it's real hot, and from there you can jump down to the Caribbean. But most everywhere has extradition back to the United States these days. You can run, but it's real hard to hide from Big Brother, once they come gunning for you."

"Let's hope it won't come to that," Marjorie said in a quiet tone.

"We're already there, Marj," Berkfield said, growing annoyed. "Didn't you hear the news J.L. just rattled off? We've already been set up by the darkside, positioned as potential terrorists . . . now the good guys are gonna start plowing into bank statements, credit cards, library cards, car notes, anything that we might have purchased even through a third party."

"Which means they'll freeze our assets," Dan said, suddenly panicked.

"You oughta know me better than that," Carlos said coolly, looking around the group as he materialized a platinum credit card between his fingers and made it just as quickly disappear. "I got most of our shit offshore in number only accounts. My old life living under radar taught me that much."

"My brother," Yonnie said, pounding his fist.

"Bigger problem is freedom of movement now just got seriously limited," Damali said, allowing her gaze to rake the group. "We're formally done—out of the music business. If we resurface again, we're going into immediate custody. From this point on, life as we knew it has changed . . . we're completely underground, strictly guerrilla."

Rider flopped back against his seat and closed his eyes. "I knew this day would come. I have just retained the right to start smoking again."

"Shoot us the images," Carlos said, his voice weighted with sudden fatigue. "We definitely need a fallback position now."

"Roger that," Doug said. "I'll alert our base-station squads that we've got our Neteru team possibly coming in hot. We'll do everything we can to throw the feds off your trail, make 'em think you're in Europe or something, and we can try to send out confusing signatures to the darkside. Also know, the Internet is your friend . . . we've got Web radio cells at your disposal, and a grid that can block theirs with Light."

"No doubt we'll get a little angelic assistance with blocking our exact whereabouts from humans so we don't have to smoke anybody," Shabazz said, fishing his favorite Glock, Black Beauty, out of his mud cloth satchel to stash in his waistband.

"That would be helpful," Rider said sarcastically. "But my main concern is not having the Unnamed One know I'm riding in a van full of explosives, but maybe I'm just paranoid."

"Well, if you get in a jam, head for the Jefferson marker," Cordell said, peering at the group over his shoulder as he drove. "See, the Washington Monument was supposed to be the first zero milestone of the city, but the ground was too unstable . . . so it now stands where they say the ground could hold it— slightly east of the north-south axis between the White House and the Jefferson Memorial. But if you stand at the Jefferson's marker facing west, you would be standing in front of a cross formed by the Lincoln Memorial in front of you, the Capitol behind you, the White House on your right, and the Jefferson Memorial on your left. If you extend two perpendicular lines from the center of this point—which is the ten square miles Banneker and Ellicott surveyed back in the day—they would terminate at the four cornerstones that are north, south, east, and west boundaries of the city. *It's a cross*."

"This riddle is about to make me pull my hair out," Damali said, clasping her locks in her fists. "A cross is squared off with a pentagram, with the White House being the exact center of the Metatron's Cube protecting it, which is also the baseline center point for a pyramid in the grid."

"Well, our stoneworkers know what to do. Ladies, you've got your position and coordinates," Carlos said. "You're gonna have to either bring us back home by frying anything supernatural that crosses the Cube or the cross-grid by supercharging that—same deal for the male tacticals on the squad."

Damali stared down at the map as the van came to a slow, rolling stop. "Two things are working my nerves. One—the Washington Monument being offset doesn't feel like a coincidence to me. I've seen this off-center arrangement somewhere before. It means something, Carlos. Two—the other thing that I keep remembering is the Washington Monument is a symbol for Ausar. It's a tekhen, a giant phallus symbol, the part of Ausar that Aset couldn't find when he was attacked and originally killed by Set or Satan, with his body scattered in fourteen segments. They only found thirteen, 'His phallus was thrown in the Nile and eaten by catfish.' "

"So they made that missing part from stone so he could be buried whole," Carlos said, wiping his palms down his face.

Every male on the team shuddered.

"Since then, that monument shape has been used in culture after culture as a symbol of fertility and power," Damali said, enthralling the van. She turned to Carlos and then to Yonnie. "Heru, Ausar's son, then came back and conquered Set—Satan—and restored his father's honor, blah, blah, blah . . . so wouldn't it make sense that, if we're following the old Kemetic beliefs as carved in the stones by the very layout of the nation's capital by its founding Masons—who also clearly believed in the ancient power of all of this—that to really get his revenge off, this particular monument would factor into the coming of Satan's son?"

"Fair exchange is no robbery," Carlos said, sitting back and looking out the window, his thoughts quickly traveling. "Baby, that's genius."

"And that is just how that motherfucker would think, too!"

Yonnie said, jumping out of his seat so he could pace in the short aisle. "He'd screw the forces of Light, in their own house, with their own dick, in front of the cross, with the symbol of their potency, their power base, and shove it right up—"

"We get the point," Marlene said. "Language, Yolando, please . . ." Her eyelids fluttered as she spoke. "There's a Heru Bedhet inside the monument above the elevators that take visitors to the observation deck."

"I don't follow," Berkfield said, looking around. "What's a Heru Bedhet?"

"It's a figure that was carved above the entrance of every temple in Kemet—it symbolizes Heru's victory over Set or Satan, as the case may be," Damali said. "Heru then ascended into Heaven to meet his father, Ausar, after his time on earth was over. But the point is, he kicked Set's butt to avenge the way his father and mother had been played. That's the foundation of Kemetic philosophy and that belief system."

"It's on my shield and on my blade of Ausar," Carlos confirmed.

"My point, exactly," Yonnie argued. "Essentially, like a Neteru tattoo at your base, bro—that Bedhet is at the base of Ausar's rock—"

"Yo, man," Carlos shouted. "TMI!"

A muffled giggle from Damali's pearl wafted up from the mud cloth bag where she'd stashed her necklace.

"I feel you, but we ain't got time to be all modest," Yonnie said, jumping up to begin pacing again. "Me and you know how the darkside thinks. So if you was the Unnamed One, wouldn't you just love to screw the entire human world and the Light with a symbol that has been erected since time immemorial, since the days of Ausar, that basically threw in your face how you lost to your adversary's kid? Wouldn't you want to bring your heir back through that?"

"He's got a point, Carlos," Shabazz said, looking at Yonnie and then Carlos. "I'm sure the Unnamed One ascribes to the mine-is-bigger-than-yours theory."

"You know he does!" Yonnie said, slapping a seat back.

"Well, what's this symbol look like—the Bedhet thing that we should keep an eye out for?" Jose asked, looking at Carlos and then Damali.

"Two winged serpents, one that looks to the east and another to the west, with the sun in the middle, and inside the sun, the six-pointed star represents Sepedet—an upside-down triangle, or female form, for Aset—and a pyramid—for Ausar—put together—"

"Forms a Star of David," Dan said, jumping up to stand by Yonnie. "That's why you got the Enoch references and had to look at the Kabbalah!"

"It's called the Thirteenth or Royal Arch Degree," Cordell said. "I know. I'm a Mason . . . and Enoch is also associated with the Royal Arch. All fits."

"Go back to the pyramid," Carlos said, too wired to sit. He stood and smoothed a palm over his hair. "If the pyramid in the Sepedet refers to Ausar, then Yonnie broke the code." He looked at Yonnie and slowly pounded his fist. "If you were the Ultimate Darkness that was operating in the shadows, you'd do the unthinkable in front of the cross, and before Ausar who's bested you in the past with his son . . . you'd use his own phallus, that is marked at the base by the symbol of the first Kemetic family, Ausar and Aset, in front of the White House—which is a metaphor for their palace—and you'd screw them with the monument that allowed them to give birth to their heir, Heru . . . the son who beat you. You'd defy the Masons, who gated you in the Metatron's Cube and set their symbol beside that in the streets, the Masonic Compass, to let all who knew how to read the architecture that they were *all* not necessarily responsible for what would arise from the pentagram—even if, perhaps, some of their early brethren who'd crossed over to the darkside might have laid those original streets in a satanic barter."

"Lotto!" Yonnie yelled in the bus.

"The Washington Monument is also the number of man," Cordell offered, fully turning in his seat as he idled the engine and put on the van's hazard lights. "Five. The Antichrist is coming as a man . . . and the monument is fifty-five-feet wide at the base and five-hundred-and-fifty-five-feet in height, a ten-to-one ratio just like the other tekhenwy in Egypt, or obelisks, as the Greeks called them."

"Hidden in plain sight," Damali murmured. "We've just gotta figure out how and where that pupa is hidden near the monument."

They waited in the van, anticipation zinging through the group. Cordell was supposed to try to gain access to the private lodge and send mental pics back to the group's seers, but the pomp and circumstance of it all was making everyone crazy. Yet, there was nothing to do but sit and wait in the van like a silently ticking time bomb. Then the first image hit her. It was the pyramid on the dollar bill.

"He's in," Damali announced quickly. "Pyramids . . . he's looking at pyramids in the library," she added in a quieter tone as her Guardian sister's eyelids began to flutter. "Cross section. Tekhen . . . he doesn't know what we need and we can't tell him because we don't know—he could be in there for hours! Dollar bill, thirteen steps on that pyramid . . . eagle tail feathers, nine. All-seeing eye. He's trying to do numerology combinations. I don't know what to tell him. Valley of the Kings built on the west bank of the Nile, our famous necropolis and many memorials to dead presidents are on the west bank of the Potomac. He's all over the place and it isn't his fault."

"Pyramids—because those are secret and they are strong and that's where the dead kings used to be buried," the pearl shouted from her bag. "It's so horrible, but that's where it's growing. I'm afraid, Damali. I don't like this at all!"

"Go back to the pyramid-cross section," Marlene said calmly. "Overlay the Queen's Chamber inside the apex of the traditional pyramid with the street design of where the Washington Monument sits across from the White House. Just like the Queen's Chamber is offset from the King's Chamber, so, too, is the Washington Monument from the White House."

"The Washington Monument could be the womb, the Queen's Chamber, offset from the male energy of the King's Chamber—the White House," Damali murmured.

"Oh, yeah, old Lu is sick . . . making Ausar's phallus symbol offset like it's female energy," Yonnie said, chuckling in disbelief, "by screwing with the ground years ago so the humans couldn't build the damned thing where they'd wanted to."

"Tell him to stay with cross sections of pyramids," Carlos said, leaning over a seat.

Damali nodded and conveyed the message. In a few moments, words began to flow from her mouth as Dan, Jose, and J.L. furiously scribbled notes.

"Potomac Avenue is equivalent to the Descending Passage and Pennsylvania Avenue to the Ascending Passage and Grand Gallery in a Giza pyramid. The old canal simulates the well shaft in those Kemetic structures. The point of the relieving stones above the King's Chamber is a direct match to Scott Circle north of the White House . . . and the junction of the Ascending and Descending Passages is a direct match to the junction of Potomac and Pennsylvania Avenues." Damali began rocking as she spoke, drawing the team in closer. "If you follow Potomac southwest in direction, right out into the river, there's a secret subterranean vault or chamber, just like in the Kemetic pyramids."

"I say we follow the juncture points and then check the vault," Carlos said. "We can't bust into the King's chamber, the White House—and the likelihood of getting smoked in the Washington Monument by human gunfire is too real—but I'd put money on it that he's hiding his heir in an easy route back to the monument. So let's start at those two places on the map," he said, pointing at where he'd drawn along with Damali's description. "We hit the junction point or head toward the Potomac."

The moment the words came out of Carlos's mouth a police cruiser pulled up beside the van and put on its popcorn lights. The team looked at one another. Doug slid into the driver's seat as Marjorie stepped up to take the pretend role as tour guide.

"Can I help you, officer?" she said brightly as Doug opened the door.

Two policemen stood wide-legged with the strap popped on their weapons.

"Step away from the vehicle, ma'am," the first cop said as more vehicles entered the street.

"Sure, no problem, sir," Marj said in her most pleasant suburban tone. "Have we violated any parking rules by stopping our tour van so these folks could take pictures? If so, I'm so sorry."

The tension in the bus crackled as Guardians held their breaths. Damali and Carlos saw it at the same time. Just behind the mirror aviator sunglasses, black static demon eyes flashed as Marj hit the bottom step. A swift tactical yank by Carlos snatched Marj off her feet and back into the bus. Reacting on instinct as Marj hit the floor and cops drew, Doug shut the door and sealed it with a tactical charge, while Carlos flung up a shield.

"Drive!" Shabazz hollered, hitting the cruisers' engines with enough charge to blow them.

Damali was up and out of her seat, sending mental darts to

Cordell. "Get out of there!" she yelled at the same time she sent the mental image and the van slammed onto the pavement to begin a wild chase.

"He'll never make it," Doug screamed, careening off the curb and into oncoming traffic. "Throw him a tactical shield or something!"

Out of nowhere, three fast-moving bicycle messengers whizzed by the two demons disguised as police. Instant recognition coiled a new level of tension within Carlos and Damali as their eyes met. The two ebony-hued sister Guardians from Philly skidded out in opposite directions, while an unknown, almond-hued male Guardian momentarily drew the demons' attention. Three names and faces pierced the Neterus' minds— Zulma, Kenyetta, Craig. Then came the urgent message to avoid a friendly-fire mistake: *Don't shoot us, we're in the Light. We came to give you cover—get out of the grid!*

Snub-nosed revolvers came out of cyclist Windbreaker jackets in a flash to spit silver shells. Demons dove behind the cruiser doors for cover and to take aim, but the cyclists' athletic maneuvers were too swift. They'd blended into the urban environment and were gone before they could be hit. Then Craig circled back around as Kenyetta slid in from one street, Zulma raced in from an adjacent one, all three now toting pump shotguns. In a split second, weapon hammers clicked back. Three blasts released, a demon splattered the cruiser interior and then burned to ash as the second one rolled under the vehicle chassis snarling. Like erratic, fast-moving lightning, the Guardians were once again gone. But they had created enough of a diversion to give the older Guardian who'd been trapped in the building time to hear the telepathic 911 and to get out.

A hail of bullets riddled the outer shields of the van and suddenly the team saw Cordell huffing down the steps. It all happened in slow motion. Guardians remained weaponless as bullets left chambers and more demon officers appeared out of thin air. Officers ducked behind cars, popping up to fire at Cordell. A stunned old man froze for two seconds too long in the crossfire. Carlos reached out, and then fell back as two-hundred-plus pounds of humanity landed in his lap.

"Thanks, young brother," Cordell said, breathing hard.

"You all right?" Carlos said, struggling to get up as Doug drove like a maniac.

"You get my father-seer? You get him!" Doug hollered from the front seat.

"I'm good, I'm good," Cordell said, crawling to a seat. "But lemme drive, boy. I can see 'round corners—you gonna get us kilt."

Choppers were in the air and sirens blared.

"This got real bad real fast," Rider said, going from window to window. "How do we know which ones are regular human cops and which are demons? Which ones do we shoot at, guys!"

"Now would be a good time to light up those stones that are on our side, ladies!" Berkfield shouted.

"We're going the wrong way!" the pearl screamed as her platinum necklace bounced out of Damali's toppled satchel and rolled across the van floor.

"No, no, no!" Cordell yelled, trying to get to the driver's seat. "You've panicked and lost your way, boy, not down that street!"

"The pentagram!" the pearl screamed and then stopped dead and went dark.

The moment the van crossed the threshold of the pentagram, the shield Carlos had put up to protect the vehicle disappeared. Blue tactical protective charges receded, leaving the van naked and vulnerable.

Guardians hit the floor as steel tore through metal and shattered glass. Then the van dangerously swerved before jumping the curb and crashing into the side of a building. Cordell made it to the front and let out an agonized wail as he pulled Doug's head back only to see a bullet wound in the center of his forehead.

"Ah . . . nooo!" he wailed, clutching the young Guardian to his chest.

"We gotta move—now!" Carlos said, trying to help the old man out of the van as sirens neared.

Disoriented, the team spilled out into the street amid screaming, fleeing pedestrians in broad daylight—looking to Cordell for which way to run.

"We've gotta get out of the pentagram!" Carlos said, shaking the traumatized seer. "Now!"

"Can't blow the van," Shabazz shouted—looking at the row of office buildings—"too much collateral damage."

"Choppers in the air," Damali said, beginning to run toward an underground Metro station. "This way!" Then she turned back for a second. "Pearl!"

"You have to leave her and energy-tag her to us later! We'll be sitting ducks underground, anyway!" Carlos hollered as they ran, pummeled the steps, and jumped the turnstiles. "We got no juice, D—none whatsoever!"

Commuters hugged the wall and backed away.

"Ladies, see what I see," Damali shouted, panting as she showed the stoneworkers on the team the cross-points and Metatron's Cube. "Light it up—magnetic-style." She turned to the male tactical squad members. "Bounce off them, electric—see if we can get enough juice to get us out of the hot-zone. We gotta do this remotely, all second-sight, no hands."

Lights lit the tunnel and then a huge explosion sounded. The first car of the oncoming train broke away from its housing in the line and came barreling into the station, empty.

"Do it!" Damali shouted.

Carlos folded the team away into the rocketing bullet as it

careened past in a blur, landing bodies with a thud on the floor, against seats, slamming poles and doors. But soon incredible heat surrounded the runaway Metro car and it became apparent that the source was right on their backs.

Thousands of miniature demons engulfed in flames chased the careening car like a blast furnace. Smoke filled the car, choking the Guardians, and every metal surface was like touching a frying pan. With no choice left, Carlos grabbed Damali's hand and pointed upward. They had to get up, had to break through the surface.

Opening the ground above them, they bulldozed to the asphalt surface, whizzing across streets, slamming through cars and traffic, moving like a missile as they skipped water on the Mall and came to a crashing thud in the manicured grass. Tactical charges cracked like thunder and lightning, keeping Guardians from colliding against the interior of the hot car. In an instant, Carlos and Damali had worked in tandem to extract the team to safety so they could breathe, but in the very near distance, sirens, choppers, and jets could be heard.

Damali held her head as Guardian messages pummeled her brain. "Local team is here—their seers led them," she said quickly, blasting the images to Carlos and her squad so they'd be sure not to accidentally fire on their own. "Michelle, team seer, one o'clock," she wheezed, whirring around, looking for the Georgia team. "Quick—military nicknamed and military trained, tactical. Three o'clock. Shaun, at your six, Carlos. Leone and Charlee are standing with Craig at your nine. And the two from Philly are in with a serious warrior from overseas, code named Dragon Rider. That brother, Craig, is with them. All our side, baby, and not civilians."

Carlos did a quick assessment of the additional squad who'd joined the fight. A honey-brown babe in ripped denim with bloodlust in her seer eyes was indeed standing at one o'clock

and ready for war with an assault rifle cocked and loaded. Not
far from her was a brown-skinned beauty, with hair in fiercely
immaculate twists, wearing a T-shirt and jeans, dual handheld
Uzis in her grip—straight gangsta, a fearless leader. The tall
Amazon-built beauty at his six made him nod with appreciation. If there was anybody to have at his six, the sister with a
pump shotgun loaded for bear was the one.

His attention whirled, making sure he had a mental lock on
all those he'd have to account for and could count on. The
petite sisters at his nine looked like they were ready to kick
things off Ninja-style. One had an L.A. salsa vibe, her hazel eyes
glittering with the rage he understood; her weapons of choice
twin Berettas. The female beside her looked like a cross between Native American and African American, her long braids
wound in silver strands and her exotic eyes spoiling for war as
she brandished a nickel-plated nine.

"Rayne," she said, her gaze hard.

"Thanks for having our backs," Carlos said.

Carlos gave a quick nod of thanks to the Philly and D.C.
teams for the assist back in the streets, and looked at the tall
woman with sandy brunet hair and the bluest eyes he'd ever
seen. "You came a long way," he said with respect.

"Was no trouble. Sandra from Scotland," she replied, hailing
Carlos and lifting her chin, then glancing around until her gaze
landed on Heather. "She's from my land, a stoneworker like I am.
I got special word to be sure she's looked after. No accidents this
time. So they sent in a Dragon Rider, me, and I'll ride those bastards into the ground if they mess with that one again." She
checked the magazine on her Uzi and stepped closer to Heather
and Dan. "I'm your new nanny," she added with a smile.

"Everybody's got a babysitter," Quick said, checking her
weapon and looking around as the sirens and choppers neared.
"I've got you covered."

"The Light ain't playing this time out—notice all the female Guardians on this watch? Quick meant what she said. The Light is making sure you've got strong female energy backup, whatever you need on the squad," Craig said, his gaze holding Carlos's. "You know it ain't normally like this. There's always been more male Guardians than females, but not this time out, bro. All the seers got the emergency vision. They call me the Kemetic One, and I heard the call to arms loud and clear. That's why I was up in Detroit with y'all. So we got your back."

Carlos and Damali gave each other a look.

"We've gotta get to a safe house, stat," Carlos said, leaning on his thighs with both hands. "The military is on our asses."

"Worse than that," a disembodied voice said, quaking the ground and opening the earth. Sebastian quickly appeared and then clapped before disappearing. "Ride this, Neterus!"

Guardians fought to stand as Damali and Carlos tried to draw their blades into their hands as the earth fissured and a massive, pale mare exited the cavern and reared on its hind legs. The translucent, phantomlike creature's black eyes gleamed with pure evil and it took off without a rider then evaporated into sheer mist. Sirens were closing in, but the ground was still rumbling.

"Fall back!" Damali and Carlos shouted in unison as thousands of shadows belched from the earth.

Try as they might to fight against the dark tide, there were just too many shadows, and human forces were closing in. Guardians fired at the shadows, keeping them at bay as much as was possible. The newly added squad covered every pregnant female on the team as though on a suicide mission; no fear. But as soon as one demon was incinerated, another replaced it. The earth continued to quake even more violently and it became apparent that there were people trapped in the Washington Monument as it began to lean. Rubble fell and people shrieked at the base as the massive structure leaned perilously. Then a blinding explosion sent it propelling forward in a pikelike spiral toward the White House.

"Vlad!" Carlos yelled, forming an energy ball in his hand and then hurling it toward the monument.

Both Damali and Carlos reached out, but the energy band wasn't wide enough to lasso and halt it; they both would have been dragged to their deaths. All they could do was watch in horror as the monument slammed into the one place in the country that was an icon for the world.

"You've just blown your load," Nuit's voice chuckled smoothly, joining in a cacophony of evil female laughter.

"Run," Lilith hissed. "And *maybe* live to fight another day."

Carlos and Damali looked at each other.

*The juncture,* he mentally whispered.

*Yeah, and the chamber under the Potomac,* she mentally replied.

They touched their swords together and sent out two blinding energy pulses in the direction of the locations they'd mentioned.

The second the charges emitted, two massive horns breached the earth—then in the next moment they were sprawled on a white sugar sand beach.

Rider was up on his feet first. "We died! This time they got us and we fucking died, people!"

Guardians stood slowly, trying to understand. Bobby bent and vomited. Krissy wept into her hands as Tara felt along her body for injuries. Each Guardian blinked, and walked in a circle, inspecting their bodies, trying to make sense of the completely senseless.

"If we're dead," Cordell said with a tearstained face. "Where's my boy, Dougie? Where you at, Dougie?"

A translucent figure stepped out of the nothingness and waved sadly at Cordell. "I messed up," he said quietly. "I took a wrong turn."

"Boy, we'll fix all that," Cordell said, weeping harder.

"No . . . it's beautiful here . . . peaceful," Doug said with a calm smile. "The angels came for me."

"We're not dead then," Tara whispered, clutching Juanita's hand.

Damali squinted as information pierced her brain. "The Philly team, DC, Georgia, the Scot—they all made it." Damali closed her eyes. "Jettisoned to a safe house in Georgetown."

"Then where *we* at?" Inez looked around.

"Bermuda," a quiet, angelic voice said. "You led us to it. We have much work to do to catch it this time. This was the last place in your minds that we could salvage. They have not won the war, simply the battle, but things back at your home have irrevocably changed. You are now outside the laws of man. Watch the news, rest, and heal . . . and await word."

"Uriel," Damali's necklace said as it suddenly appeared in her hand.

The team just stared at one another for a moment and then went to Cordell to comfort him. It was time, yet again, to bury the fallen.

# EPILOGUE

"Just in, folks . . . today is a day that will live in infamy, one possibly more horrific than all the others before it. Our national monuments were under siege by a direct terrorist hit. The White House sustained what could be irreparable damage. Hundreds, possibly thousands, of lives were lost, including workers, staff, pedestrians, and tourists alike. It was only by an act of God that our president and first lady were not in residence at the time this tragic bomb blast toppled the Washington Monument and sent it careening into the building. Our national correspondent is on the scene, where a van loaded with weaponry has been found and a significant section of the Metro system was destroyed and used as a makeshift bomb that had the kill trajectory that, it is believed, ultimately toppled the monument in this diabolical plot."

Carlos clicked off the remote control, silencing the news; Damali simply closed her eyes.

"Now what, baby?" she murmured and drew in close to him.

"Who the hell knows?"

Turn the page for a sneak peek at the second book
in L. A. Banks's Crimson Moon series.

# BITE THE BULLET

*A Crimson Moon Novel*

COMING IN OCTOBER 2008 FROM ST. MARTIN'S PAPERBACKS.

Full awareness slowly returned as Sasha opened one eye and squinted against the morning brightness. She felt as if she'd been hit in the back of her head with a sledgehammer, but she could only smile. Sun bounced off the snow and created a reflective glare that made it seem as though headlights were focused in her direction. The last thing she remembered before she'd shuddered and passed out was Hunter's strong arm around her waist as he kissed the back of her skull, mounted her, and repeatedly told her he was sorry. Hell, she wasn't.

Little by little she was able to tolerate the filtered light coming through the tent wall. A cool vacancy at her back told her that Hunter was already up, awake, and on the move. She strained to hear him through her mental haze and then inhaled deeply to pick up his scent. *What a night . . .*

Struggling to sit upright, she pulled the thick sleeping bag around her. It felt like she'd been in a prizefight . . . then she remembered. Oh, yeah, the moose. She closed her eyes and let her head fall back, taking a moment to relive the joy of it all. The sultry scent of a morning fire teased her nose and soon the smell of grilling meat drew her out of her private reverie and sent her in search of her clothes.

She shielded her eyes from the bright sunlight as she opened the tent flap and peeked out. Hunter looked up from the sizzling spit at her with a smile. Hunger made her stomach growl, but the look of him squatting by the flame, jeans drawn taut against his thighs and only a thermal T-shirt hugging his ridiculously chiseled chest and abs, threatened to get her started again. He knew it, she knew it; the situation balanced dangerously on a razor's edge and could be seen smoldering in their eyes.

The issue was, whoever crossed the line first would dictate the next shadow dance. But as badly as she wanted to just hang out in no-man's-land with him making love and forgetting about the rest of the world, she couldn't. They both knew they had a mission to complete, even if he'd been right about taking a brief break. She saw that in his eyes, too—the conflict—the same one that must have shone in hers.

Hunter stood slowly, unfurling his fantastic body from the squatting position he'd been in. The sight of him was nearly paralyzing, but her mind seized on the almost eclipsed priority—the mission.

He simply stared at her, meat sizzling on the spit beside him. If he threw back his head and howled, she'd lose it. He seemed to know that and it made his expression become more serious. No. It was only a mental whimper.

They couldn't allow the trail to Dexter to go cold; the brass had already delayed them enough with questions and reports and bureaucratic nonsense. Then again, a general had had his face ripped off in his own home, so a paranormal inquisition was bound to be had. It also didn't matter that she and Hunter had blown away almost all of the offenders involved. The brass wanted everyone and everything involved in *the situation,* as it was termed, *cleaned up*—code word for exterminated—and the vials of missing werewolf blood toxin returned. The shadow clans wanted that, too. Yeah. She and Hunter could do that—

the exterminating part—without question. It was returning the missing vials part that was going to be problematic, especially with Hunter in his condition. She had to ultimately have a conversation with Shogun, but if another male—especially a werewolf—approached her right now, at least, there'd be bloodshed. For all she knew, he might even snap at one of his own pack brothers.

If only Hunter would stop looking at her like that. . . .

They had to remain focused, now that they'd gotten last night out of their systems. He had to understand that the edges of her brain were catching fire with him staring at her as though she were breakfast.

Finding the vials would take time, and some diplomatic negotiations between other paranormal species, which often required bargaining chips or deadly force, not that it mattered to her much which way things went. But the process was time-consuming. They had to strategize. She hated that part of the gig, the diplomat part. Most times diplomacy failed. It didn't work in the same human terms people had come to expect. Working with entities was not like sitting down at a UN summit. She could only imagine what a session at the United Council of Entities would be like. However, on the flip side, the way human nation negotiations had been going lately, voting at the UCE might actually be a more civilized process.

What the brass would have to begin to accept about dealing with preternatural species was that their cultures were alien to theirs, and each one had their own history, belief systems, abilities, and prejudices. That's where the similarity between those called supernaturals and humans stopped. The same rules didn't apply. They took negotiations to a whole different level. Deadly force was acceptable at the bargaining table, which, truth be told, was more effective than sending whole nations to war. Still, she'd have to get used to seeing a supernatural world leader jump across a table to rip someone's heart out. Oh, yeah, New Orleans was gonna be interesting.

She was staring at two hundred and twenty pounds of alpha male enforcer. *Damn.* How did one explain this part of her reality to the brass? Clearly one didn't. Sasha swallowed hard and looked away from Hunter as she came close to the fire and warmed her hands against it.

Negotiators were also enforcers—in fact, that was part of the negotiation most times. Entities from the demon realms didn't do things just to be nice or for the greater good. One had to show them how it was in their best interest, or let them know that you could kick their ass, and then you had to be prepared to back up the challenge if your bluff got called. Hunter was most definitely a bluff buster, not that she was so shabby herself, but damn.

Opting for humor as an escape clause from the volatile, Sasha dramatically finger-combed her tangled hair away from her face while picking twigs out of it to make them both laugh.

"Good morning. I made breakfast," he finally said, his voice mellow and gracious. He shook his head, chuckling, and walked back to the fire.

She let out a slow breath of relief when he turned his back. The sexual standoff had ended. For a moment she thought he was gonna go straight wolf on her; it was all in his eyes. Instead of imagining the glory of that, she tried to focus on the metal cups on the ground filled with instant black coffee.

"Thanks . . . g'morning," she said, trying to keep her voice as casual as possible as she took up a steaming cup and cradled it between her palms. The heat felt good in her hands, even if the strong brew was bitter. She glimpsed the moose carcass in the brush fifty yards away and then sent her gaze toward the fire. "Some night, huh?"

He looked up from the fire he'd been poking with a stick and gave her a lopsided grin. "Yeah."

She tilted her head and raised an eyebrow as he tossed her a Bowie knife and broke the charred stick in half, offering her a skewered steak. True, it was an obvious lure for her to come closer to him, but she couldn't resist.

Warily she approached him, half expecting that he might pounce on her like he had the night before. However, gentleman that he'd now transformed back into, he exchanged a steak for a quick kiss.

"Okay, you were right. We needed the break before pushing on. Is that what you wanted to hear?"

His smile widened as he walked away from her and pulled another set of thick, crackling steaks out of the flames. He sighed heavily as he rammed the spit into the ground, suspending the meat between them. "No, but I'll take what I can get this morning."

She didn't respond, what could she say? Sometimes silence spoke volumes and she was hoping this would be one of those times.

He didn't look at her as he settled himself on the ground beside her with his coffee and a meat-laden stick and allowed his voice to bottom out to a mellow, philosophical tone. "I would have preferred to hear—"

"All right, all right, I get it," she said, laughing. She set her coffee down hard, sloshing a bit of the ebony substance onto the frozen earth before slicing at the hot, juicy meat. "But we've got to—"

"I know," he said quickly, not looking at her, and then bit into his steak without cutting it, slightly burning his mouth. "Just a passing thought."

She allowed a soft laugh to slip out around the next bite she took, enjoying the companionable silence between them while feasting beside him. Breathing, the sound of meat tearing, chewing, and the natural stillness of the snow-covered landscape, all of it was the way of the wolf. Under any other circumstances she would have fed him and he would have fed her, but that would have definitely started a shadow dance this morning, something they didn't have time for.

The sad thing was she couldn't stop watching his mouth while he ate. It was totally ridiculous how much that one part of him had become her focus . . . loving the way the muscle in his jaw worked hard . . . the way the natural juices and hot fat from his steak made his mouth glisten—*okay, she just had to stop*.

"I collected some snow in the canteens and let it melt," he finally said in his easy baritone, leaning back on his elbows as he chewed. Using the skewer as a pointer, he motioned toward a pile of heated rocks. "Water should still be warm."

She noted where he'd motioned and tried to keep her voice even as she replied. It was so sweet that he'd remembered and had even gone to the trouble to warm it up for her. "Thanks . . . appreciate it."

He gave her a sidelong glance then bit into the last of his steak. "So did I. Thanks."

Okay. There was no way to respond to that, so she would just eat the remainder of her breakfast, go clean herself up, and help him break camp. How the hell was this man gonna act this morning if she got naked in the wilderness? For that matter, how was she gonna act under said circumstances?

Sasha stood and stretched. *Enough*. Even with the cold wind whipping, it was a wondrously clear day. An intensely blue, cloudless sky seemed like it was made brighter by the stark white snow beneath it. That's what she'd focus on, the beauty around her, despite the sudden, intense warmth that made her hair damp at the nape of her neck.

Reflex sent her hand there to lift her tousled mass of now too long curls as she walked, hoping the cool breeze would provide relief. But her fingers collided with raw, sensitive skin that was healing. Damn, what a night . . . Then panic seized her as she felt for her silver chain and the amulet she rarely took off, even to shower. When she turned to look at Hunter, his was gone, too.

"Hunter, last night . . ."

Her voice trailed off as he got up in one very slow but extremely fluid move and threw his stick in the fire.

"Yeah . . . I know."

Her mouth went dry but she pressed on. "The amulets—"

"Were in the way," he said calmly, his eyes beginning to take on a luminous amber hue.

In the way? The question shot through her brain so quickly that it must have shone in her eyes.

"I'm sorry . . . I popped your chain by accident." He smiled but it somehow didn't reach his eyes.

She didn't back up, didn't move forward, but studied him very, very hard for a moment. "What happened to yours?" Why she couldn't fully remember troubled her to no end.

"You don't remember?" he asked in a low rumble that made her womb contract. "I don't know whether to be hurt or flattered."

Okay, something was definitely not right about this whole exchange. She glanced at his neck, the place where a thick silver rope should have been, and quickly became very, very worried by the deep, almost burnlike rash that she hadn't noticed before. Scavenging for an explanation, she told herself it had to be a friction burn.

"If I pulled it off you like that," she said quietly, alarmed, "I'm so sorry, Hunter. I didn't mean to . . ."

He held up his hand and came closer, his gaze cornering hers. "Believe me, I'm not complaining." His hands found her shoulders as he gently took her mouth. "Last night was fantastic."

Yeah, okay, no argument there. But when he broke their kiss her eyes were fastened to the wounds around his throat. With trembling fingers she touched the very edges of the gashes and instant alarm almost made her body go rigid. However, she tried to play it off and act like nothing out of the ordinary was rocketing through her screaming mind.

Shadow Wolves were supposed to be impervious to silver. Unlike the creatures they hunted, it was their ward, their difference, their protection. They were supposed to heal quickly from wounds, and a minor scrape from a popped chain shouldn't have left an oozing sore. In fact, her hands had healer's energy and shouldn't have sent enough pain into the site to make him wince and drop his embrace.

"You okay?" Her eyes sought his.

"It's just a little tender. No big deal."

"Hunter, we have to go get them . . . if we dropped them along the way, ya know? They're too important to just leave out here, especially on our way to a UCE meeting after we go get Woods and Fisher."

He smiled a tense smile. "The chains broke in the tent. I wrapped them up and put them in the backpacks for safekeeping, since the clasps are broken—we'll get them fixed when we make camp with the clan. There's always a silversmith around. No problem."

He pecked her forehead with a kiss and she watched him walk away. It was a logical explanation, but his delivery was way too cool for her liking. Clan leaders needed their amulets to be able to hunt beyond demon doors. It denoted not only their rank as being stronger than a local pack leader, but in Hunter's case also indicated his high rank as the North American alpha. Their amulets had been handed down within his grandfather's clan for generations upon generations, and now Hunter couldn't wear his? Broken clasp or not, it should have been shoved into his jeans pocket, on his person, in a vest, somewhere easily accessible, and not at the bottom of a backpack. Uh-uh.

Plus, the scent from the wounds that lingered wasn't right at all. Memory stabbed into her brain as she walked toward the canteens, completely freaked out. Images of Rod's demon-infected Turn battered her mind as she clumsily retrieved the water Hunter had left. The werewolf scent she'd also picked up was slight. Maybe she was psyching her own self out. That had to be it, buggin' because her hormones were all over the map. But Rod broke out like that, too, if silver even came near him. What the fuck was happening? Hunter was a Shadow Wolf!

Her hands were shaking so badly that she could barely grab the canteens' straps.

"I'm gonna take a short run while you wash up," Hunter called out. "I think that's best."

The sound of his voice nearly made her jump out of her skin. Any other day, she would have laughed and shot him a sarcastic one-liner. Today all she could do was swallow away anxiety and speak softly. "Okay, baby. See you when you get back."

As soon as she was sure that Hunter was out of range, Sasha ransacked the backpacks until she found their amulets. He'd shoved them to the bottom, rolled in layers of clothes. The clasps had been broken. She took shallow sips of air, gently trailing her fingers over the tender spot at the nape of her neck and then up the back of her scalp to where a small knot had formed, trying to focus, trying to remember.

They had transformed on a shadow run. He'd picked up the trail of large game—a bull moose. It was too big; she'd tried to signal him. Hunter was larger than she'd remembered when he'd transformed again; two hands higher at the shoulders, larger jaw, barrel chest. His eyes held something in them that frightened her.

Sasha shoved the amulets back where she'd found them and began to pace inside the tent with her eyes squeezed shut. "Oh . . . God . . ." It was coming back in fits and starts, jags of horror that she wanted to forget.

He'd outstripped her on the run. The animal they hunted turned and lowered its mantle. Hunter went up on his hind legs. Sasha opened her eyes and hugged herself with a start, breathing hard. He hadn't brought it down like a wolf. One powerful swipe from a forepaw had snapped a damned bull moose's neck!

How could she not remember? How could she not remember! *How could she not remember?* She tore around the tent looking for weapons, blood pressure spiking when she couldn't immediately find them.

Cupping the back of her head, she bolted out of the tent. Panic perspiration made everything she wore stick to her skin. Images of Hunter crouched over the carcass snarling as he devoured the animal's heart and liver brought her other hand over her mouth to keep from hurling. She could see it all clearly now—blue-black night, steam rising from the fresh kill that had been opened and gutted. Oh, God, oh, God, when did she fall and hit her head?

Backing away . . .

She'd come to a skidding halt. Their eyes had met. She was so stunned that she'd changed back into her human form and stood. He did, too, then cried out and yanked the chain from his neck . . . she'd spun to run, caught a low hanging branch, and went down. Then she was inside the tent. His arm was anchored around her waist. She squeezed her eyes shut again, remembering his impassioned voice choking out a ragged apology behind her.

Hunter had purposely knocked her unconscious, and the reason why broke over her in horrifying clarity.

Hunter was infected.

She felt a scream of rage and grief build in her throat at the thought that something like this was happening. But she swallowed it. There would be time to grieve later.

Right now survival was imperative and she needed to find her gun.

1. What potential implications does Damali's pregnancy have for the team? Are Carlos's fears justified?

2. What are the massive considerations for the female Guardians also pregnant at this time?

3. How do you envision the team incorporating infants, especially after the difficulties of little Ayana and her grandmother joining the team?

4. Now that the Neteru Guardian Team is officially on the run from both human authorities and demons, how will they manage?

5. During this "end of days" scenario, do any of the plagues and weather condition changes seem plausible? Can you cite some things that have happened because of or might have been attributed to global warming?

6. How do you feel about the loss of Father Patrick?

7. Do you believe in divine intervention and/or that good can come from bad things? Explain why or why not.

8. How do you feel about the way the Light is depicted in this series?

9. How do you feel about the way those from the side of the Light seem to move in mysterious ways—or from unseen corridors—always helping the Neterus and their team in the end?

10. Do you worry about future losses on the team? If so, which character would you be most upset about losing before the series ends?

*A Reading Group Guide*

*For more reading group suggestions, visit*
*www.the-blackbox.com*

St. Martin's
Griffin

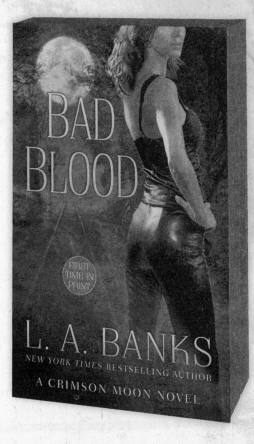